Hiding from Hope

Brittany Rianne

Cover: Leevi Crawford

Editing and Formatting: Indie Proofreading

also by Brittany Rianne

Central Sparks Series

Falling for Fury

For the girls waiting for their epic love

The girls who want a gentleman, but wouldn't mind being man-handled

Who support feminism, but are dying for a possessive caveman to growl, "Mine"

I give you, Jessie Jenkins.

Contents

1 - Lost in the Light - **Bahamas**

2 - Everybody Needs Someone - **Noah Cyrus, Vance Joy**

3 - Firework - **Katy Perry**

4 - Mr. Forgettable - **David Kushner**

5 - I am Woman - **Emmy Meli**

6 - Free - **Florence & The Machine**

7 - You're Gonna Go Far - **Noah Kahan**

8 - I Will Wait - **Mumford & Sons**

9 - Delicate - **Taylor Swift**

10 - Something in the Orange - **Zach Bryan**

11 - Ordinary People - **Blake Rose**

12 - Feeling this bad never felt so great - **Tai Verdes**

13 - Bejeweled - **Taylor Swift**

14 - Jealousy, Jealousy - **Olivia Rodrigo**

15 - adore you - **Fred Again**

16 - Letting Go - **Ziggy Alberts**

17 - Back to You - **Selena Gomez**

18 - Ocean Eyes - **Billie Eilish**

19 - Lose Control - **Teddy Swims**

20 - Scared to Start - **Michael Marcagi**

21 - Hey Girl - **Stephen Sanchez**

content warning

Book contains adult themes and is not suitable for readers under 18 years.

Included are explicit sex scenes, involving rough sexual encounters, coarse language, and moments where there is very light choking involved. Book also contains discussion and emotions surrounding a miscarriage and struggles with pregnancy in general.

Reader discretion is advised. Your mental well-being will always be the number one priority. If any of these topics are triggering for you, please proceed with caution or do not proceed at all.

If you believe any triggers have been missed, please reach out to the author so this content warning can be amended.

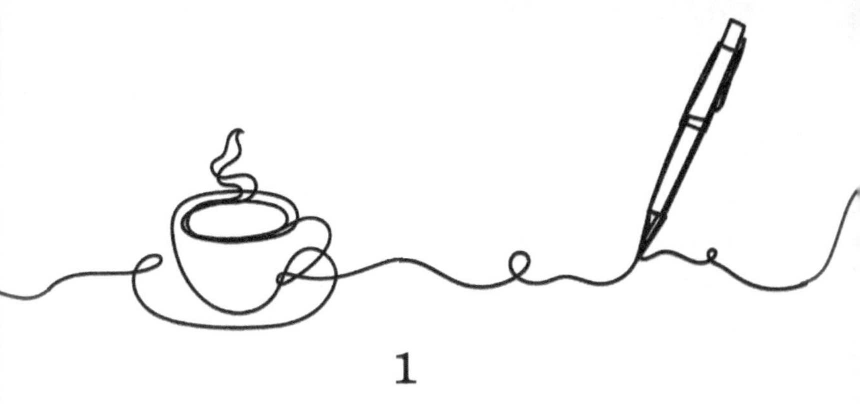

1

Jessie

"Shoosh! Everyone shut the fuck up!" Rosie whisper-shouts to the sixty-odd people currently filling the function area of Bozzelli's Bar. Addison, one of my younger sisters, has thrown a surprise birthday party for her boyfriend, Noah, roping in Casey and Rosie to help. Hence the angry whisper-shouting Rosie pairs perfectly with her trademark death stare, that essentially says, '*I'll murder you if you disobey me.*' Except, it only makes me roll my eyes at her.

Rosie and Casey have been good friends with Addison since pre-K, back when we all lived in Great Falls, Virginia, so I've known them for pretty much their entire lives, and as a result, her scare act doesn't work on me. Not to mention, Casey is like a dose of sugar to Rosie's spice. With her radiant smile and permanent glow of sunshine standing right next to Rosie, I don't think anyone is listening.

"They're here! Places!" Casey's commanding '*mothering voice*', as Addy calls it, carries over the room like a spell and everyone hushes and bundles together in anticipation for the guests of honor to arrive.

"You Addison's brother?" I turn to my right from my position in the back, leaning against the bar, and see a tall guy with an almost smile looking at me like he is ready to have a great conversation. *Oh, perfect.*

I nod and sip my beer, but instead of taking the hint, he throws his hand out. "Caleb. I'm one of Noah's friends. From college. We also work together," he supplies, despite not being asked. I look at his hand and then release the tension in my shoulders, reminding myself of the warning Addy gave me. *'Be nice. They are my friends, too. It wouldn't hurt you to socialize and make some friends, you social pariah.'* Addison's teasing isn't exactly wrong, but it's not like I'm alone by accident. I deliberately chose this life.

Friends require commitment, consistency, and caring. I'm shit out of all of that.

I reluctantly shake Caleb's hand and give him a pleasant enough smile before I direct my attention back to the entry, waiting for Addison to hurry up and drag her boyfriend through that door so I can say the obligatory *'Happy Birthday'*, and *'Good job, Ads'*, and then get the fuck out of here. He seems to take the hint, awkwardly nodding his head before he pretends to hear someone call his name and scurries away.

I love my sisters, all three of them, but really, this is not my scene, and they know that. Addison is the one I was closest with growing up. Despite the six-year age gap, she was the closest to me in personality, and we used to have a great time causing havoc for the sister between us, Ava. She was a prim princess and so fucking easy to rile up. I suppose because Ads and I only really made up properly about eight months ago, when all the drama with our family went down (dad arrested, family trust funds evaporated, parents divorced, Addison clocked dad in the jaw—the usual), I felt obliged to come when she asked. Eager to make up for the last two years that I'd been a shit absent big brother, add in her big sad green eyes that usually nail me in the gut, and I caved. It was the same look she'd give me when we would get into trouble for picking on Ava. She'd throw me the sad eyes, and I'd take the fall for the lot.

Anyway, that's why I'm out on a Saturday night socializing and not holed away in my tiny Upper East Side apartment. That is why I'm here and putting up with people trying to make small talk, anxiously twisting the ring I inherited from my grandfather that warms my pinkie, instead of sipping a whisky and finishing *The Brothers Karamazov.*

I was trying to get through my Top-Ten-Always-Wanted-to-Read list; I'm at number four. It's pathetic, especially for someone who owns a fucking bookshop.

"Surprise!" The room erupts at a stupid volume as all of Addison and Noah's closest friends and family chant to Noah walking through the door, a big grin on his face before he turns and levels Addison with a look I can only label as adoration. As much as I wasn't really on board with this relationship–with Noah's dating history–I'm glad she has someone who cares for her the way he does. I'm glad she found her happiness. At least one of us gets to.

I shake off the nervous fidgeting, straighten from my lean on the bar, and make my way to the guests of honor. As everyone embraces Noah and gives him well-wishes, Addison makes her way through the crowd to me.

"You came!" Her smile beams up at me, the short ass barely reaching my shoulders, and I pull her into an embrace.

"You asked. Of course I came." She returns the hug and then pulls back.

"Yeah, but I fully expected you to bail at the last minute." She giggles softly, the version of her I haven't seen since she was a kid staring back at me. It warms me at the same time as it sends a pang of guilt straight to my heart. I hate that she didn't expect anything but disappointment from me.

She looks a bit over her shoulder before continuing in a lower voice. "Really, though, I know how much all this bullshit makes you uncomfortable. I appreciate you coming, really." She gives me her honest smile, and it feels a little like my frozen soul defrosts. Only a little.

I toss the mop of blonde hair she has down around her face and roll my eyes. "Alright, rascal. I know you're dating a Greek, but you don't have to get all fucking sappy on me."

"Is that where Ads gets her potty mouth from?" Speak of the Greek.

"I don't have a potty mouth, you're just delicate. My gentle giant." Addison swats at Noah's chest, and the affection in which they stare at each other threatens to make my dinner escape. Whether it's twisting from the sickening thought of these two in love, or the jealousy of the love and hope they seem to beam at each other. Hope for the future, for happy things that will, no doubt, now fall into their laps.

Hope. Love. Adoration. All very foreign. At least that's how it feels now.

"Okay, I'll leave you love birds to it, then. Happy Birthday, Karvelas." I shake my thoughts, refusing to bring any of it to the surface as I nod at Noah. He returns it before I head toward the bar. A weird friendly-not-friend thing we have going on. Despite me being happy for Addison, I still think she can do better. Ava could, too.

"Hey, JJ! You came!" Casey sidles up next to me at the bar, pulling me from my thoughts.

"I was invited," I give by way of greeting to the ray of sunshine, and she laughs softly to herself.

"I haven't been to your neck of the woods in a while. I forgot how surly you were." She says it, and like always, her words sting, but her tone is kind. I honestly don't know how she manages that delicate balance.

"You too good for the boutique bookshops now, Case?"

"I could never be too good for the coffee you brew. That stuff is elite." She all but moans. This woman has never understood her presence around the opposite sex. I'll never forget the first time I escorted her, Rosie, and Addison to a bar when they all turned twenty-one. She wore a tiny piece of material people call a dress, twirled, and shook that perky ass around like it was nobody's business. I stood there on the corner of the dance floor, essentially playing bodyguard, while she gave almost every guy in there a fucking stroke from lack of blood in their brains.

Myself included.

"You drinking?" I ask as I wave the bartender over.

She nods, and her smile grows, shining as bright as a million suns. "Yes! I'll have a gin please!"

"G&T and a whisky—"

"NO! Ew, gin and *soda*, with fresh lime," she corrects, and the bartender walks away with a blush as Casey smiles at him. "Tonic is disgusting, don't ever use tonic." She levels me with a look I think is meant to be stern, but she fails and it just looks... *cute?* Is it weird to find my sister's friend cute?

"How much have you already had to drink?" I ask, noticing the glaze to her eyes and the way she is leaning on the bar.

"Oh, we pre-gamed good. Rosie said she would need the alcohol to deal with Noah's douchey friends, apparently. Although, I don't know that she has ever even met them properly." She manages to get the sentence out without slurring, but not without closing her eyes in slow motion. The bartender places the drinks on the bar, and she beams at him again. The guy practically drops his jaw and leans in as though he wants to take it further before I place my body in between them, directing Casey toward a high table. Obviously, drunk-Casey forgets about Boyfriend-Connor. Although I'm unsure why I felt the need to intervene, what she does or doesn't do isn't my concern.

She takes a huge swig of her gin and places it on the table before she takes a seat and I pull one next to her. Guess I'm babysitting the drunk tonight.

"Where's Connor? I assumed he'd be glued to your hip." The dweeb used to follow her around like a lost puppy at functions. The two of them were long-term, probably the marrying kind, considering Casey screams hopeless romantic. Seemed like a nice kid, but... he was just that–a kid. I still thought she could do better. Apparently, I don't discriminate with that line of thinking.

"Oh..." She looks stunned at me, then bursts out with a melodic laugh that almost has the corners of my lips tipping up. That realization has me shaking the stupid expression from my face.

She settles, leaning on the table with her hand propping her head up as she speaks through her trademark smile. "I broke up with Connor ages ago! Where have you been? That is like old news."

I let that thought settle in my mind for a moment.

Casey is single.

"I'm sorry... I didn't mean to bring it up," I say, sipping my drink and trying to analyze her reaction. Was it a psychotic, *'I'm going to have a mental breakdown'*, kind of laugh, or does she really not care? They were together for so long. Something sours as I remember another woman who didn't seem bothered about ending a long-term relationship. Dropping it like a bad smell, like a snake shedding a skin.

I've never been good with feelings, and not knowing where this sudden piece of information is going to take me is making me itchy. Feelings are, in my experience, just pointless. They get in the way; they destroy things. I learned a long time ago to bury those. I don't want anything to do with them.

"Oh, please, don't be. He was a child, I'm better off. Literally better at getting off–without him." I turn my head slowly, unsure if I just heard her correctly. She skulls the rest of her drink and throws her hands in the air in a '*woo!*' before she turns back to me, conversation forgotten. "Want to go dance?" she asks in a husky voice that shouldn't have any effect on me. Except, I'm a man, and she is a stunning woman, who's apparently now single and talking about getting off.

It does affect me.

Sister's best-friend.

Sister's. Best. Friend.

I silently chant the reminder as I mentally list poets and authors to reduce the swelling below the belt.

It doesn't work. Instead, I fixate. Connor really couldn't get her off? Surely, I didn't hear that right. Was he blindfolded, with tape over his mouth and hands tied behind his back? Literally so many ways to do it, and he just couldn't? What a fucking child.

I realize she is beaming up at me and waiting for an answer, and I shake my head at her.

"No. I don't dance." She scoffs and rolls her eyes.

"Boring! Fine, I will dance by myself."

She drags herself from the chair, and spins toward the dance floor, practically skipping as she goes.

I can't tear my eyes from her. She practically glows from where she spins and dances on the dance floor, the tiny spot of sunlight in the darkest room.

"Hey, man," Noah greets as he makes himself at home at my table. I nod at him in greeting and sip my drink. "Thanks for coming. And for just making an effort in general. It means a lot." I side-eye him cautiously because that was a lot of thank-you's for simply turning up at a party.

"Uhh... you're welcome?"

"I'm serious. And I don't just mean me." He holds up a hand. I normally am not one to trust this level of kindness, but the look in his eyes tells me he is sincere. "I mean for Addy. You trying, being around and filling in the big-brother shoes again, makes her happy. She missed you, and it's nice to see her get excited. Any day that she smiles and is happy is a win."

"Alright, man." I roll my eyes. "I told you I liked you. You don't need to suck up with all this sappy bullshit." He chuckles and we sip our drinks in silence. Uncomfortable emotions I can't work out sit like prickly canvas on my skin, that rolling my shoulders and kinking my neck hasn't fixed.

"I know she is your sister, and you don't want to hear about it, but she's everything to me. You'll find your reason one day, too." He sighs, all poetic and shit.

"Reason for what?" I ask the question, looking over to him. He seems like he looks off at a distance before he makes eye contact with me, and I can't help but be envious of the adoration I see in them. Happy about it in any event because he seems to make my sister happier than I've ever seen her.

"All of it," he throws a hand around the room, "A reason for every-thing."

"Do I need a reason?"

"I was trying to be poetic. I mean a girl. You'll find a girl, and you'll fall in love and all that." He rolls his eyes at me and I have to scoff. I don't dignify his stupidity with a response. Instead, we settle back into the silence, leaning on the table and sipping our respective drinks, when my eyes find their way back to the girls on the dance floor.

Mulling over Noah's words, I don't know that a girl and falling in love are in the cards for me, not sure that I even want to consider being open to it again. But I can't seem to take my eyes off Casey and wishing I could feel some of *that*. That brightness she has leaking from her. It must be nice to feel so warm all the time. The three of them dance, free and loose, like not a thing in the world matters other than that dance floor.

2

everybody needs somebody

Casey

"Who's the other guy with Noah and JJ?" Rosie shouts to Addison from our circle on the dancefloor, the music loud and lights low as we begin to slow our moves. The alcohol working its beautiful magic as it makes my skin feel light and my heart skip to the music.

"That's Caleb. He works with Noah. Him, Matt, and Ethan went to college together."

"Who's Ethan?" I ask, and Addison points to someone standing with Lucas, who is Addy's boss and also one of Noah's friends. "Lucas's older brother."

"Ooo. He is delicious." He really is. Like something out of a dirty romance novel. Tall, dark hair, and olive skin, many, many muscles. Much like Noah, I suppose, but he has a sophisticated seriousness about him, and of late, that was about enough to make me say, 'take me home, have your way with me'. I thought about accosting Lucas at one point. He has the broody bad-boy vibe, a dangerous smile, paired perfectly with piercing eyes, that I can only describe as hazel-ice, and a smattering of tattoos across his arms, and I think his torso, based on the ink peeking from the collar of his shirt. But he was friend-zoned pretty quickly after Addy made introductions. Too boyish and too perplexing, and it seemed too messy.

Since things ended with my ex, I have been telling myself I am on a man-hiatus until the right one comes along because I am done with boys, or the wrong ones, anyway. Done getting involved with children who have no idea about life or how to handle emotions. Boys who are so stupid and immature. I want a man. *Need a man*. God, I hadn't realized that I spent so much time with a boy until my first night out with Rosie after the breakup. Kieren? Kirnen? Something weird with a K, and he was tall, charming, and all it took was, "I bet you can't lift me!" and before I knew it, I was manhandled into one of the best orgasms of my life.

I hadn't known what it was like to be touched or desired by a real man until then, and now I can't go back. Every time I drink with the girls, well, Little Casey takes over and starts making decisions for me.

"Well, he's single," Addison confirms, bringing me back to reality as she states Ethan's dating status, only increasing the temptation. No, that is a bad idea. Noah's friend? Probably not a wise choice.

I look at Rosie to gauge her opinion and find her staring off in the direction of JJ and Caleb again. I follow her eyes, and Caleb seems to be staring back. No, wait, are they in a staring competition?

"What is happening right now?"

"What do you mean?" she asks, her voice sultry, but she doesn't pull her gaze away from where Caleb leans across the bar.

"Rosie, what are you doing?" Addison asks through a giggle.

"We're doing the dance," she mumbles, and Addison and I make eyes, trying to see if the other knows what she is talking about.

"What dance?" I ask.

"You know, the eye-fucking dance."

"Elaborate," Addison deadpans, and we both realize Rosie still hasn't pulled her gaze from Caleb.

"Whoever breaks first loses the power in the situation. If I make the first move, he gets to pick when we leave, where we go, and how the sex goes. If he makes the first move, well then, the control is all mine, baby," she says while twirling her hair and playing with the straw of her drink with her tongue, I assume only to add to Caleb's torment. The poor sucker has restraint, I'll give him that. The look of pure hunger in his eyes tells me she is close to winning this one, though.

"And let me guess, you never break first?" I ask through a laugh at Addison, and I shake our heads at her ridiculousness.

"Never." She throws him a wink before she wipes an imaginary drop of her drink from her bottom lip with her thumb and sucking it into her mouth. Even from this distance, I can see him swallow, and I'm certain he just growled.

"Okay, well, I'll leave you to it." I dance my way over to that super nice bartender again for another drink as Addy leaves in the direction of Noah. When I get to the bar, the fight is over, and Rosie is victorious because that is Caleb sauntering his way over to her. I throw her a salute and mentally take notes. God, it must be easy to just ooze sex like that. Mature sexy men must just throw themselves at her.

Not me. I've been single for like nine months and I haven't really been hit on once, save for Kieren/Kirnen. Maybe some nice comments here or there, but nothing like what Caleb and Rosie apparently have after one meeting. I know there isn't much to me. I'm taller than Addison and Rosie, but my *assets* are nothing to brag about. I'm a Yoga and Pilates instructor, so my muscle is lean. I don't have a big appetite, but maybe that is my almond mom more than anything else. I rarely require a bra, and I struggle to find jeans that shape to my ass, considering there isn't much of it.

"Another drink?" Jessie's deep, grumbly voice startles me from my bout of negative thoughts, and I shove them away. I have a scheduled time for them, and it isn't tonight.

"Yes! I'll order. They are super nice to me here." I give him a smile and he seems to get angrier, if that's even possible. "Are you always going to be grumpy? Or do you have, like, an expiration date on that? I'd much rather be your friend when you are done with the grump act."

"Who said we're friends?" *Geez.* I was only teasing, but he didn't have to be so nasty. My heart breaks a little bit for him because I know what he used to be like, and I know he has only been this way since he had his heart broken. I can understand needing time to grieve a relationship, but this guy has used up all his points. He really just needs to move on. Maybe I'll show him how it's done–like, show him how I moved on... not, like, *help* him move on or anything.

Not that it never crossed my mind.

I mean, like way, way, *way* back.

When we were younger, before his ex, Jenny, screwed him up and before Connor stole four years of my life. He was my best friend's hot older brother. Find me a girl who hasn't lusted over her best friend's hot older brother...I'll wait.

I shrug off his words and roll my eyes, signaling for the bartender who wastes no time before making his way over to me. Another handsome man, he has a beard, thicker and darker than Jessie's, whose is more like a farmer's scruff than anything else, adding to his lumber-jack-hipster vibe that he dons at the bookshop café he owns.

"Hey, sweetheart, what can I get you?" Mmm, even his voice is sweet. Maybe a little higher pitched than I'd like, but at least he's nice to look at.

"I'll have another gin and soda, please," I say back to him, and I feel like we should give Lucas a review. This bartender is super kind. He winks and walks away to grab the drink, and it makes my cheeks heat slightly and I try to turn away to hide the reaction from my face. I hate how it does that.

The grump next to me scoffs.

"What is your problem?" I say to him cheerily.

"He is practically salivating at the sight of you, and you're just eating out of his hand," he mumbles.

"What on earth are you talking about? The guy is just doing his job."

"Oh, please, Ace. You have to know the guy is flirting with you." *Ace.* He gave me that nickname when I was fourteen and he was twenty, and it was about the time I realized boys made my stomach do that thing. You know, like, the butterflies that let loose when the guy of your dreams looks at you, or when they accidentally touch you? That thing.

He hasn't called me that in years... it still makes my stomach do the thing.

I look back to the bartender, not believing that Jessie has any idea what he is talking about, and see he is smiling while he makes my drink. No way.

"I think you're insane."

He laughs softly through what I think is almost a smile as he sips his whisky, and the bartender comes back with my drink, and he leans on the bar opposite me with a lopsided grin.

"So, my shift ends in an hour. Feel like sticking around for a drink?" *Oh boy.* Jessie was right. The man almost chokes on his drink as he tries to hide a bigger smile and buries his face in his hand while shaking his head. If it's at all possible, my cheeks turn a deeper shade of red as I look back to the bartender.

"Umm, sorry, I'm not really dating right now." I give him a genuine smile. He is sweet, although not really my type, even though I'm not really sure what that is yet, but he doesn't do the thing to my stomach.

"No one said anything about a date, sweetheart." He winks at me again, but it lacks any of the charm I thought it had previously, and something sours in my stomach at the way he looks at me. *Gross.* I take it back. Lucas is getting a different kind of review.

The grump next to me slams his glass on the bar and stands up from his seat and basically plasters himself to my side, throwing an arm in front of me across the bar. Any humor or laughter he previously held has vanished as he essentially makes himself a barrier between me and the now creepy bartender. "That's no way to talk to a woman," he growls with his mid-century statement. I am stunned into silence and the men have a heated moment of testosterone before bartender guy raises his hands in defense and backs away without another look in my direction.

"You really need to get your flirt radar checked, Ace. That guy was practically drooling on you, and you just walked straight into it."

"I'm sorry. Are you saying that disgusting offer was my fault?" Is he for real? "You have three sisters, and you're blaming the woman?"

"No." He grunts while pulling his hand down his face in what I assume is frustration before scratching at his beard. "But you could have more awareness about you. Your lack of it is fucking dangerous in this city." I roll my eyes at him and turn to head back to the girls when that alcohol confidence from before shoots back up and I turn and pin Jessie with my best Rosie impression—the scary one.

"Why do you have to be such an ass?" I poke him in the chest, and he looks at the spot my finger jabbed, like it's nothing but an annoyance. "I feel sorry for you sometimes. You are a good person, and under all that stupid angst you've decided to live in, is a nice guy who deserves friends and kindness and love. I don't know why you push it away so much." His eyes are back at mine, his expression fierce as something resembling hurt flashes across his face, only for a second before he blinks, and it's his usual grumpy indifference again. I stand there breathing heavily, my eyebrows scrunched but I couldn't hold the angry face even if I wanted to. Regret at the horrible words hits me almost as fast as the words left my gin-loose lips. "Dammit. I'm sorry JJ, I didn't mean that." I close my eyes, my posture sags. Standing in front of his imposing and sturdy frame, I look up into his blue-green eyes. Sadness sits in them so deeply, all the indifference in the world couldn't hide the world of hurt he pretends not to harbor. Too bad Jessie, I know you better than you think.

I reach up and rest a hand on his arm and give him a soft smile. "It's just... you are such a great person. I wish you let other people see it. I know you say you like this solitary life, but... everyone needs someone."

I don't miss the way his face scrunches into a sneer, only for a second, as though the thought is something impossible, revolting to think he needs someone in his life. He closes his eyes for a beat, but then the famous Jenkins fury simmers within them as he locks them back on me, feet shuffling lightly. He's officially uncomfortable with all the feelings and conversation, and I'd normally expect him to storm right out of here, making us wait at least 10-15 business days before we heard from him again. Last time, it was pretty much two years.

But he doesn't. He stays. Right in front of me. Close enough that I can see the mental anguish, fighting against giving in, against feeling any of it.

His fury wins, and his jaw ticks. Unfortunately for him, the alcohol running through my veins causes the fight to leave me in a second and my muscles relax, and his stern look is just enough to make me want to giggle for no other reason other than he is trying to be scary, and yet I am not afraid.

I bite down on my lip to stop myself and instead I let the happiness seep into my smile as I continue. "You know, if you ever need someone, like a person," I shrug off the nervousness that tries to seep through my gin brain, shoving that nonsense right down, "I could be that for you?"

"What?" he says, confused, his eyebrows raised, eyes analyzing me.

"I know, I know, you're a big scary grump who doesn't need any-one," I mock in his lumber-jack voice while rolling my eyes at him before continuing. "But I'm an expert in grumpy people. I mean, look at Addison, we're besties. And have you seen Rosie at 5am when the coffee machine is broken, and she has a deadline? That's the scariest shit on the planet. Your act, although perfected, is not even a little scary." I bop his nose and he looks down right scandalized as his eyes bulge and he shakes his head like he isn't sure what happened. "I could be your person, JJ." I nod and plant my hands on my hips to accentuate the offer. A platonic-person-ing of friendship? That sounds like fun.

"My... person?" he repeats.

I shrug in response. "Yeah, you know, like if you feel sad, or if you don't know where they keep the star anise at the grocers, or perhaps you need new coffee order ideas, and need someone to call. You could call me. I'm always free. I always know the location of the baking aisle, where they keep the spices, and also, I'm a champ at coffee orders." I stand there and stare at him for a few beats before I start to get a little nervous with the intensity he looks at me with. His silence, I am guessing, is because he is *so* excited by my offer, he doesn't know how to voice it. And not at all because he thinks I'm a babbling weirdo who just offered a cooking-related friendship?

To feign confidence, I wink at him and shrug again before I turn and skip back to the girls.

When I turn my head over my shoulder, a tiny little butterfly dips in my stomach, only for a second before it's gone. Because JJ is staring at me and he has a soft smile on his face.

3

thirteen years ago

Casey – age 14

2011

"Make sure you give these to Lillian, dear."

"Yes, mom," I grunt and quickly pluck the container of Scottish macaroons out of the car. Mom finally let me make these on my own and they were the best batch yet. I couldn't wait for everyone to taste them. I loved baking. For a really brief second, I wondered if Addison's older brother would be home from college and if *he'd* like them too? He was always demolishing the treats mom made me bring with me every time I came to Addison's for a sleepover. I don't really know why he crossed my mind, but there was always something about his presence. I seemed to lose most brain function and my mouth was dry. The last time I came over and he was home, my stomach also did something weird. It kind of felt like I was going to throw up, but also made me want to laugh. Kind of also like I needed to pee. No one had ever made me do that before, and it was so weird because he didn't even say anything... he just looked at me and smiled.

I have to shake my head because the mere thought of seeing him was officially giving me that reaction. I was putting it down to hormones. Mom called me a late bloomer, said any day now I'll mature just that little bit more and then I'd probably be more like Grace. I knew she meant get my period, but I hardly believed I'd start and then suddenly be dying to kiss a bunch of boys. My older sister was always talking about boys and kissing them and stuff. I wasn't overly interested, but for some reason, I thought Jessie would be great at that.

Good god, Casey. He is a college student, and I am still in the ninth grade.

Walking up to the front door, I knock and wait. Hearing mom pull back down the Jenkins' stupid long driveway, I admire their home, which was epically large. After a few minutes, the front door opens, and my mouth dries up like the freaking Sahara Desert.

"The Little Baker. What treats did you bring us this time?" Remember when I said my friend's college age brother made my body do things I didn't understand? Well, imagine that, except now I was seeing him shirtless for the first time, and holy heavens. *Can boys be beautiful?* Because Jessie Jenkins was so good to look at, I couldn't stop staring.

Jessie doesn't seem to notice my obvious ogling or apparent weirdness because he just takes the container from my hands and waltzes back into the house, leaving me a drooling mess on his doorstep. I manage to quickly shake myself free of the thoughts and chase after him, closing the front door behind me.

"Hey! They were for Mrs. Jenkins, not you," I scold him, trying to steal back the container, but Jessie is tall and muscular—the kind you'd expect from a college Ice Hockey player—and I just look like a scrawny runt in comparison. His half smirk and playful eyes watch me as he continues to munch on the macaroons. Through a fully stuffed mouth, he fumbles over words I think are, "What the fuck is this? It's delicious."

"Jessie! Watch your mouth around the kids," Addison's mom calls out from somewhere close but out of sight, and I roll my eyes.

"I'm not a kid. And also," I leap when he isn't expecting it and manage to steal the container, "these aren't for you. I made them for your mom."

"You are a kid. Well, a baby-teen, anyway." Jessie shrugs and licks the remainder of the powder from his fingers. "You made these? Shit, Ace. Not bad."

Jessie just gave me a nickname. *There goes that weird butterfly-stomach thing.*

"Ace?" I ask and he just shrugs. I can't help but stare at him, watching the way his neck works as he swallows his mouthful, the way his tongue flicks out to lick his lips and the way his long lashes frame his light eyes. Eventually he seems to forget my existence and turns to head upstairs, and now I was just watching his back–his bare back–the muscles move with every step and his bum. Oh my god. Can bums be attractive? Is this what happens with adult hormones?! They melt your brain and turn you mindless? I was becoming worse than Grace.

All the Jenkins' were beautiful though. Addison was the prettiest girl in all of our classes, and her older sister, Ava, had boys constantly chasing her, although she just started dating the football captain that every other girl seems to be obsessed with, Matt something. I didn't really pay attention because, for whatever reason, the only one of the male species that seemed to steal my attention long enough to make me notice things was Jessie.

"Do you need any help, Mrs. Anderson?" I ask the Jenkins' family cook. They don't have her over all the time, but I love when she is in the kitchen. It's a lot more fun than when Mrs. Jenkins is in here.

"It's just Mary, love. Did you mind setting the table for me?" she asks, her gentle smile firmly in place as always and I nod, heading toward the cutlery drawer. Addison was having a shower before dinner and I was bored waiting in her room, so I figured I'd come to my favorite place in any house. Except, you should see their kitchen–epic.

We work in silent tandem, Mary finishing the plating of the food while I set out the cutlery when I hear heavy foot falls on the stairs and then down the hall toward us.

"Smells excellent, Mary," Jessie compliments as he enters the kitchen, heading straight for the fridge. Despite the fact that I feel my cheeks instantly heat with his presence in the kitchen, I pretend not to care and keep at my task.

"You better not be spoiling your dinner, JJ." I hear the sound of her smacking his hand and JJ's deep laugh from the kitchen before it's silent again.

"Need any help?"

"Gahh!" That stupid noise leaves my mouth and I die of embarrassment. The sudden closeness of Jessie's voice scares the crap out of me and I spin on a yelp, dropping the hold on the remaining cutlery in my hand.

"Woah, Ace. Sorry, didn't mean to sneak up on you." He laughs and bends, efficiently collecting the dropped cutlery and placing it on the table. "You good?" he asks, a slight furrow in his brow as he searches my face. My brain must be broken again because I can't say anything, instead I just stare at him again. Thankfully, this time he has a shirt on, but his hair is messy in kind of a cute way, and he has a slight crease under his eye when he smiles softly like that. I realize in this moment I've never seen him smile really big. Like the kind of smile when I found out I was in the AP program, or when dad made it to my first dance recital. Actually, I smile big all the time. Why doesn't he?

"Why..." I shake my head. *That is a weird question, Casey. Don't ask that question.*

"Why?" He tilts his head, looking confused.

"Never mind," I breathe and hope he doesn't keep asking. His eyes dart to the pin at the top of my head. I hadn't bothered to style my bangs today, so I needed them out of the way.

"You pinned your fringe back," he says, and he taps a finger to the pin on my head. I swear the air got thicker in here. Not being able to say anything, I just nod, my eyes locked on him, unable to blink.

"I like it. You can see your eyes better," he responds nonchalantly, like a simple fact.

The sky is blue. The sun rises. Jessie Jenkins can see my eyes.

I'm cutting my fringe off tomorrow.

I stand there like a frozen statue, and he turns, heading back over to Mary.

"Hey, you okay?" Addy asks, and my heart lurches at the second jump scare in as many minutes. If I'm not careful, I am going to have a heart attack before I become a woman.

"Oh, yeah... fine." I clear my throat and continue with the table. Addison picks up some of the cutlery and helps.

"Why is your face red?" Addison asks, and I refuse to make eye contact, not giving her an answer, either.

"Do you think I should cut my fringe?"

"If you want, I like it, though," she responds, and as we finish at the table, we head to the kitchen counter and wait for Mary to be done. Jessie seems to have made himself scarce and I can't explain the little pit of disappointment sitting in my stomach.

"Do you think you can see my eyes better without it?" I push, and this time finally look up at her. She assesses my whole face, actually considering the question.

"Mmm. Maybe? I don't know. Do you like it?"

"I don't think I do anymore." I shrug and play with the ends of the braid over my shoulder, trying to give my nervous hands something to do.

"I guess let it grow, then."

I guess I will.

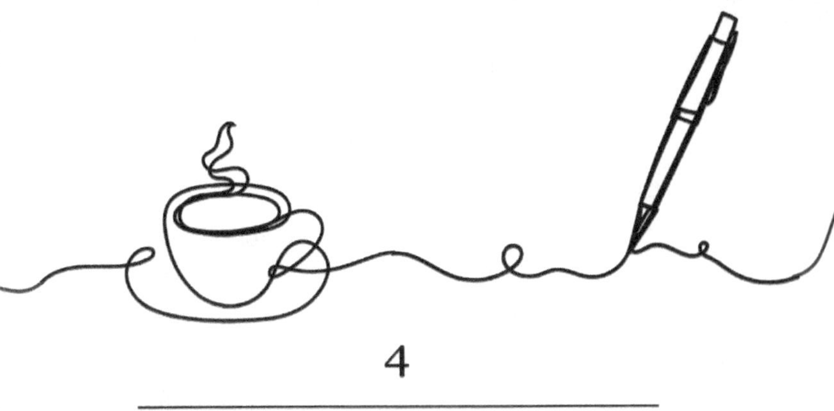

4

eternally curious ray of sunshine

Jessie

Present Day

"Just the usual, thanks, handsome," Betty, my 70-year-old Monday regular, orders as I place her exact coffee order on the counter. Betty has been ordering the same large, full fat, no sugar–*because she is sweet enough*–coffee order since I opened. Like clockwork, every Monday, and right at 10am.

"Here you are, Betty. See you next week." She winks at me before leaving another generous tip and heading back for the door.

What *doesn't* happen every Monday at 10am, though, is Casey skipping through the door like she's riding a fucking rainbow into the sun. And, of course, she steals all the air from the room as she does it.

"Morning, Jay!" Her sweet melodic voice makes its way over to me as she saunters over. Casey has called me *Jay* for years, like JJ wasn't already short enough. It was a nickname I told her I hated and to never call me, which only made her use it more and with a disgustingly large smile every time. I hated it.

Because I didn't fucking hate it at all. That was when I really started to notice Casey.

It was easy when she was sixteen. Sure, she was adorable, and being around her made me feel light and full of joy. Things I now hadn't felt in years. But then, I was an adult, and she was a teen. A mature, funny, and cute teen that was my sister's best friend. I might not have been attracted to her at the time, but I definitely enjoyed her company. The lingering looks I left in her direction, the way she started to elicit reactions I had no control over, only started at Addy's twenty-first birthday. The first time I really *saw* Casey as a woman, outside of being my sister's friend.

And now she was here, beaming all her sunshine at me and calling me familiar names that were threatening my solid walls of apathy.

"What weird concoction you ordering this morning?" I level her with a bored tone, ready for her to place a ridiculous order. Casey has a habit of trying the strangest coffee orders, of which she thinks I apparently need help with, considering she offered to be my... person? Whatever that is.

She bopped me. Literally bopped me on the fucking nose like some witch with her magic bop, and it made my stomach flip and I nearly laughed right along with her. Seriously, what is it with this fucking woman and throwing every single brain cell up in smoke?

"Hmm." She taps her chin, biting her bottom lip as she reads the menu on the wall above my head.

Why can't I stop looking at her lips?

"You don't have anything new since the last time I was here." She seems disappointed and something inside me sinks, making my chest feel tight. "Can you surprise me?" She leans her hands forward on the counter as she asks, her bright blue eyes practically glowing in the scant rays of the morning sun, painting her auburn hair in a glow that is angelic. Fitting.

"I have a few new syrups I haven't tried out yet. Give me a sec," I mumble as I drag a hand down my face and turn to head out the back. Needing the air, needing the space. Needing to pull myself the fuck back together.

I hadn't seen her here in a long time. When my relationship with Addy was strained, she and Rosie both stopped coming around as often. If Casey ever did, she was usually alone and never stuck around long. Perhaps a touch of sadness to her expression, but she was still always perfectly her. Rosie wouldn't give me the time of day and I knew I needed to apologize to her too before she started coming around again. I made her best friend cry, so she added me to her murder list.

I grabbed the two new syrups and with effort dragged myself back to the front where Casey stands staring out the window. We were only just coming out of summer, so the air was still warm with a slight breeze, and the sun was hiding more often than not, but she still found the single ray of sun, which she seemed to do everywhere she went. She doesn't notice me right away, and even though I shouldn't, I linger in the doorway, away from other patrons, but enough so that I can drink her in. Her creamy skin glowing in a pair of yoga tights that should be illegal, a loose tank top, and a sweater tied around her waist. Her hair is half pinned back with a pale blue bow at the top of her head.

Innocent and pure.

The thought alone has me heading toward other thoughts. Ones of me testing out that innocence, dirtying up that pretty and clean look she has going on. Releasing the bow and using it to secure other things.

"I have black cherry or Turkish delight. The rest are normal flavors," I announce as I force myself from the inappropriate thoughts.

Sister's best friend.

Sister's best friend.

As I find my way back to the counter. She turns to smile at me before locking eyes with the syrup bottles I'm holding up.

"Oh, yay!" She claps her hands together and then leans on the counter, considering her options before she practically leaps in the air. "I'll do Turkish delight, but add extra cream, a dash of caramel and then chocolate on top!" I roll my eyes at the absurdity of her order, but begin the prep.

"You're insane," I mutter.

"Nope, just eternally curious."

"About coffee flavors?"

"Of course? Don't you worry there could be something amazing out there that you'll miss out on because you were too chicken to try it?" I know she is talking about coffee, but it just feels like so much more than that. Refusing to analyze any of it, I ignore the question and continue with her ridiculous order. While she waits, she roams over to the bookshelves nearest the coffee machine, analyzing the titles, tilting her head as she goes.

"So, what are you doing on this side of town today, anyway?"

"I actually have a favor to ask you." *This should be good.*

She turns back to face me, slowly pacing near the shelves. She tries to give me a look of mischief, but again, she just looks cute.

"Let's hear it, then." I wave a hand at her, gesturing for her to proceed.

"The studio girls never got to have a Christmas party. We had landed a new studio, so the funds were tight. Grace and I want to throw them a little something, and I was looking into these Paint & Sip classes. They come out, set up mini tabletop canvases, there is wine, and everyone paints, drinks, laughs, and has the best night of their lives!" Case has this way of talking about things that make it feel like the most exciting thing in the world. She always had, and I'm convinced it is why Addy kept her as a friend. I mean, who wouldn't want her around? She makes you feel like the only one in the room, like you're the most amazing person she has ever met.

"I'm missing what this has to do with me? If this is an invite, I strongly decline."

She laughs softly and rolls her eyes. "No, you grump. I need a venue. I was wondering if you would be the best person EVER and let me host it here?" She brings her hands into a prayer under her chin. Her eyes bulge, big, blue, and heart-achingly adorable as she levels me with her puppy dog eyes. A groan works its way up my throat, and she must feel I'm about to cave because she continues. "I can organize all the catering, I'll bring all the wine, and I'll even pay for your staff's time. You don't even need to be here, just open up. If you're happy to give me a key, I can even lock up. Or I can text you when we're done, and you can come lock up." I stare at her for a beat and try to work it out in my head.

Obviously, I'm going to accept. *You* try denying Casey Baker something when she smiles like *that*.

"I'm licensed, Case. Tell me what wine you want and I'll order it. If they're buying drinks and food, I'll make a bit, so you aren't paying for staff. I'll just work it myself." I handed her over a food menu, and I avoid looking into those bright ocean blue eyes that try to suck me into their depths. "Pick a few hot and cold items from here. I'll have the chef prepare and we can do roaming plates. No fucking handouts, though, they are paying full price."

"Of course! Grace and I were going to fund the lot and we can put it on a tab. I want the girls to eat and drink for free, so if you could put everything on an invoice and we'll put it on the business. Did you want a deposit?" Now that I knew it was all her money, I felt kind of bad for being such a dick about it.

"I trust you, Ace. No deposit is fine, just confirm numbers a week out. When is it?" I pull out my phone and open the calendar. She doesn't speak, and when I look back at her, she has her eyes squeezed and is biting her bottom lip. Before I can ask what the fuck is happening, she opens one eye in a squint and answers.

"Umm... this Saturday?" Her voice is a squeak.

"Jesus Christ." I run a hand down my face. Of course it fucking is. Now I really had some work to do.

"I'm sorry! I know it's last minute. We planned to do it at one of the studios, but there were issues with food safety, prepping, and cleaning because our staff kitchen is not built for catering. Grace and I decided maybe it was just better if we held it at a hospitality venue." Her eyes are just big round blue circles of pleading, and it gets her right off the hook.

"It's fine. I'll make it work." I pop her coffee on the counter with a little more frustration than I should have, and she leaps for joy, clapping. "Thank you, thank you! You're the best!" She comes around the corner of the counter and leaps on me. Wrapping her delicate arms around my neck. Hugging her docile body against mine, I stand frozen in place.

Fuck, she smells good. I don't know what it is, flowers? It feels like fresh air in my lungs and, for some reason, it makes me relax. I land one hand on her upper back and pat awkwardly, trying to maintain some semblance of control and actively avoiding the thoughts of the blue bow and her bent over this counter.

She finally extracts herself from my space. "You're the BEST ever!" She declares before going back around, picking up her coffee and sliding over a bill to pay for it. She tilts her head after taking a sip, assessing the flavors on her tongue, and then looks at me with wide eyes. "Oh my GOD! That is freaking delicious! You have to try this one."

She basically shoves the coffee into my face, and I politely push it back in her direction. "I'll take your word for it."

Casey giggles to herself before she pulls out her phone. "This one is going in the record books. You should make this a proper flavor. It's incredible." I roll my eyes at her dramatics before she slides the phone into the side pocket of her leggings.

"Thanks, Jay! I'll confirm numbers tomorrow, I promise. See you Saturday!"

I am suddenly looking forward to the weekend.

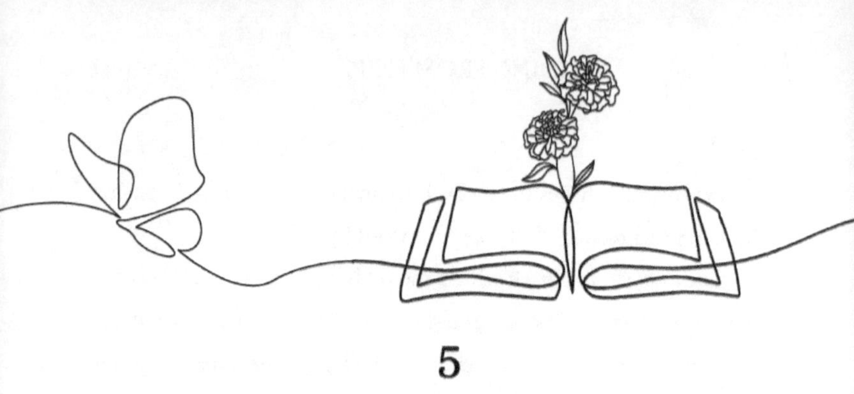

5

lost in caramel bananas

Casey

"Beautiful work today, ladies! I hope you're feeling as relaxed and refreshed as I am after that!" I declare to my Wednesday Mom's class. Nods and sighs fill the room, each of my clients having a relaxed smile on their face that makes me feel happy. Satisfied with a sense of achievement that I've been the person to bring these hard working and tired moms a bit of peace on a Wednesday.

This one is my favorite of the week. The women relax as we enjoy a slow stretch meant for de-stressing, flexibility, and relaxation. "Join me for a few still moments of seated meditation to bring us back before we enter our chaotic day. Close your eyes and breathe deeply through your nose." I love this part. Everyone becomes still. The room is quiet, as my older sister, Grace, and I ensured each of the studio rooms were properly sound proofed at construction. Expensive or not, we wanted to make sure our clients get the best experience possible. The only way for them to really get the best out of their yoga and meditation is to do so in the perfect setting. That meant not hearing the hustle and bustle of New York City.

I peek my eyes open just to make sure everyone is deeply within their meditation as I walk them through the exercise. Satisfied that I have successfully lulled my class into a trance, I close my eyes again and let myself just be. I go to my happy place. This is usually somewhere light; there are flowers and books, coffee, and comfy couches. Never a bra, always sweats. There is a slight breeze and I sit back in a deep-set couch breathing in the fresh air, the scent of sandalwood, a scruffy beard that tickles my neck... *woah.*

My eyes snap open and I quickly analyze the room and check that no one saw inside my mind and the traitorous direction my brain went just now. Grumpy lumberjacks will not be invading my happy place. No siree.

After ten minutes—and a few failed attempts at securing the proper happy place—I finish up the class and we pack away our mats. Elle, one of my staff who attends this class, comes over as the rest of the clients leave. "Hey, Case! I'm so excited for Saturday. Who else is going?"

"So far everyone has RSVP'd! It should be such a good night. You'll love JJ's, super vibey."

"I don't think I've ever been." She tilts her head.

"Oh, you need to go! It's a Bookshop Café! Next time you go, ask for a Turkish Delight, extra cream, caramel, and chocolate on top. Thank me later." I wink at her, and she laughs as she leaves the room. I pull out my phone and see I've missed a FaceTime with my parents, so I make a note to call them back. Since they retired, they have been busy traveling the world. At the moment, they're still in the US, but doing the country tour around Arizona, so I am sure they just wanted to brag about all that they have seen. I get a text pop up from my group chat with Rosie and Addy, and every time I see the group name Rosie gave us when we moved into the apartment together, I swear I'm going to change it.

23A Sluts

Rosie: I have a gap in between meetings, feel like lunch at Pucks?

Addy: On my way!

Me: Sounds perfect.

I mean, I don't know if perfect is the word I'd use, a sports bar in the middle of the day isn't exactly what I want, but it is chilly outside, and Pucks is warm in the bistro area so, it'll do. Plus, the girls love it there, so I don't mind going for them.

I check the time quickly. I don't have another class until 4pm, which means most of the day is all mine. I wave to the other staff on my way out and head in the direction of Pucks, a short fifteen-minute walk from the studio on the Upper West Side.

On my way, I walk past a drugstore, so I pop in quickly, then get distracted at a bookstore and find Rosie's recent edit, so I grab that, too. I manage to walk straight past the flower shop without picking up a bunch of marigolds–which is extremely hard. I do, however, get sucked into the thrift store, and it is like the universe rewards me. There is a gorgeous Vintage Chanel jade green clutch for fifty dollars that I needed to get my hands on, because I know exactly who this would look perfect on. The same person who would never buy herself such a thing.

I finally manage to make it to Pucks with arms full, immediately spotting the girls. Rosie is hard to miss with a head of tight dark curls that sit just above the caramel skin of her shoulders. Her go-to style of jeans, tank, and purple blazer, paired perfectly with ankle breaking Jimmy-Choo's. She calls it *'Rosie-casual'*, which I think is Rosie for, 'I wear what I want, and I dare someone to tell me otherwise'. Addison wears her Bozzelli's shirt, jeans, and Converse, like every other day she works in the bar, her long blonde hair pulled back into a tight pony sitting primly on top of her head.

They notice me as I get closer, and both look at me as if they expected nothing less.

"No wonder you were late. You buy up the whole strip between the studio and here?" Rosie accuses analyzing my full arms.

"No, I just happened to have a run of luck. I got another copy of that book! Can you please sign this one? I want to make sure I'm rich when it's vintage." I push the book in Rosie's face as I drop into my chair.

"You know I was on an editing team... I didn't actually write the thing."

"Doesn't matter. Still proud." I shrug while grabbing the drug store bag and giving it to Addison.

"What's this?" she asks.

"Cranberry tablets," I respond while I grab the other amazing find. "I also got you this!" I practically squeal as I hand Addy the vintage purse.

"Oh my GOD! Casey, is that Chanel!?" Rosie screeches, and I nod enthusiastically.

"Yes! The thrift shop had no idea the value of the item they held, and I just couldn't leave this baby in there all alone. Unsafe. Unloved." Rosie nods, completely understanding.

"But... why? Why give it to me? You should have it!" Addison says, while holding on tightly.

"Because you have that gala thing with Noah this weekend, and I thought it would go amazing with that black dress and shoes. Compliments your eyes." Addison looks like she is going to cry, hyper-emotional that she is, and I laugh at her.

"You're incredible, Case. I love you." She hugs me and I return the embrace. "Wait, how'd you know I needed cranberry tablets?" she whispers.

"Because you went to the bathroom like ten times last night," I whisper back. But then my eyes widen and I look at Rosie for a split second before we both look at Addison and say at the same time. "Oh my God, are you PREGNANT?!"

"Shhh! And NO! My god. What is wrong with you women? Your original assumption was correct... I'm just a little uncomfortable, think it might be a UTI."

"All that dirty Greek sex you're having." Rosie wags her eyebrows at Addison, who just rolls her eyes and sips her drink.

We eat lunch and have a quick farewell, checking home arrival times when Addy informs me she is at Noah's tonight and Rosie has an adult sleepover, so she'll sneak back in at the early hours–depending on how good or bad her date is. The girls dart back off to their jobs and I catch an Uber home. The walk would have been nice, but maybe in the warmer months. When I make it back, I immediately dump my bag and head straight for the best place in the house: the kitchen.

It seems cliché for a woman to love being in the kitchen, but I do truly *love* cooking. I like to keep an array of hobbies; crafting and rebinding classic books is a favorite. Hobbies mean keeping busy, keeping busy means never needing to stop, never having time to waste over-analyzing things. Outside of meditating, the kitchen is the only real time I feel peace.

Baking, experimenting, the lot. The even better part is the compliments. When you try something new, or finally master a skill, and everyone loves it. It is my all-time favorite thing to do. I bake when I'm sad, I cook when I'm inspired, I try something new when I'm feeling stuck. No matter where I'm at, being in the kitchen helps.

Today, it feels awfully close to that time of the month. Not *that* time, but the scheduled time. Where I take a day to process emotions. All the busyness in the world can't hide the craziness of life and the way it all inevitably builds up. Sometimes, life is just... hard. It's challenging, people are complicated–or just plain rude. Sometimes I miss my parents, or being a kid with no responsibilities, sometimes I get sad and dwell on my strained relationship with my sister, her inability to connect with me, or lack of desire to, I suppose. And sometimes I miss having a person. Of course, Rosie and Addison are always there for me, but Connor was, for a time, my person. The person I could be a mess with, let my hair down and go crazy with. He wasn't that for at least the last twelve months of our relationship, and I guess, lately, I have really missed that.

Seeing the overripe bananas on the counter, I decide I'll make a dessert for after dinner: banana caramel self-saucing pudding. *Yum.* I grab all the ingredients out and set up the oven and mixer, walking to the Bluetooth speaker and setting up my baking playlist.

This is like an alternate version of my meditation sessions. It pulls me from my head, my mind wrapped up in the therapeutic nature of creating something with my hands. You combine a bunch of things that are ordinary, or even boring, on their own, and together they create something delicious and amazing. It's magic.

I get lost in the kitchen. *I am Woman* by Emmy Meli plays in the background when my phone rings. It startles me and pulls me back into the space, reminding me there is a world outside this place. Quickly stopping the mixer and turning down the music, I grab the phone and answer before even checking who it is.

"Hello?"

"Ahh…" A cough and some shuffling in the background before the man on the other side continues. I pull the phone away quickly and realize who called. "I didn't expect you to answer so quickly." My stomach does a dip at the sound of his voice over the phone and the fact he called at all.

"Hey, Jay! What's up?" I skip over to the couch and plant myself down, staring out at the gloomy view or New York.

"Ahh, well… I was thinking of a way to mend the bridge with Rosie. You know… for being such a dick to Addison. I thought you could give me some ideas." I giggle into the phone at the memory of this grump being as soft as butter under all that angst.

"Well, what did you have in mind?"

"Originally, I thought I'd build her a bookshelf. But that felt too… weird. So, I am currently looking around the shelves at the café. I was thinking instead a good book would work. She likes reading, I like reading. It could be something that bridges that gap." I hum into the phone and consider. He isn't wrong. You buy Rosie a book and you have a friend for life.

"If you're buying a book for Rosie, it'll need to be a dirty one. They're her favorite, and if you're apologizing, I feel like that's all she'll accept. Especially because it'd give her immense satisfaction at how uncomfortable it'd make you to buy her a smut book." I hear him grumble over the phone and it makes me laugh again. Jessie is a reader, but he is a reader of classics, painfully emotional or mentally challenging general-fiction, or even non-fiction and biographies. There was a time we bonded over our mutual love for classics, but I gravitate to the profound romantic style as opposed to the tortured life-lesson type. "Just make sure it isn't a book her publisher printed, because she likely already has them."

"Right. Well, thanks. I appreciate the... information." He sounds anything but thankful and it makes me laugh at him again. Such a grump.

"Why'd you call me, anyway? Why didn't you just ask Addy?" Biting my thumbnail–a dirty habit I've had since college–I stand and walk over to the window, needing to fidget at the turn in the conversation I took us on, the anticipation for him to speak making my stomach flip. There is a pointed silence from the other side, and I feel like I can see him clearly, see him rubbing his hand down his face, scratching at the scruff he refuses to shave and pressing his brows into that concentrated furrow he has practiced so much.

"You said..." I can hear him swear under his breath, and it's all I can do not to laugh out loud at his forced friendliness. Not laugh *at* him. Of course not, I'm all for grumpy lumberjacks finally connecting with their emotions. But I do laugh at the image of him stomping his foot and scowling so deep he forms permanent marks in his forehead. "You said you would be my person," he all but mumbles, and I bite down on my lip, not wanting to laugh and stop him from continuing. He is silent for another moment, but I say nothing, hope gripping my throat. "Do you think... Well, will you... you know, be that?" His tone is set with defeat, and it makes me squeeze my eyes shut and do a little happy dance in a circle. Maybe my eternal sunshine–as Addison calls it–has finally warmed up JJ's icy heart.

I let a little giggle go before I respond. "I can be your person if you want, Jessie." He is silent and I hear him release a breath before he just grunts something that I think meant he agreed. Perhaps wanting to say yes, without admitting he'd like me to be his friend. I can't help but bite down on my thumbnail again, still trying to suffocate the laugh wanting to escape me. Those earlier emotions that felt like they were brimming to the surface seemed to have dissipated. Between JJ thawing and getting lost in bananas and caramel, my chest feels much, much lighter this afternoon.

"Well, anyway. Thank you for the recommendation. I'll see if I can find an Elle Kennedy. Those squealing Book Club girls don't shut up about her," he grumbles. "I'll see you... I guess." He stumbles his goodbye and hangs up before letting me also say goodbye.

I lock my phone and turn and skip back to the kitchen, changing the song. I do a little dance on the spot and whisper to myself as *Free* by Florence + the Machine plays through the kitchen. *"Yes!"*

6

star of the sea

Casey

"What do you call that?" JJ's deep soothing voice trails over my shoulder as I sit, trying to paint a replica of Van Gogh's *Starry Night*, except I think my interpretation might be off.

"It's the village." I tilt my head and analyze the yellow and blue blobs on my canvas.

Jessie just *harrumphs* from behind me, standing so close I get a whiff of his scent, something that reminds me of the fresh smell of a new book mixed with something like vanilla or sandalwood. Something so very him that it skitters across my skin, leaving goosebumps everywhere.

You said you would be my person.

"Maybe if you pull up a chair and have a go yourself, you'll see how not very easy this is." I swing my head over my shoulder to give him a glare and notice how close he is standing behind me, bent over, resting his hands on his knees. Our lips are barely a breath apart and it makes me pause. The blue of his eyes is more intense from this close, but with tiny speckles of gold scattered throughout that it creates a mix.

Maybe that's where the slight green comes in. He takes a beat, but he eventually realizes he has invaded some of my personal space—not that I was all that worried about it. He stands quickly and rubs the back of his neck, walking back behind the counter. Forcing a swallow, I take a deep breath to slow my heart rate, which, for some reason, decided to nearly beat out of my chest. *He needs a friend right now. Not some idiot lusting over him.* I chastise myself and try to wrangle my hormones.

Looking back at the canvas, I suddenly can't concentrate. "Everyone good for drinks?" I ask the girls, who are happily painting, giggling, and nibbling on hot food from the plate in the middle of the room. I notice a few empty glasses, so I get up and make myself busy at the drinks table when Elle approaches.

"Umm... who is the sexy brood who keeps looking at you like his next meal?" I almost drop the glasses from my hands.

"Who are you talking about?" I ask, completely in denial that she is talking about Jessie. He *is* sexy. Like a rugged lumberjack who retired and tried to carve out his own bit of quiet peace within the heart of the city. Except I try to pretend that I don't notice this because he is my best friend's older brother, and I'm almost certain he still sees me as the annoying kid who used to run around his childhood home. Even if he didn't, it's Jessie. He isn't looking like I'm his next meal, he just looks like that. Permanently frowning. It only looks like *hunger* because his eyes are so intense, between the blue, gold, and green, all framed with dark lashes. Besides, the guy wouldn't know emotions if they walked right up to him and introduced themselves.

Elle gestures over her shoulder toward said lumberjack.

"Oh, that's Jessie. He is the owner."

"I know that much. What's he to you? You guys seem close?" She bumps my shoulder with hers, her tone teasing as though she knows something I don't.

"Oh, we kind of grew up together. He is my best friend's older brother."

"Girrrrl, that is like the ultimate trope. The hot older brother? I can't imagine going through my hormonal teenage years with *that* kind of eye candy. How did you handle it?" *It was very difficult.* I bite back the retort as I remember being sixteen and standing in the corner of the hallway facing JJ's room. I wasn't being a stalker or anything. I had just stepped out of Addy's room and was on the way to the bathroom. JJ was back from college for the weekend. His room was next to the bathroom, opposite Addy's room, and he had just gotten out of the shower. His door was ajar, his dirty blonde hair a damp and messy mop on top of his head, with droplets of water dripping down through the ridges of the muscles that lined his abdomen. I was frozen in time, imagining what it'd be like now, as adults. If he caught me, would he open the door wider? Would he drop the towel around his waist and let me lick the droplets from his skin?

Oh my god! I shake my head and snap myself out of that ridiculous sentiment. It is just the little break I've had from sex and the lack of meditation this week. My hormones are on fire, and I can feel my cheeks heat as I try to pull myself out of the stupor, coughing to clear my throat, and shrug like I didn't just have a wet dream while completely awake.

"Oh, no. It was fine. I barely even knew he was around," I lie and turn to deliver the drinks we just poured to the rest of the group.

The party was a hit, and I finish drying the remaining wine glasses as JJ packs away the chairs to their usual setting. "You know, you didn't have to stay back and help me clean up," he says, almost mumbling.

"And you didn't have to let me host here on such short notice." I keep the lightness under my tone, despite sleep pulling at my bones. I only managed one glass of wine amongst organizing everyone, making sure they had what they needed, were fed, drinking, and enjoying themselves. Grace, of course, had no qualms settling in for a drink and letting me manage our staff.

"Your staff seem quite happy. They enjoyed themselves. You and Grace are good to them."

I shrug. "I mean, it's the least I could do for them. They are the most amazing staff, and Grace and I wouldn't be where we are without them."

"You pay them," he says, as though it answered a question.

"Of course?"

"No, I mean, you pay them, so of course they do their job. You don't have to..." he turns to me then, waving his hand around the room, "do all of this, too. They'll keep coming to work without the flare, Case." *Ugh, grump.*

I roll my eyes and stifle a laugh.

"What?" he asks, his usual scowl in place.

"What do you mean what?"

"Did I say something funny?" When I look up in his direction, I find his eyes locked on me. Confusion marring his handsome face as though he missed the joke but understands he's the butt of it.

"You know that you can be kind to people just because?"

He shrugs. "Not everyone deserves kindness," he says deeply and under his breath. I nod my head and put the last glass away, turning back and walking in his direction.

"No, they don't. But these girls do." I walk past him and wander to the bookshelves at his back. I feel him turn; his gaze trained on me.

"Do you think I deserve kindness?" he asks, except it feels like he didn't mean to, like he hated every word as it left his mouth. The rawness of the question, the vulnerability I haven't heard from him in a while, has me twirling in his direction with speed. His brows are furrowed, but his eyes hold so much pain it makes my chest clench. I take a step toward him and rest a hand on his chest, reminding him there is a heart in there, even if he refuses to use it.

"Of course. One of the most deserving." His eyes search mine for a moment, neither of us breathe, both of us aware of where my hand currently warms his chest and I feel his heart beating rapidly under his skin. The zap of energy reminds me that this is Jessie Jenkins, and I am Casey Baker, and this is inappropriate.

Clearing my throat, I give him a gentle smile and go back to the shelves. "Did you find a book for Rosie?" He takes a moment, but he finally answers, the tension in the room dropping, the air cooling slightly.

"Ah... yeah. I couldn't get any Elle Kennedy that I'd heard of, but I found this other one that was about a different Ice Hockey player, and apparently that sends the girls feral, so I'm hoping my mortification wins me points." He grunts the words out as he walks to the coffee machine, putting a lot of distance and objects between us.

I laugh softly and turn to him, leaning my back against the shelves. "Dirty one?"

"Apparently so. I refuse to find out for myself."

"You never know, maybe you'll learn something."

His eyes meet mine, but they seem a bit darker. "Nothing I don't already know, Ace." And the words skitter across my skin like a dirty promise. I think my eyes bug out of my head and any retort dies on my tongue, brain empty of words and instead replaced by dirty images. Not dissimilar to the awake wet-dream I had earlier today.

He averts his gaze, and thank the Lord, he continues so that I don't have to, "The Book Club girls said there was something about an Uber and Taylor Swift singing *Cruel Summer.* That was enough for me to grab it and leave the conversation. I'm sure it'll do."

I shake myself and pretend his previous statement was in my head and didn't actually happen as I stumble on something that might be a laugh, commencing the thumbnail biting like a child. "I'm sure it will."

Sensing that this little bit of openness, this tiny slither of friendship I seem to have been able to pull from him is as much as I'm getting tonight, I grab my bag and walk to the opposite side of the coffee counter. "I guess I'll be on my way. Feel like making me that Turkish delight special to go?"

"What's the M?" He ignores my question and I follow his gaze to the lettering on my purse. The C.M.B. my parents had personalized on the last gift they brought back from their travels. "Oh, Moira. My middle name." I look back up to his eyes, and they are assessing, his lips pulled slightly to the side as he huffs a breath, almost like it was a laugh?

"Something funny?" I smile at him, enjoying this soft, relaxed version of the grouch.

"Just... it makes sense." He looks back to me, his slight smile still firmly in place. I tilt my head as he continues, "The star of the sea. Guiding lost sailors home. It's just fitting for you." I have no idea what he means or what he is saying, but I smile and nod. "You have Scottish family?" he asks suddenly, and I have to think before I answer.

"Ah, yeah, I think so. Distant on Mom's side. I think Moira was like a great grandmother or something. How do you know all that?"

He looks around the shop as though the answer is obvious before he answers. "I read. A lot." He places the Turkish Delight deliciousness on the counter in front of me. "Your strange concoction. To go." He pushes it forward at the same time that I grab it and I brush his fingers gently, a zap of energy again coursing over my skin. I quickly pull my hand and the drink away and take several steps back toward the door, making a mental note to do *something* about my body's constant reaction to this guy. "Thanks, JJ. For tonight, and for this. You do deserve kindness, you know. Maybe you'd get more if you gave some yourself." I sigh, biting my bottom lip to stop a laugh from tumbling out at his expression. He looks both constipated and amused all at once, and it's refreshing. To finally see a range of emotions on someone who I haven't seen express anything other than anger in the last few years.

I don't wait for his response before I turn and leave the shop, rapidly breathing in the fresh air and heading toward my pre-ordered Uber.

7

a horrible worthless dick-bag

Jessie

I stand in front of apartment 23A and remain solidly in place, without having even knocked. I raise my fist, then drop it. Taking a breath and running a hand down my face in exasperation. Whether it's because Rosie's acceptance means I win a point with Addison or because I have no idea if Casey is here or at the studio, and because I can't work out why the fuck I hope she is here. But then I also don't want an audience to me actively swallowing my pride and apologizing to a woman for being mean to her friend. This all seems very... childish. *You are a grownup.* I chastise myself, and on a quick gust of confidence, I knock rapidly on the door.

It swings open, Rosie answers and the moment her eyes lock on mine, her smile drops and she just says, "Nope," before slamming it closed again.

I fight the urge to grunt, and I try again. "C'mon Rosie. I'm a grown ass man, don't make me beg."

The door swings open again, and her usual scowl is in place. Not the one she gives innocent men she sets her sights on. This one is saved specifically for me. And probably anyone else that she thoroughly loathes.

"What?" she spits as she crosses her arms and leans on the door frame.

I lift the book, which I suddenly realize I haven't wrapped. "Truce?" *Great apology, Jessie.*

Her eyes lighten for a split second as she sees the book, before she corrects her facial features and looks back up to my face. She raises an eyebrow, which I take as a win. She is probably counting down from five before she slams the door again. I have to make this good. I take a deep breath, swallow my manhood, and give the best apology I can muster with my arm still outstretched, holding the book. "I'm sorry for making Addison cry. For hurting her when she was already hurt, and for not being there for her when she needed me." She blinks expectantly and tilts her head like she hasn't heard enough. I scratch in frustration at my beard before I force out the rest. "I'm a horrible and worthless dick-bag, and I deserve to burn in the pits of hell because Addison is amazing and I'm the worst." I recite the words Casey texted me. The words she said would work as a last resort if the book didn't win me any leverage. I hadn't asked, but she said she had last-minute nerves for me and was really just hoping I had a win.

I was just lost on the tiny, inconsequential fact that Casey had been thinking about me. Cared about my feelings and wanted to help. Whatever the hell that meant.

After a few tense seconds, Rosie's entire face changes. She plasters a big, toothy smile on her face, leans forward, and snatches the book from my hands.

"Oh my god. Jessie? It's so nice to see you. It's been a while!" She announces it like she is genuinely pleased to see me and didn't just listen to that apology. She turns to head back inside, leaving the door open in what I assume is an invite. I hadn't planned to stay, but I'm on dangerous footing, so I follow her in. Before I can get any other words out, my chest tightens slightly as I find Casey in the kitchen and Addison on the couch with Noah.

"Ahh..." Great, I had an audience.

"Good job, Jay," Casey whispers, with her back turned to everyone else, and my entire soul feels like it warms inside me. I quickly shake off her praise and the way it makes me want to do *more* things that Casey likes. Makes me want to get more of those smiles.

"Lovely selection, Jessie. How'd you pick?" Rosie questions as she joins Addy and Noah on the couch. Noah raises an eyebrow, his expression knowing as he enjoys watching me squirm. I don't know why he looks so smug; Rosie scares the shit out of him, more than she does me.

I shrug at Rosie, and she narrows her eyes. *God, this woman.* "The dirtier the better, am I right?" I sigh. She throws her head back in a howling laugh and Addison just shakes her head, burrowing into Noah's side.

"Food's up!" Casey calls from the dining table, unnecessarily. Sure, the apartment is larger than mine, but we are all still technically in the same room.

"Oh, I didn't mean to intrude. I'll catch you guys later." I turn and head for the door.

"Don't be ridiculous! Stay, there is plenty!" Casey swats me on the arm as she makes her way back to the kitchen.

It brings me back to the moment in the café on Saturday, when she left her hand in the middle of my chest, burning a path straight through me as she told me I was the most deserving of kindness. It was all at once shocking and unbelievable. That she firstly thought I was worth someone's effort in kindness or forethought, and secondly that her simply saying so made me want to throw her on the counter, rip her clothes from her body, and do dirty, exciting, and unspeakable things. I had to mentally slap myself out of it. She is best friends with my sister. She is the epitome of love, happiness, and kindness. This woman who has me so fucking confused and frustrated. The one person who I have no right feeling confused or frustrated about, no right marring with all my baggage.

"You're going to want to stay. Casey made her chicken pesto, and it is honestly the greatest thing ever." Addison groans as she pulls herself into the chair. Noah and Rosie quickly sit down, leaving the only empty seat next to Casey. I pull a tight smile in her direction and take a seat, instantly unsure if this is a good idea. The dinner and the proximity.

She sits down but waits. I don't know what for, but I guess maybe I should wait, too? Maybe she prays?

I watch as everyone digs in, returning my eyes to Casey, and I realize *she* is waiting for *them*. To compliment her food, to enjoy it. She bites nervously on her thumbnail, something she seems to do a lot, a small line appearing between her perfect auburn eyebrows. She is genuinely afraid they won't like her cooking. The bubbly, happy, and confident woman goes and surprises the fuck out of me by suddenly being shy, anxious, and uncertain of herself. I almost want to grab her shoulders and shake her. Ask her how she could possibly be concerned, how there couldn't be a soul on this planet that wouldn't immediately fall in love with Casey Baker.

The room fills with the sounds of people enjoying their meal, but I just watch Casey. A glorious smile spreads across her pretty face, and it just somehow makes her glow brighter. She bites her lip instead of her thumb. She does what I can only describe as a little dance from her seat as she looks around at everyone enjoying their food. One word coming to my mind: *marvelous.* Watching her and seeing the rare moment of insecurity disappear, replaced by that warm smile. Seeing it right now feels almost like a little bit of magic.

It isn't until her eyes make their way to me and startle that I realize I'm staring at her. Sitting completely still next to her, and my eyes haven't wavered. It's like an eclipse. You want to look so bad, want to never tear your eyes away because you don't want to miss the magic or the beauty. Even when it's better for your health if you avert your eyes. In my case, it's better for Casey if I avert. All her clean and pristine happiness, mixing with the tar and dirt from my gloominess. It's unfair, and she doesn't deserve that.

What a jerk I'd be.

And yet... I just can't look away. Can't... stop.

I reluctantly pull my eyes from hers and try out the pasta everyone is moaning about—

"Oh my god," I also moan around my food.

"See!" Addison beams.

"You like it?" Casey asks self-consciously next to me. Honestly, she could serve me cold stale bread with out-of-date butter, and I'd shove it in my mouth and tell her it was amazing.

"I honestly don't think I have ever tasted anything better," I say quietly to her, and her eyes dart to my lips, like she needs to see the words come out to believe them. Before I get lost again, I look back to my food and remain in silence for the rest of the dinner. Feeling somehow contented just being here and enjoying the comfortable happiness that Addy, Casey, and Rosie exist in.

I'm happy my sister has this place to be herself in, but I find myself jealous of her situation. We both suffered similar demons and the same tragic parenting, and somehow, she seems to have pulled herself out unscathed. Without the loneliness and self-hatred that clings to me with a death grip.

Despite where my thoughts lead me, I stay, soak up the bit of joy everyone seems to think is so good for us before I think up an excuse about an early start and head to the door. I get almost out the door when two little arms aggressively wrap around my middle. I turn and find Addison looking up at me with soft eyes and a smile. I soften slightly as she says a quiet, "Thank you."

"What for?"

"Making up with Rosie and staying for dinner. For... trying." She shrugs and I do the same, giving her a small smile.

"Baby steps," I say.

She shakes her head and laughs. "No, these are big steps. And I know you're making them because you feel like a shitty brother. But I do love you, JJ. I forgive you, and I'm glad you're around more. I like it when you're around Little Rogue." She punches me in the shoulder, her nickname makes me laugh a bit, too.

"I like being around, Big Rascal." That little bit of honesty settles like a heavy puddle of warmth in my stomach. I toss her hair and she swats my hand as I turn to leave, and she closes the door behind me.

I can't even recognize myself as I somehow end up back at my tiny apartment. The uneasiness that swims at the back of my mind. I do like being around them. My sisters, Noah, and Rosie. Casey.

But relationships, friendships, connections they all risk leading to that same place. That goodbye, that never really comes, just slammed doors, retreating steps and hateful words. No one really stays, not forever at least. And how could I trust that anything new is real? How do I know I won't fuck it up and make them leave? Or that they won't just get sick of the same old boring waste that is my life, and just bail the moment they can?

The thoughts spin in a loop as I mentally battle my way through my apartment and collapse on my bed. Exhaustion pulling at me as I replay the evening, seeing the way they all seem to unknowingly orbit around Casey. She has perfectly constructed herself to be their gravity, to ensure they are all where they need to be and have whatever it is they need to be comforted. And instead of affording herself the same, she sits in a silent happiness. Like their comfort is the sole thing that brings her joy. Lying here now, alone in the dark quiet of my room, the usual way I like it, remembering her, it feels like I am in a completely separate galaxy being swallowed up by a black hole. And I desperately search for any excuse to find the sun again.

8

eleven years ago

Casey – age 16

2013

It was incredible. That a specimen could be designed this way.

I was innocently making my way to the bathroom to relieve myself. It wasn't *my* fault that Jessie left his bedroom door open as he toweled off his hair after his shower. Thankfully–or perhaps, unfortunately–he had his boxers on, but that was it. And it was magnificent.

I watched as the water droplets from his hair dripped down the smooth lines of his back and he was slowly turning. Somehow that didn't make me move to at least pretend like I wasn't ogling him. Instead, I just soaked up every new bit of skin revealed as he turned to face me. His door was only open a sliver. The hallway was kind of dark, so maybe he couldn't see me? I don't care–he had abs, and they were incredible.

Addison had mentioned Jessie was in the back workshop further down their property, playing with bits of furniture when he was down. He'd injured himself in hockey and was off the team. I guess he found a new hobby. A hobby that gave him a new kind of muscle definition that was mouth-watering.

"Whatchya doing there, Ace."

Busted.

Mid-ab-appreciation, Jessie spots me in the hallway, and with faux confidence and trying my best to hide my blush, I clear my throat and approach his door. He opens it wider, at some point having pulled on a pair of gray sweats.

"What's that?" I point to a dark spot on his forearm... like it was the sole reason I was staring at him. He seems to notice my slight embarrassment at being caught, and he one hundred percent knows I was checking him out, but thankfully he just goes along with my pretend ignorance.

"Dropped some wood when I was in the shop earlier." He shrugs, turning back into his room. I take it as an invitation, walking closer but leaning on the door frame, remaining safely on the outside of his room and the masculine scent of it.

"What are you working on out there?"

"New bookshelf." He gestures to the current one in the corner of his room before he spins and sits on the edge of his bed, facing me. "Old one has had it."

"I didn't realize you were an avid reader?" I ask, squinting at his collection to see if I recognize anything.

"You can look." My eyes dart to him, and he grabs a shirt to pull on, tilting his head to the shelves. "Go for it." Swallowing to wet my dry throat, I steel my spine and remember that I am a strong, confident woman and I don't need to be anxious around any boy. Even if it was the one guy who muddied my mind. I enter the forbidden zone and beeline straight for the shelves, reading the titles.

"*Gatsby, To Kill a Mockingbird, Catcher in the Rye, Dracula... Age of Innocence,* a lover of classics, I take it?" I giggle.

"It's the best kind to read." He sighs.

I turn my attention to him for a moment, and he just stares in my direction, his expression relaxed, but there is still something so intense about having his attention on me. I look back to the shelves. "I've always wanted to read that last one."

"You can borrow it."

"Oh, no. That's fine. The school readings are enough right now. But I have them all on my list." I straighten and go to head for the door when Jessie continues.

"You read much?"

"Nothing of your taste, I'm sure." I smile and turn when I make it back to the threshold of his room, leaning on the door frame once again.

"I might surprise you." His lips pull into a half smile, and it has my stomach dipping in that familiar way it does when he is around. His piercing eyes of green and blue search my whole face.

"Jock, nerd, handyman. Is there anything you can't do?" I mock and he laughs huskily under his breath, but doesn't respond. My eyes scan his room for a brief moment, and I note the trophies on the top shelf and a few picture frames. He has... *are they flowers?*

"They're Jenny's," Jessie informs me, obviously noting where my gaze had snagged. "She won an award at cooking school, and they gave her a bunch of roses." He rolls his eyes and my nose scrunches as I smile.

"Roses are the worst. So cliché," I joke.

"So cliché," he agrees with a gentle laugh and that comfy silence washes over us again, nothing said or needing to be said before he breaks it, "I thought all women loved roses."

"Well, I guess I'm not all women, then." I sigh and go to head back to Addy's room, but his deep voice pulls me back in.

"What's your favorite, then?"

"Hmm?" I ask, turning back and seeing him leaning forward, his attention stuck on me like he is hanging on for the answer.

"Flowers. If you don't like roses like every other woman in the world, what are your favorite?"

"Marigolds," I respond, feeling the smile grow on my face as I recall the bunch Mom just planted in the backyard. "They are bright and bold. I swear they shine. Like a bunch of little suns you get to hold in your hands. You can't look at a marigold and not feel joy." The corners of his lips tip up, and his eyes grow slightly wider as he opens his mouth to say something. Except we're interrupted.

"JJ, you ready?" Jenny pushes past me into Jessie's room and grabs her purse from the end of his bed. He stands at attention quickly when she walks into the room, his cheeks slightly pink and no longer making eye contact with me. He clears his throat.

"Ahh... yeah. Casey was just asking about the books." I don't know why he had to explain that, but Jenny doesn't seem to care. She rolls her eyes and slides on her shoes.

"C'mon Jessie. I'm hungry. Let's go."

"You guys aren't staying for dinner?" I ask them both, but direct to Jessie. Jenny isn't usually the nicest person, and I don't really know what Jessie sees in her.

"Heading to her parents' for dinner. Celebrate her award." He gestures back to the roses and grabs his sweater. I nod and back away to head to the bathroom. My bladder is officially screaming at me to stop thinking with my hormones and finally go do what I was on my way to do when I got distracted.

"Well, have fun." I force a tight smile and turn toward the bathroom.

"Later, Ace," Jessie says as they start to descend the stairs, and when I look over my shoulder in their direction, Jessie throws me a wink and then he's gone.

Like none of that even happened.

9

omelets are for sharing

Casey

I knock again, because I don't think my first three were heard. If they were, I'm certain he would have answered. I know he is home because the café doesn't open until 7am, and it is 6:23am according to my phone. I check again–6:24am.

"Jay, I know you're awake. I can see the shadow under the door."

Jessie opens the door and gives me a bored stare, like my presence here is the last thing he wants. "Why are you here, and why so god-damn early?" He doesn't phrase it as a question, but I wouldn't have been able to answer even if he had... because he is freaking shirtless right now.

Jessie Motherfucking Jenkins, in all his glory, is bare chested, with low cut jeans and a tea towel over his shoulder and just standing there like he is a six-foot version of Charlie Hunnam, ready for a cowboy photo shoot. I haven't seen him this revealed since I was sixteen. And I *certainly* haven't felt this woozy about a guy since... well, since I was sixteen. "Umm..." is all I manage, and instead of acting like a grownup, I peruse the male specimen in front of me, taking in the tower of muscle and the way his skin looks both smooth and rugged. The boy I had ogled eleven years ago is now a man, and he must have been busy with his hobby of furniture making because he is *stacked* with muscle.

I shake my head and snap my eyes back to his, not missing the knowing smirk he has on his face.

"You alright there, Ace?" His voice is deliciously rough, and it teases me. *Good lord, Casey Moira Baker, you need to get laid. Fast.*

I waltz into his apartment, eager to pretend I'm completely fine and not tingling in places I have no business tingling in, and head to his one single living room window. More pretending as I look out to the view, but all I see is the memory of Jessie shirtless, and I continue with the words of the English language that form the sentence I came here to say.

"Are we friends?"

There is no response, and so I turn. *Thankfully,* the Husqvarna model found a shirt to put on and stands by the stove as he looks over at me. "Well?"

"Do you *want* to be friends?" he asks, or rather, grumbles.

I roll my eyes and then plop myself down at his dining table. "Well, of course I want to be friends."

He rolls his eyes, that familiar scowl firmly in place as he shakes his head slightly, returning his attention to the stove and releasing a big sigh. "What are you doing here, Casey?" he asks as though I am a bother. *So much for friends.*

"Well, I, firstly, came to determine if we're friends."

"And secondly?" Still not looking at me.

"I need to find the first thing out first." He looks at me over his shoulder, an assessing look before his brows furrow and he faces back on the pan. From the scent, I think it is an omelet. Also, it smells *delicious.*

"We're friends." He doesn't sound pleased about it at all. Still hasn't offered me an omelet.

"Do you like being my friend?" I ask and lean forward on the kitchen table, propping my chin on my hand. "Because it doesn't seem like—"

"Is this line of questioning going somewhere? I typically like my breakfast in peace." *Well, okay then, grumpy pants.* His tone cuts through the room like a knife as he turns the stove off, flips the omelet on to the plate–still hasn't offered me one–and practically throws it back to the counter. I swallow deeply as he pinches the bridge of his nose, his shoulders tense, but I refuse to let him get to me, so I roll my shoulders and sit straight, making a mental note to move up my scheduled emotional time. I'm feeling a bit more sensitive than I should be. Feeling like the edging on my control is not the typical type of edging I'm usually down for.

"It's okay, I'll leave. I'm sorry I interrupted you." I give him a soft smile and stand for the door.

"Don't do that," he scolds.

"Do what?" I tilt my head and beam at him, because I'm not letting some guy ruin my internal strength.

"Pretend I didn't hurt your feelings."

"You didn't. But I know when I'm not wanted, Jessie. I'll leave you be." I pluck a blueberry from the container on my way out and make a show of popping it in my mouth before offering him a closed-lip smile and making for the door. The picture of calm and unbothered.

"Wait." He puts a hand up in front of me and steps in front of my path to the door. He mutters a low *dammit* before he continues. "I'm... sorry. I didn't mean to snap. I haven't had my coffee yet. And I wasn't expecting company. You're also very... sunshine for this time of day." I don't have the energy to laugh at him. My emotions aren't as easy to control today, so I just smile and get the words out that I came to ask.

"Okay, well, I was just coming here to ask if we were friends. And then, if you said yes, I was going to ask you a friend question."

He drops his hand and sighs while shaking his head and this time, it's him who is smiling and laughing instead of me. "We're friends, Ace. What is it?" I narrow my eyes and assess him. Only for a minute before my excitement gets the best of me.

He grabs the plate and heads for the table. As I turn to follow him, he pulls my seat back out and gestures for me to sit down. I say nothing and take the seat. He pushes me in, like some kind of 19th century gentleman and then takes a seat on his side. I shake my head and ignore all of those things as I continue. "Well. I have a self-defense class tomorr—"

"What happened? Did someone hurt you?" His voice is rough, and his eyes pinch together with what I can only describe as a mix of anger and worry, which has me relaxing into the seat.

"Chill, nothing happened. I am *hosting* a self-defense class at the studio. We have an instructor coming to teach a class to see if it is something we are going to start adding to our roster moving forward." He visibly relaxes and starts on his omelet, gesturing with his hands to continue, and I try not to salivate at the smell. *Why has he not offered? Mid-century manners, and yet, still a caveman.* "Noah was supposed to come with us to be the dummy we practice on, but he got called to Chicago for some work thing and isn't going to be around. I was wondering..."

"Isn't that what the instructor is for?" He looks at me, puzzled. And I still look at the damn omelet. I wonder what he puts in it to make it smell so good?

"Well, no, they need someone for us to practice our moves on." I look back to his eyes and I feel like I've been busted reading porn.

"Would you like an omelet, Case?" he asks on a sigh, defeat coating his tone. I bury my neck in my shoulders, biting my lip to smother my grin as I nod. But instead of making me a new one, he pushes his plate across to me.

"Oh. No, I don't want—"

"Just eat it." He leaves no room for argument and that smell leaves no room for my protest. I take his fork, dig a piece out, and shove it right in my mouth. I close my eyes because the taste is sensational, and I'm officially jealous.

"Okay, this has no business being so delicious! What do you put in it?"

When I look up at him, he is leaning back in his chair, a peaceful smirk on his face as he brings his coffee mug to his lips. He shrugs and just says, "Secret. Can you not practice on each other?" It takes me a minute to understand he has changed the subject back to the self-defense and is not talking about us practicing anything on each other. *Which I was surprisingly ready to accept, regardless of what it was.*

I mean, that would make sense, but the instructor had said we should see if we could get a guy to volunteer, show women a more accurate representation of what it would be like to try to take on a man rather than another woman. Not that women can't also be strong and tall. But the strong and tall men are typically who we are protecting ourselves from, so we should probably learn *with* a strong and tall man. I don't say any of that. Instead, I just take his rejection in stride and stand to leave, but not before polishing off his breakfast. If he is going to be rude, then so will I.

"It's okay, you don't have to. Noah said he might be able to get Caleb to do it." I give him a tight smile and he stands quickly.

"Wait. I didn't say no. I was just trying to understand why you needed *me.*"

"But you don't have to. It wasn't really *you* than it was just a man who was tall and strong." And Jessie is certainly strong. He winces at my words but recovers quickly as I stand there wondering if he has like '*I go to gym*' muscles, or if it was the kind of muscles that are honed by labor. Given the hobbies, it is likely the latter. Just naturally occurring muscles, the kind that are earned from dirty, strenuous work.

Good god, get it together, girl.

"When do you need me?" He ignores everything else I say and the way I'm probably peeling his shirt off with my eyes.

"Today at three?" I say softly and he stays standing, his omelet I finished all but forgotten, and he walks the four steps between us and stands directly in front of me, his frown in place, his messy hair tempting me to tame it with my fingers as that same vanilla-sandalwood wraps itself around me.

"See you at three," he says, so low. A deep baritone that makes my mouth feel dry. I nod quickly and dart out of the door without a goodbye.

I jump around on the mat, loosening up my limbs and rolling my neck to warm up my shoulders. This class isn't typical for a yoga and meditation studio, but it felt typical for empowering women, and that's really what I'm in the business of. Giving women the movement of their body, the control of their mind and now, with this, the confidence and strength to protect themselves, too.

I quickly check my watch and notice the time is 2:50pm. He isn't here yet, but he said he would be. And he said we were friends, too, so he'll come. I shake my head.

It doesn't matter if he comes or not; the guest was a suggestion, not a requirement. And, anyway, he has his own life. I'm only being an inconvenience by dragging him out in the middle of a workday.

I check my watch again. 2:51pm.

I really don't recognize this version of myself. Don't understand what any of this means, so I chalk it up to needing to have an emotions day so that I can get back on track and focus. I mentally prepare myself for that day to be tomorrow. It's a Sunday. I have no plans. Addy is away with Noah, and Rosie... I'm sure she'll keep herself busy.

"Lovely to see you ladies here today. I'm so glad you're here and ready to learn to protect yourself, give yourself strength..." the instructor claps his hands together and displays a gorgeous smile as he continues, "and, of course, have some fun." The women in the room giggle, but I'm certain it is less a reaction to his humor and more a reaction to cover the effect I'm sure this man has on women everywhere. Did I say hot? Because holy handsome.

The door opens and closes from behind me and instructor Dan smiles gorgeously again. I wasn't going to look because, *damn, Dan.* But then vanilla and sandalwood wrap around me and I can't even help myself. I turn toward the door and Jessie has his eyes locked on me. He has a soft smile on his face, and it brightens my whole day to see that he actually came.

"You're here?" I ask as he comes to stand next to me. He looks down at me for a couple of seconds, his eyes scanning my face.

"I told you I would be." I force myself to swallow, and instead of answering, I just give him a smile and we turn our attention to instructor Dan.

"I assume this will be our volunteer today?" Dan asks.

Jessie nods and throws a hand up, pulling his face into a forced smile to the rest of the women around the room. I see the way they also light up at seeing Jessie here, and as I take in each of their reactions, some kind of strange possessiveness overtakes me, and I have to actively tamper down the need to stab a flagpole on Jessie, *"This one is mine. I was here first!"* I quickly shake away those thoughts. Jessie is here to help the class as a whole. And in any event, he isn't mine to claim.

Dan moves us each through a warmup and some starting positions before he pulls Jessie to the center to go through some practiced maneuvers.

"Okay, we're going to walk through some of the more common ways that you might have to defend yourself against someone. I need one of the ladies to volunteer, and I will walk you through the movement with our pretend attacker here." He says with his hand on Jessie's shoulder. Every single hand in the room flies up and my jaw hits the ground. I almost want to chastise them for being so goddamned eager. My hand, of course, is down, and Jessie stares at me like I'm a dummy and should have beaten everyone to the punch. Now I feel like a horrible friend because he is already uncomfortable in big social settings and now, he is going to have to fight off twenty horny women who look at him like he is a piece of meat. *He does look delicious.*

"How about I start? I've done a few of these before, and maybe it'd be good for the girls to watch first," I announce, stepping forward while still actively shoving down the cave woman who wants to get on all fours and bark at the women gawking at JJ.

Relief passes over Jessie's face before his cool indifference is back. Dan nods and gestures for me to walk forward, placing his hands on my shoulders to gently direct me in front of Jessie. I watch as his body goes rigid, his eyes staring at the place where Dan's hands rest on my shoulders. His face pulls into something mean, but only for a second. The moment he looks back to my eyes, it's gone.

"Closer," Dan says to Jessie, using his grip on my shoulders to turn me around. Before I know it, the warmth of JJ's front is almost completely warming my back. I feel his breath hit the back of my neck and that same delicious scent wraps me up. I should really tell him to cash in on that. Bottle and sell it; he'd make millions.

"So, for the first one, we will demonstrate an escape if you were attacked from behind." He says to the class before turning to us. "Jessie, could you please wrap your arms around Casey's middle, pinning her arms like you're an attacker?"

Jessie does what he is told, except my body completely betrays me because this doesn't at all feel like I'm being attacked. Maybe by my hormones, sure, but this is not the kind of attack my brain, or Little Casey, wants me to fight off.

"Okay, good." Yes, *good*. Jessie's arms are firmly wrapped around my body, his face is in my neck, and I swear I can hear him take a deep inhale. I have to physically restrain myself from falling back into him, to stop myself from pushing back and demanding he start exploring with his lips and his hands.

"Now, Casey, the slow movements are to grab onto his forearms here," he points to where Jessie's arms are held tight under my breasts, "and pull yourself in." I follow his instructions as he slowly walks us through it. "Then swing your hips to the side." I do so and he stops us. "To get momentum and an advantage, this gives you good range to injure your attacker, weaken their grasp on you, and be able to escape. Now that you have swung your hips to the side, with a closed fist, you can swing a punch backward into the groin of your attacker several times." He says this mostly to the class while indicating the new open space from me moving my hips out of the way. I clench my fist and go to swing. "Woah! This is just a demonstration. We will get him some protection before you go injuring the goodies." Dan chuckles as he grabs my fist. I look back at Jessie to apologize and his face makes me burst out with laughter.

"I think I just saw my life flash before my eyes," he chokes out, and the girls laugh alongside me.

"I'm so sorry! I can't believe I nearly knocked out the golden berries!" I say back to him, quiet enough just for him.

His arms are still firmly wrapped around me, and he leans in, so his response is just for me, too. "Did you just call my balls the golden berries?" Amusement coats his tone, but it still makes my cheeks flush. I shrug in response and *thankfully*, Dan takes back the focus.

"After you've gotten a few strikes to the groin in, you should have the momentum to spin and lock your hands behind your attackers' neck." Dan grabs my shoulders, and Jessie's grip on me loosens only slightly as I'm turned in his arms. Dan grabs my arms and lifts them, placing them around Jessie's neck, and suddenly our faces are extremely close. I feel every bit of warmth where our bodies touch and Jessie's hands on my hips—

"No, you should place your hands here. Naturally, after you've just been punched in the sack, you probably want to hold and beg for mercy," Dan says it low enough, like he needs to remind us this is public, and we are not currently in an embrace. Jessie snatches his hands from my hips like they burnt him and leaves them near his front.

"Good," Dan announces to everyone else. "Now, Casey, locking your fingers together behind his neck, you need to pull him down a touch." I do as I'm told, and with Jessie's tall frame, he is bent over, his head being lowered as I pull, and then I realize exactly where his head is.

Right in front of my breasts.

I hear a groan from Jessie and his hands tighten into fists at his side.

"Sorry, am I hurting you?" I whisper to him, letting go of my pull slightly.

"Not in the slightest." He grunts out, but he still sounds like he is in pain.

Dan turns to the rest of the class. "From this angle, you'll be able to get a few good knees into the groin area to further incapacitate your attacker, giving you the opportunity to run." Jessie's hands snap to his groin with speed as I raise my knee. "Woah! Again, just a demonstration. Until the man has some protective padding, please don't unnecessarily make him infertile," Dan jokes, and my cheeks heat. I lean in further and whisper an apology to Jessie. Dan rests a hand on Jessie's back, a quiet indication we can stop. "Okay, good. Let's get him in some gear and we can all practice. Jessie can take turns giving the ladies an example of being attacked by some strength and height, but the rest of you can break off into pairs and still practice together. The more it becomes instinct to react this way, the safer you'll be," Dan announces to everyone before striding toward the gear he brought with him. I release my grip on JJ's neck without removing my arms completely, and he rests his hands on my hips to straighten to his full height. I'm stuck in place, looking into those confused blue-green eyes, the speckles of gold twinkling and the way his half smile grows on his face. From this close, I notice the scruff on his face is neatly trimmed, like a groomed businessman who has an attachment to his beard. I have this impulse to reach my hands and scratch at it, but I remain somewhat sane as I don't move. His eyes flit to my lips and hold. It makes them feel dry, and I lick them to rid myself of the sensation, but he only bites his as he follows the path of my tongue. *God damn, it is hot in here.*

Someone clears their throat, and it's like a bucket of cold water. I snap my arms away from Jessie and take a few steps back. Elle stands off to the side, a knowing look on her face, and my cheeks heat like never before. I force a smile to pretend like we weren't just caught about to kiss as I turn toward the bathroom. "Be right back!" I announce. And practically run.

Did we almost just kiss? Was Jessie about to kiss me? Surely not. I *definitely* imagined that. There is no way Jessie Jenkins felt the same tension I did. He isn't the one harboring a crush since he was sixteen and on a sex hiatus that is sending his hormones wild. That is just me. There is. No. Way.

I barrel into the bathroom, standing at the sink, and splash cold water on my face before I give myself a few gentle slaps. "Get it together. You are a professional and you are an example. Strong independent woman who needs *no* man!" I point at myself in the mirror. I close my eyes, straightening my spine to full height and rolling back my shoulders. Taking a deep inhale through my nose, I slowly release it through my mouth. Feeling the pale blue ball of calm centering joy spread its way through my body. Traveling my arms, my legs, and through my center before making its way to each of my fingers and toes. I breathe slowly and when I open my eyes, I feel centered, calm, and in control. "You are strong. You are fierce. You are in control." I say it to myself and then release the final breath. A smile spreads across my face as I feel a sense of satisfaction spread through me. Yes, I am absolutely in control.

10

who did this to you?

Jessie

Sunday morning is the one morning I let myself have off. The day I get Eugene to open and man the shop for the day. He's a good egg. I was originally skeptical because he didn't read or really know anything about books. His one redeeming quality is that I'm pretty sure he can brew a coffee better than me. Not something I will openly admit to, but the little creations he can form with the foam are truly something else. So, I took the morning to sleep in, bum around the house. I finished the book I was reading and moved on to *The Odyssey*. Except, despite being perched in my reading chair, surrounded by books, the type of peace I usually spend daydreaming of, I can't focus.

Instead of reading the words on the page, I see the tiny auburn flyaways at the base of Casey's neck as I had held her tightly to my chest in the studio yesterday. I see the rise and fall of her breasts as she breathed heavily. We were pretending, and providing a demonstration, and yet, when she pulled me toward her chest it took every single cell in my body not to grab the neck of that ridiculous tank, tear it down to bare her perky breasts to me so I could devour her.

I shake my head and re-read the same sentence I have re-read for the last ten minutes. Except all I see are the same words on a loop in my head.

I can be your person.

Here was this kind, selfless woman, agreeing to befriend a lonely grump. Maybe it's that I woke up at thirty-three and have never felt so lonely. It feels pathetic to be so desperate for a connection; it's even more pathetic that I'm struggling to swallow my pride and just behave like a normal guy. But *fuck,* I can't get her out of my head. Imagining her in all kinds of places, most of them naked and with me inside her, that blue bow tied around her delicate wrists so I could take everything I wanted. It feels forbidden, wrong, like a betrayal to Casey, me lusting after her when she had agreed to be my friend. *Ugh, friend.*

I aggressively turn the ring on my pinky for a distraction, trying to focus on the feel of it twisting on my skin, but I still can't stop thinking about the way Casey re-emerged from the bathroom with a solid indifference. She chatted with her staff, we ran through a few more movements, and it was like the electricity I felt with her around was only one-sided, like I was imagining the whole thing in my head. *Right?*

I'm officially going insane. And it's all thanks to a small chestnut pixie.

Thinking that she didn't also feel this pull toward each other. That the moment we were in the same room, the air didn't thicken and make rational thought impossible. I mean, *of course* she didn't. There was no way she was attracted to the likes of me.

This infatuation was stupid, ridiculous, inappropriate, and perhaps that was why I decided on another distraction. I walked into my room and pulled out the manuscript. The one I wrote a year ago before promptly shoving it to the back of my closet. I pull it out and dump it on the reading chair, pacing the space before it, twisting the ring again as I mull it over. Ready to finally complete another edit. Maybe if I polish it again, I'll feel ready to show the world?

No one wants to hear what you have to say.

Why would they? This book is just a tormented, fictional spin on the tragic story of a boy who had his heart torn from his chest by the sun of his sky.

No one cares about that story.

Another frustrated grunt as I run a frustrated hand through my hair. I spin, grabbing my keys from the counter, and leave the apartment, slamming the door behind me. Unsure where I'm going or what I'm doing. I forgot my coat, and the New York air is unforgiving, but the heat thrumming through my veins is doing its job so far in keeping me warm. The streets are busy with people in their activewear, their fashionable coffees in hand, walking their pets. But it all passes me in a blur, as though my subconscious has a one-track mind. Like I'd planned this, my insanity has taken over my motor skills and now I have somehow ended up at the Garcia building, standing in front of apartment 23A.

I raise a fist to knock and instead throw my head back in exasperation. "What the fuck are you doing, Jessie?" I chastise myself and turn to leave. But I make it four steps, then pivot, and before I think about it anymore, I raise my fist again and knock. Possibly heavier than I meant to.

The door opens a crack, and I see the warm auburn hair that I see in my dreams spilling over her shoulder as she leans through the gap. "Oh." Her voice is softer than usual, something off in the way she speaks. She quickly closes it, and before I can protest, she opens it again, a smile I can tell is forced plastered to her face. "Hi, Jay, what... what are you doing here?" She tries to pretend, but I hear the wobble in her voice, see the stains on her cheeks and the way her lips have puffed slightly. She was crying.

Something tightens within me, like a wrath and an urgency. I want to simultaneously save her from her woes and destroy the perpetrator all at once. Whoever made Casey Baker cry or feel sad was going to meet a painful demise, and I'll be damned if it wouldn't be by my hand.

I push the door open wider, stepping right up to her, planting my hands on her face. "Who?" I practically growl at her. She looks shocked, but after a few tense seconds, she melts and leans into my touch, lowering her eyes to her feet. I urge her with my hands to lift her gaze to mine. If she won't tell me with words, I'll get them through her eyes. I don't care. "Ace, tell me. Who made you feel like this?" I try to soften my voice, try to dim down the rage while I map out the ways I'd ruin someone for hurting her.

"Me," she says on a whisper and big sad tears drip slowly down her pretty pink cheeks before she squeezes her eyes shut, releasing a sob. Before I know what I'm doing, I pull her to my chest and wrap my arms around her, walking her backward into the apartment and kicking the door closed behind me.

She wraps her arms around my waist and just cries. I feel strange, a mix of rage and pain. I want to make it stop. Make her not hurt, but at the same time, I selfishly take pleasure in her coming undone in front of me. That she is letting me comfort her, allowing herself to lose a little bit of that control she holds onto so tightly.

It dawns on me then that I have no idea what I'm doing. I don't know how to comfort, I'm not good at helping heal or talking through emotions. I pray to *God* she doesn't want to vent. The only emotion I'm well acquainted with is anger. And I feel like that won't do much use here.

I use a hand in her glowing reddish-brown locks to gently massage her head, a firm hand between her shoulder blades, and we stay standing near the entryway of her apartment like this for minutes.

She breathes in, then steps out of the embrace, leaving the safety of me, and taking with her my sanity in not being able to cure her unhappiness. She self-consciously wipes her cheeks and turns and heads to the kitchen. I can't even help it; I follow her like a lost puppy as she finally speaks. "How come you're here, Jessie?"

She isn't mad, but she is embarrassed, and I hate that.

"Well... I was feeling like shit." I shrug and subconsciously twist the ring on my finger. "I was going to see if you wanted to... hang out or something," I mumble because I feel like an idiot. The only reason any of these honest words are coming out is because when she is in the same room, I seem to lose all sensibility.

She turns and looks at me, a quick sight of shock, before reaching and grabbing a glass to fill with water at the sink. "Oh, you wanted to hang with *me?*"

A lot of responses come to mind. None of them make it past my lips. When she looks up to me, she must find the answer she was looking for and a soft smile replaces the pain she held previously. She brings her thumb to her mouth and chews it again.

I step back into her space. Gently prying her thumb from her mouth, I run a soft finger through the line formed between her brows. The rarity of the imperfection only adding to her magnificence. Operating on autopilot, and this suddenly desperate need to take away any pain she feels, I twist and slide my grandfather's ring off my pinky, sliding it onto her thumb. She looks at it, a pink blush covering her cheeks. "Now, every time you go to bite your nail, you'll see the ring and remember to stop." She breathes heavily for a moment, then blinks rapidly and shakes her head.

"Why?" she whispers.

"Because doubt and worry are two things you have no business entertaining. I can see you feel them when you bite your nail. But you're exceptional. You don't need to give in to those bullshit emotions." I tuck her hair behind her ear because I can't help it, but I manage to restrain myself from running my thumb along the sharp line of her cheek or pressing my lips to her puffy ones. I'm a man, not an animal. *Yet.*

I decide then that earth shattering attraction and desire aside, perhaps we both need this. A person, a friend. If she was easily so willing to be that for me, I sure as hell could do that for her.

"You know, Ace, if you need a person, too, I'm here."

"Oh, no, I'm fine really. I just—"

"Don't lie to me." I grip her chin and force her to look into my eyes. "Stop pretending to be okay. Be strong enough to exist in your shit. If you can't do it for yourself…, do it for me." I fail to tamper down the anger, but it's hard when I watch her put up this façade. When she changes who she is to ensure other people are comfortable, to keep the peace. Her eyes search mine and a blush rises from her neck to her cheeks as her lips part on a breath. I use every ounce of control within my soul to keep my eyes on hers and my face not within kissing distance. She nods and grabs my wrist, not removing my hand, but instead leaning into the touch. I small twitch of my cock at the passing thought that she likes it firm.

I quickly step away and shake my head, and she breaks the silence.

"So… you wanted to hang out? What did you have in mind?"

"Well, what do you usually do when you have… these feelings?" I gesture and mutter as I stalk for a seat at the kitchen counter, trying to put solid objects between me and the walking temptation.

When I look back to her, her smile has grown. The light I usually find in her eyes is back, and she looks every bit as beautiful as always. "I bake."

"Well, then I guess we're baking."

Casey's baking playlist fills the kitchen, Zach Bryan singing *Holy Roller* setting the soundtrack to the way I watch Casey float through the motions. She looks truly at peace when she bakes. The sadness and sorrow from earlier but a distant memory, and I'm selfishly glad Rosie was called into work today because I get the real Casey. She isn't putting on a show, there are no fake smiles, and she doesn't pretend to have her shit together.

Watching Casey exist in her feelings, though, makes the echoing heartbreak from Jenny ring harder in the back of my mind. The bullshit I buried and refused to deal with. Our departing words and the way she just *left*.

But this new leaf is meant to be forgetting and moving on. If Casey is willing to give me the time of day, well, I'm holding onto it until she realizes that she is slumming it with the likes of me.

"What now?" I ask her from the stove. I'm stirring some kind of sauce mixture while the cakes bake in the oven. Casey is behind me at the kitchen island beating cream and she turns it off, leaning around me to look in the pot, she dips a finger in and my heart lurches in my chest, "Case, that's hot!" I go to grip her hand, but she instead licks the sauce mixture from her finger and moans with her eyes closed.

Jesus Christ. A new kind of urgency wraps itself tightly around my chest.

I watch in silence, and when her eyes meet mine, there is mischief and joy floating in their depths. She smiles brightly, and the air leaves my lungs. She nods. "You're good. Turn off the heat and set it aside. Once the cakes are ready, we can pour on the sauce and the cream and we're good to go!" She claps and goes back to the cream mixture.

I do as instructed, and when I turn back to her, I want to give her a taste of her own medicine. All the teasing smiles, little puffs of breath and moans she throws out there, having no idea the number of men she could bring to her knees with just a look. This walking, talking temptation needs to understand that two can play this game.

I slowly stalk behind her, placing a hand on either side of her body, caging her into the bench. Her body goes rigid, and she turns her head to the side. "What are you doing?" Her breath is short, and she tries to eye me.

I reach a hand into her bowl of cream and drag my finger through it, bringing it to my mouth and licking it, moaning as she had done. Except I leave my eyes open so I can see her delicate neck work as she swallows and licks her lip, see the blush that races up her neck and hits her cheeks. "Just taste testing," I tease her, dropping my voice. Satisfied the cream tastes sweet enough, I place my hand back to the counter and lean down. I test the waters even further, dragging my mouth past her ear and inhaling that intoxicating scent of flowers and soap. "Delicious."

She gasps and turns so she now faces me, and *fuck,* I want to throw caution to the wind, throw her on this counter and really get it messy. The air between us pulls taut, the tension unprecedented as I watch her chest rise and fall to the rapid rate of my heart.

Backing up a few steps and leaning against the stove, I cut the tension as best I can. "Have you made these before or first time?" I place a bored expression on my face, one I've mastered over the years, and hope she can't see through it.

She is far too good for me.

After a long pause, she shakes her head and goes along with my distraction. "Yes, this one is a favorite for Ads and Rosie. I make it often." She is breathless, and it brings me a special kind of satisfaction to know she is as affected by our chemistry as I am, despite the fact we can't act on it. Casey and I don't make any sense and it's best we don't cross those lines.

"Can you tell me why you were crying earlier?" I lean forward, casually resting my forearms on the counter next to her, and assess her from this distance. She looks back into the whipped cream bowl and scrapes at the sides mindlessly.

"It was just needed," she says quietly, and I crane my neck to get her attention.

She looks up at me and rolls her eyes, trying her best to smother a smile, but she fails and turns to the stove, her back now to me. "I try my best to keep everything under control. I don't like to think I am someone who feels things on the surface because I'm stronger than that. But you know... sometimes it's just hard. So, I give myself a scheduled time of the month to exist in my feelings. I stay home alone and I cry. I watch silly rom-coms, read sappy romance books, and I cry. Then I bake and eat my feelings. I sleep for nine hours and wake up fresh and ready for another month of being my best." She says it all, rehearsed, practiced, and certain. She holds no shame at her emotions, and I admire her so deeply because of it.

"That's..." I can't find the word, but try, anyway.

"Lame?"

"Lonely." I straighten as she turns back to me. Her head is tilted like she didn't believe I'd say it. My chest tightens out of frustration. Frustrated that she has all these big feelings, and instead of feeling safe to embrace them in the moment, she holds on to them. Because she feels undeserving of them? Because she feels responsible for ensuring she doesn't burden others? I get the feeling it's both and I can't work out why that makes me even angrier.

"You should stop that. Stop pretending like you have to be on all the time. You're as entitled to feel shit as the next person. You can exist in your feelings when you get them."

"But I can't, not really. People rely on me. How can I be there for them if I'm too wrapped up in myself?"

"And who is there for you, then?"

"What do you—"

"Don't bullshit me, Case. If you spend all this time looking out for others, who is looking out for you?"

"I don't need to be looked out for. I'm a functioning adult. I can look out for myself."

I nod, but I'm not convinced. "How do you feel right now?" I ask.

She tenses her shoulders and drops them, letting go of a breath, and I can see it. The way she is taming herself, calming and centering herself to react in a way that she believes she should. "Better, now that I baked."

"Liar."

She has the audacity to look shocked at me calling her out and her brows draw together. Something about it gets my heart racing, and I stand straighter as she fully turns from her position at the stove and stalks up to me.

"Okay then, hot shot, tell me. How am I supposed to feel right now?" she questions, anger I've never heard from her before laces her tone and it makes me smile, makes me want to coax more from her and have her unleash the real Casey, even if it is just for me.

"You're just supposed to *feel* whatever it is that is actually in here." I raise a finger and point to her chest, at the area holding her heart.

"You're not supposed to hide, not here in your home. Not here with me. Don't hide. Just be you."

"Rich coming from you, Mr. '*I hate emotions*'."

"Well," I pause briefly, trying to spit the words lodged in my throat, "maybe we can both be better at being real."

She searches my eyes, whatever for I don't know, but she finds something because that crease between her brows disappears and a soft smile forms on her face. Exhaustion evident in her eyes, and she rolls them before she groans and leans her head against my chest. "You're a dummy," she mumbles into my clothes, and something soothes the tightness I previously felt at how comfortable she feels around me. That she can fall into casual affection without blinking. A rough laugh releases from my chest as I wrap her in an embrace.

"I've spent too long around people who lie and pretend. If you want me to be open, then I'm going to need you to be real," I say, and she pulls her head back and narrows her eyes, pursing her lips like she was listening to some hidden message. I raise an eyebrow at her inquisitive stare, and she wraps her arms back around me too, a heart-stopping smile spreading across her face, and she nods.

"Deal."

11

so many bad ideas

Casey

23A Sluts

Rosie: Gangs headed to Pucks, who's in?

Addy: Who is "gangs"?

Me: Also asking

Rosie: One day you girls are going to be fun and just say yes when I ask something

Addy: And on that day, we might just end up arrested.

Me: Or in the hospital

Rosie: The Greek God, sex-pest, the tall one, crazy eyes and Lucas.

> **Me:** How come Lucas doesn't get one of your fancy nicknames?

Rosie: He is an enigma, I'm yet to work him out. Until I do, he just gets his name.

Addy: Please elaborate on the other nicknames. But also, would enigma not work as a temporary nickname?

Addy: I'm also bringing Riley; she needs a break from Mom.

> **Me:** I'm bringing JJ – that guy needs socializing.

Rosie: YAY FRIENDS

"So, which one is 'sex pest'?" I ask Rosie as we stand out in front of Pucks waiting on Addison. The early winter air isn't as brutal today, but we are both wrapped up in our coats and shaking our legs, trying to keep warm as we wait. Uncertain why we couldn't just wait inside.

"Caleb."

"WHAT?! You slept with Caleb?"

Rosie waves off my astonishment and rolls her eyes, searching the street for Addison.

"It was one time. After Noah's. He is like a dog with a bone, too. If I'd known he'd become obsessed, I wouldn't have even gone there." She is pretending to be annoyed, but I can see the slight smile on her lips. Taking this rare opportunity for the two of us, I bump her shoulder with mine to get her attention.

"Would it be so bad if you had a repeat? If he is one of Noah's friends, I'm sure he is a good guy." Rosie's cheeks blush but she holds tight to her look of indifference.

"Oh, please. He wasn't even *that* good." She fusses her hair out of her face as she looks around. I don't miss the way she bites her bottom lip to hide a smile.

"Oh my GOD!" I slap her shoulder. "You liar!" I laugh and she covers her face with her hands. "I don't think so, spill everything NOW! You would never let Addy and me get away with such blatant lies." She grunts and throws her head back.

"Fine! It was..." She looks at me, narrows her eyes, then rolls them to look away from me. "Earth-shattering. Show-stopping. I saw through space and time and felt like my soul left my body, before I came back down and found myself in the body of a goddess who was gifted her three wishes before being given a whole other genie bottle to wish for more. It was like..." I watch as she runs her fingers over her lips, and I plaster a hand over my mouth to stop the laugh from tumbling out. "Case, it's bad." Her big brown eyes widen and lock with mine as she whispers intensely.

"What's bad?" My head tilts in confusion because I wouldn't describe what she just said as being bad sex. If it is, then I really need to evaluate my own sexual experiences.

"It was *too* good."

"Is that a thing?"

"Yes! It means I'm ruined. I can't have sex again. My sex-life is over!"

"Or you could just repeat."

"I don't repeat."

"And why not?"

"Because people get attached, they get their hopes up, and that's when disgusting things like love happens." She shivers as though she inhaled a bad smell.

"I don't think love is disgusting. And would it really be so bad if you did find love? It sounds like you finally found your equal. Someone as wild and crazy as you are. Maybe he's your soulmate?"

"Ew." Rosie enacts a pretend vomit, pointing her finger into her mouth and screws up her face. "Thank you." She turns and nods, now smiling fully.

"What on earth for?" I ask, barely able to withhold my laughter.

"Saying all of that fuckery. I think you cured me."

"You are something else, Rosie Garcia." Rosie winks at me, and I shake my head as Noah's car pulls up.

Noah and Addy exit the front, with Riley swinging herself out the back and leaping onto the sidewalk, as another exits the car. The sex-pest himself.

"Garcia." He winks at Rosie.

"Ugh, pest." She rolls her eyes at him. "Okay, let's wait for everyone else inside. It is freezing out here."

"I'll just wait for JJ."

"Huh?" Riley pins me with a look.

"As in our brother, JJ?" she asks, tilting her head to the side.

I shrug, not sure how to explain that we have kind of been hanging out without everyone getting the wrong idea. Because there is no idea to have. There is nothing going on between us, and after my emotional day that turned into a wholesome baking-friend-date with my new *friend,* I think it's safe to say my unbridled desire is officially cured. Especially after I realize how completely unaffected he is and how easily he can switch from teasing to indifferent.

"Yeah. I ran into him a few times at the coffee shop, he helped me out with a studio thing, and he just seems like he could do with expanding his social circle." It feels like a little bit of a lie, a little bit of a betrayal, like he is a tragic person in need of saving, when really he is just a person who was broken too many times and needs someone to show him he is worth the love and care everyone else is.

"Just doing your bit for the community, Case." Rosie taps me on the shoulder. Riley breaks out into a laugh, but Addison's eyes narrow on me as the guys head into Pucks.

"You know what you're doing there, Case?" Addison says, just low enough for me to hear as she follows everyone in.

"What do you mean?"

"That guy has been broken before. I really only just got my brother back. Not that I think you'll hurt him, I just... could you be careful?" My cheeks heat and I shake it off.

"Of course! Really, things with JJ are purely platonic. He's your brother, anyway." She nods, but her eyes search mine. I give her my best smile that I hope says, *I have never had a sex dream about your brother. Not at sixteen and not now.* She seems satisfied as she turns and heads in while I wait for my... *friend.*

"Jessie? I think we met at Noah's?" Ethan throws a hand out to JJ as we enter and take our seats at the table. It took a *lot* of convincing, puppy-dog eyes, and smiles to get JJ to agree to come out. He was very adamant that socializing with his sister's friends was *'worse than death by Lingchi'*–which he eventually had to explain was known as a death by a thousand cuts–but once I said, '*This is what being real is, despite all the sorrow and crap we feel, we show up for people we care about,*' he grunted and rolled his eyes. Some choice curses under his breath, but here he is.

Jessie shakes Ethan's hand and gives him a tight smile. Similar in-troductions are made with Lucas, Caleb, and Stella–who I am putting together is the *crazy eyes* Rosie was referring to.

Stella works at Bozzelli's with Addison and Lucas, the crazy eyes part I think might be that they are so dark they could be black, but she also has this kick ass winged eyeliner that makes me envious of her wrist control to be able to pull that off. The one time I tried winged eyeliner, it looked like someone was trying leech therapy on my eyelids. Rosie had laughed herself sore before she was scrubbing it off my face. *'I cannot, as a best friend, let you try to get laid with that on your face.'* Needless to say, makeup is not my strong suit.

"Drinks?" Rosie announces as we sit. "I'll get first round." She grabs her purse as people call out their orders.

"I'll help!" I move from the seat, and just as I go to ask JJ what he wants, I clock the pleading look from his eyes. I wink at him. "I'll be right back." He stiffens and swallows before nodding and returning his attention to Addison and Riley. The latter steals my seat and intertwines her arms with her brother's, whispering something that makes him laugh. Something loosens inside me. A warm unfurling that makes me feel light and happy. That Jessie is here, putting in effort and bridging gaps, not just socially, but with his sisters.

"Girl, JJ is hooked," Rosie grunts as we head for the bar.

"What on earth are you talking about?" I shift my bag on my shoulder, and Rosie wraps an arm around my shoulders as we walk.

"He watches you like you're the sun and you're the first sunrise he has even seen." I laugh and smack Rosie's side.

"You are insane. Good simile, though. That editing is softening your heart."

"Nonsense. There is no softening. I'm just excellent at my job. But seriously, do you know what you're doing there?" Her tone takes a serious lilt and between that and Addison's warning, I'm starting to get a bit frustrated.

"We are just friends. We don't all have a sex agenda, Rosie." She takes a step away from me like I just slapped her, and I have massive instant regret. The shock that those words left my mouth hits us both. I must look as stunned as I feel because Rosie softens and starts laughing, a full belly laugh that has her falling forward, bracing her hands on her knees.

"Would you look at that, Casey has claws. Maybe Jessie *is* good for you, too." She smacks my ass and skips the rest of the distance to the bar. I shake my head and swallow past the lump of regret in my throat. I am not sure when I became so defensive or snarky toward my friend, but I'm not sure I like that version of myself.

"So, have you decided where you're going to live, Riles?" Addison questions from across the table. The whole crew is finally here. I put together that *the tall one* is Ethan because he is the tallest of the lot. Lucas just does his usual thing of laughing when something was funny, getting the shout on his turn, small jabs and barbs at the guys when they arise, but otherwise he sticks quietly to himself and just... watches.

"I'm going to see if I can find share-housing or something." She shrugs and sips her drink. "Everything is so expensive. And since Dad decided to go rogue and ruin all our lives, I can't afford college or my own apartment." The tension at the table becomes thick. Riley has never had a filter and sometimes it makes for awkward conversations, except our enigma at the opposite end of the table laughs deeply under his breath, which has a domino effect on Rosie and Stella, and suddenly we are all laughing with Riley.

"Nicely done, Riles," Addison grunts as she downs her drink. Noah wraps a protective arm around her and squeezes her shoulder. A small comfort I notice softens her as she leans into his touch. A little bit of jealousy pokes at my chest before I shake it off and shove it down.

"Lucas, you have a spare room, right? Didn't Lenny move out?" Noah questions.

I follow the table's gaze as it lands on Lucas. He has a moment of shock, eyes widening before he corrects himself and nods. "Ahh... yeah, I'll have a spare room at the end of the month... if you need." His eyes nervously flit to Riley as he answers before fixing his gaze on his drink.

"Oh... thanks. I'll see what happens." Riley shrugs and sips her drink. I feel Jessie stiffen next to me. He watches Lucas with an unsettling frown, his hands on his legs closing into fists.

Before we have an unnecessary display of misplaced brotherly concern, I discreetly place a hand on his under the table. Prying his fingers apart and hopefully goading him into relaxing. I keep my attention on the table conversation, but I feel his gaze snap to mine before his eyes look to where my hand touches his. My plan is successful, and I feel him relax, turning his palm over, twining his fingers with mine. It feels oddly intimate, but also right, like it was just the right amount of grounding I needed and the right amount of calming he needed.

A smothering blanket to a grease fire... Okay, my similes are not as good as Rosie's.

"How's the shop, JJ?" Addison asks.

"Ah, good." He nervously sips his beer, frown in place, and I squeeze his hand. He squeezes back but doesn't continue.

"That new menu looks popular. I saw it on the socials," Rosie says from my other side, leaning forward.

"New menu?" I ask, because I hadn't noticed he had a whole new menu. A bit of excitement at the new flavor possibilities zings through me.

"Oh... yeah, just an idea I had. Seems to be going well."

"The *Baker* Brew, right?" Rosie asks again, and my head twists in her direction. I catch the tongue-in-cheek look she gives me before focusing back to Jessie. I do the same because I'm sure I didn't hear that right and Jessie is about to correct her.

"Right." He tries to clear his throat before he disentangles our hands and nervously rubs his palms on his thighs. "It's kind of like a build it yourself menu. Encourages people to try different flavors and explore the options we carry. Then I don't have to think of it and people use the stock I order. It's a good way to get rid of some of the shit that doesn't commonly get used in standard orders." *Don't cry. Don't cry.*

Happy tears prick the back of my eyes as my heart tries to explode out of my chest. My stupid romance heart wants me to read into this *so* much more than it should, and it takes every ounce of control to remain impassive at this little piece of information.

"Oh, that sounds amazing!" I say as I clap my hands and try to swallow past the lump stuck in my throat. "I love it! Different flavor options every time? Yes!"

"Right up Casey's weird coffee alley." Addison giggles from Jessie's other side.

"That's actually a great idea. I might steal it, if you don't mind," Lucas chimes in, his face serious, but some amusement sits there.

"By all means," JJ says while sipping his drink, and I feel like my happiness meter is going to explode. Between JJ actively engaging with my friends, but also... *The Baker Brew?* Like c'mon, how am I meant to *not* have butterflies around this man?

"I'm not sure coffee suits a speak-easy bar, Lucas, but nice effort." Rosie pats him on the back condescendingly, and it still shocks me how this little Latina manages to make six foot tall and intimidating men look and feel like they are the size of an ant.

Lucas is a good sport, though. He shakes his head and laughs before responding, "Hilarious, Garcia. I was talking about the idea in general. I could do a DIY cocktail station. Get rid of some of the stranger ingredients by letting people create something horrible themselves."

"Or maybe they'll create a bit of magic," I say through a smile in Lucas's general direction. His eyes are severe as they snap to mine, their bright-hazel blue color that pierces through his dark Italian lashes, and a sobering smile that grows across his face.

"Very true, I suppose," he mutters in my direction before we both sip a drink and return to the rest of the table.

I let my gaze float past JJ, and I note his eyes locked in Lucas's direction. Fierce and feral, and I have to distract him, again. This guy really needs to be socialized more often.

"What are you reading at the moment?" I ask him as the rest of the table breaks out into their own conversations.

"The Odyssey," he responds tightly, but the moment he turns to give me his attention, he softens.

"Oh… nice… what's it about?" I tilt my head, because the only thing I know about that book is that one George Clooney movie, and I'm doing my best to think of anything other than the Baker Brew.

"Greek poems. Broken into a collection of books, but it tells the story of Odysseus…" He looks to my eyes, which must illustrate my confusion, and he shakes his head. "Never mind. It's not that interesting." I see the light in his eyes wink out. I wonder how often he hides the things that interest him because he doesn't think anyone would care. I rest a hand on his arm.

"No, tell me, I am interested. It's why I asked." I give him my best smile, which he stares at for a few beats before he snatches my eyes and continues.

"The Greek hero Odysseus and his journey home after the Trojan War." He searches my eyes for a moment before he nervously plays with his drink. "But really, it's about the profoundness of the human experience in the journey of life. Determination and resilience." His attention switches from the drink to me, and I can see every ounce of his gentle soul peeking through that grumpy façade. I give him a soft smile, encouragement to continue. Not that it's an effort, he'd never know, but it wouldn't matter if he was talking about the ingredients of paint. I'll always hang on every word he says. "It's about a man's resolve to reunite with his family, and it reflects the universal human longing for connection and belonging. The pain and the strength, at once intense and unavoidable."

He talks about this interpretation like it is a love letter, the way he speaks, like he is Odysseus himself, feeling the effect of trying to push on through, to find his love. My heart beats a little faster.

My hand rests on his thigh, facing each other in our chairs, his arm rests on the back of my chair. We almost breathe each other's air.

Rosie clears her throat discreetly next to me, and I'm thankful for the reminder that we are at a table of our friends and not alone. *Although I desperately wish we were.* So much for that unbridled desire disappearing. I'm going to have to find other tactics.

"You've a cute nose." Jessie bops me on the nose as I try to assist him through his apartment door.

The night was a success in terms of socializing him. He got along swimmingly with the guys, so much so that he is now wasted, and I am a glorified babysitter.

He gasps and points to the reading chair. "I made that." I giggle slightly at the pride in his words, but before I can say anything about it, he continues. "Made that, too." He points to the coffee table. "Doo like them?" he asks, as he turns his face in my direction, his warm breath hitting the side of my face, and I have to breathe through the lust.

"Mmhmm. So good, Jessie. Now let's get you into bed."

"Oh, no. You can't come to mibed. You Adinson's friend. Off limits," he grumbles, punctuating the last two words perfectly enough that it makes my stomach sink just a little. I already knew all of this but hearing him actually say it leaves the bitter taste of disappointment. He turns to look at me and raises a wonky eyebrow. "I don get you," he says low, the scent of whiskey enveloping us as I haul him through the living area to his bedroom.

"What don't you get, Jay?" I ask, but not really focusing on the conversation because I am trying to haul a man triple my size through an apartment.

"Why you hang aroundme. Why you've hope." He says it as we make it to the bed, and it's a good thing because I'm so shocked by his question that I stop and he falls, the mattress catching him.

"I... what do you mean? I think you're great."

"Butthass what I dongettt." His words slur, and he says all of this without looking me in the face. "No one thiks I'm great, I'm aggressively *not great*. I'm like..." he fumbles for the words as he tries to peel his pants off. He must forget I'm in the room and he isn't just undressing by himself. I turn to face the door, trying to give him some semblance of privacy. "I'm college sex, good. Not exciting, spotspona-*you know*, friend material, good, you know?" *No, Jay, I don't know.*

"I think you're a bit drunk, Jay, and I *do* think you're exciting."

"Yeah?" He looks up at me, now shirtless, pants-less, and sitting on his bed in just his boxers, looking like an absolute dream, even with his glassy eyes.

Holding on to hope that he just passes out and forgets I'm even here, I nod and smile, walking over to him and smoothing his wild hair. His eyes close at my touch and he leans into my palm. "Yeah, Jay. I think you're the greatest." He starts to nod and lay back to the bed. When I think he is going to fall asleep, his deep husky voice fills the room. "Can you call Jenny'n tell her that? Maybe... maybe if she hears it from you, she'll change her mind." Something sharp and painful spears itself in my stomach. A pain I have no right feeling because I *knew* he was still hung up on Jenny. I knew he was healing and shut off from everyone for a reason. It was the whole point of me being his friend. It is just a cold and sobering reminder of why this stupid crush I have is pointless and a waste of my energy.

I pick up Jessie's discarded clothes and hang them on the back of his door as I respond. "Why would hearing it from me mean anything to her, Jessie?" I know he is drunk, and yet I feel confident in my responses, like it's the only time I'll get any honesty from him.

"Because you're special. Youcould leadher back with your magic." Okay, there is honesty, and then there is just plain delusion. It hurts maybe even a little more that, in this fantasy, I'm the fairy godmother that grants his wish. Just once, it'd be nice to be the prize. I wasn't prize enough for Connor to bother with any effort. Not prize enough for my sister to really give me a whole lot of attention. Apparently, my *magic* extends only as far as bettering people's lives until the next best thing comes along. And for Jessie, that isn't me.

I don't respond this time, I just close his door and try to tiptoe my way out of his room—

"*Ow!*" I try to whisper-scream so I don't wake the drunk baby. I stub my toe on his reading chair on the way out of his room, and when I look down at the stupidly placed furniture item, my eyes snag on a stack of paper peeking out underneath. I use my foot to nudge it and realize it's bound together. I pick it up and—

"Oh, it's a manuscript," I whisper to myself, reading the title, *'Fragments of Me' by Jessie Jenkins.*

"Jessie wrote a book!?" I whisper-shout again. "Oh my god!" I sit down on the reading chair and flick on the light, immediately turning to the first page and diving into the first chapter.

A tear drops to the page, and it brings me back. I quickly wipe it from the page and realize I've been sitting here for 2 hours, already nine chapters deep and weeping like a baby. *Oh, Jessie.* My heart feels like it's being pulled in two different directions. It breaks for the pain and sorrow he feels deeply, that is evident within his words, but also so incredibly impressed because this... this is an amazing piece of writing and I wish he had the confidence to show it to the world.

"Immediately unthink that idea, Casey," I chastise myself. Because what I'm thinking would be a really, really bad use of a new friendship. It feels like a gross betrayal of his trust. I snap the book closed and stand, grabbing my bag and wiping my eyes. I throw the manuscript on to the chair and stare at it.

Bad idea.

Bad idea.

"Dammit," I mutter to myself. Snatching the manuscript, I run for the door.

not being enough still hurts.

Jessie

Water. I need water, Advil.

Maybe a bullet.

Fuck.

How much did I drink last night? It feels like a thousand suns burn through my window, searing my eyeballs and causing my skin to dry as I wake the morning after... well, after whatever the fuck happened last night. *How did I get home?* I vaguely remember soft auburn hair being tangled in my fingers in the back of an Uber. I somewhat recall Caleb, Ethan, Lucas, and I in a shout for shout after everyone else bailed. Except not everyone bailed. Casey, she was there. I don't know what she was doing, but I remember her sitting on her phone in the corner for a while.

BANG BANG.

"No," I barely get out. My throat feels like a desert as I try to throw a pillow on my head and ignore the knocking on my front door. I don't care if it is a Tuesday. It isn't my opening shift, anyway. I literally have nowhere to be until at least 11am.

"Go away."

"Unlikely. OPEN UP!" Riley's voice shouts from the other side.

"We brought goodies!" And that sounded an awful lot like Ava.

"Uncle JJ!" And *that* is my favorite six-year-old.

The sound of Mia's voice pulls me from my bed. I throw on a pair of sweatpants and a t-shirt that were folded over the reading chair–which I don't remember laying out–and make my way to the door and open it. Mia runs straight into my legs and makes me almost lose my balance. "Hey, kiddo," I grumble out, still trying to pull my eyelids open.

"Woah. What died in here?" Ava asks as she strolls in, followed by Riley and also Addison. *My soul* is what I don't say.

"What are you three doing here on a Tuesday? And where is Ollie?" I try not to sound so inhospitable; I *am* trying to be more accessible as a brother, but I still would like to exist in my hangover alone for a while before they all start collectively breaking my balls.

"He's with Matt. I needed a non-contact morning. If that kid bites my tit one more time, I'm going to scream." A shiver rolls down my spine at the image of my six-month-old nephew breastfeeding. Instead, I ignore the comment and stand aside for them to pile into the apartment.

"I spoke to Ava this morning and told her about your rare moment of socialization last night. She got jealous and convinced us to go to brunch. Mimosa?" Addison explains on the way to the kitchen counter. The thought of more alcohol makes me queasy, and I shake my head while closing the door and picking up Mia. I walk her over to the couch with me and twist her to sit as I lay down. Hoping she just plays around me instead of expecting me to play *with* her. Addison busies herself at the kitchen counter before they all eventually follow me down to the couch. Mia flops onto her stomach on my chest and pulls absently at the hairs on my chin.

"So, how'd you get home?" Riley asks as she drops a coffee–thank the heavens–on the coffee table in front of me.

"No idea."

"When did you leave?" Addison asks.

"No idea."

"Is there anything you do remember?" Ava laughs and the three of them take a seat opposite me on the couch.

"Caleb buying Fireball shots. Ethan said something about me being cooler than Addison." I give her a wink at her gasp. "Lucas just asked about Riley as a roommate." I turn my head reluctantly and squint in Riley's direction. "Think he might be worried you're a slob." I give her a teasing smile and she throws a pillow that I catch before it knocks Mia over.

"You stink, Uncle Jessie."

I sigh heavily. "I know, kid, I know."

Because I haven't had a chance to shower and probably reek of whiskey and cinnamon. Can't imagine that is a great combination of smells.

"Since when did you and Casey start hanging out?" That has my head snapping in Riley's direction and my brain fog clearing. *Maybe if she hears it from you, she'll change her mind.* The events of last night flood me like the worst bout of hang-xiety you could have.

Before I left the apartment on the way to Pucks last night, I was torturing myself with a scroll on the Instagram of *Petit Délice*. The French restaurant in the heart of Paris, of which had an announcement that their head Patisserie Chef was engaged, with a wedding in the summer. It felt like my whole world collapsed in on itself. Jenny and I hadn't been together in over two years now, and yet it felt like she had left all over again.

'You have no ambition. You can't live your life surrounded by books,

Jessie. One day, you're going to have to grow up. I can't live here anymore. I feel like I'm being suffocated. You suffocate me. Goodbye, Jessie.'

The words and all that they implied, all the damage they did, had swept through me like a hurricane. It threw off any goodness I had tried to do over the last couple of months. While I knew I wasn't in love with Jenny anymore, it was a punch to the gut, leaving me feeling winded. The strong burn of those Fireball shots the only thing that seemed to make me feel lighter again. I guess she found someone who made her feel alive. She found and fell in love with someone else. Someone to spend her life with. And instead of me doing the same, I just continued doing everything she called me out for. I sat, stewed, and sulked in my own darkness and pity. Never moving on, giving up on hope, and telling myself I let the best thing in life go. I didn't deserve a second chance. Not with her, not with anyone.

"JJ?" Ava's concerned voice reminds me that I haven't answered Riley's question.

"Oh, she hosted her work thing at the café. And when Noah bailed on that self-defense thing last week, I helped her out. We aren't hanging out; just a couple of chance encounters." I swallow the acid that rises in my throat at the words. It feels like an understatement. I don't mention the moments where it had felt like my heart was waking up from a deep slumber, or where she drove me so crazy I forgot how to behave like a gentleman. Completely ignore the fact I caught her crying and she let me stay and hang out with her. Leaving out the little fact that our grandfather's ring that used to warm my pinky finger now sits on Casey's thumb.

Platonic from the outside. Extremely confusing on the inside.

The damage of Jenny's engagement makes it clear I'm in no position to be anything to anyone, though. I can't get involved with Casey. As much as my dick really wants me to, my heart is ice. I don't have the ability to give her the whirlwind romance she desires. Can't give her love, I would only drag her down. Only bring her into my sadness, suffocate her like I almost did to Jenny, until all that sunshine was snuffed out. And I refuse to be the reason the world loses a star that shines as bright as she does.

"I'm glad you're branching out. You could do with some friends," Addison chimes in.

"Yeah, the guys weren't too bad."

"I told you they were great. You just have to get to know them," Addison encourages.

"So, does that mean you're, like, part of their group? Are you going to see them again?" Ava asks reluctantly.

"We aren't like you women. We aren't going to gush about a new friendship and braid each other's hair, for fuck's sake. I enjoyed a few whiskies with a couple of guys. If I see them again, I'll join them for a beer, or I won't. Who cares?" The three of them collectively eye roll and scoff at me and it makes me laugh. Mia flops around on my stomach, making an *oomph* leave from the way her elbows dig into my chest as she props her chin on her hands and stares into my eyes, the biggest grin on her face.

"Fuck's sake," she replies. *Fuck.*

"Mia! We don't say those words!" Ava chastises, but Mia ignores her.

"Do you have a girlfriend, Uncle Jessie?"

"I do not."

"Why not?" Six-year-olds have no business asking such loaded questions. I tilt my head to look at the three stooges and see if I will get any assistance. Ava and Addison just laugh, but Riley gets that mischievous look in her eye and leans forward, pretending to whisper just for Mia.

"Because he is a big baby and is scared of girls." I roll my eyes, but before I can correct her, Mia sits up abruptly.

"You're scared of GIRLS!?" she shouts and starts laughing. That kid-cackle that makes everything in the room feel wholesome. "You can't be scared of girls, Uncle Jessie!"

"Why not?"

"Because! We aren't scary. We're just smarter, silly." Mia shakes her head and continues to giggle as I shoot a knowing look at Ava, who just shrugs and sips her coffee.

"She isn't wrong." Again, I roll my eyes because this is the worst hungover conversation I've ever had.

"I'm not scared of girls. I just keep my distance to avoid hurt feelings," I mumble.

"Theirs... or yours?" That bucket of cold water, of course, is tossed by none other than Addison. The only person in the world to ever call me on my shit seriously. The other two poke fun, but Addison gets right in there and digs deep. It is both the thing I love about her and the thing that makes me burn with rage. I grunt and lift Mia to the ground before I stand.

"You're all welcome to leave." I try to push my way through the door and ignore the frown on Mia's face as she climbs onto Ava's lap–who makes no effort to leave.

Addison stands and I hear her trail behind me.

"Oh, no, you don't. Don't you lock yourself away again. We were just getting you back, Jessie. If hanging around Casey is what you need to bring you back to us, then good. If it's the Monday night at Pucks with just the guys, great! But don't you dare lock down because you think you don't deserve joy. Because you're afraid of feeling *something* again."

"Jenny is engaged." It comes out as a whisper, and the room goes deathly silent. I don't know if it is the hangover or if it is the fact that I haven't felt this close to my sisters in a while, but for some reason, my defenses drop and I turn. Riley and Addison share a similar look of pain and anger, while Ava just looks sad. The same kind of softness that makes me want to lock up and not feel. I don't want their sympathy or their pity.

"Who cares about that bitch?" Riley's words sound almost like a growl.

Jenny and I were what people donned *high school sweethearts*. We even made it through college, lived together, and were starting to plan our future together. Or at least that is what *I* thought we were doing. Jenny was applying for restaurants across the world, wanting to jet off and 'explore herself'. The carefree, gorgeous brunette who coaxed me out of my introverted shell in high school, made me fall desperately in love with her, only to jet off and leave me behind, like it was nothing. Easy. I was just a dead weight she needed to drop in order to breathe.

"*Riley!*" Ava hisses and pins her with a stare. It makes me laugh a bit, but then I look back to the blonde devil standing in front of me. Addison's face scrunches into a scowl, her eyes searching mine, and I watch her go through about four different emotions as she wars internally on how to react. Curious to see how she tames her rage, I wait her out, letting her see into me, letting her know she doesn't have to feel frightened of that anger. The same anger I learnt to burn and churn years ago. Finally, she closes her eyes and breathes out in a long breath before she just falls forward and wraps her arms around me tightly.

"I'm sorry." The words sound like they reluctantly slip out of her, and it makes me smile wider. "She didn't deserve you, anyway. But I'm sorry you're hurting. I'm sorry that you still love her." I hold her tight for a moment and Riley and Ava share a knowing look behind us before Addison steps out of the embrace. "Do you want to talk about it?" I shake my head.

"You *should* talk about it." Mother Ava to the rescue.

"I'm not still in love with her."

"And I'm an otter who can't swim," Riley mutters, the rest of us turning in her direction. "What? I thought we were telling obvious lies?" She puts on a smile that is deceptively sweet, and I walk back to the couch.

"I'm not, though. It just... it was a surprise. I guess because I used to picture my future with her, I couldn't see it with anyone else. It was her or there wasn't one. I guess... she just didn't feel the same way. But that's part of moving on. I don't love her anymore, but it doesn't mean knowing I wasn't enough doesn't hurt." I lean forward, my elbows on my knees, and head in my hands. The couch dips from either side of me as Riley and Addison lean into a hug. I'm enveloped by two of my sisters as Ava places Mia on the floor between my legs and she flops my hair around. "You'll get there, Jessie. Just let people help you, or at least let us. We might be scary girls, but we know you better than anyone." Ava has the same soft smile as mom and when I turn to look at Addison on my left she winks, then Riley, on my right, nods and pats me on the back.

"Our baby boy. Such a big softy under all that gwumpiness," Riley says in a mocking baby voice. *Right, that will do.*

"Okay, we're done now. You can leave. I need to... eat meat and lift weights or something." The three of them laugh and I stand. They grab their stuff and head for the door. As they leave, Addison lingers and turns to me. "You're going to be okay, Little Rogue." She says it like she can predict the future, using our childhood nickname to send a pang of nostalgia straight to my heart.

"Thanks, Big Rascal."

13

dinner or dessert?

Casey

"Dinner!" I call to the girls from the kitchen, and it feels an awful lot like I am a mother. I don't mind cooking dinner every night. In fact, I *love it* and would promptly kick the other girls out of the kitchen if they tried it, but I also wouldn't mind a meal cooked for me at some point, too.

"What's on the menu, chef?" Rosie asks as she strolls in and plops herself at the dining table.

"Nothing fancy today, just spaghetti. I'm exhausted."

"Oooo, big night?" Rosie gives me the waggly eyebrows and I scoff at her, turning back to the stove to plate up.

"Hardly. That Monday night wiped my whole week. I didn't get home until 2am because I was busy being the DRA for a bunch of drunk idiots." And I stayed up even later when I got home binge reading Jessie's manuscript. But I don't tell anyone that. "Then I've been covering all of Grace's classes this week because she is sick." She is actually pregnant, and can't keep her food down right now, but she isn't ready to tell people, so I keep the fact I'm going to be an aunty to myself. She hasn't even told our parents! I was surprised when she called to tell me. Perhaps it is more because we are business partners and I needed to know why she couldn't take her classes, but I fully expected to be the last person to find out. We aren't close in the way Addy is with her sisters. We don't socialize or talk like sisters; we don't have sleep overs or visit each other. I don't really know why, she just always kept me at a distance, and I let her.

"DRA?" Rosie questions.

"Designated Responsible Adult." A collective, *ahhh* from the girls fills the room.

"Quiet weekend this time, then?" Addison asks, sitting down, joining Rosie. The rare night where she isn't with Noah or he isn't here. The two of them are usually inseparable.

"Actually, I have a date this weekend," I say it on a sigh, like I'm not flipping out about it.

I discreetly downloaded SoulSwipe and managed to match with a guy named Ian. I deliberately kept this from Rosie because I knew she'd say something about how he sounds like a forty-five-year-old accountant and I'm in for a night of the worst sex of my life. But I really need this. Like, really, *really* need this.

I need to get a certain dirty blonde coffee brewing king out of my head so that I can function and behave like a normal single woman in her mid to late twenties. I need a... *release* because it has been too long and Little Casey is getting restless. I need a good man to *take me* properly and make me forget about the way Jay makes me feel like every nerve ending has been set on fire. I need to get over this stupid crush on a guy who is hung up on his ex, and most notably, not interested in me.

"Do tell?" Rosie says as I grab my plate and sit with them at the table.

"His name is Ian and—"

"Ugh, he sounds like a forty-year-old who believes the male orgasm is superior and women should be grateful for missionary," Rosie grunts and I pat myself on the back for knowing her in advance.

"Actually, he is twenty-seven, so same age as us, he is in med school, and lives in the Upper East Side. His pictures made him look like a brunette Tom Hardy."

"So, short king?" Rosie questions, and Addison and I both almost choke on our pasta as we laugh at her.

"I guess. He didn't advertise his height and I really am not that bothered," I reply.

Rosie nods, but her face suggests she isn't done with her comments.

"Goodness me, Rosie, if you bite your tongue any harder you won't be able to eat your dinner," I coax her as Addy, expectantly, shovels pasta in her mouth without coming up for air.

"It's just..."

"Don't stall, spit it out," Addison says over a mouthful of food.

"Well, I thought you had a thing with Jessie?" Rosie narrows her eyes at me, and Addison chokes, properly, on her food next to me.

I vacantly pat her back as she regains her air. "I don't have a thing for Jessie." I laugh, but it's void of humor. Really, the response is, *Jessie is still in love with his ex and too busy pining for her to notice me.* Instead, I say, "We're just friends." Turning my attention to Addison before I continue. "You guys have been through a lot. You have Noah, Rosie, and me. Jessie didn't really have anyone, so I figured we'd hang out. It's no big deal. Really." They both nod, except Rosie narrows her eyes and studies me. I had handed her the manuscript after I redacted Jessie's name. She doesn't know it's him, but I wonder if she is suspicious at all. She looks at me now like she knows a secret.

Addison steals my attention by placing a hand on my arm.

"Thank you. For being there for him. I'm glad he has someone like you looking out for him." She says it gently and smiles. It makes me feel warm but also guilty. She thinks I'm out there looking after her brother, but instead, I'm trying to actively get him out of my system. Dreaming about him, thinking about him while trying to sleep, while showering, while meditating. It was becoming a problem. I've surrendered to finding ways to distance myself from him. I have no idea how to be his friend and not physically want him. That was why I ended up on SoulSwipe. If I fell in love with someone else, I could be around Jessie without wanting him to touch me, without feeling like I can't catch my breath or think properly.

My phone rings from my pocket and I reach to answer it, looking for any excuse to avoid talking about JJ any longer. "Sorry, have to get this." I excuse myself from the table and answer as I duck into my room for a breath.

"Hello?" *Oh yeah, there is someone on the other side of the call.*

"Oh. Hi..." I pull the phone away and... *fuck's sake!* I really can't catch a break. "Jessie? What's up?"

"I have a dinner with Mom in a week, and I was trying to work out what to take? I was instructed on a dessert. Help?" His tone is flat, there is shuffling in the background, and it makes my shoulders relax. The usual warm buzz his voice sends across my skin softens and slows my mind.

I bring my thumb nail to my mouth out of habit, except I see a flash of silver. Looking at my finger, I see the ring he slid onto my thumb last week when he showed up in the middle of my scheduled crying time. '*You're exceptional. You don't need to give in to those bullshit emotions.*' My stomach dips and flutters at the memory of Jessie holding me, saying those words and then just *being* in my space in a way that felt the opposite of intrusive. I didn't feel smothered or embarrassed. It was just... nice.

"Ace?"

"Oh... sorry. What about those chocolate lava cakes we made? How many are you baking for?"

"Just Mom and me." *Why is that so sweet?* I really need to sort my crap out.

"Let me look at my recipe book and I'll flick you some options." I smile through the phone. JJ making time for just him and his mom is special, especially after the horrible divorce and trauma she went through. This feels like something that should have some thought into it, something that deserves to be remarkable.

"No worries," he says, but we both hang onto the line, or at least I do. By the sounds of it, he has me on speaker in the background and has probably forgotten about me.

"Thanks for Monday, for coming out with us," I say, because I have no idea how else to bring it up. If he remembers how he got home or what was said. *Whether he notices a missing manuscript.* I instinctively use my pointer finger to twist the ring on my thumb, feeling it burn through all my betrayals.

Just as I feel like I'm about to come clean, Jessie speaks. "I'm sorry, Case."

"What for?" I whisper, because my voice won't work.

"For what I said about Jenny."

"Oh, don't be ridiculous. You love her, it's total—"

"I don't, it's not... she's engaged. I found out that night, so it just..." My heart shatters and I blink back the tears. Stupid empathy tears because the love of his life is marrying someone else, and I forced him to come and be social. I'm an idiot.

"Oh, Jessie, I'm so sorry. If I'd known, I wouldn't have forced you to come out. I'm so sorry."

"Please don't be sorry. It's fine, really. She doesn't mean anything to me anymore. It was just a shock." He has always been good at lying to himself.

I say nothing, and neither does he. Just a few seconds of tense silence.

"Okay, Jay." He releases a breath on the other line.

"Okay," he says back.

What else is there to say? In this moment, though, I know I'm not going to let him hide again. Maybe we'll both find our one true love and find a friendship, as well.

"Well, I better get back to the girls," I say, awkwardly.

"Oh, of course... I'll see you..." He ends the same way as last time and hangs up before I can say goodbye.

"You look incredible." Ian leans closer to me at the bar of Bozzelli's as we wait for our drinks. His hand rests respectfully on my hip as we stand toe to toe. He is, as Rosie had described, a 'short king'. Even in my semi-heel, I am at least four inches taller. He is pretty though, like textbook pretty, I'm sure he could model for Calvin Klein, you can't see height in photos.

"Thank you. You clean up well yourself." I bite my lip and try my best to flirt, but at this point, it's forced. Despite the way he appraises me, I still feel no attraction to Ian. I don't feel the butterflies, I feel no desire to get naked. I *do* have a desire to experience sex ASAP, though. I need to get other images out of my head, so I'm betting on a drunk buzz to give me the desire to go home with Ian and hopefully find a release.

"So, you're a yoga instructor?" he questions and leans closer, his hand roaming gently on my lower back. I wore a tiny dress that I wouldn't normally wear, but I explained to Rosie it was a dire situation and she said this would be the one to end the spell, so here we are. "I am. My sister and I own a studio." Creepy bartender guy from Noah's party puts our drinks in front of us. He raises an eyebrow at my date and pointedly looks around, as though he is waiting for some tall lumberjack to come and chastise this guy, too. *Honestly, he would if he saw.* And I know it, too. Jessie might not be interested in me, but I know he still wouldn't think much of Ian here.

"That mean you're flexible?" And suddenly his touch on my skin feels like an acid burn.

I pull my lips into a tight smile and swallow the retort while nodding.

"Mhmm."

"That's hot." *Ugh.* Men. "Feel like dancing?" he asks, while trailing his eyes down my body. I slam my drink on the bar, because I can't seem to calm the frustration that builds inside me. "Sure." I turn and pull his hand toward the dance floor and scan the area. I'm determined to get laid. If it isn't with this man-child, it will be with someone else.

I pull my stupid date onto the stupid dance floor and let him crowd behind me. I let him put his hands on my hips as I tune out to the music around me. I close my eyes and will the ball of frustration out of my body through dance. I feel the movement and let the music wash over me. I pretend it's just me here, enjoying the music and letting my body move as though it is an instinct—as though there isn't a douche feeling me up right now. I open my eyes and the dance floor is packed. There are people everywhere. Rosie and her date are in here somewhere, because I refused to date without some kind of backup. As I scan the darkened dance floor, my eyes stop on a man to my left.

Tall–or tall*er* than me–brown hair neatly combed and styled. He is wearing a shirt that gives away his muscular build, has a jawline that could cut glass, and a strong nose. *Yum.* There are those tummy flips I've been waiting for.

I hold his gaze, forcing my eyes to a half-mast, and decide to tease him with my current date. He hovers, a small smile pulling at his face as he narrows his eyes and sips from his glass of what looks like whiskey. His eyes tell me he knows the game I'm playing; his body language tells me he enjoys it.

I take a dip and grind my way down Ian, pushing my ass out as I come back up and sexy-tall guy smiles wider and winks. *That's my cue.* I turn to Ian. "Going to the bathroom, be right back." He looks a little disappointed, but shrugs and keeps dancing.

I look back to my left, and sexy-guy is nowhere to be seen. I head for the direction of the bathroom, anyway. If it was a missed opportunity, at least I can take a few breaths then bail.

As I head toward the bathroom, a hand wraps itself around my elbow and drags me into a dark corner. I yelp until the hand spins me into a hard body, and I meet the face of sexy-guy up close and personal. "Oh." I breathe and bite my bottom lip. "I thought you bailed."

"Not at all, just wanted to get you somewhere quieter." He pulls me against his body and wraps his arms around me. My body is enjoying it, but something in my head is giving me red flags. I ignore the bells and whistles because that is why I have gone this long without sex. I can ignore red flags if it means good sex, right?

"Is that so?" I taunt him and lean in for a kiss as he reaches down and palms both ass cheeks. He leans down and takes my mouth in his. The kiss is both searing and dangerous. The kind of kiss that they write about in dirty romance novels, and it causes the red flags to turn to green as I wrap my arms around his neck and pull him closer.

"*Fuck, you're hot,*" he growls into my lips, and I claim him again, urgently, and his hands frantically search my back. One hand breaks away and comes to my front. "Can I touch you?" he whispers, and my heart starts rapidly beating out of my chest. I look to him and search his eyes. I imagine Rosie hearing this request and slapping me for pausing. Unable to verbally agree, because I'm worried I'll chicken out, I nod, and he takes me in another kiss. His hand makes its way under the front of my dress and rubs gently at my center, over the top of my panties, eliciting a dirty moan I had no idea I was capable of releasing. The foreign noise snaps me from my daze and I push gently at his chest, "Wait. I—"

"Sorry, sorry." He looks a little embarrassed, but still reaches for me and I let him.

"I just... I don't even know your name." A laugh tumbles out of me at the absurdity, and his smile grows to a whopping size that has me biting my lip. "Lane," he says roughly. "Yours?"

"Casey," I breathe, and he leans down and kisses me again.

"Casey." He says it back to me like he is testing it out. "Feel like getting out of here, Casey?" *God yes.* I nod my head and he steals my lips with one more kiss before he turns and guides me out. On the way we run into Rosie.

"Um, bitch, that ain't the guy you arrived with?" Her face pulls into a mischievous smile as her gaze widens and takes in *Lane.* I squeeze my eyes shut at being outed in swapping a date, but when I look back to Lane, apology in my eyes, he wraps an arm around my waist, pulling me to him as he leans down to Rosie.

"No, but it's me she is leaving with."

Rosie gasps audibly, forming an *O* with her mouth before she high fives me and leans in to whisper, "*Yes, bitch! Get it!*"

I whisper back that I shared live location–we can be spontaneous, but we can also be vigilant.

Lane pulls me toward the front, and as we exit, I twirl to face him, his fingers interlaced with mine and that smile of his dangerous. "Where are you taking me, Lane?" I add a slight moan to the end of his name, which has it's intended impact as he practically growls and hauls me against him, taking my mouth in another searing kiss as we walk slowly backward toward the street. We pull apart as he goes to answer my question, but we bump into someone.

"Oh, sorr—"

"Ace." *Oh god.*

"Jessie. Oh... Hi!" The words squeak out of me at an embarrassingly high pitch. I shake my head and try again. "*Hi.*" Okay, that was basically a growl. I am officially an idiot.

Despite doing nothing wrong, I feel strangely like I'm being busted doing something illegal. I plaster on a happy smile, like I'm so very pleased to see him. Except he is the last person I want to run into because, of course, everyone pales in comparison to him.

He is taller than Lane, sexier and more rugged than Lane. The word *dirtier* comes to mind, even though, technically speaking, he is actually clean.

But he just... he just... *ugh.* You just *know* it'd be dirty with him, and I hate that now I'm thinking about it... *again.*

"What are you doing out tonight?" I ask sweetly and wait for the moment where I can imply to Lane that this is not my boyfriend.

"Catching up with an old friend." He gestures to the stunning blonde next to him and that stupid unwanted pit of sour gummy worms falls heavy in my stomach. *Jessie is on a date.* Of course he is on a date; I'm also on a date.

Because we're friends.

Nothing more.

He might be hung up on his ex, but at least he's found *someone* to help him pass the time.

I get itchy skin at the sadness trying to take me down. At the very solid reminder that I wasn't good enough to be that person for him. That he could never look at me and see anything other than his little sister's friend.

I nod at him and smile. "Well, Lane and I were just leaving." I gesture to my date and step into his embrace, which seems to perk up his ego, and he wraps an arm around my shoulders.

He awkwardly nods his head at Jessie before looking down at me and smiling. "Should we go?" he asks, except it feels like he is asking something else, something like, *are you sure you're leaving with me?*

"Yep!" I look back to Jay. "See you around?" I plaster my best smile on and will my heart to slow. Jessie scrunches up his face, but, in a second, the look gone back to that same solid indifference that makes my heart sink. I don't know what I expected. Jealousy? Him to throw a caveman-level tantrum about Lane having his hands on me? Why would he, though?

He levels Lane with a severe look, delivering some kind of message that Lane seems to answer with his eyes. Whatever transpires between them, it seems to be enough because Jessie looks back at me. "Yeah, I'll see you." Before he nudges his date with his elbow and they enter the bar. He never introduced me to her. She didn't say a thing, just smiled and looked at her shoes like she was trying not to laugh. *Stupid bitch.* I'll give you something to laugh about.

Ugh. I'm sure she is a super nice lady, and probably not a bitch at all, but for whatever reason, I can't seem to reconcile that with this stupid jealousy.

As Jessie leaves and I try to reign in my facial features and the abundance of mixed feelings, Lane pulls his phone out and orders an

Uber.

Between the cool night air and the run in with Jessie, I'm feeling very sober. "You good, red?" Lane coos into my ear, causing goosebumps to trail my skin. I turn into his embrace and ignore the odd nickname. He rests his hands on my lower back as I wrap my arms around his neck, walking us backward so he leans against the outside wall of Bozzelli's as we wait for the Uber.

"I'm good," I whisper and steal a chaste kiss. He smiles into it, then pulls back to analyze my eyes.

"What?"

"Who was that?" He nods in the direction Jessie left.

"My, my, Lane, are you jealous?" I tease and bite my lip as I curl the back of his hair with my fingers. He laughs gently and uses his hands to grab a fistful of my ass.

"Not at all, sweetheart. But I think he was."

"Oh, no." I laugh at his insane assumption. "He is my friend's older brother. We're just friends," I explain.

"Mmhmm. I'm sure he only sees you as a friend," he says, that sexy smile still in place, his hands still searching.

"What do you mean?"

"Well, he looked at me like he was ready to clock me. He looked at you like you were dinner." He hums the words in my ear, not even dirty talk and it has me shivering. Probably because I'm picturing Jessie, and me, and—

"And how about *you*?" because I desperately need to not picture Jessie right now.

"What about me?"

"What do you think about me?" I trail a finger across his jawline and let my eyes wander his pristine face.

"Mmmm, I think you'd be perfect for dessert." He says it into my lips before he steals them in another kiss. A car pulls up behind me and I pull out of his embrace, walking backward to the car.

"Let's find out, shall we?"

"Oh, sweetheart, you're speaking my language." He follows me into the Uber, and we make it safely to his house.

And I do everything I possibly can to *not* think about Jessie.

14

lame lane

Casey

I am unbothered.

I breathe through my morning meditation and repeat the words, trying desperately to unclench my jaw as I say them out loud.

I, am unbothered.

Breathing again and repeating, trying to relax my muscles *and* my jaw.

"Iamunbothered."

"It *sounds* like you might be bothered."

My eyes snap open as Rosie's voice pulls me from my relaxa— Oh, who am I kidding? I couldn't mellow out even if I had weed gummies.

I am very bothered.

I grunt and stand up from my position on the floor of the lounge room and make my way into the kitchen. It's 5:30am on Monday, so of course, Rosie and I are awake, and Addison is sleeping like the dead.

"I thought you got laid this weekend?" Rosie asks as she watches me stomp my way into the kitchen.

"I did." Except it was horribly anti-climactic... or, at least, for me.

The guy gave major BDE and yet... under performed. Way too much, '*Is this okay?*' and, '*Can I touch you here?*' Like, c'mon, man. I love consent as much as the next person but... for the love of God... TAKE CONTROL! Rip my clothes off, throw me on the bed, and tell me how you like it. Is it too much to ask for? Has the world gone insane? Am I being irrational?

"Okay, this is SUPER fun. I have never seen you like this. Can I have all the gooey details?"

"He crossed the finish line, and it was *not* a relay race. Instead, it was a one-man fucking marathon, and I was left at the water station," I grunt out and Rosie audibly chokes on her cereal as she tries to get her laugh out. Grabbing my *bend and flex* yoga mug, I pour my second cup of coffee for the day and give Rosie a deadpan look.

"So many metaphors. Swearing from Casey Baker? My goodness, he did a number on you."

"Want another? His name was Lane... should have been *Lame.*" That gets me a full-on cackle from Rosie, and I can't help myself. I join in.

The worst part is the lack of orgasm isn't even the full reason I'm pissed. I went home and sorted myself out. No, I'm pissed because a certain someone *else* seems completely unbothered. *And who the hell was that blonde?!*

"It's not really about Lame Lane, though, is it?" Rosie questions as she shovels more cereal into her mouth. I sit my mug on the counter and hang my head in my hands. Unable to hide anything anymore, I shake my head and mumble, "No."

"It's Jessie?"

"Yes." I groan. "What is wrong with me, Rosie? I've haven't been able to shake this stupid, *stupid* crush since I was a teen! I had a boyfriend in between, and yet, we spent one day together and it's like

I'm a dog in heat."

"Maybe you guys need to like... bang one out."

"Bang one out?" I ask, unsure if she is actually being serious.

"Yeah, you know, like, get it out of your system." In theory, it sounds splendid. Practically speaking? Horrible disaster. I know for a *fact* I would just fall harder. And falling for someone completely unavailable is out of the question. Been there, done that. Really not interested in *that* again.

"He isn't even interested in me. This is a one-way thing. Plus, he had a date on Saturday."

"So did you."

"But that wasn't a *real* date."

"Maybe his wasn't either." She winks at me when I narrow my eyes at her.

"No, he is the one hung up on his ex. He really does just need a friend and I'm happy to be his friend. I just..."

"Want him to pick *you,* " Rosie says softly.

I shrug and look down at my thumb, twisting the ring on my finger. Completely conflicted about the way he has acted in the past versus the version of him from Saturday night. Unaffected and completely unbothered. Making it abundantly clear that this is very one sided.

You're exceptional.

"Yeah. I guess it'd be nice to be chased instead of doing the chasing. I spent four years in a relationship with a guy who never made an effort. Never showed his emotions, never had a real conversation. And now, I'm lusting after a man who is so beyond heart broken by his ex that he has no room for another love. Am I just destined to fall for emotionally unavailable men? Is that like... my trope?"

Rosie laughs and hops down from her position on the stool, stalking around to meet me in the kitchen. She puts her hands on my shoulders. "There is no such thing as a soulmate, Casey. I know that soft romantic heart of yours is waiting for your knight in shining armor to swoop in and manhandle you into a swoony love bubble, but that isn't real life. You're going to trip a few more times before you fall properly."

"You can tell you're a romance editor. You're excellent at romantic declarations." I smile down at her, and she pulls me into a hug.

"No more self-deprecation for men who don't deserve it, okay?" She points her delicate fingers up at me. "Be a good feminist with a great sex life and you'll live happy and fulfilled." She nods and flicks my nose before she turns and struts back to her bowl of cereal.

I try to listen, except she says, *'great sex life,'* and I immediately wonder how great Jessie would be in bed.

I'm screwed.

I walk through the coffee shop and the door chime jingles, and for some reason, I was hoping to enter unannounced. Instead, my entrance gets his immediate attention, and it's like a million and one emotions pass his face, and I can't tell which one he lands on.

Plastering a smile on my face, I skip the rest of the way, reordering my emotions, shoving down everything that makes me horny and sad when it comes to this broody man. I am determined to hold my promise to him and be his person. That means showing up even when I really don't want to. "Morning, Jay!" When I make it to the counter and hoist myself up so I sit, facing him, he straightens and there is a half-smile on his face before he shakes his head and leans back on the counter opposite the one I prop myself on.

"Good morning, Ace." We stay staring at each other for a few seconds that feel like minutes. His eyes are intense as they hold my gaze, like he is trying to read my mind.

All the weirdness I thought would be there, isn't. Instead, it's like the sexual tension just exploded by a million. It's like he knows that I spent the morning wondering if he would have let me leave without finishing the job properly. It makes me wonder how he'd rectify the situation if I told him.

My face must tell him something of what I'm thinking because he asks, "How was your weekend?" Except, with the way his voice sounds, it's more like a dirty promise than anything else.

"Good—" I cough to clear the husk from my throat, which just makes him smile wider. "Good. You?" I twist the ring on my finger nervously and he tracks the twitch before he takes a few steps forward and comes to stand directly in front of me.

He places his hands on either side of my thighs that sit on the counter, his face level with mine, and his eyes land on my lips. "Could have been better." *Oh, and don't I know it.*

I force a swallow. "I came to try the new Baker's Brew menu." It comes out as a breath and his eyeline lifts from my lips and steals my gaze. Without looking, he uses his left hand to grab something and place it on my lap, but he doesn't step away and doesn't remove his arms from this cage. He just continues to watch my eyes. So many questions he wants to ask that he won't. So many feelings he wants to feel, but won't.

I look to my lap and see the menu sitting there. I grab it and flick my hair off my shoulder, trying to wrangle my pulse so as to appear unbothered. Jessie just stays where he is.

"Oooo, Cotton Candy! That could be yum."

"It's terrible."

I look to him and narrow my eyes. "Is that an honest assessment or coming from someone who hates joy?" I raise my eyebrow in challenge, and he bites on the inside of his cheek to hide his smile, as those gold and blue eyes alight with amusement.

"Touché." His voice is deep and rough and sounds dirty, and I hate loving it so damn much.

"Maybe..." I trail off and read the rest of the menu, trying my best not to be distracted by his proximity, by the smell of vanilla, books, and *man,* and the way he completely envelops my senses, especially from this close. "I'll get Cotton Candy, with blue heaven and banana. Extra cream." I slap the menu down and place my hands on the counter next to me, inside his embrace, and lean forward. I smile and bite my lip. "Delicious," I whisper, repeating his taunt from that day in my kitchen.

Our faces are so close, I could lean forward a fraction and we would kiss. Our lips would touch, and I'd be lit on fire. Everything in me screams not to do it because it crosses the final line I'm trying to hold between us, but *God* do I want to know. He seems to sense my growing desire and takes one for the team as he steps back and toward the coffee machine.

"You are utterly insane, you know that?"

"What do you mean?"

"Did you hear the order you just gave me? It is a toothache waiting to happen."

"Nonsense. It sounds like every kid's dream." I plop down from the counter and move to the book stacks that line the wall opposite the coffee machine in an attempt to get some air as I try to find a way to casually ask about that blonde he was with, without crossing friendship lines and entering jealous girlfriend territory.

"You're not a kid anymore, Ace."

"No, but don't you wish you could be again?"

He chuckles and nods his head.

"So…" I linger and turn away from him so he can't see my blush. "What did you do this weekend?"

"Same as you." *Ugh, vague.* "Went to Bozzelli's for a drink," he continues. I nod and try to pretend I am reading the titles of these books.

"Walk of shame, or did you stay for breakfast?" I put on my best teasing voice, so it sounds like a question from a friend and not me satisfying my own curiosity.

"Neither." *Dammit,* that gave me nothing. I spin on a heel and see him looking at me, a shit-eating grin on his face.

"What is that look for?"

"Just amused," he says before he puts his attention back on making my beverage.

"And what is *so* amusing?" Now I'm annoyed. I walk back to the counter but remain on the customer side and cross my arms as he leans on the counter and pushes my finished drink forward.

"Casey Baker, you're jealous." I steal the drink and scoff.

"Am not." Are too. "I was simply being a *friend* and trying to see if you had as successful of a weekend as *I* did." I throw Lane in his face and leave out the fact the guy couldn't find a g-spot if I drew him a map.

"Well, for the sake of your curiosity, I dropped Chloe, my old college friend, home to her *wife*, at about 11pm." *Ohhhhhhh.*

I internally slap myself and try my best not to wear my embarrassment on my face. Except, I must fail because Jessie's face lights up, but when his gaze moves to my neck, the light drops, and he turns to busy himself at the counter. "Seems like you had a great night, though." I raise a hand to cover the giant hickey Lame Lane left.

Friends, we're being friends. And I need to bridge this weird gap I created with my misplaced jealousy. "Was great on the surface. Lane was pretty lame." He turns his head over his shoulder and laughs.

"I could have told you that."

"Mmm, but you didn't." Challenge set in his eyes as he turns.

"And what would you have done if I'd said something?"

"Well, what would you say?" I ask back, narrowing my eyes and biting on the straw of my drink.

"That you won't find what you want with that pretty boy," he says it low and deep, like a caress, as he stalks forward again.

"What exactly do I want?" The air in the café grows thicker and I feel like I'm a thousand degrees with no escape.

"That's the million-dollar question, Casey." His face sets in an emotion I can't name, and his eyes snatch to my lips as his voice drops. "What do you want?"

For you to take me against these bookshelves and remind what it's like to be desired by a man. "Extra chocolate," I respond and wink at him, swallowing all the unspoken words. Because I can't. I can't sit here and want a man that probably, most likely, doesn't even want me. He shakes his head and lets go of a soft chuckle before he grabs the chocolate shaker and leans to dust the chocolate over my drink. He does so without dropping eye contact, and I take a few steps toward the door. "Well, I should probably get going." He nods and smiles at me softly, but when I go to pull out a note to cover the coffee he puts his hand over mine and shakes his head, that same soft smile in place.

"Okay," I whisper. "See you later?" I ask and smile at him from the door.

"Yeah, I'll see you." Again, no goodbye, before he turns and busies himself, and I leave the shop.

I leave, feeling both empty and satisfied. Conflicted but content?

What on earth does that even mean?

15

princess-worthy romance

Jessie

I have no idea when I fell asleep, but the only reason I notice I was asleep at all was because of the knocking at my front door.

"Open up, Jay!" Casey's melodic voice floats through and like a pirate to a siren my heart beats faster, my muscles relax, and I'm stalking for the door without a beat to think about it. I was halfway through the *Odyssey* when I apparently dozed off. It's late out, maybe 9pm, my reading lamp the only light on in the dark apartment, every blind open, letting the lights of the city set my small apartment in a glow.

"What on earth are you doing out in the city alone this late at night, Ace?" I grumble at the thought of this walking ray of sunshine skipping through the dangerous streets of the city, completely oblivious to her own fucking safety.

I barely get a chance to greet her as she waltzes on past me, her arms full of grocery bags. It's nice to see her confident glow back, considering the last time I saw her was Monday when she dropped by, I assume, to suss out the success of my weekend. I did take great pleasure in seeing her get jealous over me with Chloe. Chloe also found it amusing. The moment we got inside, she let go of the painfully loud cackle she was holding on to and just teased me for being *'a lovesick idiot'* for the rest of the night. I hadn't admitted anything. Chloe only said the sexual tension was so thick she almost needed a snow plough to make it out–her words, not mine. So fucking dramatic.

The joy in her jealousy settled like a sour pit when I saw the hickey marring her skin. A mix of rage and frustration took over, and I had no idea what to do with it. Why had she come? To rub it in my face? She was jealous of my date, that much was clear. But still went home with someone else? What kind of fucking game is she playing?

Her soft humming on her path into my apartment brings me back and I kick the door shut so I can trail after her, grabbing the heavy bags from her arms as she tries to protest.

"I found the perfect recipe for you date with your mom! I thought I'd grab everything, and we could make it together." She hits me with the sharpest smile that steals the breath from my lungs as I place the bags on the counter and repeat the same mantra I've been trying to beat into my brain since that day I found her crying in her apartment: *just friends. Just. Friends.*

"This time of night?" I ask, confused why she'd go out of her way to do this. More confusion. More frustration.

She shrugs, but her smile remains. "I couldn't sleep, anyway, and Elle is going to take my classes tomorrow."

"Why couldn't you sleep?"

She purses her lips as her eyes dart around the groceries as she tries to come up with a lie. "Couldn't stop thinking about this recipe, and I didn't want you to embarrass yourself with your own mother, soo…" She trails off as she pins me with an amused smile.

"I didn't need you to come and make it for me. I know my way around a kitchen." Her smile drops and I try to clarify. "Not that I *don't* want your help… I don't want to put you out. I appreciate it—"

"Don't be ridiculous." She waves me off and laughs under her breath as she swings her long auburn hair into a knot on her head, baring her slender neck, which makes me need to close my hands into fists, so I don't grab her. Don't succumb to this stupid caveman desire to feel my lips on that bare patch of skin. She is oblivious to my internal struggle as she heads to the sink to wash her hands. "This is an old family recipe. I wasn't going to let you fumble around and ruin it. What kind of a baker would your mom think I am then? No pun intended." She says it sweetly, and I ignore all the annoying reactions my body is having at her being here as I start unpacking the grocery bags.

"Fine," I grumble.

Seeing her leave with *Lame Lane* on the weekend, then finding out she actually did sleep with him–add to that the fucking hickey–I was vibrating with sexual frustration. I was close to wrapping my fist around that strawberry-blonde pony, yanking her to me and wiping any trace of his touch from her. Replacing every mark with one of my own. I don't, of course. Instead, I try to shake it off and remember: she isn't mine to possess. I have no right, and this stupid lust-filled obsession needs to stop. Friends, we are friends, and she is damn good at it.

And now she's here in my kitchen.

"You have a Bluetooth speaker?" I point in the direction of the speaker near the TV and glare at the back of her as she skips toward it.

Her floral scent filling my senses, filling this room.

Taking over my mind, body, and soul.

"We need an epic soundtrack for this one." She smiles and bites down on her bottom lip as the song she picks starts to play through the room. She skips back over, *adore u* by Fred Again fills my small apartment, and she looks like the picture of joy as she fills my space with her smile.

I can't help it. I'm drawn to her. I want to be in whatever space she's in. I want all those smiles. I want to hear every laugh. I want... *her*.

"So, what is this recipe?"

"Scottish Macaroons. Was flipping through my mom's old recipe book and found it. It was actually the first thing Mom let me make on my own when I was a kid."

The memory tugs on my mind. "Wait, I remember that. You brought them over, and I polished off the whole container. They were delicious."

"You remember that?" she asks, a bright smile on her face, but a gentle blush heats her cheeks.

"Of course. I remember all the things you made over the years."

"No way," she chuckles in disbelief. "I brought a container of food over like every weekend from the age of six."

"I said I remembered everything *you* made. Not the food you mom made for you to bring us." She seems stunned, and when I search her face, I see her big blue eyes blink rapidly, like she is trying to understand something. I leave her to her shock and turn to line up the ingredients from the bag. I wasn't lying. Casey's mom made most of the desserts she brought over, but every now and then, the treats were Casey's, and they were always epically delicious. She has such a talent in the kitchen.

"Where is it?"

"Where is what?" She looks puzzled as she responds.

"The recipe book." She looks at me over her shoulder, a mischievous smile slowly growing on her face. Leaning slightly toward me, she lifts a finger to her temple.

"It's all in here, Jay." I couldn't stop myself if I tried. I stare at her lips as she bites down on them. We're close now. Close enough that if she just pushed up on her toes and I leaned in slightly, I'd finally know if she tastes like the floral scent of her hair. Whether she makes a little moan as I swipe my tongue through those pretty pink lips. I'd finally be able to replace that fucking hickey with one of my own.

"Umm..." She swallows, clearing her throat, and I realize I've inched forward ever so slightly and we're now sharing breath. Breath that is ragged, as her chest rises and falls at the pace of mine.

Fuck's sake. I can't be around this woman for more than five minutes without sporting a semi and wanting to be balls deep. I run a hand down my face and try to think of grandmas and sick dogs, trying to will away the lust-filled haze we seem to constantly find ourselves in.

"Let's start then, shall we?" I say as I pull out a baking tray and a bowl.

She nods and then blinks rapidly, plastering on a fake smile as the song plays, and that weird universe thing happens where the words of the lyrics fit perfectly for this exact moment.

'You walk through life just like a dancer, if I had my way, every day would be your parade, oh, I adore you.'

"Okay, we'll pop them in the freezer for forty-five minutes and then the fun part happens." She claps her hands, the same beaming smile plastered to her face as she closes the freezer.

"What's the fun part?" I'll be honest, I've never questioned Casey's baking, but... there is potato in this dessert and I'm a little concerned.

She smacks my chest and then leans on the counter opposite me, crossing her arms against her chest. "You're supposed to say the whole thing was fun." I roll my eyes amusedly as I nod and pad over to the bookshelf.

"What, you didn't have fun?" she asks, but her tone is teasing, a small chuckle lining her words.

"Yes, Ace, I had fun. Can't wait for what's next." My words are low and sarcastic as I hunt amongst my stack of books, an absolute mess that it is.

"What on earth are you looking for, Jay?"

"I got you some— There it is." I reach and grab the special edition that I had picked up earlier in the day.

"You got me something?" She sounds confused, like it is absurd that I, or anyone, for that matter, would think of her.

"I did." I nod my head as I hand it to her. Her eyes bug out as her mouth opens in a delicate *O* and it warms my chest. "You like it?" I try not to sound nervous, try to hide the way my palms clam up in her silence, anticipating her response.

"Jessie." She whispers my name as she gently swipes a hand over the white canvas hard back cover. The yellow and orange indented foiling under the lattice pattern and the cursive title that reads, *Age of Innocence*, flashing through the angles of the overhead lighting. "You... remembered?" I assume she means the day she searched my bookshelves and discovered my love for literary fiction. I noted her special attention to this title in particular. I shrug and scratch a palm at the back of my neck as I try to remain relaxed and calm and not like my heart is exploding out of my chest at her delight. *I'll buy them all if it means you smile at me like that.*

"I saw a couple of re-bound canvas classics at your apartment. I knew they were yours, because there was no way they were Rosie's with her dirty book obsession, or Addison's with her aversion to reading classics. I remembered that day in my room, you had them all on the list to read. All of the ones you had were there, re-bound in different covers." I shrug again. "I just thought you'd want to finish the collection. I didn't see *Age of Innocence* amongst them, but I can have it swapped if you already have it."

"It's... it's so beautiful, Jessie." Her eyes have a soft sheen to them as they look up to me, wide, the blue of them dark in this corner of the apartment, like the deepest part of the ocean.

"I love it. I don't have this one yet," she replies. I give her a soft smile, and I can't add anything else before she wraps herself around me tightly. I stop for a second before I close my arms around her and hold her to me. Allowing myself a moment to soak up her floral scent.

"Usually, I buy them, then re-bind them and shelve them *after* I have read them." She pulls back, only enough to look up at me, her show-stopping smile in place, keeping her arms wrapped tightly around me. I soak her in, giving her my natural smile for what feels like the first time ever.

"I never pegged you for a classics reader. Or an arts-and-crafts person, either." I chuckle.

"Of course, I am. Everyone needs hobbies, and I need something to channel all my pent-up sexual energy into." Her smile drops as she registers the words that left her mouth, and she straightens awkwardly out of the embrace and keeping her gaze off mine as I try to ignore all the ways I'd help her burn through said sexual energy. "Besides, all the best heart-breaking and princess-worthy romance stories come from classics," she continues, admiring the hardback, and I let her steer the conversation away from where I'd prefer to take it. "They always seem to find the perfect way to twist your heart, steal your breath, and make you believe in soulmates with just a few words." I raise an eyebrow in disbelief at her as her gaze finds mine again, and she brings her hands to her chest–still clutching the book–to feign offense.

In the next breath, her smile spreads across her face as she turns and heads to the couch.

"*I wish you to know that you have been the last dream of my soul.* That one is Charles Dickens, *A—*"

"*A Tale of Two Cities.* I know it well." I can't fight the smile on my face, and I trail after her as we sit on the couch next to each other, but enough distance for her to sit sideways, facing me, folding a leg up as her gaze falls on the book in her hands, moving over the cover appreciatively.

"*Whatever our souls are made of, his and mine are the same. Wuthering Heights.*" She says that one in a different tone of voice, one I hadn't heard before, and when she raises her eyes to mine, there are words within them that I can't pick, can't name. "*'I am in you, and you in me, mutual in divine love.'* William Blake." Her smile softens as her eyes search me and it feels like I'm right back in my childhood home. The two of us, in the quiet, comfortable silence, sharing something we can't quite work out. Like I was then, I'm trapped. I can't tear my gaze from her, can't drive my mind to find a distraction or think of all the reasons it's bad to want her.

This intelligent, light, funny, and stunning woman. It feels like... like... "*'I am yours. Don't give myself back to me,'*" I say, my voice rough from my dry throat. Her eyes bug before she blinks, and they go back to normal. Her chest rises and falls to the pace of my heartbeat.

"Rumi," I finish. It might not be from any one classic, but it fits all the same.

She wets her lips, and I track the motion before her gaze drops briefly. Before she looks back up to me and her eyes sparkle, the ocean in the morning sun as her mischievous grin—my favorite of hers—spreads beautifully across her face. "*You are, and always have been, my dream.*" I tilt my head, not recognizing that one, and narrow my eyes at her as she smiles even larger. "*The Notebook*." I laugh, louder than it deserved, but purely because she found herself hilarious and I can't help myself.

"Ace, that is not a classic." I shake my head, the tension there but not as taut.

"Well, it's a classic for me. That is where all girls first learned about love."

"What did *The Notebook* teach you about love?"

"Well..." she trails off, leaning her head against the couch and looking to the ceiling for answers. "You know, really, not much." She laughs and then looks back to me. "Maybe that it's normal that I can't make decisions. Except if my future husband yells at me for it, I think I'd slap him instead of cry." She returns her gaze to the book and continues to laugh at herself.

"Maybe the lesson is not to settle for someone who will yell at your indecisiveness. Instead, find someone who knows you enough to make the decision for you. Or wait you out until you're ready to decide," I say simply, finding it completely unacceptable that she'd settle for a husband who would be anything but patient, loving, and obsessed with her. Indecisiveness or not. Or he could fucking grow a set and anticipate her needs. She's Casey Baker, not a fucking Akkadian script that needs translating.

She looks at me with big blue eyes and a surprised smile, but pushes on with a big breath, falling further into the couch. "But it would be nice to find a guy who promises to build me a big house with a wrap-around porch, on a nice bit of land by a pretty lake. Now *that* would be a dream."

"You want a big white house and a lake when you grow up, Case?" I ask, trying to sound like I'm poking fun. She giggles softly and almost bites her thumbnail, and I watch as she stops and stares a moment at the ring I gave her. A content smile warms her face as she slowly twists it and then replaces her hand in her lap. "I always imagined I'd move somewhere more remote, away from the crazy city, have land, space, and *maybe* a lake. Then I could raise my hoard of kids in the safety and tranquility of open air and spacious land. My little section of peace in this world." She's wistful as she says it, all the while looking out the window behind me, to the city.

"Sounds like a fantasy," I say softly. She has plans and a whole life to make them happen.

She smiles and nods, her attention back to the book. "I really do love this gift. Thank you, Jessie." I nod and pull my lips into a tight smile, trying to find anything to keep her here. Something to keep her talking to me, despite me trying to ignore my attraction and desire for her. It's impossible not to notice how thoroughly she clears the sting of loneliness. Looking at me with those big blue eyes and heart-breaking smile. I want her to fill this space, every space, and never leave.

"So, walk me through the rest of this recipe. Mom's going to ask me about it, and I need to not sound incompetent." Her laugh fills the room as she throws her head back on the couch, and no matter how hard I try, I can't stop myself from seeing how perfect she looks here. In *my* space.

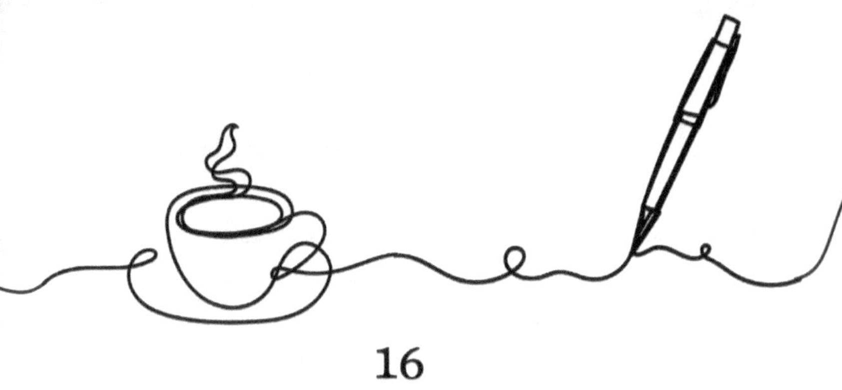

16

comfortable friendship or painful pining?

Jessie

"Door's open!" Mom calls after I've knocked. I swing it open, letting myself into her quaint apartment. It's in an older building, but the owners before her renovated. It has the classic moldings, higher than usual ceilings, original wood flooring, with creamy colored walls. She's decorated it with minimalistic designs, from artwork to greenery, the furniture simple, but elegant. Very Lillian.

"I'm so happy to see you, Jessie!" she coos from her side of the kitchen as I make my way in and put the dessert container on the counter. I make my way around her, place a kiss to her cheek before grabbing a beer from the fridge and sitting at the table.

"You made something?"

"You asked me to?" I raise an eyebrow at her.

"Well, I figured you'd buy something. I didn't know you baked." I shrug at her.

"Jenny taught me some things back in the day." Something uneasy settles in my stomach at the thought of bringing Jenny up, when Casey was the one that helped me make the Scottish Macaroons. "I actually had help with this one, though. A, uhh... friend, she picked the recipe and showed me how to make it. A family recipe, apparently." I'm rambling and my nervousness must be evident, because I never speak to mom about this crap and she gives me a knowing look.

"A female friend?"

"Don't look at me like that. We're just friends."

"And when do I get to meet this friend?" She pulls her lips into her mouth to smother a laugh, and I roll my eyes.

"Relax, you already know her. It was Casey, Addison's friend... from Great Falls."

"Oh, *finally.*" She slaps a hand on the counter and starts laughing before busying herself with the rest of dinner.

"What the hell do you mean by finally?" I sit up straighter, suddenly defensive.

"I saw the way you've looked at that girl since you were twenty-two. I know you were both kids when you met, but you've always had a connection; it was clear as day. I just wasn't sure you were ever going to *do* anything about it. Finally, that wench, Jen—"

"Alright, that'll do," I scold her and get up from the table to pace. To do something with the weird energy coursing through me.

"I'm just saying," she lowers her voice and rounds the counter, stopping in front of me and resting her hands on my shoulders. Her blue eyes roam mine, and she gives me a pitying smile. The same one that used to send Addison into a rage. "I'm glad you're finding someone who cares about you. I know you loved Jenny. But you were both so young, and she wasn't ready to be thinking about anyone other than herself. I'm not about to fault a woman for chasing her career—" I give her an incredulous look because, up until recently, she most definitely would fault a woman–her daughter, Addison, in fact–for such things. "Don't look at me like that. I'm still growing.

I'm... doing better." Glad for the pivot opportunity, I shrug her off and head for the kitchen, trying to busy myself by cleaning up and putting things away.

"Speaking of, have you caught up with Addison recently?" I glance up at her and she nods, a sad look on her face.

"We're doing much better. I have a lot of ground to make up for. I... well, I caused more damage than I thought I had." The sadness in her tone cracks open a slither in my chest.

"You'll get there. She loves you." She nods.

"Where's Riley tonight?" The sarcastic comments and dramatic storytelling the only things missing from this small apartment. Even though Riley was actively trying to find anywhere else to live, she hadn't managed to nail down a roommate.

"She's out with friends. I presume she'll stumble in at some point later." She heaves a sigh, more of exhausted effort than anything else. Riley is a free spirit. I prayed for anyone that attempted to tame her in the future.

"Have you reached out to your father?" *What the fuck?*

"Uh, no. Why the fuck would I?"

"Jessie! You might be thirty-three, but I'm still your mother!" she chastises me and I send her a guilty look.

"I'm sorry, but why? Why would I do that?"

"He is still your father, Jessie. Despite his faults, he helped raise you. You are a part of him." I scoff and shake my head, trying to bite down on the colorful words I'd like to throw his way.

"I love you, Mom, but please, don't push this point. That chapter of our lives is done. I have nothing to say to him." Especially not after the way he was with Addison. Watching her smack him in the jaw was the highlight of the entire shitshow. A warm flame of pride lit in my chest as I watched her defend herself, to fall into her fury, feel it and embrace it.

"I really hope you don't ask Addy this shit when you see her." She scoffs this time.

"I'm not that much of an idiot," she says under her breath and it makes me chuckle. She brings her eyes to me and she laughs lightly, too.

"So, how come you haven't invited the girls, too?" I ask. I'm aware my relationship with Mom is different to the girls, at least with Riley and Addison. They struggled with Mom, and maybe that was because Mom was going through her own shit toward the bitter end of her marriage, but I would have thought bridges would be made.

"I just wanted some time with my boy."

"You know this is why they get pissy and call me the golden child?" I tease, and she slaps me on the chest.

"I love all my children equally. I also know that I haven't been the best mother to my daughters, and they need more time. Space. Also, women can be horribly dramatic, and I like that you are honest with me." I roll my eyes again, but refuse to put my two cents in. No point arguing.

"And speaking of honesty, tell me about you and Casey."

"Nothing to tell. We're just friends, Mom." I sigh, and when I look at her, she is pulling the same look that says she knows more than she is letting on.

"What? I'm serious."

"Mmhmm." She shakes her head. "You lie just like your father," she says under her breath, and some of that deeply buried fury rises to the surface at the hit of her words. I know she doesn't mean it to cut, but it does all the same. Comparing me to that manipulative liar and cheat.

I will never be like him. Not in a million years.

I roll my shoulders and bite my lip to hold back words that would do nothing but cut.

"C'mon, let's get this dinner on the table so we can eat, and you can talk to me about your day." She changes the subject, and we finish up in the kitchen.

"Where the fuck is it?" I grumble, internally berating myself because I'm thirty-three and a fucking mess. I could have sworn I left my manuscript by this chair, and yet, it's nowhere to be found. My phone pings from my pocket, distracting me from my manhunt.

Ace: Lol please laugh at this with me.

That was accompanied by a picture of a cat riding a llama, and the laugh that tumbles out of me is directed more at her sending this than the random picture.

I shake my head and pocket my phone, returning to my search, just as it pings again. I plop myself on the reading chair and settle in for the slew of texts.

This has been the pattern for the last couple of weeks. Since Casey came and took over my kitchen, we've fallen into this comfortable friendship, or rather, painfully pining from a distance, in my case. But it's been nice, having someone to just be around. Nothing is forced, and we can exist comfortably in silence together without any expectations.

I think I'm suffering from denial, though. I have to remind myself that she offered to be my person simply because there was no one else. I needed to remember that this *thing* between us will be over the moment she finds someone suitable to spend her life with. But, *fuck,* am I struggling with continuing to hide how goddamned badly I want her. I had resigned to avoiding her in person, which, of course, only made her force herself into my space more. Not that I am sorry about it.

"I haven't seen you in three days, so I'm checking for signs of life," she had stated as she skipped through my door a couple of days ago. She brought the special edition book I got her, and we sat in a peaceful silence together as we read. I say silence, but it was anything but. This was how I learned she is a loud reader. She coos, *'aw's,'* and, *'oh my god that was so beautiful',* as she throws her head back and hits her face with the book. The most dramatic and expressive reader I've ever met.

And I fucking love it.

Ace: Laugh.

Her text demands when I leave the llama picture on read.

Me: Ha ha.

Ace: Better. Now, what are you doing tonight?

I try to think of something–anything. Because it's too much, pretending like I don't spend every fucking shower thinking of her. Like I don't wake up seeing her incredible smile. I'm closer to losing my control every time we hang out, and I can't bring myself to pretend today. Before I have to think of an excuse, the sky opens and drops luck right into my lap.

Noah: Guys are headed to Pucks, you in?

Manuscript hunt is put off as I flick a confirmation text to Noah, standing from the living room and walking for the front door. Telling myself to keep the olive branch open and not tell Noah to quit inviting me to his regular Monday night at Pucks with the guys.

> **Me:** Heading to Pucks with the guys.

> **Ace:** My lone wolf is actively socializing?! I never thought I'd see the day.

I roll my eyes and hide a laugh and instead fixate on those two letters.

My.

"So, what's the deal with you and Casey?" Noah asks from beside me, and I try to hide my intake of air as I sip my beer.

"There is nothing with Casey and me." I shake my head, avoiding eye contact. Caleb, from my other side, scoffs and Noah just chuckles.

"Yeah, okay. How long you plan on sitting in denial for? We did this with Noah already, and it's kind of old," Caleb responds. I roll my eyes but take the deflection.

"What did Noah do?"

"Pretended he wasn't head over heels for your little sister." *Ugh.*

"You know what, I actually don't think I want to know about that," I grumble, sipping my drink, and Matt leans over and tips his beer bottle against mine in agreement.

"Don't you pipe up, De Luca. I want to hear none of your shit, either." His face is shock before the rest of the table breaks out into laughter and Caleb takes the opportunity to barb further. "Might have to add Lucas to your hit list." Lucas spits his beer slightly as he wipes his mouth and hits Caleb with a reprimanding look.

"What are you talking about, Smith?" he asks, and I turn my attention to Caleb, who pins me with his shit-eating grin, that usually makes me what to knock someone out, except, for some reason, on him, it's not as punchable.

"Well, I heard that Riley was taking the spare room at Lucas's joint at the end of next month. How many guys live with you, Luke? Was it four or five?" Caleb taunts, and I see Lucas's face change from concerned to annoyed as he rolls his eyes, and I clench a fist at the thought of my baby sister in a house of four twenty-five-year-old boys.

"Other than me, it's one. Lenny is moving out, so there are just me and Damen." He says it leaning back in his chair and pinning me with a stare I can't read.

I sip my drink and swallow the words that threaten to end this small circle of acquaintances I've made.

"It's all right, JJ." Ethan rests a long arm across the back of Lucas's chair and slaps him on the back a few times. "Little bro here has no game. Least of all when it comes to the likes of Riley Jenkins."

"What, you don't think I could pick her up?" Lucas challenges, humor lacing his tone, and I have to white knuckle my beer to keep from throwing it at him.

"You usually go for the pretty, timid ones. You know, less bite to them, so you can just waltz in and charm. Less work. I've seen you at the bar on your nights off," Caleb replies, and Lucas rolls his eyes before he turns back to his brother. Ethan and Caleb, of course, are far more intelligent than Lucas, having goaded him into a foot-in-mouth situation. If more words leave his mouth, I might get kicked out of this venue.

"Please, I'd have Riley eating out of my hands in no time." I slam my beer to the table and level a glare in Lucas's direction. A warning. I will hear no more where my sisters are concerned.

"You're quiet over there, De Luca. You gave me shit for weeks about Addison. But nothing about Riley? Really?" Noah teases Matt, who laughs.

"That's because I knew you had a chance with her. Riley isn't giving Lucas the time of day. He's too quiet. She'd eat him alive." That releases a tension in my chest, because he isn't wrong. Riley can be fucking insane. Still, I keep my gaze on Lucas, and he gives me a subtle nod, pulling a tight smile to his lips. I hope, in a mutual understanding.

"You know, if you dickheads are going to spend every Monday talking shit or discussing the details of where my sisters are concerned, you can drop the invite. I'm not interested in suffering a slow death," I grunt out, which causes Caleb to beam a pleased smile and chuckle, completely satisfied with how worked up he got me.

"Lighten up, dude, we're just poking. Does it make it better that the woman I'm chasing isn't a Jenkins?"

"Makes me like you a hell of a lot more than everyone else at this table." I give him side-eye, and his face beams a boy-ish grin that has my rage cooling. Not a bad guy, I decide.

"So, back to Casey," Noah redirects.

"Oh, for fuck's sake, Karvelas." I rub a frustrated hand down my face. "You lot are worse than the women. Can't you talk work and sport like normal guys?"

"But women are so much more interesting," Noah provides, his smile growing as I roll my eyes at him.

"There isn't anything to know. We're friends."

"Ava and I were friends once, too." A low laugh spreads across the table. As I meet Matt's eyes, he smiles and winks at me. *Prick.*

Still, I can't help but let a smirk hit my face as I sip my beer.

"She's young, free, and happy. We just hang out sometimes. I think she honestly enjoys the peace and quiet my apartment offers. Between

Rosie and Addison, there is a lot going on. Plus, I've helped her out with a thing at the studio. It's just... normal." I shrug and spin the beer in my hands.

"Except, she is super into you," Lucas chimes in.

"And you'd know?" I challenge with a half-smile.

"You see the way she looks at you?" he provides, still looking straight through me with his clear hazel eyes. I shuffle on my chair and look back to my beer.

"Casey is like a deer in headlights on the best of days. You see the way she looks at a Blue Heaven and Banana Latte? Ridiculous," I respond, but struggle to hide the little chuckle and smile that hits my face, remembering the look Case gave me as she tasted that latte for the first time. When I finally look up, I have five sets of eyes looking at me incredulously. "What the fuck are you all looking at?" I demand.

"I correct myself. Have you seen the way *you* look when you talk about her?"

I turn to Noah. "If I'd known your catch up was an inquisition into the love lives of your friends, I would have declined the offer."

"Oooh, love life?" Fuck's sake. I run a frustrated hand down my face at Caleb's taunt and Noah chuckles beside me.

"Fine." I lose the battle of pretending. It's too damn exhausting. "I'm into Casey. But she *is* just a friend. There isn't anything there. She got out of a long-term thing, and she's... well, she is good. She could do so much better than me. Deserves better." I mumble most of it as I sink back into my chair and skull the rest of my beer.

"They all could and do deserve better than the likes of you lot." Ethan gestures between Noah, Matt, and me. "But you can be selfish," he provides.

He's wrong, though. I can't, not where she is concerned. I'd rather never see her again than force her to settle for something as mediocre as a life with me. Not with the dreams she has, the hopeless romantic that she is. I shake my head at Ethan's response and Noah chimes in.

"Have you asked her?"

"Asked her what?" I sigh, officially over this interrogation.

"What *she* wants." I turn to look at him because... well, no, I haven't. But it wouldn't be me and I can't bring myself to face the rejection. *Again.*

"My guy, you're about as approachable as a starving lion, and she is like a delicate flower. She isn't coming to you, despite how much she probably wants to. Your move." Although I disagree with their description of Casey, because the time we've spent together recently makes me think she actually has incredibly thick skin and could smack a man down if the situation arose, but it still makes me consider. A tug-of-war starts to tighten my chest. Between wanting to avoid the rejection and losing a friend I've grown to need in my life, and perhaps actually succeeding and having Casey in all the ways I've only dreamed about.

Officially over being the topic of conversation, I point the knife in a different direction. "You're awfully quiet back there. What about you?"

"What about me?" Ethan tries to shrug off the question.

"You're almost as old as I am. What? No *crush* the guys fucking hammer you about?" I grumble back and Ethan just waves a hand in the air, trying to remain casual.

"Too busy. No one interesting enough, I suppose."

"Oh, sure," Lucas says under his breath.

Ethan levels him with a look mid-sip, and Caleb latches on to the information. "Oh, here we go." Caleb claps his hands together. "What have you got for us?" He leans forward, eager to hear the response. Noah, Matt, and I just watch in apt fascination.

The silence is deafening as the brothers spend a few moments in a death stare before Ethan drains his beer and gets up. "Hitting the john," he says as he departs, and Lucas chuckles to himself.

The guys move on to better topics than grown ass men not knowing how to discuss feelings, and I remain mostly silent for the rest of the night. We all seem to have had enough of early week hangovers because we leave Pucks by 7pm, and I thankfully make it home sober and with no embarrassing stories.

Except, when I make it inside the apartment, I can't help but notice how empty it is. The space is small, and yet it feels way too big with just me.

Me: Busy?

Ace: Depends, what's the offer?

Me: Movie? Just some reading? Whatever.

Ace: Feel like going to the night market? I want to get some more binding materials and the craft stall has some pretty canvas paper.

Me: Sold.

"Have you ever thought about writing a book?" The question pulls me out of the peaceful daze I had lulled myself into as we casually stroll through the stalls of the market. Casey's gaze is fixated on the shelves holding a collection of used books as we meander through the state library's stall. I do the same on the opposite side, both of us seeming to avoid eye contact.

"Uhhh, no," I lie. "I don't have anything interesting to say." I haven't told anyone about the book. Thought about submitting it to publishers, but the story felt too personal, too vulnerable, and I'm not exactly ready for people to see the wounds of my soul. It feels like some kind of betrayal to lie to her. I know deep down Casey would only shower me with praise and support. Perhaps it's the latter that scares me. I know she'd encourage me to publish. In fact, I'm almost certain she'd go as far as sourcing editors, publishers. Fuck, she'd probably design me a cover and become my manager.

I turn my head over my shoulder, and there is a delicate pink on her cheeks that makes me want to brush my fingers against it and follow the trail to see how far down her neck it spreads. It makes me want to get rid of this friendship label, so I don't have to have restraint. So I can touch her and learn her in every way. So I don't have to hide how my heart is slowly growing, warming, and it is just filled with Casey.

She doesn't continue to ask, so I take the opportunity to change the subject. "Have you ever thought about offering the re-binding as a service? I feel like people would pay good money for those covers." She releases a self-deprecating laugh and I turn to her as we exit the stall, and she looks up at me.

"Not at all. But I like that it's just for me." She says it with a sweet smile, and *fuck,* I want to kiss her.

Your move.

Noah's words from earlier taunt me. I want to make a move. *God,* do I want to make a move. But I don't want to ruin... whatever this is. The last few weeks, I've felt more like myself than I have in the last two years. Sure, I've been making more of an effort, but I know the lightness and happiness I wake up feeling every day is solely because of

Casey. The fact I can get through a day without chewing off someone's head has everything to do with Casey. The prospect of seeing her, talking to her, or even spending the slow café afternoons thinking about her, makes me feel like I can get through the day again.

I know she doesn't feel the same, and I'm not losing the only friendship I've maintained in order to trial a stupid fantasy.

We turn and continue down past a few more stalls, Casey loads up a basket of craft materials before checking out–that I then proceed to carry for her–and we continue for a few more minutes in peaceful silence, taking in what's on offer until we get to a crepe stall.

"Hungry?" I look down at Casey and ask as she practically beams up at me.

"Yes!" She skips over to the crepes, and I can't help but stare after her, can't hide the awe in my face if I tried.

We order and continue to walk. Casey holds a huge, folded crepe in a cone, covered in chocolate spread, strawberries, and powdered sugar. She ordered two, so now I'm also getting a toothache at the sweetness. I usually can't stand these kinds of desserts, but when she turned at the stall and asked if I was getting one, too, I couldn't say no to that smile.

We walk until we find ourselves at a table and chairs off to the side of the market. The lights are lower, the air slightly cooler, and the quaint world of the market slips away as the busy nightlife of the city creeps in.

We spend a few moments eating in blissful silence before Casey drops a moan that has my eyes snapping to hers and I watch as her long eyelashes fan out across her cheeks and her lips pucker as she chews on her food.

"Oh, God. This is honestly heaven." She mumbles over her food, the sounds sending flames of desire across my skin. I watch her for a moment, and it does nothing for my self-control. She pulls away and her eyes look at me for a second before looking to her crepe and snapping back, probably realizing I'm staring at her. "What?" she asks, still fumbling food in her mouth. The incredulous look is so adorable on her, my heart beats a little faster.

"You have shit all over you, Ace." I smile at her, and she tries to wipe the chocolate from her face, missing it completely.

Still beautiful, even if she has chocolate and powdered sugar smudged across her cheek. I shake my head at her mess.

"Did I get it?" she asks and then tries again, missing again, and this time, I can't help myself, a laugh tumbles out and I scoot slightly closer to her.

"Here." I drag a thumb across her cheek and wipe the chocolate from her perfect skin. I linger longer than is necessary and I watch as her lips part on a sigh. I wipe again, nothing there, but selfishly, I can't help myself. The touch burns across my skin, and seeing her physical reaction as she leans slightly into me has my self-control flying out the window.

With the chocolate off her skin and now on my thumb, I do the only thing my man brain can think to do, and I place my thumb in my mouth and lick the chocolate clean off. The same chocolate that was on my now forgotten crepe, and yet it tastes a thousand times more delicious. She swallows and her eyes track my thumb as her crepe lowers in her lap. We sit close enough that she is practically in my lap. She bites down on her lower lip, and that previously mentioned slip of my self-control snaps entirely.

Fuck it.

I move fast enough to not second guess, but slow enough that I don't startle her, as I grip her chin and pull her in to seal my lips on hers. The second my body registers the taste of Casey, all blood leaves my brain and heads south. Relief flooding me when her body softens, her perfect lips mold against mine, and I swallow the little moan she releases when she relaxes against me. A gentle swipe of my tongue against the seam of her lips and she opens for me. The taste of her is chocolate and sugar and so incredibly sweet I think I might die. I *could* die here, right now, with Casey Baker kissing me.

My crepe finds its way to the ground as my baser instincts take over. Gripping her waist, I haul her onto my lap, and she wraps her arms around my neck without missing a beat, pulling her chest firmly against mine.

She feels incredible, the warmth of her seeping through our clothes, with her legs falling to cage my thighs and my hands exploring her back until my fingers tangle and pull on her soft auburn hair. *Fuck,* the need to lay her out on this table and fuck her mindless is like a restless energy I struggle to control as it vibrates through my veins.

Our tongues dance desperately, her lips soft against mine, as I learn the responses of her body. Her moans, the way she delicately rolls her hips, have me remembering how very public we are and how very carried away I'm about to get. I pull back, reluctantly breaking the best fucking kiss of my life, and lean my forehead against hers to catch my breath.

I pull back further to look at her, gauge her reaction, and pray to God I don't find any regret. My heart is in my throat at what I find. Stunning blue eyes sparkling back at me, a light pink blush dusting her cheeks, and a dazed smile across her pretty face. My expression must reflect whatever she was hoping to find because she bites her bottom lip to suppress a smile, and a small laugh, that is beginning to be one of my favorite noises, tumbles out of her, her eyes flitting back to my lips.

"Umm."

"Yeah," I respond. Both of us unsure what happened. Only that I kissed her, and she fucking kissed me back. I'm desperate to not break the spell, to keep her here, panting in my lap. Even if I could bring myself to pull away from her, I'm going to need a minute.

"Why?" she whispers. The one question I was dreading, the one that forces me to face the possibility of rejection, to come to terms with the fact that Casey Baker is not in my future.

"Because I wanted to," I say softly back, and for the first time in a long time, I don't care about the consequences or what any of it means, because somehow, even if she isn't into me, Casey is the only person that makes me feel unbroken.

"Me, too," she whispers back, biting down on her smile again, and I feel that familiar fire burn under my skin. It takes everything in me to wrangle back control and not wrangle her into an Uber, take her back to my place, and properly lay claim to her. Instead, I stand, her still wrapped around me, and I release my grip on her hips to lower her to the ground. Before I can say anything, the sound of her phone ringing pierces the perfect bubble we'd been floating in.

"Dammit," she mutters as she squeezes her eyes closed and leans her head on my chest. I chuckle softly, but my grip remains on her lower back. She withdraws the phone from her pocket, her eyebrows pulling taut when she sees who's calling.

"What is it?" I ask, and something tugs on my chest, making it feel tight.

"It's... It's my sister." She looks up to me, worry lining every part of her face. "I'm sorry. She doesn't ever call me. I should get this; it could be important." She searches my eyes as though she needs my permission.

"Don't apologize, of course, answer it," I rush out, hoping she just fucking answers it before it ends. She does and rushes out a greeting before her spine snaps straight and her face drops. Casey Baker, for the first time in history, is as ashen and pale as a ghost, and it feels like my own chest caves in.

She turns away from me, and I grab her bags as I follow after her. By the time I catch up, she is practically jogging to the entry of the market. "Ace, talk to me. What happened?" She spins and I see the unshed tears that have my chest clenching.

"My... it's Grace. She..." Casey's breaths come in heavy and fast as she shakes her head, a few tears dropping down her face. "Grace lost the baby," she whispers as a sob leaves her lips. She looks like she might fall, but I drop the bags and wrap her close to me just as her knees give out. I hold her and she cries, the full body sobs shaking her as I hold her up against me. Losing the moment we had feels disappointing, but seeing Casey break like this? It feels like I'm shattering into a million pieces.

17

six years ago

Jessie – age 27

2018

"I can think of a number of places I'd rather be."

"C'mon, Jessie... please? Mom and Dad are being assholes about this, and they won't let me go without a chaperone. At least this way I know you'll leave us alone and I can tell Mom there is an adult with us. Plus, it's for Casey's birthday. You aren't going to make her go out by herself, are you?"

Escorting my sister and her friends on their first night at a bar is seriously not something I saw myself doing... ever. But Addison looks up at me through her pleading eyes, green and sad looking, and my chest tugs slightly. Jenny is at some cooking school gala thing tonight that I wasn't invited along to, so I guess it is this or brood alone at home. I'm not sure what is going on with Jen lately. She is distant and short. She is always busy and bailing on plans we'd made. I mean, I know she is working hard at her career. She wants to be a pastry chef, and I am doing my best to support her, but she doesn't seem to care about my own dream. I snagged a small corner building in New York, the city she said she wanted to move to, and I was going to set up a bookshop café there. Put both my literature and business degrees to use. Sure, the apartment the lease came with is small, but it won't be forever. It is just a steppingstone. The day I signed and wanted to celebrate, she said she already had plans and sent a, *'Congrats babe, that's cool,'* text with a thumbs-up emoji. It is starting to feel like one foot out the door with her, and I am starting to get really fucking tired of it.

Not being able to come up with any excuses or able to fight off the sympathy Addison's pleading look gives me, I roll my eyes and give in.

"Fine."

"Yes! Thank you!" She launches forward and hugs me, making me feel a little better about the decision.

"What time are we leaving?"

"Case and Rosie are on the way here, and then we wanted to catch a cab to Reston, a new bar opened we want to try." I knew the one.

"I'll drive. We can take the truck." I am stoked with the new car. Dad had helped me pick it up the other weekend. He wanted me to get one of those sporty idiot mobiles that he and all his country club losers drive around in, but I am happy with my truck. It is practical. The bed of the truck is perfect for drive-in date nights or camping. It allows me to drive most roads and was practical when I needed to help Ava move out of her dorm and into her new apartment with her boyfriend.

"Sweet! Okay, I'll let you know when the girls are here." She darts off to her room, pulling out her phone to call the girls, I assume. I head back to mine for a shower and to change. I have some errands to run in town before we left, anyway. I flick a text off to Jen to let her know my plans have changed. She was going to come over later, but I might just head to hers after I drop the girls' home.

"Jessie, the girls are here, let's go!" Addison yells from the bottom of the stairs. I grab my keys and coat and head down. Checking my phone, I see a text bounce in from Jen.

> **Jen** 💙: I'm tired after tonight, anyway. Don't worry about coming over, I'll see you Tuesday. x

Cool. I pretend like that's fine, and it doesn't make me fill with a ton of rage. I just fucking miss her. I miss conversations, laughing, comfortable silence, and just being a fucking couple. Sure, it'd been a while since we'd slept together, but at this point, I'd give up the sex for some kind of connection. Anyway. I'm sure this happens to all long-term couples. Maybe the change to the city will help. We move in a few months. Things will get better, I am sure of it.

I head for the stairs and hear the giggling of the new adults in the kitchen as I descend.

"We going?" I am ready for this night to be over. I head for the front door and hold it open, Addison rounds the corner, friends in tow.

"JJ," Rosie greets and I nod at her.

"Hey, Jay!" Little miss sun—*what the fuck is that.*

"Are you wearing that?" The words leave my mouth before I can think better of it and my jaw slams shut. My comment has shock registering on the rest of them as Casey halts so quickly she nearly trips, Addy and Rosie spinning too.

"Sorry... I didn't mean it like... it's just—" I raise my hands in defense and the front door swings and hits me on the ass, making me nearly fall over. "I mean, you girls know you're going to a nightclub, right? Not only is it freezing, but... well, you aren't kids anymore." How did I politely and not creepily tell my little sister's friend—stupidly attractive friend—that what she is wearing is leaving very little to the imagination?

I love my girlfriend. Jenny is more than enough for me... but I am still a man and not completely immune. Plus, I don't know what it is about Casey, but even when she was sixteen, she just had this aura around her. Her smile, the way her hair practically glows, and it feels like the sun follows her path. Add to that, she was now completely grown, with a woman's figure, and my brain and body are betraying me.

"Forget I said anything," I grunt out at Rosie's and Addison's reprimanding looks, and they start to head out. Casey hangs back, and when I turn to see what the holdup is, I curse myself again. She has her arms wrapped around her waist and something like sadness across her face.

"Maybe I should change?" she mumbles.

"No way! You look hot as fuck. We are all finally twenty-one, and we get to let our hair down," Rosie reassures her.

"Yeah, ignore this fucking idiot," Addison, as classy as ever. "He's just been out of the game for too long, he has no idea what it's like out there anymore. Such an old man." Addison delivers the insult with a feline smile and smacks me on the back of the head as she and Rosie head out to my truck. I turn back toward Casey and see the same look of hesitancy on her face.

"I'm sorry, Case. You do look... good." There is no other appropriate way to say that. "I was just... well, you know, it's been a minute since I saw you girls." *And I hadn't realized she had turned from a smiling little girl to a glowing, drop-dead gorgeous woman.* I was at least smart enough not to say that, though. "There isn't anything wrong with what you're wearing." I feel my cheeks pink uncharacteristically and a small smile pulls at her face as she scrunches her button nose. The brightening of her face has me remembering, "Oh, wait here," I tell her and dart quickly to the living room, returning with the gift in hand. "Happy birthday, Ace." I hand over the bunch of flowers and her face brightens even more, something in my stomach tugging at me. I don't even know why I bought them for her. I was down the street to grab shit for my new truck and they had these on display in the flower shop next door. I remembered that Casey mentioned they were her favorite flower, and well... I mean everyone deserves flowers on their birthday, right?

"Oh... they are so pretty, Jay," she whispers, a huge smile on her face as she brings them to her nose and sniffs. "I can't believe you got me marigolds."

"You said they were your favorite."

"And you remembered?" She looks at me with confusion. I have no idea how to answer that, so I just shrug. She walks over to the hall table and places them down. "I'm sleeping over tonight, so I'll take them home with me in the morning." I just nod again, holding the front door open wider for her to head to the truck.

"Umm..." Her voice is soft as she takes a few steps closer to the door. "Do you... well, I haven't, like, been out before, or really dated." She shrugs and looks down at her feet.

"Okay?" I have no idea what she is asking me.

"Well... do you think... would guys, like, react like you? Or... do you think, maybe... they might find me pretty?" She looks up slowly, so much insecurity in her voice, and her cheeks are bright pink. My heart softens slightly, and I almost want to pull her into a hug—a platonic hug, of course—and comfort her.

Instead, I just give her an easy smile and nod, and that seems to be enough to settle her nerves. Her shoulders relax and she smiles a little brighter as she struts past me, heading out to meet the girls in the car.

I wait a beat, closing the front door behind me and following behind, I whisper just to myself, "So, so pretty."

18

he i could build you a house kind of muscles

Casey

Present Day

"Okay, I got you some supplies in this bag, and some new clothes in this bag. Just comfort ones, nothing flashy. Oh, and some couch snacks because then you can just relax... or at least try to. I also got some lavender, and I bought you a new diffuser because you said the other week yours was broken. Oh, and bath oils. You're going to need lots of relaxing bath moments. I even bought some DVD—"

"Casey, you're rambling. Again," Grace scolds, her face pulled into a bored expression, despite the tear stains lining her cheeks. Grace's strawberry blonde is more blonde than strawberry compared to mine, but she has the same fair skin, blue eyes, and lanky build.

She turns, leaving the entryway of her apartment open as invitation. I swallow the guilt and enter, closing the door behind me and heading straight for the kitchen. Grace disappears into the apartment and her husband Evan meets me.

"How is she doing?" I ask.

"How do you think she is doing?" Evan's rough response has me wincing. He scrubs a hand down his face and releases a long sigh. "I'm sorry, Case, you didn't deserve that. It's just... we'd been trying so long, you know? She doesn't let me in, and I—"

"Don't know how to help?" I finish for him as he braces his hands on the counter and hangs his head. I rub his back gently.

I try my best to hold back the tears, refusing to be another thing they have to worry about. Grace was wild and felt everything freely when we were growing up. It used to send our parents into chaos at the best of times. It was just easier to try to keep the peace as much as possible. Mom was less likely to forget me at the library when I did.

"I'm here, and I'll stay and come back as many times as you or her need. I have all her classes, so don't worry about it at all." He nods slightly and starts to unpack the bags I brought, while I heat the kettle and pop the heat pack in the microwave. After we've finished unpacking everything, I pull out the beef and vegetables I bought for dinner.

"Right, I'm going to make us a casserole." I nod in determination.

"It's 9pm," he deadpans, but I don't dignify that with a response. It is never too late for dinner. Evan doesn't fight me; he just nods and heads out.

"Here," I grab the heat pack out and pass him the cup of tea, "take this to her. Suggest a lavender bath, but she might refuse for the first few days, which is fine. You can't force her to talk to you, Ev, you just need to let her process. She wanted this as much as you, if not more. The difference is her hormones convinced her it was happening. She biologically fell in love with that baby before she even knew she was pregnant. So don't hold this against her. Let her grieve." His eyes are red-rimmed as he nods again, taking the heat pack and tea from my hands and heads in the direction of Grace. We might not communicate or be as close as Jessie is with his siblings, but I still love Grace with my whole heart, and I'll be damned if I'm going to let her suffer. At least not without Mom's beef casserole.

"This tastes just like Mom's," Grace says from where she sits bundled on the couch, the bowl of stew in her hands. Her voice is devoid of emotion, but she doesn't hesitate to finish the dinner, which brings me a special kind of warmth. "Where were you when you ditched to come play nurse?" I'm sure she doesn't mean it, but her words sting, especially their delivery. I know in my head she is doing it to feel something because she hurts so badly right now, so I shake off the pain. I can be her punching bag if that's what she needs right now.

"I was at the night market with a friend." Jessie caught the Uber with me and rode to every pit stop on the way to Grace's, and I assume he took it home after I got here, but I didn't really stop to check. I know he hadn't wanted to impose, and I hadn't the energy to do introductions or even think about what happened.

He kissed me. Jessie had actually kissed me—no, he kissed the *crap* out of me. Damn could he kiss. It felt like... what was it that Rosie said about Caleb? Her soul left her body, and she came back down in the body of a goddess? Yeah. Jessie *for sure* made me travel space and time with that goddamned kiss. And I couldn't even remember what I said after. Just that my heart broke into a million pieces. And now here I am.

"One of the girls?" she asks.

"Oh, ahh... no." I push the beef around with my fork. It is just like Mom's. But I don't really have an appetite.

"Oh! A boy?" She says it like I'm sixteen and have a crush again. *Well, same guy, I suppose.*

"It's nothing. Really." I fail at hiding my smile but refuse to make eye contact with either of them. Evan laughs softly under his breath.

"Spill the beans, Case. You never give me the gossip. C'mon, is it someone I know?"

I shrug because I don't even know if Grace remembers my friends, let alone their siblings.

"Well, we aren't anything. We're just friends. You remember Addison's older brother Jessie?" I look up to her then and she nods through a mouthful of stew. "Well, I wanted to get some more book-binding supp—oh, shit!" I stand from my seat and mentally assess my belongings that I came to their apartment with. *Dammit!* I left my purchases... I don't even know where. The seat where Jessie melted my brain? In the Uber?

"What is it?" Evan panics.

I hold my head in my hands for a second, frustration threatening to make me lose it completely before I remember that, right now, today, is not about me. It would just be nice if something went my way.

I take a breath and shake it off. All of that is replaceable. Maybe not the money I spent on it, but I can earn it back and re-purchase. "I bought some things, and I think I left them there. It's fine. I'll go again during the week and get some more stuff," I say calmly as I breathe out, letting go of the irritation. The room goes so silent, and it isn't until a fork clatters in a bowl that I look up.

"Grace." Evan's voice is soothing as he goes to stand, except Grace raises a palm to cut him off as she pulls her face into a scowl.

"No, I'm sick of it." She slams the bowl down on the table and stalks straight for me. My heart lurches in my throat and she stands above me. "Stop it. Stop fucking doing that." She points at me with so much anger, and I work to try to recall what I said, what I did?

"Grace... wha-what are you talking about?" I whisper because shock has lodged itself in my throat. I've never seen her react this way to me. She barely looks at me, let alone spends energy directing her emotions at me, at least not since we were teenagers. I struggle to wrangle my tear ducts into submission and remember that Grace is suffering a surge of hormones. This is just the hormones, not her.

"Stop molding yourself. Stop pretending. Stop trying to make a bad situation good. Be a mess for once in your pathetic life, Casey. No one cares if you aren't the prim and proper princess. Just fucking exist in the real world for one goddamned day and get off your high horse. Just once!" Her tone gets progressively more aggressive and higher as Evan comes up gently behind her, gripping her shoulders and pulling her away from me. The fury in her face has tears pricking the back of my eyes.

I'm speechless. I—

"I... should go," I say softly, my eyes never leaving hers. "I'm sorry, I didn't mean to upset you Grace. I'm so sorry." I blink back the tears, although some escape, and I quickly wipe them from my cheeks. Shock numbs me as I try to make sense of everything that just happened.

"Sure, leave." She scoffs at me. "At least not being here is an honest decision." I bite back the furious retort to that and swallow before I say a bunch of things I know I'll regret. *She is hormonal, it's normal.*

I nod at her and make quick eyes at Evan, who hits me with a sympathetic look before he pulls Grace into the bedroom.

I leave quietly and without any goodbyes.

I practically fall out of the elevator in our apartment building, slowly trudging around the corner, sleep pulling at my eyes, my brain, and my limbs. I fumble for my keys and there is movement—

"Jay!" I raise a hand to my chest. "You scared the crap out of me." I try to smile, but the exhaustion must be evident on my face because the concerned look in his eyes hasn't changed.

"You okay?" he asks softly. His hands leave his pockets to take the bags from my hands, along with the bag of—

"Oh my GOD! Is that my stuff from earlier?"

"Uhh, yeah, I was bringing it in for you, but I knocked and no one answered. Addy messaged, said she and Rosie were out tonight. I didn't want to just leave it, so I figured I'd wait." He shrugs and a blush hits his cheeks, my chest expands so rapidly that I might finally cry the millions of tears I've been desperately trying to hold back. "Oh, Ace, don't cry. I'm sorry—"

"No, don't apologize. I'm... I'm just wrecked. I need bed," I say, and he grabs the keys from my hands to unlock the apartment, following me in and closing the door behind us. I don't even register what he does with my belongings, or whether he locked the door before he left, only that I found my way to the shower, turned it to hot, and let go of every single tear that had been burning my eyes since that devastating phone call.

The hurtful things Grace had thrown in my face sting like a fresh burn. I feel buried under guilt and shame. Embarrassed that I've spent the last twenty-six years being a nuisance and a bother to her. Maybe that's why she never connected with me? I have no idea where I went wrong or what I'm even meant to do about it. I just... I only ever wanted the best for her, only wanted to care for her.

I heave and strain over the body shakes that come with the full-on sobs, and I just let it out. Holding back nothing until there are no tears, no more sadness I need to expel, to leave only that aching numbness that follows a good cry. Under normal circumstances, I would make a cup of tea and get lost in a reread of a classic romance, but I can't. I can barely dry myself without falling asleep.

Need. Bed.

I pull on an oversized T and tap on some under eye cream in anticipation of puffy eyes tomorrow and head back to my room, shocked to find the curtains drawn and all the lights off, save for a side lamp. That one lamp has the soft blues of my room shaded a warmer hue, and that intoxicatingly delicious scent of vanilla-sandalwood envelops the room.

"I thought you left," I whisper across the room. Jessie stands, leaning against the door frame between my room and the hall that leads to the kitchen.

"I wanted to say goodbye first." He stands, and I watch as his eyes trail my legs to the hem of my shirt, which falls to my upper thigh, and I watch as he flexes his hand by his side. I'm suddenly so glad he didn't leave.

"Jessie?"

"Yeah, Ace?" His voice is rough but soothes and warms the numbness currently coating my body.

"You could stay?" He stares at me for a moment, and I take the few steps between us to close the distance. Close enough to see those gorgeous eyes, but enough space that we don't yet touch. His eyes search my face, a few seconds of silence before he nods lightly.

"I can stay in Addison's room." He says it quietly, but his eyes remain locked on me as I shake my head. I wrap a fist in his shirt, pulling him into the room as I walk backward toward the bed. He kicks the door behind him. Understanding dawns on him, and I'm no longer dragging him, instead he walks voluntarily.

"I want you to stay with me, Jessie," I whisper. His hands grip my waist and he pulls me against his body. I keep my grip on his shirt and my eyes flutter closed at his proximity.

"Are you sure?"

"Certain." My response is a breath. His eyes fall to my lips, but instead of giving me one of those earth-shattering kisses again, he leads me to the bed, pulls back the covers and guides me in. I have no idea what I'm doing. What *we* are doing. The only thing I know is that, right now, when I feel hollow, a shell of myself, I need him. I need his warmth, that dominating presence that consumes me. Makes the noise in my head silent and the ache in my chest less painful. I can think of consequences tomorrow. Tonight, I just want to be selfish.

He toes off his shoes, and he stares at me for a beat before reaching over his back and peeling his shirt from his body, uncovering the expanse of muscles my memory did not do justice.

I feel like my original thought was right; they aren't gym muscles. They're '*I work in the yard*' muscles. The '*I could build you a house*' kind of muscles. *Damn.*

His gaze still hasn't left mine, despite the ogling I do of him, and his pants are gone as fast as his shirt, and it finally dawns on me that Jessie Jenkins is in nothing but his boxers. In my *bedroom!* An internal squeal happens in my head and sixteen-year-old Casey passes out as Jessie climbs into my bed. I bunker down under the covers, and just as I go to roll over so I can freak out without being caught, Jessie wraps his big bear arms around my body and drags me into the safety of his warmth. "Get over here," he practically growls. With his chest to my back, he nuzzles my neck, and it makes a stupid squeak release from my throat. He chuckles coarsely.

"Sleep, Casey. Your problems will be there tomorrow. Right now, just sleep."

Sleep?! I feel like my adrenaline just kicked up to level one thousand. I try, though, to pretend I'm still sleepy and nod my head.

"It feels like I'm holding a fucking baby rabbit," he mumbles, his lips at the shell of my ear. "Your heart is going nuts, Case. Just breathe. It's just you and me, and we're going to sleep. You need rest." His voice is so deep and soothing, my shoulders drop and I relax. But I need to work extra hard to force myself–and little Casey–to calm the F down and not get *any* ideas.

"Night, Jay," I whisper, unable to hide the giant-sized smile on my face.

He lands a soft kiss to my temple before he pulls me tighter against him and whispers back.

"Night, Ace."

19

stop pretending that we're just friends

Jessie

A soft moan is what pulls me from sleep. I take quick stock of my surroundings, my eyes snapping open when I start to feel the dizzying sensation of all the blood in my body flowing south. It's still dark out, my hands touch, or rather grip, smooth delicate skin, and I realize my hands have made their way under Casey's nightshirt of their own accord. A perky breast and taut nipple held in my hand, as my other hand is splayed out against her flat stomach, pulling her into my lap. My lap which is currently sporting a boner so fucking hard I'm surprised Casey hasn't woken up.

What the fuck am I doing?

We kissed, but then Grace lost the baby and Casey went into protector mode. Cuddling is one thing. Being there for her while she cried and allowing her to rest is what a friend would do. But I can't be doing *this*. This is bordering on taking advantage, and I'll be damned if I ruin the best thing in my life right now because I couldn't get a hold of myself. I'm better than this.

She deserves better than this. Than me.

Maybe climbing into her bed and holding her was a bad idea. She asked me to stay, and after I listened to her cry in the shower, or heave out her heart more like, I couldn't bear to leave. It took everything in me to not storm into that bathroom and hold her. Protect her, or at least try to take away her pain. Listening to the gut-wrenching sobs felt like a stab in the chest. So when she looked at me with those sad and hopeful doe eyes, I caved immediately. Didn't even bother pretending like I was going to leave.

That same moan happens again, and Casey rears her ass further into my lap and my grip on her tightens as a growl works its way up my throat. I need out of this situation right fucking now. Reluctantly pulling my hands from her incredible body, I extricate myself from the bed, my dick yelling at me to stay, which has now pitched a tent in protest.

As I flip the covers to leave the bed, I get a fantastic flash of Casey, her smooth creamy skin, those sorry excuse for panties as her shirt lays bunched near her tits.

Perfection.

I drag a hand down my face and shake off the thoughts, forcing myself to enter her bathroom. Ordering my mind and my dick to get a fucking grip. How did I get us into this situation? Openly groping her in her sleep and doing fuck all about stopping it from happening. I splash my face with cold water. It's still the middle of the night, but I need to snap out of this. I stare at myself in the mirror. "You're a grown fucking man. Pull it the fuck together."

Stepping out of the bathroom, I sneak into the kitchen for a glass of water and some fresh air on their balcony.

Staring out at the city, the scent of the air is fresh, the frost kisses my skin, cooling the heat that radiates off me in waves. The early hour scent washes over me, the one where you know daylight is coming in another couple of hours, but enough people are still sleeping that there is a lull of peace. I close my eyes and let the breeze softly wash over me. Leaning my elbows on the railing I try to talk myself out of making a huge mistake. Casey is possibly one of the greatest people I know. She literally skipped back into my life, and she has just turned me completely on my head. She is all I think about, all I dream about. When I'm alone, I want to be near her, and when we're together, I could listen to her laugh or watch her reading for hours. Literally hours. When I'm with her, I'm an addict. I can't get enough.

I'm in way too fucking deep. But I've already learned my lesson, and I can't let myself do this again. Can't put myself back into a place where I lose my mind and shut myself off from everyone who loves me. Addison, the way she looked at me all those months ago, like she didn't know me. The way pain spread across her face when we would speak. All because I had my heart broken.

I won't do it again.

I can't.

"Jay." Casey's voice pulls me from my depressing spiral of thoughts, but when I turn to see her stepping out onto the balcony, she steals those thoughts, along with my breath.

Her auburn hair is sleep-messed and pouring over her shoulders as her sleepshirt falls to only the top of her thighs, leaving her perfectly long and soft legs completely on display.

"What are you doing out here?" she asks softly, her lips forming a delicate smile, and *fuck,* I want to kiss her again.

"I couldn't sleep. I didn't mean to wake you." I try to give her a soft smile back, but my chest just aches. I'm telling myself to keep my distance, but it's hard to hide the very prominent thoughts and feelings that flood me the moment she is in the same room as me.

I want her. I want her *so* badly. In every way.

I clear my throat and shrug as I push past her to enter the apartment and refill my glass of water. The soft padding of her bare feet against the oak flooring tells me she has followed behind me, and I have to stop myself from openly grunting.

"Is everything okay?" she asks gently.

I squeeze my eyes shut and round the counter, fixing my facial features before turning to face her. She stands on the opposite side, the kitchen counter the only thing between us, and words evade me. Something like a groan climbs its way up my throat, and I pull my gaze from hers as I fill up my glass.

"Jessie, what's wrong?" This time she comes to stand next to me and places her hand on my arm, the heat singeing me, and I shrug her off.

"I can't do this anymore, Ace," I say under my breath. I feel her tense beside me, and she steals her hand from my arm like I burned her.

She has no idea that it is her that burns. Melting everything inside me.

"Do what?" Her tone is laced with concern, and when I finally lock eyes with her, the look on her face is a punch to the gut. The last thing I wanted to do was hurt her.

"I can't keep acting like I'm not losing control every time I'm around you," I respond. Placing the glass in the sink and turning to her. Our bodies almost flush, she steels her spine and stands her ground. I watch as her face hardens. Whoever said Casey Baker was delicate doesn't know the first thing about her.

"I can't keep sitting on the couch pretending to read with you." I take a step closer, and she turns her back to the counter. I brace my hands on either side of her, giving them something to do so I don't act out the very indecent thoughts that tiny bed shirt gives me.

"I can't stand in this kitchen and bake with you, pretending to hear what you're saying because really I'm trying to stop imagining you on this fucking counter, covered in the batter of whatever delicious masterpiece you are making while I eat it clean off your skin." Her eyes bulge and her lips part on a sigh. The fact she feels the same desire and electricity between us makes the hold on my control that much harder. I watch her neck as she tries to swallow and the way her breath increases.

"I was doing just fine controlling the way you make me want to turn into a feral animal. But then I kissed you. I tasted you. And you kissed me back. Now I can't stop wanting more."

"Oh," she breathes.

"You spend so much of your time taking care of everyone else. Thinking and anticipating everyone else's needs and, *fuck*, Ace. I really want to take care of you. I want to stop pretending that we're just friends. I want to anticipate *your* needs." I search her face for a reaction. Search for something that tells me to take a step back. I'm coming on too fucking hot, just like I told myself I wouldn't.

Her breathing hasn't slowed, and instead of listening to reason, I reach a hand to tuck her hair behind her ear, using my thumb to trail her pretty bottom lip and watch as the blush hits her cheeks. To hell with caution, I don't have the strength to fight it anymore. If that makes me weak, then so be it.

"Please, let me look after you. Let me give you what you need. What *I* need," I whisper to her, our lips now only a breath away.

She nods frantically, and it's all the permission I need as I close the final gap between us and slam my lips to hers. She moans at the touch and a growl of pleasure works its way up my throat as I feel her melt against me. Her petite and lithe body docile in my arms, and I grip the back of her thighs, lifting and placing her on the counter. She opens her thighs for me to step between. With one hand, I grip the back of her head, pulling lightly on the strands of soft strawberry hair that tangles between my fingers, using my free hand to grip her waist, pulling her closer to me.

Our kiss is hard and desperate, like a race against the clock, or perhaps trying to soak up as much of each other before common sense catches up with us. I swipe my tongue with hers as I desperately try to taste every inch of her. Memorize the way her mouth moves with mine, her lips soft and plump. Her hands are around my neck, nails digging into my scalp as she moans and that little leash I had on my control in this moment is out the fucking window. I untangle a hand from her hair and push it under her shirt, bunching it and trailing her perfectly soft skin until her breast is cupped in my hand. She gasps, but I kiss her deeper, drawing her closer, and gently pulling her already puckered nipple between my fingers.

"*Jess,*" she moans, and fuck if hearing her say my name like that doesn't make me even harder. I lean my forehead against hers, my hands trailing every expanse of skin they can find, trying to catch my breath. Trying to stop this from going too far. Her eyes are wide and searching mine as she pants against my mouth.

I bend and slowly kiss up the line of her delicate neck, lightly dragging my teeth across her ear. Pulling on that same nipple again, and I see her eyelashes flutter.

"What... what are you doing?" she asks between breaths.

"Trying to hold onto some self-control. Because I want you, Ace. So fucking bad." I punctuate my statement by gripping her hips and pulling her against me, pressing into her as I lightly bite her neck. I hear her breath catch as her head falls back, giving me more room to caress and feel her heart rate skyrocket.

"Tell me to stop, Casey," I beg, she has one last chance to not cross this line. To give us time to work this out before it becomes something we can't stop, that I can't take back. That she'll regret.

"Don't you dare stop," she demands. The hand massaging her tit reluctantly lets go as I reach up and grip the front of her neck, bringing her full attention back to me, allowing me to drown in her blue eyes. She doesn't move, but something changes in them, and it is the permission I need. My hand tightens on her skin and I pull her face to mine, so I can grab those perfect fucking lips between my own. My other hand dances around the edge of her panties. I stall, not yet going to where I desperately want to be. Waiting, seeking one silent and final reprieve. For her to have the chance to change her mind.

She moves a hand between us, searching for access to my briefs, and I grab her wrist and pin it to her back.

Fuck.

She has no idea how beautiful she is. This sight before me. My hand grips her neck, as I pin her arms behind her back, and she pants, barely able to catch her breath. Something primal rumbles in my chest and my lips tip at the corners.

"Not tonight, Ace. Tonight is all you," I whisper and return to trailing kisses across the smooth skin of her neck, collarbone, and shoulder, trying to compensate for the very caveman-like way I hold her. Wanting to be rough, but tender all at once.

My hands release her and reach the hem of her shirt, quickly pulling it over her head, and I groan. *These fucking tits.*

"But I want to—"

"No."

She lifts her gaze to make eye contact with me. Easing the look of confusion, I cup her cheek, swiping her skin with my thumb, my other hand teasing the inside of her thighs, her abdomen, and finding the start of her panties. The tiny bit of cotton stops me from getting to where I'd rather be.

"Let me take care of *you*, Case. You're not great at being selfish or looking out for yourself, and that's okay. But you sure as fuck are going to let me do it." I steal a soft kiss of those pretty lips, lingering on the softness, on the way she sighs the moment we touch. I pull back and watch her, my gaze searching over every detail of her face as I trail my fingers up the inside of her thigh and dip them into her panties, tracing a soft finger lightly through her seam and—*fuck me.* The softness of her delicate skin, how wet she is already. She is making me go insane. I pay special attention to those delectable lips and the way her mouth opens into a small *O.*

"*Oh, God.*" She moans as I gather and spread her wetness.

"All this mess just for me, Ace?" She bites her lip, and the uncertainty in her eyes has my chest tightening with anticipation. I can't wait to watch her come undone and to be the one to put her together again.

"I'm going to take care of you, Casey. I'm going to make a fucking mess of this pretty pussy, and I want you to be a good girl and let me." The words are emphasized by the mess I spread across her. She bites her lips to hold in her moans, and I focus on the little bundle of nerves that has her opening wider for me.

"What'd'you say, Ace? You going to make a mess on my fingers and let me clean you up?"

She moans softly, incoherent almost, but nods quickly as I slide two fingers into her tight wet center, feeling her clench down on me and grip me. "Fuck, you feel perfect." I groan as I trail my teeth back up her neck.

"Oh, God," Casey moans again, reaching a hand to thread through my hair and pulling, she uses the other to grip my forearm, holding me in place, nails digging in, making me near feral. If I wasn't set on taking this slow and getting on the same page with her, adamant to make this real and not fuck it up, I swear I'd rip apart every layer separating us and fuck her so hard she'd need to replace this counter.

"Jessie, I want you." Breathless and writhing as I slowly fuck her with my fingers, I pick up the pace, using my palm to tease her clit, feeling her clench around me.

"I can't wait to have you spread out below me," I growl, taking a bite of her neck and licking away the sting before repeating it on her shoulder, while I continue to work her with my fingers. "This pussy, dripping and open, just for me." Bite, lick. "The sounds you'd make, your fingers in my hair." I curl my fingers, and the sound she makes is almost animal. Exactly how she makes me feel. Biting and licking this perfect fucking skin. "I can't wait to make a fucking meal out of you." I wrap my free hand around her waist and pull her to the edge of the counter. My grip on her is strong, and she opens wider, giving me room to put in a third finger, the expanse of my palm cupping her, as she sits impaled on my fingers. The pace increasing as I lose any sense of control, curling my fingers, grabbing that special spot as I feel her orgasm grow closer, the walls of her clenching around me, the sounds of only her wetness and moans filling the room.

"Oh, *fuck!* Jessie, I'm—"

"Yes, Case. Make a mess on me. *Come.*" The demand is a snarl, the rumble in my chest fighting against my self-control as I fuck her perfectly tight pussy with my fingers.

"Ohhh, GOD. *Jessie!*" I bite on her shoulder to smother the roar I feel as she shatters around me. I keep the pace intense until I feel her clench and come down from her high, riding out her orgasm and trying to will away my own. The sounds of her, the feel of her, everything about her is sending me insane.

"Good girl," I whisper, peppering her with soft kisses across her skin as she catches her breath. Withdrawing my fingers, I drag them down her thigh so she can see the evidence of her need. What a pretty mess she is, just for me.

I place a hand on each of her thighs and lean in to kiss her soft lips, which are still parted as she tries to catch her breath. Her gaze dances around me, refusing to look at me.

"Don't hide from me now, Ace." I give her a gentle smile, trying to will away the very painful boner straining against my briefs.

"That was..." she breathes, finally letting me see her eyes.

"Fucking incredible," I whisper back to her.

"But... what about you?" She tilts her head, locking her legs behind my back, holding me perfectly in place between her knees. She reaches up and loops her arms around my neck as she starts to come back to earth. With her tits pressed up against my chest, any effort I made in taming my dick dies a painful death.

"Are you kidding me, Casey? That was the hottest thing we've done in this kitchen." I lean my forehead against hers and run a warm hand up her back as I try to picture anything other than the view I just had of her. Trying to soften my dick so I can get a little more sleep with this beauty in my arms. Before the sun rises and life goes back to normal.

"But—"

"No more buts." I emphasize with a slap to her perky ass as she gasps and giggles. The sound brings a sudden lightness to my chest, and I find myself smiling. Her expression changes to what I can only label as shock.

"What?"

She brings a finger up and traces my lips. "Your smile. I haven't seen that one before."

I'm speechless as I look into her eyes.

"You're stunning," she whispers as she continues to trace my lips, and something in my chest clenches. Embarrassment or apprehension, something heats my skin, and I look away. Gripping her hips, I lift her from the counter. With her still wrapped around me, I walk us back to the bedroom and kick the door closed behind us.

"I know you have a lot going on right now. I have no expectations, Casey. But I do expect you to let me take care of you. If you're going to be busy with other people's needs, I'm going to busy myself with yours. Not because you're a burden. Not because you *need* it. Because I fucking want to."

"Oh." Her voice is delicate, and when I place her down on the bed, throwing the covers over and pulling her to my chest, I look down at her. The look I find makes my heartbeat faster and my lungs struggle with air.

Hope.

This perfect ray of sunshine, with eyes as deep and as full as the ocean, is looking up at me with so much hope I feel like I've been dropped out of a plane. Falling to a death I can't stop from chasing because that look grips me and makes me want to fulfill every single one of her dreams. I want to watch every one of her wishes come true, and I so desperately want to be the one to give that to her. Despite the way she looks at me, I know I'm not in her future. But if this little pocket of happiness is all that I get, I'm going to soak up as much as I can for as long as I can. Until she finds her forever. Until that hope fizzles and she moves onto the next big thing, I'll take whatever she'll give me.

I place a chaste kiss to her forehead, and I feel her sink deeper into me and let sleep pull us both under, as I hold in my arms the one woman that, if I had any hope at all, could have been my future.

20

have an orgasmic day

Casey

Early morning sun wakes me, which is unusual for me because I'm usually up before the birds. Usually have a coffee, meditate, and do my morning yoga, maybe even some light cardio, all before the sun and Addison are awake.

But nothing is usual about this morning.

I'm deliciously relaxed, and I feel myself wake slowly, unsure where this lightness comes from, and then I start to *actually* wake up and remember yesterday.

Jessie kissing me.

Grace losing the baby.

Grace losing her temper at me.

Jessie staying over.

Jessie making me co—

"Oh my god!" I squeak and sit up so fast my head spins. I search my room, which is empty, placing my hand on the side of the bed that Jessie had been lying on. It's cold. He must have left a while ago. For some reason, my stomach sinks at the thought, but noise in the kitchen pulls me from my thoughts, and I peel myself from bed in a daze.

I open my bedroom door and zombie walk to the kitchen where I see Rosie trying, and somehow failing, at making her cereal.

She glances in my direction and says a half-hearted good morning before her gaze snatches back to me and she tilts her head, assessing.

"Hey, you okay, Casey?" I nod because I can't form words.

"You slept in. Big night?" she asks again as she pulls the carton of milk from the fridge.

"Mmhmm," I say again, nodding, my gaze still frozen on Rosie. My mind racing, unsure what the heck is happening right now, or what happened last night. What do I do with today? What day even is it?

Jessie...

"Jessie finger fucked me into oblivion on that counter at 2am this morning."

I thought I said that in my head, but the splatter of a milk carton on the floor, followed by a loud crash, and someone choking behind me makes me think that I perhaps said that out loud.

"What the fuck!?" *Oh, no.* That was Addison.

I turn around and see Noah standing by the window near the living room holding a takeaway coffee cup and hitting his chest like he just inhaled and choked on the contents. Addison now kneels on the floor, trying to pick up the remnants of a broken dish as she stares at me, white as a ghost and disgust written all over her face.

"Morning," I whisper to them before I look back at Rosie, who has the biggest smile on her face, eyes bright with delight as she drops a bundle of paper towels to the floor. I assume to mop up the spilled milk.

Rosie doesn't drop her gaze, which remains locked with mine, and she approaches me like I'm a scared animal, her arms raised, her smile humongous.

"Um... *what*?!" she squeaks.

"Mhmm. Yep. Wasn't even a dream," I say, still trying to wrap my head around it.

Jessie did that. My best friend's older brother, whom I've crushed on since I was sixteen, made me come harder than my boyfriend of four years ever did. *What. The. Heck.*

Addison strolls into my line of sight, her mouth open in pure shock, and her eyebrows are pulled tight, like she isn't sure if she feels shock, disgust, or anger.

"Umm... I'm just going to... I'll wait in Addison's room." Noah continues to cough through his sentence as he bails straight to Addison's room and closes the door. Rosie and Addison both look at me with opposite reactions.

"Oh my god, I want so many details. I want every single bit of information. Details. All of them. Oh, God, I need it. Casey! Speak!" Rosie is practically bouncing on her feet, and Addison looks between me and Rosie, still confused how to feel.

"For my friend, I would also, normally, want details. But I really also want to throw up because it's my brother. Can I have highlights, like the G-rated version, and then you can give Rosie all the disgusting details when I leave the country after being scarred for life from this information?" Addison turns and heads for the couch, understanding that we are very much going to need to sit for this conversation. Rosie turns to the fridge and then meets us on the couch, shoving a takeaway iced-latte cup into my hands. I see JJ's logo on the front and look up, confused.

"Jessie dropped us all coffees this morning. Said this was yours and not to wake you." She winks, and I look at the coffee.

"What...?" The question dies on my tongue as I read Jessie's handwriting on the side of the cup, *record-breaking Turkish delight latte (with a twist).*

Not being able to help myself, I immediately take a sip and the flavors ignite on my tongue. Jessie took my original Turkish Delight order and mixed in the banana from the last time I was there, instead of the chocolate. It sounds positively disgusting. But it's like an orgasm in my mouth.

"Yum," I murmur, staring at Jessie's cursive handwriting, pretending like I can't feel the stare of Rosie and Addy burning through me.

"You need to start from the beginning," Rosie demands, the excitement evident in her expression.

"And please, for my sake, spare the gory details." Addison grimaces.

"Save them for me later. I want to know everything," Rosie confirms.

I start at the night market, giving them, as requested, step-by-step details of the night. From the binding supplies to the crepes. Rosie nods along and is practically bouncing with energy, while Addison looks like she knows what details are coming and wishes she didn't ask about it.

"And then… he… Jessie kissed me." The last part is a whisper, and I briefly bring my fingers to my lips, like I can still feel the dominance of his touch on me.

"Rosie, it was like that thing you described, I think my soul left my body. It was the best damned kiss I ever had. He kissed the ever-loving shit out of me." My gaze is stuck somewhere vacant, staring, unable to focus as my mind goes back to that park bench. The fairy lights of the night market, the bustling of the city dropping away as Jessie's blue-green eyes sparkled with emotions I couldn't figure out. The tension pulled so tight I could barely catch my breath, and then he was just kissing me and, *damn.* I wanted to kiss him all night long. But—

"Then Evan called me from Grace's phone." I look up at the girls then and I think they can sense something in my voice because the excitement is gone. I tell them. Everything.

Rosie's excitement drops and both she and Addison scoot closer to me on the couch. Rosie throws her arms around me in a hug, and I tilt my eyes to the ceiling, forcing myself not to cry. Addy rests a hand on my thigh, her expression firm but gentle. Her way of supporting without pity. That girl hates pity.

"Evan called me because Grace had been a mess, and he didn't know what to do. She had lost the baby a week before. She didn't call me or tell me. Had been calling in sick, and I just never knew what was going on." I shove away the pain. That she never wanted to tell me. That she didn't want me there, remembering the hateful words she threw at me.

"I left Jessie, or he came with me then left. I don't really know. I went to Grace's. I just needed to be there. I needed to make sure she was okay; my heart was breaking for her." I feel a tear slip down my face, and I quickly swipe it away. "She wasn't that happy I was there. I made mom's casserole, and we ate and everything was fine. I don't know what I said or what I did. She just *lost* it. I think it was just the hormones. I'm sure everything is fine, but... anyway, I left."

I swipe at my eyes a few more times, and the girls stay plastered to my side, not offering any words, and I've never appreciated them more.

"I was exhausted, so ready for bed, and I came home, and Jessie was at the door."

"He had messaged me last night, asking to unlock the door so he could drop off some things?" Addison questions.

"Well, he had my stuff, because I'm an idiot and I completely forgot about the binding things I purchased. I lost my head. I couldn't think straight."

"But then he stayed?" Rosie asks and her smile grows again. I nod.

"He stayed. I asked him to stay." I look at Addison, nervous about her reaction. Wondering how she feels about me and her brother. Whether maybe I shouldn't say too much.

"Umm... I asked him to stay. In my bed." I bite on my lower lip, and she forces a smile that is part disgust, but she pats my knee and nods to continue while Rosie bounces in excitement next to me.

"And he did. But he just wanted to... cuddle?" I'm also still confused about that. Addison starts laughing, her head thrown back, and Rosie looks at me incredulously.

"Cuddle?" she deadpans. "That burly lumberjack wanted to just... cuddle?" Rosie's tone matches my confusion. I shrug and nod, and Addison laughs harder.

"Oh, my brother. He is so dumb sometimes."

"He said that I needed rest and to just sleep. I guess I eventually did, and then I woke, and it was still dark out, but the bed was empty. I walked out and found him on the balcony. He looked so..."

"Broody?" Addison asks while rolling her eyes, and it makes me giggle.

"Yeah, like he was contemplating life's biggest mysteries."

"He does that. Hasn't changed in the thirty-three years of his life. He always looks like he has some big mystery to solve." Addy shakes her head but looks at me to continue.

"Well, he said some things to me. I followed him back into the kitchen, and he said more things—"

"What things!?" Rosie pleads.

"Is this the part where I leave?" Addison squeezes her eyes closed and I laugh again.

"Highlight reel: he said swoony things that made my heart skip. Then he lifted me onto the counter, kissed the shit out of me again, and... well... his barista hands know what they are doing." I sigh and fall back to the couch. Remembering the way those big rough hands just dominated my whole body.

"Ew! Okay, yuck. Done. I'm done with that part. Please move on." Addison covers her face with her hands and Rosie just laughs and jumps up.

"Yes! But also... ew, on the kitchen counter?" She points and looks at the kitchen with a curled lip.

Sighing, I nod. "Yeah. On the kitchen counter."

"Then what?" Rosie sits back down, bringing her knees to her chest, and beams at me. Like a kid ready for the rest of the story.

"Well, he carried me back to the bed. Said even more things, and then held me, and then I fell asleep. Then I woke up, and he was gone." I try to hide the way my heart sinks.

"You didn't—"

"Do not answer that question!" Addison chastises Rosie and squeezes her eyes shut, and I laugh.

"I didn't. But he also wouldn't let me. Said he wanted to take care of *me*." Rosie's jaw hits the ground, and Addison's face changes to a confused mix of what I can only describe as, '*awh*', and, '*yuck*'.

"So, you didn't even find out if he is..."

Rosie holds her hands up in measurement and drills her eyes into mine with meaning.

I laugh, hard this time, shaking my head. "I didn't."

"Stop! I don't want to know or hear anything about that." Addison covers her face again.

"Addy, does this bother you?" I question, slightly scared about the answer.

"Hearing about my brother's dick? Yes. It bothers me a lot!" she exclaims.

"No, I mean... me and Jessie?" I bite my bottom lip, not sure about how that sounds.

"Is there a '*you and Jessie*?'" she asks, and the sympathy in her face makes my heart sink. I guess I don't even know the answer to that question. He said no expectations, but nothing we said meant this was anything, right? He probably was overcome with lust, but that doesn't mean he has *feelings* for me. Caring about someone isn't the same as having feelings for someone. Only the other week he was hung-up on his ex.

I look between Rosie and Addison and see the matching looks on their faces. Sympathy and pity, like I'm the last one to work out that I'm in love with someone completely unavailable. Well, I'm not *in love*. I'm just infatuated. I just need to meet someone else. Or I need *him* to meet someone else, so he becomes off limits. I throw my hands to my face and groan, and the girls fall to either side of me on the couch, sharing the same exasperation.

"I have no idea. I don't even think I have the energy to contemplate it." Addison pats me on the leg.

"I love my brother. But he hasn't quite mastered the ability to be vulnerable. The stupid bitch Jenny ruined him, and I worry for you, Case." Dropping my hands, I turn to look at her.

"Even if he had some feelings for you, I don't know that he would let himself have them. He doesn't believe he is deserving, and I don't want you to get hurt. He is my brother. He was my best friend before you two. I just don't want to lose you if you can't be around him." That realization hits me like a ton of bricks. I'd like to think I could be mature and not have this effect on my long-standing friendship with Addison, but the truth is, being around Jessie is hard enough as it is. If he made me fall and then didn't fall right back? God, that would be hard.

I nod and Rosie grunts.

"I lost Addy to love, and now I'm going to lose you, too?" She sounds exasperated.

"Relax, we had a moment. I don't think this means much. Like Addy said, he isn't emotionally available. Also, I have way too much going on right now, and I don't want to come between you two," I direct at Addison. "I'll go see him today. Clear the air. Set boundaries, you know?"

"That doesn't mean you guys can't... you know... help each other out." Rosie emphasizes her point with the wiggle of her eyebrows, and Addy grimaces while I giggle.

"I don't think I could do that with JJ without getting my heart involved."

"Wow. His fingers must be good," Rose retorts wistfully.

"Ew! Rosie, God. Details! I don't want them!" Addison gets up and heads for her room before she turns and pins me with a gentle smile.

"I'm happy if you're happy, Case. Just... be careful. With your heart, and his." She nods and then pins Rosie with a glare before she leaves. Rosie laughs from next to me.

"Okay, now that she is gone, I want *every* detail. I want words, sounds, descriptions. Everything!"

"Gross, Rosie," I say, while laughing.

"Think of it as research. I am an editor with a love for smut. I need to know real-life experiences so I can make my author's work pop." She emphasizes her point with a little pop of her lips.

"Don't you have enough real-life experiences for the both of us?" I ask, turning to look at her. She scoffs and scoots down the couch.

"Not lately," she mumbles.

"Oh, what's that now? Rosie in a dry spell?"

"It is *not* a dry spell! It's just... I'm having a stretch of dull dick." That makes me lose my shit, and I tumble forward laughing and slap a hand to her knee as she grunts.

"Shut up. Look, in my defense, work has been super busy, and I've been super tired and haven't been bothered to chase much. I'm just in a rut. I'll get back on it, don't worry," she instructs, like it is very serious, and I shake my head at her.

"Well, I need to get ready. I have both mine and Grace's classes for the next however long, and I need to fix the rosters." Rosie nods.

"Fine, details later. With wine. Have an orgasmic day, *Ace.*" Rosie winks before she giggles and struts with emphasis back to her room. I roll my eyes and head for mine.

My heart jumping and my stomach taking flight with a flurry of butterflies.

Is there a me and Jessie?

No. There can't be. I know that. I hate it, but I know that. He is broken over Jenny. I have a lot going on with family. Honestly? I don't think I could go there with him. Not now. Especially not when he isn't willing to give himself completely. There is too much he is holding on to, too much of himself that he guards. He has every right to guard his heart, but I already spent four years of my life with someone who didn't give me their all, and I won't do it again.

I nod at myself, finding my reflection in the mirror of my bathroom, and a spark of pride and confidence grows deep within my chest. He isn't ready.

And that is okay.

Jessie is important to me. A friend, and I care for him.

I'll wait. But I won't risk my heart. If he wants this–wants me–he is going to have to come right out and say it.

21

surprises with a side of dinner

Casey

"Sorry everyone, Grace is away for the next couple of weeks, so you are blessed with me in her absence." I smile to the group of women—and one man—before me. Taking Grace's inner-child class today. She was always so good with this one, helping others heal through breath work, stretching, and movement.

"Let's start in boat pose." I walk them through the breathing, setting up the posture, and ensuring we practice with the right muscles engaged, adjusting beginners as required and challenging the more experienced regulars.

"Let go of what you've been holding on to. Use those emotions to power you through, stoking the fire that drives you, keeping you strong. Relaxing your face muscles, let go of all that tension, while bracing your core, keeping your navel drawn to your spine. And breathe. Holding for 3, 2, 1, lowering all the way to a long body stretch." I demonstrate and stretch my arms up above me, feeling my spine stretch along the mat, my muscles relax, and the coolness of letting go washes over me. I think about the tension I hold through every day, the weight of expectations, and trying to anticipate the needs of everyone to make sure the people I love are cared for.

"Notice how you feel. Don't dwell, just note it. Label it, and file it away, keeping your breaths deep, your face relaxed with a gentle smile." I softly instruct as I fall deeper into the stretch, trying to take as much advantage of the exercise as my class engages in theirs.

Memories start to come to mind, fleeting, but they're there. Grace sneaking out after Mom and Dad were asleep; at first, she didn't know that I knew, but after the first few months, I started waiting for her. I wanted to know where she was going. I needed to know who she was with. What would happen if one day she didn't come back? I would need to tell our parents. They would need to know where to look, would need something to give the police if she went missing. I felt responsible for making sure she was back safely. That was, until the night she was busted. Man did that scare the crap out of me. My parents have always been pretty level-headed, at least up until that point. I'd never seen Mom lose her cool like I did that night.

Grace was grounded, of course. But it changed the direction of everything. Mom, Dad, and Grace started getting into a lot of fights. A lot of things, I thought, could have been avoided with just a little communication, anticipation, or thought.

Grace getting mad that none of her clothes were clean; Mom losing it because she never put her clothes in the wash.

Grace having a tantrum because she had lost something; Dad getting angry because Grace was careless with her belongings.

When Mom and Dad lost it at Grace, they lost it at each other, at me. It got extra bad when Mom dropped me off at the library for study group in high school, but then forgot to come get me because she was busy chasing down Grace after a particularly heated argument she'd had with Dad. They ended up eating dinner and getting ready for bed.

Rosie's nanny—yes, nanny...even in high school—had picked me up and dropped me home, and then my mom cried because she felt so horrible that she'd forgotten me.

After that day, I just found it easier to help. I'd made sure Grace's clothes were washed if Mom wasn't home to do it. I had convinced Grace to send me her location when she'd sneak out and give me one contact number—she wouldn't tell me the name of the person, and said she'd murder me if I ever used it for anything other than an emergency—but I saved it, nonetheless. I started keeping track of Grace's jewelry that she'd lose or where she'd put her keys. The house started to resemble some peace.

And then Grace started snapping at me.

Mom and Dad were exhausted. They would sigh, beg Grace to relax, and then just let her go on her rampages. But it was okay. I was okay. As long as we could sit and have dinner, as long as Dad would remember my recitals and Mom would pick me up from the library on time, I could handle Grace.

I breathe deeper, reminding myself not to dwell. The fleeting memories are only that–memories. I'm happy and healthy in my life. I know I struggle with being a chronic support person; I know I tend to take on the feelings of those I love, but it's hard not to. I just don't want people to feel sadness, to hurt. I know I can handle it, so I want to take it from them. If I could heal the world by taking the pain for myself, I would in a heartbeat. Flaw or not, I don't think I'd change this one piece of myself.

Walking the class through the next few stretches, we find ourselves in a standing, bent over position, instructing the class through the pose. "Bending your elbows in toward your body, with palms flat on the ground and knees slightly bent." I breathe deep and demonstrate.

"Resting your right shin on the back of your right arm, heel lifted off the ground. And relax."

I turn to watch the class follow, watching for any bad posture or poses to avoid any injuries when we take it further. "Good. Remember to keep breathing through it." They do as I instruct, and a bubble of pride rises through me, watching each of them follow with ease.

We repeat on the other side, then with both knees at the same time.

"Leave some weight in your toes, keeping your gaze up in front of you, keeping your face gentle and relaxed." Excited for this next part, I remind myself to stay calm and breathe. I love the feeling of my body moving through these movements. The feel of my strength, the feeling that I can do *anything*. Be anything.

"Fire up your core and transfer your weight, powering through your hands. If you can, if you feel supported, and your core is engaged, lift one foot." I pause to look at the class, and see each of them trying and succeeding, a few strained faces. "This is designed to go only as far as your ability takes you. This is not a competition. Just breathe. Remember to keep your breathing even, don't push past your body's needs, tailor it to be perfect for you." I watch a few drop their feet and their heels, and I smile gently.

"For anyone who'd like to take it further, lower your foot and try the next. Play with this pose as much as you like, filter through the rising of your heels, the lifting of your feet. There is nothing wrong with your level of need for this position. Play with it. Let that inner child play and connect." And I feel my inner Casey frown at me. I feel her ache for play, for carelessness. To be free and frenzied and fun. But I feel disconnected. I don't know how to be those things; they were never in the cards for me. I have never been able to be those things, because if I did, everything would just... fall apart.

I make it through the rest of the exercise, walking the class through the final meditation and reminding everyone to care for themselves and be gentle with themselves as they go about their day. I realize I can't dwell on any of it because I need to get to the next class.

I wave a quick goodbye and duck into the next room.

"Sorry, everyone. I'm here!" I quickly make my way through to the front, where the mat is prepared, and I take a quick look at the schedule on my phone. This is the mom's class.

Right, okay, I've got this. I take a deep breath to relax. This class deserves my best, so I will give it to them.

"Let's start in child's pose."

I'm exhausted.

You'd think a day of Yoga would just make someone flexible and energized. But I'm wrecked. It's heavy emotionally, a strain on my muscles and my voice. Socially depleting, my mouth hurts from smiling, and my brain hurts from just being 'on' the whole day.

Five classes, it's 7pm, I'm home, finally. I managed to do the grocery shopping. I had popped home to do some laundry, but I haven't had a chance to even blink, really. I have all the ingredients for chickpea and sweet potato curry, but I am so tired I don't know if I can stand to be in the kitchen.

"Hey, girl, how was your day?" Rosie asks from her position on the couch. A glass of wine in hand and Netflix paused. She rests her chin on her hand as she looks over at me.

"Long," I respond. "Addy in tonight?"

"No, she is with Noah, said she might be there for the week. She has a few long shifts and wants to spend as much time with him as possible. You know, gross couple things." She waves her hand at me and rolls her eyes. It brings a lightness to my chest, and I chuckle at her.

"What do you feel like for dinner?" I ask, grabbing a glass and meeting her on the couch.

"You haven't planned it already? That is unlike you," she says, eyes narrowing on me when I fall to the couch. My head thrown back, I close my eyes and take a deep breath.

"No. I did. I can start in a minute." The words are barely a breath, and I rest the wine glass on the coffee table before I lay on the couch. Rosie puts her glass down, too, and throws me a pillow.

"Chill for a bit. I got this." My eyes snap open at her, follow her as she makes her way to the kitchen. I sit up and watch her as she opens the fridge.

"Uhhh, what are you doing?" I ask, confusion fogging my brain.

"I'm going to MasterChef you a meal. Momma Case needs a break," she tsks as she fumbles her way through the kitchen cabinets.

"Rosie, I saw you struggle to make a bowl of cereal..." Rosie whips her head in my direction, a look of offense plastered to her face.

"Excuse me. I'll have you know, I'm an excellent fast learner and extremely resourceful. Lay your pretty head down. I got this." I stare at her skeptically, but am far too tired to fight her on this. Instead, I do as she says. I will just order pizza if this doesn't work out. At least she is trying.

I don't know how long I nap for, but it's long enough for a meal to be cooked, and I'm woken by gentle fingers sliding against my cheek as I hear my name whispered. A deep, soothing whisper.

"Wake up, Ace. Food is ready." My eyes snap open.

"Jessie?"

"I called him because I was trying to work out what the ingredients you purchased made, and then gave up because, what the fuck? And

Addison was out with Noah, so... I didn't know who else to call."
Rosie stands behind Jessie, who has crouched down in front of me on
the couch. When I look to her, she over-exaggerates her wink, splits her
fingers into a V and pokes out her tongue before giving me a thumbs
up. My blush is instant, and when I snap startled eyes to Jessie to make
sure he didn't witness that atrocity, I see the tenderness in his eyes, the
gentle smile on his face as he looks at me like there is nothing else in
the room.

"You cooked me dinner?"

"I did. I assume you were making a curry? I'm sure it isn't like what
you had in mind, but I witnessed Rosie attempting to dice the potato,
and, well, I really needed to take over." He chuckles, straightening, and
putting a hand out to help me up from the couch.

"How come... why are you..." I cough to clear my throat and Rosie
slaps a hand across her mouth to stop a laugh. I throw her a glare over
Jessie's shoulder, and he lowers his head, chuckling.

"Uhhh... I'm just confused. Why are you cooking me dinner?"

"Just taking care of you, like I said, remember?" *How could I forget?*
He shrugs and smiles again. That same smile, which has apparently
been stuck on his face since yesterday. I stand from the couch, letting
him pull me and drop me into a seat at the table. Rosie grabs wine
from the fridge and pours me a glass. As Jessie plops a bowl of delicious
smelling curry and rice in front of me.

"Oh my god, it smells *amazing*."

"It's no Casey Baker meal, but it'll do," he says, not able to make eye
contact. I look at Rosie as she does eye tennis between JJ and me, her
mouth open in a wide smile, like she has no idea how to react.

We settle into a comfortable silence, and taking a bit of the rice and
curry, it melts perfectly in my mouth. It doesn't taste like the one I
usually make, but it's delicious. I practically moan as the fork leaves

my mouth.

"Jessie, where the hell did you learn to cook? Between this and the omelet?"

He shrugs self-consciously and scratches the back of his head. "Um, a... friend... in high school, sh—they taught me. I used to spend a lot of time at their house. Cooking was one of the things we did a lot together." He doesn't look at me, and I know he is talking about Jenny.

Something hurts in my chest. Food, cooking, baking is something that I find comfort and joy in. I hate that I'm jealous he did the same thing, but with someone who broke him. I hate that he still has that with her, and it isn't something shared with me. I nod and continue with the food.

I'm certain I'd lose my appetite if it just wasn't so damned good. Rosie still hasn't said a word, and when I look up at her, she is just smiling like a total idiot and looking between us.

We sit in awkward silence for a while. And when we finish, I waste no time grabbing the plates to clean up before Rosie stands and shoves me back in the seat. "I might not be able to cook, but I am excellent at cleaning. Sit down and let me." She gives me a look, and I slink back down into my chair. She clears the table, heading to the kitchen, and Jessie shuffles awkwardly in his chair.

"Thank you for the coffee this morning," I say gently, not really sure if we're acknowledging what happened or if we are going to pretend like it never happened. For the sake of our friendship, I hope we forget, but I know if he pretends, it'll hurt more than I'd care to admit. *God, I'm a mess.*

He nods, looking at his hands, which rest on the kitchen table. He fiddles with his pinky finger, where a ring that is no longer there used to sit. Because it rests on my thumb. I grab it on instinct, like seeing him reach for it makes me need to do the same, and I twist it on my finger.

"What time did you wake up?" he asks, and his voice is rough, his eyes finally looking up at me.

"Um, about 8ish. I didn't feel you leave?"

"I didn't want to wake you. I needed to be at the shop, but I opened early and brought everyone back some coffee. I knew you'd need it. I was hoping you would rest," he says simply. Like it was a completely normal act of kindness.

"Have you spoken to Grace today?" I shake my head and keep my focus on the thumb ring, twisting it up and down my thumb. Grace hadn't even reached out. No calls or texts. It feels so completely selfish being upset that she hasn't. She has so much going on right now; she really doesn't need to be thinking about me.

"I was going to go see her tonight, but it just got so late. I might go during the week sometime." He nods again, and I look up to find Rosie giving me another look. One I think means she wants me to try. Honestly, I don't know what we're doing here. I don't know how to address any of it. Maybe it's better if we just clear the air. Be friends. It was a moment of high emotions, of intensity, and we were both spent and tired. It doesn't have to mean anything or ruin anything.

I open my mouth to speak, but Jessie beats me to it.

"Well, I should probably go. I didn't mean to interrupt." He gives me a forced smile, standing from the table.

"Oh. Sure, okay. That's fine." I smile back at him.

He stands there staring at me for a bit, giving me his fake smile. I can't tell whether he knows I know it's forced, or whether he actually believes I think he is smiling at me. He nods again, and I follow him to the door. Rosie watches us with fascination as she tries to multitask between cleaning and watching. Jessie nods at her as he passes, and she does something with her hand that I think is a wave, but she is so far into her shock she doesn't really do anything except fling soapy water across the floor.

I follow Jessie to the door. He opens it and turns to face me on the other side of the threshold. Holding onto the frame for balance, because his proximity always knocks me around, I stare up into his greeny-blue eyes.

"I'll see you?" he asks, softly.

"Yeah, I'll be around." I nod, biting my lip, because all the words I want to say just don't feel right. He isn't going to talk about what happened. I guess that means we're pretending it didn't happen?

He steps closer to me, a hand on the door frame above mine, and leans in.

"Good," he says, low enough just for me, his mouth hovering just above mine, and when his eyes dart to my lips, I lose my breath. He leans in and places a soft, chaste kiss to mine that has electricity coursing through my entire body. His one touch lighting me on fire, but it's gone the moment he pulls away. I take a step back, and when I look to him, his eyes seem darker.

He hits his fist into his palm and takes rapid steps back, biting his lip to hide the real smile I've been dying to glimpse again, before he turns without another word and rounds the corner to the elevators.

c'mon, man, we're buddies!

Jessie

"That book club has been in twice this week, and the romance sales have increased so much in the last couple of weeks, I think we need to expand the collection," April informs me. "I have a few Indie authors I follow and they're super popular. I can send you some recommendations if you like?" Groaning, I rub a hand down my face. Why can't general fiction or a love for classics be what trends? Even biographies? I'd take that over this glorified porn the kids are reading these days.

I say kids, but I'm well aware it's just women everywhere. Including my sisters.

I hired April, who's just started college, as a sales assistant on the bookshop side of things. It was also because I, too, recognized the change in customer base to young women and knew that I wasn't going to be of much assistance to them.

A shiver courses through my body, and I nod at April.

"Okay, get me a list. I'll price it and see what we can do." She nods and continues with her box of new stock that she is shelving. Grabbing another, I place it on a stool next to her.

"These have to go away, too, but some are up there." I point to the taller shelves. "Just leave them. I will do them later." I turn to head for the coffee counter after hearing the door chime sound, indicating new walk-ins.

"Oh, I can just use the ladder?" she retorts. But a workplace claim is the last thing I need right now.

"No, it's fine. I'll get to them. Anything above your reaching height, just leave out back. I'll do them tonight." She nods and continues with what she is doing.

As I head to the front counter, I see a greasy man in a suit. Short and slightly overweight, his comb-over doing nothing to hide his balding, and the hairs on the back of my neck prick up.

"What can I get you?" I ask, assessing him.

"Is the shop owner around?" You'd know the answer to that if you stopped to look up from your phone.

"He is." My voice lowers, and I cross my arms over my chest. He remains silent, I assume, waiting for me to continue. When I don't, he looks up at me. Raising a brow, I wait for whatever genius this moron is about to come out with.

"Oh, nice to meet you. I'm Tom, I work for Ryder Developments. Nice location you have here." He throws his hand out to shake and plasters on a smile that just makes me angry. My lips curl in disgust as I look from his hand back to him.

"What can I get you, Tom?" I ask again, not uncrossing my arms.

I know exactly what he wants. My shop.

The location is perfect, hence why I fucking bought it. It is surrounded by mid to high scale residential apartments. Some business types and some 'hipsters', as Rosie calls them, both great for my customer base, and I'm also a short walk from a corporate district. Which means I get lunch time walk-ins and some post-workday drifters, needing something to perk them up or help them wind down.

The location is perfect. And I'm ready to tell fucking Tom the same thing I told the last developer. I'm not fucking selling.

"Well, you have a great location here, heart of every corner, and, well, it would be great if we could have a chat. Discuss numbers? I know the right buyer who could set you up for life in purchasing this from you. Take away the burden. You wouldn't have to worry about a thing."

In case you're wondering, this is almost identical to the last developer sales guy. Telling me how much of a burden having the shop is. How I'll practically thank them for taking it off my hands.

The difference with this time? I don't have the endless cash flow from my parents for the bad weeks. I can no longer coast on just enjoying the store and the lifestyle it affords me. I'm officially a small business surviving on a terrible economy, with taxes, wages, and general overheads biting me in the ass.

I'm not in the red, and we'd have to continue like this for at least another year before I'd need to look at down-sizing or even selling. But I'm not giving up on this.

Not yet.

"You want a coffee?" I ask, staring into his eyes, hoping he sees the very real 'fuck off' I am trying to communicate to him.

I watch him gulp and nervously laugh.

"Uhh, sure, I'll just take a latte." I nod and get busy making the latte as he starts to walk around the shop. I watch him as closely as I can, not trusting this slime ball.

I make quick work of the latte and slide it across the counter. He throws down a few bills, well and truly over the price of the coffee, and it makes my skin heat with anger. This fucker thinks he can throw some cash around like a big swinging dick and I'll just fall at his feet?

I bite down on my tongue, wanting so badly to tell him to whip it the fuck out and let's really see whose is bigger.

Fucker.

"Anything else?" I ask, barely louder than a growl, and I hear the door chime ring again, but I don't remove my eyes from the slimeball.

He slides over a business card. "Call me once you've had a chance to think it over." I don't move to take the card, but he winks at me and heads for the door, passing two guys on his way out.

I double take and notice those guys are Noah and Caleb. Great.

"What do you fuckers want?" I grunt and slap a hand on the business card and the cash, pocketing both. Making a mental note to shred the card later. I don't need Caleb or Noah witnessing any of that.

"Thought you'd be in a good mood considering you finally got laid—OW!" Caleb says before he shouts at Noah, punching him in the arm. His words have me glaring at Noah.

"What the fuck are you talking about?" I say under my breath. "What bullshit you spinning?"

Noah raises his hand in defense before he levels Caleb with a look, who rubs the arm Noah punched and looks at me apologetically.

"I didn't realize it was a secret," Caleb says between gritted teeth.

"Casey might have said some things," Noah fills me in. What the fuck?

Noah must see the rage on my face because he continues. "She didn't know I was there! She didn't even know Addison was there. Actually, I don't think she even knew she was speaking out loud." He raises his hands again, and I look around the shop to make sure no fucker is listening to this drivel.

"I didn't have sex with Casey," I say quietly, but clearly, omitting the fact that I spent the morning wishing I had and, instead, pictured the face she made when she came while I fisted my dick three times. I was insatiable for Casey.

Noah drags a hand down his face and snaps his head to Caleb.

"Can you just keep your mouth shut for once? I never said they did."

Caleb shrugs. "So, he gets freaky on the counter and then, what... just goes to sleep? How the fuck are your balls after that?" Blue as fuck. I obviously don't say that, or clarify that I left early the next morning so I could relieve myself before my shift started.

I look at Noah and point to Caleb. "This is who manages your sales team?" My point comes across, and Noah closes his eyes and sighs heavily while nodding. Understanding that his best friend is a fucking idiot.

"What!? What did I say this time?" Caleb spreads his hands like he honestly hasn't any idea.

"Can I get you guys a coffee? Or are you here to talk about shit you have no idea about?"

"We came for a coffee. But also to hang out. When you off?" This coming from Noah, and I narrow my eyes at him, trying to pinpoint the joke here.

I'm sure they want to hang out so they can talk shit about me and Casey. Although I have no idea what to even say about it.

Freaky on the counter is one way to put it. Really, she just destroyed my mind, and sneaking out of her room was the single hardest thing I've done. But if I didn't, the counter wasn't the only place we were going to get freaky. Casey is vulnerable right now, and I didn't want to cross a line we couldn't come back from. Physical attraction is one thing. I know she is attracted to me. I see the way she reacts to me, but it's just that, attraction. And I don't know that I can move beyond that. I don't know how to give myself over completely.

"Shift ends at four."

"We're meeting Luke and Ethan at Bozzelli's. You should come," Caleb offers, as he sits at the counter, Noah following his lead and they pick up a menu.

"Why?" I ask, looking between them.

Noah looks up at me and raises an eyebrow. "Uh, because we're fun?"

"Don't be lame. Come have a beer," Caleb says, not looking up from the menu. "Hey, what does Rosie usually order from here?" he questions, still not looking up, and it has Noah and I turning in his direction, puzzled looks on our faces. Caleb looks up and notices our staring, his cheeks heat uncharacteristically. "What?"

"Rosie doesn't really order here. When she does, it's just a black coffee."

"Black coffee?" he says, his eyebrows drawing together. He looks at Noah for confirmation, who shrugs and peruses the menu again. "Really?"

I shrug in response. "She says she likes her coffee to match her soul." Caleb's jaw drops, and Noah just chuckles under his breath and replies quietly, "That sounds about right."

"You fuckers ordering or wasting my time?" I flip a tea towel over my shoulder.

"I'll just have a latte. We'll get it to go and get out of your hair, but you should come by Bozzelli's." I nod and start on the latte.

"Caleb? Coffee?"

"Uhh..." He clears his throat and rolls his shoulders, mustering what I assume is confidence. "Yeah, I'll just get a black coffee." He stands, bobbing his head like we can't see right through him. He slides his sunglasses over his eyes and plasters on the biggest boyish grin I've ever seen. I roll my eyes and finish making their coffee.

Sliding it over to them, they stand and take it, sliding over a note each in payment.

"Bozzelli's?" Noah asks. I nod.

"Yeah, yeah, I'll text you when I'm on my way."

Caleb throws out a fist, and I look at it, then at him, raising an eyebrow.

"What? C'mon, man, we're buddies!" he says, exasperated. I shake my head at him, but knock my fist with his, shaking off that odd feeling.

I haven't had 'buddies' in a while, and I hate thinking about that. After high school, my life revolved around Jenny. She consumed me. I wanted nothing other than to be around her.

Perhaps that was our downfall? Maybe I really did smother her.

I lost contact with all my college friends. Well, really, I just shut myself off. I had Chloe, but Jenny wasn't comfortable with her, so I also closed myself off from her, too.

It's oddly comforting to have people who seem eager to hang out, who appear interested in my company. Oddly comforting, but also gives me an itch, like I'm waiting for the other shoe to drop. I suppose I can stomach it, put up with these idiots, as long as it doesn't turn into the Spanish Inquisition of my fucking love life again.

I came home to shower before I met with the guys–still plagued with those images of Casey. I sorted myself out, again, before getting distracted with a fresh word document open on my laptop. Writing had become my escape. Spinning a world of fiction from my own baggage as a way of dealing and processing. Getting lost in another world, another mind, where nothing else matters. It allowed me to sleep, sometimes dream, where I could control the story, what it looked like and where it went. Now, with two thousand words written, I am officially shocked. This time doesn't feel like the first manuscript. This time is different. I hadn't wanted to escape reality because it was too painful, instead I want to exist in a dream where I allow myself what I actually want. I am officially lost in a world where there are no consequences for going after what–or who–I want.

I can't find my other manuscript, no matter how hard I've tried to search for it, and maybe it's a sign. Too much pain and misery. This one–I think this one is different. I don't really know where it's going, but for the first time in a while, I feel a little spark of hope.

Noah: You coming?

"Shit." The downside of writing is that I usually lose track of everything else. I check the time and quickly close the laptop, flicking a quick response back, and head for the door.

The bar is only a fifteen-minute walk from my apartment, so I head out. The air is cool, the closer we get to the end of the year, so I grab a coat. The sun is setting, sitting close enough to the horizon that the sky is painted in navy blue and purples, lights lining the streets, which are just as busy as they are at every minute of the day in this city. Admiring the landscape, taking in the park, the warm oranges and yellows of the fallen leaves, as I cut through, maybe making the walk longer, but it's certainly a more scenic route when my phone chimes again.

Ace: Hey, would you be interested in doing a partners Yoga class with me?

We've barely spoken since the other night. She came so hard on my fingers, I kissed the fuck out of her pretty face, and then I cooked her dinner and said goodnight. It was the best, most domesticated and confusing twenty-four hours of my life, and I have no idea how to talk about it.

I knew she was going to say something at dinner. I knew it was going to be something I hated. She was going to tell me it was a mistake, that we should forget, but I couldn't if I tried, and I don't want to put pressure on her. I also know I can't label it. I saw her wanting to talk feelings, and I just fucking bailed. And now? Partners Yoga?

Me: Why?

Ace: Boo! You're such a grump.

Ace: I usually do it with Grace...
You don't have to, though. I can find someone else.

Like fuck.

Me: I'll be there.

I arrive at Bozzelli's and tuck my phone into my pocket. Navigating through the throng of people and finding the table with the guys. Caleb throws his stupid knuckles at me again, and the rest of the guys nod in greeting.

Stella walks over with their order and stops by me. "What can I get you?"

"Whiskey, neat. Thanks." I nod at her, noting the dark circles under her eyes, but look away quickly enough not to stare. A small pit of concern for her forms low in my stomach, but I work to bury it. Finding the energy to even be here with the guys was hard enough, let alone branching out into a personal conversation about an acquaintance's well-being. I didn't need the added guilt for not asking if she was okay, so I try to bury those sudden and frustrating feelings. Her eyes narrow slightly, obviously clocking my split-second look of concern, and somehow, I feel like she just read my mind. Appearing on the same page as me and wanting to avoid the socialization, she turns around as I tune into the table conversation.

"I'm telling you, it's the long game. As long as I pretend she doesn't exist, but give her little looks every now and then, she'll be begging me to take her home," Caleb informs us as Noah and Matt laugh. Lucas and Ethan just share a similar eye-rolling, exasperated look.

"What poor innocent soul are you targeting tonight, Smith?" I ask him, and his boy-ish grin hits me from across the table.

"Your three o'clock." He tilts his head in the direction and I look over. Seeing who he is referring to and dropping my head in an honest chuckle before returning to him. She's a pretty little thing, dressed in a pencil skirt and blouse and looks to be giggling with her friends. She couldn't be less interested in Caleb's gaze, and from the way her male companion is cozied up to her, I'd hazard a guess she isn't even available.

I'm sure that isn't much of a hurdle for our resident fuckboy, though.

"Not a chance," I mumble as Stella walks by, dropping my whiskey, collecting empties, and heading back to the bar, and I catch Ethan's lingering stare, the concern matching mine from a minute ago before it's gone. Good, let him concern himself with her wellbeing. I have enough bullshit to work through.

I sip as Caleb darts his confused eyes from me to his next victim.

"Why not?"

"Because she is out of your league, like we've already said." This coming from Lucas.

"You need to get realistic, Caleb. This isn't the long game. She just isn't fucking interested." Ethan provides in a bored tone, Matt and Noah almost thoroughly losing their shit as they struggle to contain their laughter. Caleb's annoyed expression grows as he sips his drink and analyzes his target with new eyes. Probably realizing what we've been trying to tell him.

I settle into the camaraderie, and whether it's the whiskey or lack of sleep and mental clarity, it has me opening up a lot more than I had planned.

"You guys ever heard of Ryder Developments?" They each turn their gazes to me, and Ethan leans forward from his relaxed position in his chair to rest his elbows on the table, giving me his full attention.

"They're known for buying up old buildings, knocking down, and re-building stupidly expensive residential apartments no one can afford to rent," he informs me with his signature furrowed brows.

"And the CEO is a huge dick," Matt supplies, and I roll my eyes. Figured.

"Why's that?" Noah queries.

"Stopped by the café. Gave me his card," I mumble and sip my drink, mulling over my choices.

"Your building isn't that old. Why would they be interested in you?" Lucas asks.

"I'd say it's the location." That gives a knowing nod across the group.

"Was that the wannabe suit who was leaving when we arrived?" Caleb all but forgets his latest target as he settles back into the conversation. I nod as I sip my whiskey. Noah's and Caleb's lips turn into different versions of a snarl, and I feel comforted that my instincts of the sales guy were correct: slimeball.

"I wouldn't trust him as far as I could throw him," Noah supplies.

"Mmm. They do pretty well, actually. They're extremely successful, and from the deals I've heard of, the people they buy off make good coin." Ethan, pragmatic as always.

"Didn't you just say they price them too high?" I deadpan back at him.

"I did." He nods and sips as I raise a brow at him. "Both facts can exist at the same time," he provides, and I roll my eyes, running a hand down my face.

"Are you considering selling?" Lucas asks. And I stare at him in contemplation. I really don't know how to answer the question. Do I want to sell? No. Should I sell? Maybe. Not yet, though. If I did, what else would I do?

I shrug in response, my focus landing on my glass, and I twirl it self-consciously. A ball of fury and frustration starts to grow inside me, knowing they're all looking at me expectantly.

"I don't want to."

"Do you need to?" Ethan asks, albeit gently, but his eyes are serious, considering, and the rest of the table feels the same. Again, I shrug.

"Look, if you need, I can look over your books. Run some numbers, help you out?" Ethan provides. I knew he was in finance, but if I'm honest, I really have no idea what his actual role or job description is. I look into his dark eyes, intense and assessing, and I feel the left corner of my lips tilt in an appreciative smirk.

"Thanks. I'd appreciate that, actually. We're not in the red. Every bit helps, though." I nod and he does the same, pulling out his phone for me to input my number. I do and hand it back.

"I'll reach out next week and we can catch up." And with that, they return to their usual casual conversations. It feels unusual to rely on other people. To be handed help and amity without any expectations, but something warm spreads in my chest and I realize I feel less of a need to avoid or escape, but instead feel perfectly content to just be in their space and their presence.

partners yoga was an excellent idea

Casey

"It's not that bad."

"It's partners Yoga, Casey. It's not that great." I struggle to hold my chuckle in as I watch Jessie shift on his feet. We are currently in the lobby. Elle's hot Yoga class is running over time, probably because everyone in there is exhausted, but I'm not worried. The extra time to make Jessie overthink this whole thing is hilarious.

Am I nervous about being in close and suggestive positions with the guy I have been trying super hard not to crush really hard on? Yes.

Am I enjoying tormenting him and looking forward to watching him try not to be attracted to me? Also yes.

I mean, how could I not? Just look at that frown and sweaty upper lip.

Finally, losing the battle to withhold my laugh, I lean forward and rest my hands on my knees in a cackle. He looks down at me, unimpressed.

"It's really not that bad. If you didn't want to do this, you could have said no." I smile up at him and he crosses his arms. I hadn't really explained to him just how much it meant to me that he came with me. It was the one thing Grace, and I did together. It's a great workout for strength, flow, and flexibility, and was a way for us to have our own time without taking away too much from our own teaching. But of course... I couldn't exactly come with her now.

Asking Jessie, though, felt easy. I hadn't even thought about it, really, just knew he'd come through and that it'd be comfortable with him, like everything else is.

A tight frown forms and he makes some noise that is a mix between a scoff and a grunt.

"So you could press up against and bend over in front of some other guy?" he grumbles, and I just innocently shrug, biting my bottom lip, knowing it'll make him insane.

"Over my dead body." His response is quiet, almost growled, but I catch it. I love it and hate it. Because who is he to get jealous of someone else? It's confusing as all heck and yet I'm still not complaining.

"It's going to be fun, you'll see." I watch him roll his eyes and shift again when the hot yoga class starts filing out of the room.

After a couple of minutes, letting the room cool down and air out, the couples file in. There are twelve of us, being six couples, and we each find the mats and take a seat. Elle takes this one, too, with her husband, who is also an instructor but doesn't work at our studio. He just comes in to assist this class, but otherwise works as a PT for one of those flashy gyms that trains celebrities.

Jessie and I take the front. I do this as a courtesy, as I am obviously comfortable in a yoga class and can assist in demonstrations.

Jessie is still shifty, though he has tamed it down now that we're in class. He is probably also shifty because we haven't spoken about last week. The counter, the dinner, the kiss. We've seen each other sporadically. I've popped into the café for a new coffee blend, and each time he's refused my payment. Sometimes he'd drop a coffee off to me here at the studio, he'd invite me over for dinner and ask me to make him something from my mom's cookbook again. We'd sit in silence in his apartment reading, almost snuggled on the couch together.

Snuggled, literally legs intertwined, a shared blanket over our laps and whispered words–snuggled.

It has been... wholesome. That appears to be the only word I can seem to come up with. There have been no other sexual interactions, but it isn't from a lack of tension because, my god, was there tension. It feels like we're both in a constant state of panting. But it's comfortable, there is no awkwardness. It just feels... right. Like it's exactly where we're meant to be.

I know Addison and Rosie are my best friends, but we all have busy lives. It's different with Jessie. He fills a space I hadn't realized felt so empty. He just fits, and now I don't remember a time before him.

Before us.

We get walked through individual warm-ups before we start moving into the pair work. The moment Elle announces the first one, my stomach sinks. The yogi box. It isn't that it is overly intense; it is that it is close. And requires some strength and trust. I don't know what I was thinking, doing this with Jessie.

"You done this one before?" Jessie whispered as we move into the starting position.

"Yeah, but just with the girls." I nod back at him.

"Partner A, lie on your back, with your hands in the air, as we demonstrated, and Partner B, ready to grip the shins just above the ankles," Elle instructs, and she walks the room to check form and assist as I focus on Jessie. Partner A requires more strength and is better for the larger of the couple, so naturally, that is Jessie. He takes the mat, lying flat on his back and lifting his arms. I swallow and take a deep breath. Centering my mind, I try to do everything I can to focus on the exercise and not on Jessie's strong legs. On the way his exercise shorts are practically gripping his thighs and the way his T is giving away every single muscle. Every dip of his cut torso and rippled stomach.

I try to swallow again, but my mouth is suddenly dry.

"You going to start soon or just stare at me?" Jessie's deep timbre voice pulls me from my staring competition with his body, and I try to shake myself. Focus. Focus on the movement, not the body.

When I look to his face, he has the audacity to hit me with a smug smirk. He knew I was checking him out.

This is the dance we've been doing all week. Catching each other ogling the other. Knowing that we are both a breath away from tearing clothes and lighting each other on fire. But we've also both been comfortable in the almost touch, content to not be the one that takes the next step.

It takes edging to a whole other extreme, and I am ready to lose my mind because of it.

I reach down and grip the space just above his ankles and lift mine one at a time and place them in his hands.

This is the moment I realize my mistake. We're in a glorified six-ty-nine-plank position, with me suspended above him, and I feel my skin heat where he grips my ankles.

"Umm..." I try to breathe through the feelings that are flooding my system, trying to shut down the screams of Little Casey as she begs me to take Jessie home and cross the final line I keep trying to draw in the imaginary sand. "So, from here, we need to jack-knife up." My voice is a pant and from the way Jessie has his eyes scrunched closed and the grip on my ankles tightening, I'm not the only one affected.

"Okay. Great," he says through gritted teeth.

"Are you okay?" I whisper.

His eyes snap open, and lord, if I wasn't already a hot and sweaty mess, that look of hunger in his eyes would do me over.

"Your ass and pussy are basically in my face right now, Ace. I'm not sure okay is the way to describe anything right now." I stumble between a pant and a laugh. Thoroughly enjoying his pain, but also, I just really want to be naked with him right now.

"Okay, let's just get this over with. Maybe it was a bad idea," I say between giggles, and he just shakes his head, a delicate smile gracing his handsome face.

I haven't seen one of those devastatingly stunning smiles since that night on the counter. I keep trying to get one, but he keeps them locked up tight. I won't give up, though. I'm determined to get another.

While I'm usually pretty quick to engage my muscles, my core is always switched and ready to go, I hadn't counted on the fact that Jessie is six feet of muscle, and compared to my five-six gangly sack of bones, I barely have to think of a muscle because Jessie sits straight up, lifting me like I weigh nothing, and his face is level with Little Casey.

A grunt comes from deep within his chest, and I watch as his eyes trail my body and make it to my face.

"Nah, I think this was a great idea."

I can't even respond. Words evade me. That same look of hunger burns a path over me, and I can practically see the dirty images flying past his thoughts.

Being Jessie's friend and not climbing him is going to be very hard after today, I think.

"Want to grab a coffee?"

"Sure." I nod to Jessie as we file out of the yoga room.

After the surprisingly intimate pose that we had jack-knifed into, we managed to keep our eyes off of each other. If not, just out of utter desperation to make it to the end of class without tearing into each other than anything else. But this easiness we fall into immediately after the hot and heavy is something I've come to love. The way we can exist in each other's space and it just be a little slice of peace.

"I can't stay long. I promised Evan I'd pop over. I made Grace some freezer stock meals because Evan has to go interstate for a work thing, and he's worried about her not eating properly." Before we leave the studio, I head for the freezer in the staff break room, pulling out the bag of meals I had stored here when I arrived, knowing I would stop by Grace's before I went home.

We make it onto the street, heading in the direction of the café on the corner. Jessie loops around me to walk on the side closest to the road.

"Do you speak to her much?" he asks gently, and I shrug.

"I've tried to call her. Sometimes she picks up and sometimes she doesn't. I just want to be there for her and she won't let me. I know it's selfish, but—"

"It's not selfish to want to love your sister."

But why won't she let me love her?

"Well, anyway, we haven't really spoken about the fight. I've just passed it off for now. I think we are going to need to have a conversation in the future, and I'm dreading it." He nods, understanding. On one of our quiet reading dates in his apartment, I told JJ all about the things Grace had said that night I went over there. He didn't offer advice, and I didn't ask. He just listened, and then when he vented about the shop and the nosy developers, I didn't try to fix it. I just listened, and he talked.

"Have you seen that sales guy again? From the developer?"

"No. I don't know if he'll come around again. I think that was a one off. My lack of response was probably answer enough." I nod.

"Did you ever take Ethan up on his offer?" I smile because he gives me a side eye like he knew this question was coming. "It's okay to rely on your friends, Jessie." A small chuckle makes it past my lips.

"Ethan is Noah's friend, not mine. And I don't need him to look at anything. The shop is fine." I just nod, not pressing, because I know he isn't ready.

His parents' divorce is still relatively fresh. He is still somewhat overcoming his ex, and I know this guy isn't the best with change. If he is anything like his sister, it's likely panic-inducing. So, I just let him sit in his thoughts.

"Ethan is definitely your friend," is the only response I give as I bump his shoulder and skip ahead.

Lattes in hand–chocolate banana today, perfectly boring–we stop in front of the coffee shop. I need to go left, and his apartment is off to the right. Jessie looks at me, and as he reaches a hand out to tuck an errant hair behind my ear, he steps closer and speaks. "Want to hang at my place tonight?"

It's an intimate question from this close. I can also see the vulnerability swimming in his mixed eyes of blue and green as he searches the depths of mine. Despite the fear the closeness and intimacy gives me, it also makes me feel light and warm. Makes me feel a little like I might be burning up. But to keep from squeaking something weird, I just bite down on my smile and nod quickly. Holding onto that lightness, I take a leap of courage and press up on my toes, lightly dusting my lips to the corner of his in a delicate kiss.

When my feet are planted back on the ground and I'm stepping backward away from him, I see his stunned face watching me, his free hand fisted by his side as he white knuckles the coffee in his hand.

"I'll text you when I'm on my way." I give him a wink–honestly, who am I right now–and I turn and head for Grace's.

The walk there is short. This studio is the one closest to her apartment, which is why I run the other one, but I pass a convenience store and pick up a treat for her, anyway. I knock once on Grace's door, and she answers with a soft smile. Foregoing hello's, she just turns and walks back into the apartment, leaving it open in invitation.

Her apartment is decorated similar to the studios, but with dark laminate flooring and greenery everywhere. I spot Evan in the kitchen and nod in hello as Grace leaves us to it. I store the meals and walk out to the living room to find her lying on the couch. I sit, grabbing her feet to lift them and place them in my lap.

"Here." I hand her the chocolate bar. Or I try to. She looks at it like it offends her, then back to the TV.

A frown pulls at my face and I place the bar on the coffee table. The heaviness in my stomach souring. At least she is letting me hold her in some way.

"I don't know how to make this better, Grace," I say quietly into the tense air that surrounds us.

"It's not your job to make it better."

"I meant with you and me. I don't know how to be a better sister. I'm sorry for whatever I've done that's hurt you. I just want to be good with each other again. This distance hurts," I say gently back, trying as hard as possible to be sensitive to her situation, but also aching to have a relationship with my sister.

"Stop trying to fix everyone and everything around you and we'll be just fine, Casey," she says in one breath. I just nod at her, but the awkward tension in the room doesn't dissipate.

"Okay." I rub gently on her leg, trying to give her some affection in the only way she seems to allow it. I love her. I know she is hurting, and watching her hurt like this makes me just want to cry again.

I don't know what the heck is wrong with me, or when I became like this. I used to have a great handle on my emotions. I could bundle them all up and let them go on demand once a month as needed for an outlet.

"Well, I've stocked the freezer for next week. I know that Evan isn't going to be home. I'm only a phone call away. Maybe we could have dinner together a couple nights a week?" I ask, except I must have said something wrong again because a humorless laugh makes its way out of her mouth as she pulls her legs from me and sits up. Shaking her head, she levels me with a look of hatred.

"I'm no insolent child who can't take care of herself. I don't need you mothering me. Did you forget I'm the older sister?" She doesn't even wait for me to answer, she stands from the couch and storms for her room.

I've had just about enough of this.

"Grace, for the love of god, stop walking away from me," I shout after her, losing my grip on my emotions.

The apartment is so quiet you could hear a pin drop. Grace has stopped, but her back is still facing me and I see her shoulders rise with her erratic breathing as she works to calm herself.

"All I want is to love you. Why won't you let me?" I ask, blinking back the sting in my eyes and willing myself to hold it together.

She spins slowly and those same angry eyes stare coldly back at me.

"You shouldn't be so desperate, Casey. It's not a good look." Her upper lip curls slightly in disgust before she continues to storm back to her room. I see movement at the corner of my eye and watch as Evan's face drops, looking at me apologetically.

I grab my bag from the counter on my way out and angrily swipe at my eyes. Before the door to the apartment slams behind me, Evan stops it.

"Casey, I'm sorry, she... she has just been upset. Please don't stop trying. She is pushing everyone away, and she really needs us right now." My chest feels hollow, my heart aches, and I just want a warm blanket and a good cry, but I nod at him and try to paste on my most positive smile.

"I'd never give up on her, Ev. She's my sister," I whisper before I turn and leave. Heading for somewhere that feels warmer.

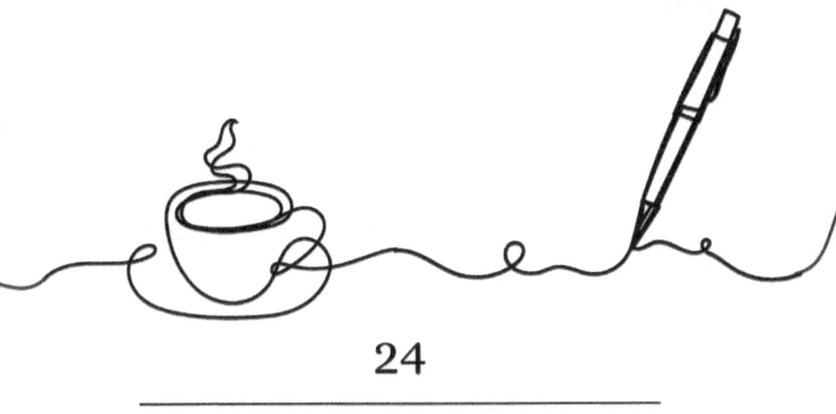

24

you're not ready.

Jessie

"You're right, you're not in the red, but the projection also isn't good. Without an increase in cash flow soon, a relatively large increase at that, in order to still make a profit, you'd have to look at selling in at least the next three to six months. Maybe eight, if you're lucky." Ethan's grim delivery about the shop's finances floats through the phone and makes my skin prickle.

"And if I don't?"

"Well, if you don't sell, you'll end up being forced to close in twelve months, at most. Because without that injection of funds, the business will begin to lose money, and it won't be worth enough to cover your losses and make a profit in selling. Look, I hate to be the one to give you that information. I just hate to see you go down with the ship."

I grunt in response, and he keeps going.

"Looking at it, the sales are good. You just need more, mostly with the books. Have you thought about an online store, more traffic that way? Maybe a new building so you could expand the selection?"

"I can't afford a new building. Otherwise, I would have done that already." Hadn't thought of the online store, though, that isn't half bad.

"Say you do accept the developer's offer. Maybe you can have them sweeten it and allow a settlement to link with you finding another building?" Another idea I hadn't thought of.

I grunt some sort of response, feeling the early seeds of failure take root. I've been running this business for five years, I should have thought about these options already.

"Think it all over, anyway. If you have any questions, I'm happy to help you out. You wouldn't need to make any decisions for at least another month. Unless the developer's offer has a deadline," he gives, and before I can answer, there is a light knock on my apartment door.

"Someone's at the door. Speak to you later. Thanks, Ethan." I mumble the end, and a light chuckle hits me from his side before he responds.

"Anytime, JJ." And the call ends.

Shutting the laptop and storing the papers back in the cabinet by the reading chair, I head for the door and swing it open.

"Casey, wha—"

Before I can finish that sentence and ask what she's doing here earlier than I had expected, her small body wraps around me tightly and she shudders in my embrace. Sobs leaving her lips as she cries into my chest.

I wrap my arms around her and kick the front door closed.

"What happened? What is going on, Ace?" Panic grips my chest and her knees almost buckle as I feel her weight drop. I reach an arm below her knees, bridal carrying her through my apartment. I sit on the couch with her in my lap and hold her. No responses leave her, instead she just cries and hiccups through her breath.

I try not to push, but uneasiness sits heavy in my stomach as I wait out the sobs. Eventually, they begin to slow, and I lean back, bringing a finger below her chin to look into her deep ocean blue eyes. Filled with only joy and mischief not two hours ago, they suddenly are filled with a deep aching sadness that makes the rage in me wake and rumble, wanting to ruin whatever or whoever did this to my sunshine.

"Talk to me," I beg her in a whisper.

"Grace. She... I just... it hurts, and I don't know how to fix it."

Casey is a people-pleaser. Probably to a chronic level, and I know this sense of helplessness in her stems from watching someone she cares for break and only being pushed away instead of being allowed to help. I just don't quite know how to tell her that this isn't hers to fix. To stop trying and she maybe won't hurt so much.

I just want her to stop hurting, and fuck do I want to storm over there and tear shreds off that witch for making Casey cry.

My Casey. My sunshine.

"Maybe you just let this one go. Don't force it and don't fix it." Instantly, I regret the sentence as she pulls back from my grip on her chin, her brows furrowing.

"She's my sister, Jessie. I'm not going to abandon her." The pinkness returns to her cheeks as she swipes angrily at her tears.

"I didn't say abandon her, but you can't change her, either. Give her some space. Or ask her how to help. But you can't keep turning up and doing the same dance and expecting a different outcome." I try to say it as gently as possible, but by the look on her face, I'm failing. She pulls herself out of my lap and stands like she is going to leave, except I'm instantly there.

"She is my sis—"

"Your sister, I know. But she isn't your problem." I step into her space, her stance strong as she stares angrily up at me, and as I raise a finger to swipe away one of her tears, her face softens. The contact of her skin is warm and inviting, and I want it all over me. To feel her everywhere.

"She isn't your problem, Casey. You deserve as much happiness, respect, and love as she does. Don't reduce your wants and needs just to fit hers. If she can't see how special and amazing you are, then that is her loss. She'll come around. Maybe just give her some space." She blinks up at me, but doesn't lose her frown. Instead, I trace the frown lines with my fingers until they soften and she leans forward, resting her head on my chest.

"I'm so tired, Jay," she breathes, and my body relaxes as she fists my shirt and holds me close to her.

"I know," I whisper back, rubbing circles on her back.

A brief pause. The comfortable silence between us always settles my mind, bringing me a peace I can't seem to find anywhere else.

She takes a large breath and just as she lets it go, she whispers, "Why haven't you kissed me again?"

This time I'm caught off guard by her words. Pulling away slightly, I look down as she looks up. Those same sad eyes hit me.

"Do you want me to kiss you?" I ask back, but she gives away nothing. Steel determination in those big blue eyes, it almost makes me chuckle. So, instead, I ask her, "Why haven't you kissed me?"

"Because you're not ready for me." Again, she whispers, and where I'd expect shyness is only confidence. Because Casey Baker knows exactly who she is and never apologizes for it. Still, her response once again catches me off guard. While I have no idea what we're doing or what is going on in my head, I couldn't care less how complicated this gets. I've got a feeling she's all I'm ever going to want. Ready or not.

"And what if I kissed you now?" I grip her lower back and push my body into hers, running a hand across her cheek to push a hair behind her ear and holding her in place, my lips dusting hers gently as I speak the words. Her eyes hood and her chest rises with her breath.

"I'd let you, anyway."

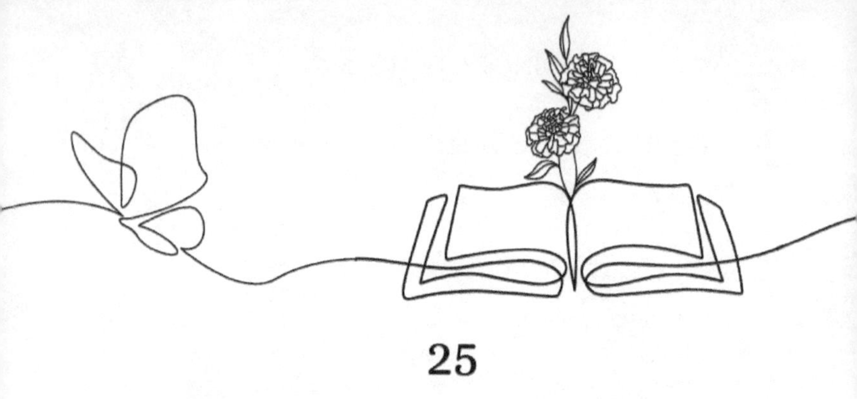

25

you pierce my soul

Casey

Jessie's lips are on mine in a blink. Instead of the rushed and desperate passion our last couple of kisses have been, this one is soft, delicate. Loving. Our lips are sealed until his tongue dances with mine, and I breathe a soft moan that he steals. I grip his shirt tighter, trying desperately to eradicate all the distance between us, to feel him on me. His hands leave my face, trailing down my body, and in a flash, I'm off the ground, my legs instantly wrapping around his firm waist, his lips never leaving mine.

The room is quiet, nothing but the sounds of our lips, breath, and moans as I taste him, feel him, and savor him. My back arches on instinct, unable to stop from squirming, searching for friction, for more. Instead of the counter, which holds a very specific appeal right now, he walks me blindly to his room. Kissing the absolute shit out of me, I wrap myself as firmly as I can around him, and when the door is closed, the room darkened by the closed shades, he slowly and gently lowers me to my feet in front of him.

"You better tell me to stop." I'm practically panting. He better not stop. Shaking my head and taking a step back, retreating to the bed, I watch as Jessie becomes the predator I've been looking for. He takes a step forward, never allowing the space to grow between us.

"What do you want, Casey?" I can't tell if he means right now or between us, but I get the feeling it wouldn't matter what my answer was. He'd give me everything I asked for right now.

So I ask for what my soul shouts for. After everything with Grace, I am so exhausted from trying to be everything for everyone. I am done anticipating everyone's wants and desires, at least for right now.

No. Now, I want to give in to myself, I finally want what it is I desire, what I want.

I want the beast, to be the beauty who is ravished by him.

"I'm tired, Jessie," I breathe, and I watch as his lips tip up at the corners, understanding everything I'd just decided without me even needing to say it. He continues to slowly stalk toward me, and when my knees hit the bed, I sit, and he remains standing in front of me. "You know what I've always wanted but never bothered asking for?" I continue, trying to hide just how turned on and desperate I am for him right now.

"Tell me." His response is a deep, strangled groan, and I can see his control slipping. Desire and need pool between my legs, aching for his attention.

"I want a gentleman and a savage." Slowly, I peel my shirt off over my head and look him dead in the eyes. "I want you to choke me and tell me how pretty I am."

His control snaps.

Before I have a moment to know what's happening, he grips my calves, yanking me to the edge of the bed and flipping me to my back as I gasp in surprise, biting back a giggle at how quickly he went from caring about my tears at the door to a caged animal in the bedroom.

In one swift motion, he yanks my yoga tights down.

"You want to fuck a savage, sunshine?" he asks.

A whimper leaves my lips, and I swear my pussy clenches in antic-ipation at the sound of his voice like this. Rough and full of desper-ation. In a blink, my panties lay in pieces as they're torn and my bra discarded to the ground.

The desire on his face, the way he appraises me, has me hot and squirming. God, I need him. I have never needed someone this way before. Reading my desperation, he teases me, slowly dragging his shirt from over his head and flicking the button of his jeans.

He hesitates for only a moment, but in that moment, I see it. The longing, raw look of hunger. Stripping off his jeans and boxers, his length springs free, and it makes me swallow, my mouth suddenly dry.

I might have been a little too confident, because, oh boy.

He strokes himself once, and I have to bite my lip to keep the moan from escaping. Returning my gaze to his, I reluctantly tear my eyes from gaping at the size of him.

Before I can say anything, he steps into my space, gripping my chin and lifting my face to look up at him. Confidence oozes from him in a way I've never seen before. He is in charge, this is all him. And I've never been more turned on in my life.

"Move up the bed, lie down, and open for me." I do as he says, simply because I couldn't come up with a retort if I tried. I lie on my back, keeping my gaze locked with his, as I slowly drop my knees, opening for him.

His eyes trail down my body, stopping only briefly at my breasts, enough time to stroke himself again before he lands between my legs and groans. Like the beast I asked for, he climbs to the bed, but lowers himself between my legs, his grip tight on my hips, my legs over his shoulders. A single swipe of his tongue up my middle and I gasp.

"Jess!" The single word unleashes him, and he does what he had promised that night on the counter.

He makes a meal of me.

His lips, tongue, and teeth devour me, like a man starved, teasing and nipping at my little bud. The sound of my moans fills the air, and I grip at his hair, guiding him as I ride his face. Those damn teeth lightly graze my clit again. "Jess!" I'm a panting, squirming mess, and he can't get enough.

"I knew this pussy would be delicious." His voice is raspy with desire and vibrates through me as he removes the grip on my left hip and spears two fingers inside my soaking heat, feeling that orgasm at the edge as I grip him.

"Oh, god! I'm going to come." My words are a mix between a moan and a groan, and it pushes him further as he curls his fingers and drives me closer to the edge, his tongue working me closer. I feel the build, the tingle in my toes, the way it tightens, and I squeeze my eyes closed, ready for the euphoria his magic tongue will send me to. Just as it crests, he pulls back, biting my inner thigh. I groan in complaint, and he chuckles lightly as he looks up from between my legs, licking me from his lips.

"Needy," he whispers and kisses a path up my stomach, his fingers running an achingly slow path down my middle, trailing the link from where I desperately need him, to my sensitive swollen peak.

"Please," I beg.

"You said you wanted a savage." I did. I so badly just want him unleashed. His lips reach the shell of my ear as he continues to whisper. "Turn around and put that delicious ass in the air, sunshine. Tonight, you're coming on my cock."

Oh my god.

I can barely see straight from the desire fogging my brain, from the need shaking my core, from the way I am dripping for this man and ready to be and do anything he wants. Following instructions, I roll to my stomach, to my hands and knees, shoving my ass back, but before I can get into any sort of position, he is gripping my hips and dragging me to the edge of the bed, the tip of his cock teasing at my entrance, spreading the wetness.

"You are so wet for me, Ace," he grunts, and then I feel his warm hand firmly press up the length of my spine, and a sound I can't even begin to describe leaves my throat.

Pleasure. It is just pure animalistic pleasure, and I have never felt more desired than I do under his touch. His hand continues its trail until it wraps around the front of my neck and pulls me up, making my back flush with his front, his grip firm on my neck as he bites my ear and whispers, "You're so fucking pretty."

Then, in one whole thrust, he sheathes himself completely. A loud, almost scream leaves my lips at the same time a deep growl comes from him. Losing my breath for a moment as I adjust to the size of him.

"I knew this tight little pussy was going to fit me perfectly. Look how well you take me." He slowly pulls out, almost to the tip, before he pushes back in with the same power as the first time, and I squeeze my eyes closed... too much. Oh, god!

"Jessie," I moan, because I can't form words. Everything evacuates from my mind, and all I feel is him. He's everywhere.

"I'm not going to be able to stop after this, Casey."

"You better not stop." I think I'd sue if he did.

His pace increases, and my body comes alive. The feeling of him as he slides inside me is like ecstasy. I'll never get enough of this. Of him.

"I couldn't quit you if I tried," he spits between clenched teeth, and like the final tether on his control is snapped, he leaves the grip on my neck, pushing my chest to the bed as he holds my hips and fucks into me again and again, like the savage I asked for.

"God, Casey, you feel so fucking good," he growls before he drives deeper, harder into me, my knees barely on the bed as he holds my hips and takes me over and over. I feel the tightening, the way my desire pools and soaks me, feeling the tingles in my toes as I grip him.

"Fuck! Jessie, I'm going to come! Please, make me come!" I shout at him, and he drops my hips, laying his chest to my back, his pace never ceasing as his hand reaches under me and plays with my clit.

"Oh, fuck!"

"That's it, Ace, make a mess. Come on my cock, I want to feel you everywhere." He bites down on my shoulder, at the same time, he pinches my clit, and I come in an explosion. Dark spots invade my vision, and I lose my breath as each wave of my orgasm overtakes me.

He doesn't stop, he keeps going.

"Fuck, your pussy is strangling me. God, you feel amazing." He pulls out, but before I can argue, he flips me on my back and is on me in seconds. His cock thrusts again, and I wrap my legs over his hips, needing him closer as he pistons inside me with speed, his lips sealing with mine.

"Another. I need another one," he pants in my ear and kisses down my neck. "Lift your hips for me."

I think my brain is on autopilot, because without knowing what I'm doing, I lift my hips. He slides a pillow under me and I nearly come undone completely by the change in angle.

"That's it," he praises and grips my neck again. "Look at me. I want to see those pretty eyes when you come. So, be a good girl and fucking come," he demands, and like my body has become completely his, it obeys, the sheer speed of his thrusts, the angles, the way one hand grips my neck and the other pinches my clit, I fly off again, trying to hold those incredible blue-green eyes as euphoria takes over me. After another thrust, I feel him go, too, and we ride out the wave together, coming down from the high as he stills and lays above me.

"You are magic," he whispers, and when he raises his head to spear me with those eyes, he barely looks before he kisses me. Gently and softly.

He pulls out slowly, and it is only in this moment that I realize he had actually used a condom.

God, I hadn't even thought about it. In the throes of the passion and desire I was flooded with, I hadn't even cared. I'm glad he at least had half a mind to do that.

He disposes of it in the trash can in the corner of his room, and before I can leave the bed, he bends and lifts me in another bridal carry.

"What are you—"

He ends my question with a kiss. Another gentle one, full of longing. A lazy, delicate, and sated kiss that pulls on my forgotten heart strings. Sending an ache to my chest, one I needed desperately to shut down.

He kisses me so thoroughly I hadn't realized we were now in the bathroom. He sets me down on my feet, leaning behind me with one arm to turn on the shower, allowing it to get hot.

We don't speak any words, but instead hold each other's gaze. His fingers drag lazy circles on my lower back and mine find their way to the nape of his neck, massaging and tickling. "You pierce my soul." He smiles gently as he whispers his words against my lips.

"Jane Austen," I whisper back, our usual game in play, seamlessly. I bite my lip to suppress the smile and the way he lights up my heart, but feeling my chest grow heavy as I hear the omitted quote in my head. The words he didn't say. *I am half agony, half hope.*

He can't give all of himself to me. He is still fighting it.

Jenny.

Without another word, he pulls me into the shower, soaping up my whole body, dotting my clean skin with kisses as he massages, caressing away any doubt, making me forget the mental warning. That I might be falling for someone who is in love with someone else.

He turns me gently, in every which way, before he is at my back and massaging in the shampoo.

Being the second half of my request. Jessie Jenkins: the savage and the gentleman.

"I could get used to this." I hum happily, my eyes closed tight as those barista hands work their magic.

"Me, too."

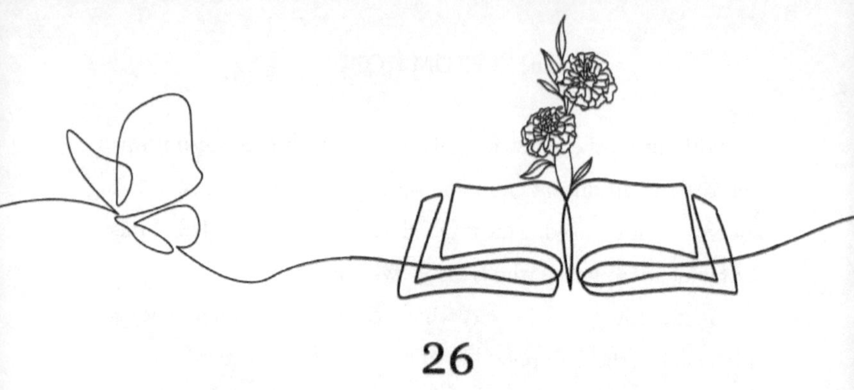

26

my darling

Casey

I'm achy.

Like, the good kind of achy where every time I stretch out my muscles during each pose in my classes today, I feel good and a small smile forms on my lips.

Then I get flashes of yesterday. The man and the beast. The gentleman and the lover. That shower led to three more orgasms. Jessie hadn't let me leave his embrace until I snuck out this morning for my first class at 5am, and I hadn't a moment to check my phone or have a break since, to really piece it all together.

Now I am in the cooldown of my last class, it is 7pm, and I am too exhausted to even try to think about what happened and what it all meant.

I've been taking Grace's classes for a couple of weeks now, and if I don't hand ball some of them soon, I am going to fall on my face. We have two studios and five instructors. Four with Grace out, and I can't keep this up. It isn't good for me.

I'm barely registering the goodbyes as the staff file out, and I pull my phone from my bag as I lock up the studio. It's ringing the moment I turn to walk up the street toward the apartment, and because I'm about to start sleep walking, I answer it before I see who it is.

"Hi, sweetie!" My mom's melodic voice travels through the speaker phone and a kernel of warmth hits me as I blink back the tears of relief. Hearing Mom's voice when I feel this crap wins over any control I try to have over my emotions.

"Hi, Mom! I'm sorry I haven't called you back in a bit. It's been a bit crazy over here."

"I know, darling. But it's all going to be okay," she assures me, and even though she can't make those kinds of promises, hearing them from her helps, even if it's just a bunch of empty words.

"Thanks. How's Dad? Where are you guys at the moment?"

"Good. My turn on the driving, so he is napping. We're stopping in Kansas City, making our way back, but might stop in Memphis and see Grandad before we head on back to Virginia," she explains, and I can hear the smile on her face at the excitement in seeing her dad. We don't get out that way very much.

"Send him my love."

"I will. Casey—"

"I don't want to talk about Grace, Mom," I almost whisper into the phone because I can't muster the strength or energy to hash it all out. I am sure she has some story or another from Grace, but thankfully, Mom has a habit of taking Grace's stories with a grain of salt, and coming to me for the accurate details.

"Okay, that's fine, sweetie. But you're going to have to talk about it soon. I know you're going to store all this in your head until you're too tired and implode. I don't want you to implode on your own. I hate to think I can't be there for you or Grace." Mom might be aware of my tendency to bottle up and cry alone once a month. With the way my emotions have been running, I think, at this rate, I'm at once a week, but even if I did return to my ways, something tells me I wouldn't be alone this time.

"I'm not alone, Mom. I have the girls and—"

I stop myself before I say too much. My need for sleep is affecting the seal of my words and my mom gasps at my silence because she is a genius and can read me like a damn book.

"Casey Moira Baker... is there another boy on the scene?" Her joy at that sentence makes my eyes roll.

"No, Mom, I haven't even been single a year."

"Don't you lie to me; I can practically see your shifty eyes. You get that from your father."

That makes me chuckle, and I hear a grumble in the background as Mom also chuckles to herself.

"You can keep your secrets for now, miss. But we'll be in New York in maybe two or three weeks. You and Grace will start talking and your secrets are coming out. I want to meet Mystery Man." She is jovial, but I have to catch my words again before they flood out. She is going to have a heart attack when she realizes the man who currently lives in my head rent free is the same boy that she used to hand the container of sweets to at the front door when she'd drop me off at Addison's house for sleepovers in elementary school.

My stomach is suddenly twisting with nerves.

"I better let you go. Focus on the road. I'll call you next week."

"Love you, sweetie. Smile big!" Her typical motto that she's given Grace and me forever has me rolling my eyes again and chuckling.

"Love you, too, Mom."

23A Sluts

> **Rosie:** Adult sleepover tonight – see you sluts tomorrow!

> **Addy:** I'm at Noah's for the rest of the week and then we fly to Chicago for E's grad and Thanksgiving. Back around the 30th!

> **Me:** Have fun! Miss you girls xx

> **Rosie:** I'm literally still here. I'll see you tomorrow...

> **Me:** lol

I giggle to myself at the texts with the girls, and I assure Rosie that we'll have a girls' dinner tomorrow night when she is home. It'll be a Friday, and I finally have a day off on Saturday and can indulge in some wine and sleep in.

But it means tonight, I'm home alone. And I really don't want to be.

Like he can read my mind, as I pull up Jessie's chat, a text comes in.

> **Jay:** Plans?

Whatever is happening here feels different. I can't tell if I'm disappointed this isn't some swoony love message about how he misses me, but then, also, I have no idea how to answer this glorified booty call because... well, I have no idea what we're doing.

My heart feels heavy because despite how far I try to bury my feelings, I know I'm falling, and I'm falling hard and fast. Like a train derailed, I can't seem to stop. He's hung up on Jenny. He can't let himself fall, and even if he were, he'd stop himself. He'd pull back. And pulling back when I'm falling? Who would catch me?

> **Me:** I'm beat, going home to crash. Another long day tomorrow x

So I don't second guess myself. I lock my phone and pocket it. I can't let myself dwell on the what ifs. I don't want to think about whether we made a mistake crossing that final line. I honestly can't even think what I'm going to have for dinner, let alone mustering the energy to contemplate my... situation-ship.

The rest of the walk home is a blur, the trees and cars all merging to one as I let my brain empty and I try to focus simply on walking my tired sack of bones up the stairs, into the elevator, then through my apartment door. By the time I'm inside, the apartment is dark, cold, and lonely. I flick a switch... and for the first time since I moved in, I hate it.

I hate its emptiness. I hate the space and how clean it is. It smells like Rosie's lemon cleaner and Addison's indoor plants.

I want it to smell like home. I want it to feel like home.

Somehow finding the energy, I change into my pajamas, connect my phone to the speaker, hit play, and head for the kitchen.

Wildfire by Cautious Clay plays and my heart does a little skip.

"I love this song." I pause a beat to turn it louder, singing along to the lyrics and getting lost in kneading the pastry for my apple cinnamon slices. It's an easy recipe. After the pastry is made, you simply peel, slice, and coat the apples. A delicious buttery cinnamon spice mix, lay them on the pastry, cut into rectangles and bake. It's nothing flashy, but these apple slices were my favorite post-school snack to bake with Mom. Back then, it was with store-bought pastry rather than homemade. But I need this today, need to get lost in the song and in the therapy of making some magic out of something plain.

The moment the tray of apple slices is in the oven, the song changes and Noah Reid's rendition of Simply the Best comes on, making my heart pull tighter. I'm a tired silly idiot and I've put my love playlist on shuffle, and instead of powering through my tired bones, I feel the aching loneliness from before sink back in.

I need to stop doing this to myself, stop wallowing—

"Jesus, you scared the crap out of me." I had turned to change the song, and instead my heart leaps out of my chest. I must have missed the front door opening and closing. With a hand to my chest, I lean back against the counter to catch my breath.

"No god here, sunshine, just me." Jessie winks and smiles with the delivery of his line, his shoulders relaxing, and he takes in the room as he walks with purpose toward me. Not stopping to pause or taking a moment to feel any awkwardness, Jessie uses a firm hand to grip my jaw and pulls my lips to his. His kiss is quick, demanding, and breath stealing as I feel him surround me.

As quickly as he approached, he turns, stealing a glass from the cabinet above me and filling it with water and walking into the living room.

"Umm, what... I mean, not that I'm upset by the kiss and all... Jess, what are you doing here?"

"I like when you call me Jess," he says in a low voice, his back to me as he leans over Addison's plants and tips a bit of the water into them. "Addison gave me a key for while she is gone, to water her plants, so I'm watering her plants."

"But, I live here?"

"You do live here." The smug bastard is almost chuckling as he finishes watering the plants and saunters back over to me.

"Why would you need to water the plants?" I cross my arms and tilt my head, trying my best to understand what the hell is going on here.

"She didn't want you to be stuck with that because she knows how busy you are. Plus, I wasn't going to say no to the key."

"And why's that?" He closes the rest of the distance between us, placing the glass in the sink before he comes to stand in front of me, wrapping his arms firmly around my lower back and pulling me to him.

"Because then you can't retreat into your head and avoid talking to me about all the things we need to talk about." I swallow. Oh. "Why'd you blow me off, Ace?"

"I didn—"

"You did. Why?" His question isn't aggressive, just sure. Because this broody lumberjack is suddenly full of confidence, and with the way his eyes trail a burning path across my face, he can see everything. I bring my hands to my face to cover the blush and hide the way I want to cry, scream, and fall asleep all at once.

"Jessie, you aren—"

"Say I'm not ready for you." He pulls my hands from my face and forces me to stare up at his serious eyes. "Say I can't handle you or take care of you. I dare you." I hope he didn't hear my attempt to gulp down air.

"Your message was a glorified booty call." I slap at his chest, but his eyes just darken in challenge as a half-smile pulls at his lips.

"As much as I'd love to have a repeat of last night, it wasn't a booty call. I knew you were busy and wouldn't have eaten." True. "I was sussing your plans because I wanted to take you out." He kisses my cheek delicately, and without my permission, butterflies take flight in my stomach and my chest aches.

He can't give himself to you.

"What about Jenny?" I ask, knowing it was delivered with a knife, but it gets me the space we need while we talk about this because he takes a step back. I hate the way he looks at me, like I just slapped him.

"What about her?" That sexy lumberjack frown is back, and I want to trace the lines between his strong brow until they disappear. Like he does for me. Instead, I settle for twisting the ring of his that rests on my thumb. He tracks the movement, and I watch his jaw clench before he shifts on his feet and looks back to me.

"You've been hung up on Jenny for years, but suddenly you're not?" I smile gently and shrug, but continue. "It wasn't that long ago, Jessie, when you were drunk and you asked me to call her and tell her how great you are so she'd take you back."

He pinches the bridge of his nose and shakes his head, his eyes scrunched tight and his shoulders tense.

"Wait a damned minute. You thin—I am not in love with Jenny, Casey. That was years ago. I was hurt, but I'm not fucking hung up on her,." he throws back at me, and finally his back is up. Good. If he's angry at me, this will be easier. I can put some distance between us and get over this crush before it crushes me back.

"It's okay, Jessie, really. Maybe we shou—"

"Don't finish that sentence," he growls and then he is in my face again. "Don't you dare say you regret last night in order to push me away. Not unless that's how you feel. Do you regret being with me last night?" His angry eyes burn holes right through me. The hunger gone and in their place is the cold green fury of the Jenkins family. I don't hesitate; I shake my head. I don't regret our time. I couldn't if I tried. I just regret crossing a line we now can't take back.

"Good." His face softens, and he places a hand on each of my cheeks, ensuring my eyes can never leave his. "Then let me make myself perfectly clear." That bedroom voice from last night is back, and I have to physically restrain myself from gripping his shirt and settle instead for curling my toes.

"I. Want. You." I swallow, but can't seem to find words.

"I haven't thought about Jenny in a long while. Not until you just said her name. You are all I can think about, Casey. And after last night, you're all I taste. In my sheets, you are all I can smell. I see only your warm smile and soft freckles when I close my eyes, and when I dream, it's of oceans as blue as your eyes." Oh no.

I'm... oh god, this broody grump is going to make me fall in love with him.

"Was that clear enough for you?" I nod, but still can't bring myself to speak. I just... I can't... I don't know how to...

"Good. I don't know what this is, what any of it means, Casey. I just know that this is more than attraction. It simply is just... more."

"Okay," I whisper, biting back the greatest fear that has lodged itself firmly in my throat. That I'm falling too deep too quickly, and I don't want to have my heart torn from my chest when he bails. He analyzes me through fierce eyes before he breathes a sigh and plants a soft kiss to my lips.

"Slow," he says quietly.

"Slow," I repeat. The weight of all that is left unsaid sits heavy on my chest, but I smile gratefully, which he returns.

"Was I right?" His lips tip at the corner, and I tilt my head in confusion.

"About?"

"You didn't eat dinner, did you?" I roll my eyes and peel myself from his embrace as he chuckles.

"No, I didn't. But I made Mom's apple slices."

"Well, anything that is a Momma Baker recipe is bound to be delicious." I level him with narrowed eyes and pursed lips, which makes his smile beam as he laughs.

"Your recipes are just as exquisite, sunshine." His deep voice covers my skin in warmth, and I want him to wrap me up again and never let me go. But... space, time, slow. I really, desperately need to slow my heart down.

The apple slices are promptly pulled from the oven when the timer dings, Jessie grabs water from the fridge, and I plate up the slices with a scoop of ice cream and a sprinkle of cinnamon sugar before we are cuddled on the couch, once again. When I think about switching the TV on, he throws the remote and pulls my legs into his lap, his plate balanced on his knee as he uses one hand to massage my feet and the other to feed himself.

"How was the studio today?" he asks and the domesticity of this has me shaking my head to regain normal enough thoughts to answer him.

"Uh, good. Long day. I think I need another instructor. I'm wrecked."

"Did you ever end up doing those self-defense classes?" he queries, and it suddenly hits me why my brain is foggy, and confusion has me feeling fuzzy. Jessie is asking about my day. Like, bare minimum, but he is looking at me like my answers are important and if I told him I had a problem or was upset, he'd jump to my rescue.

Connor never did that. Ever. It's the sudden and depressing realization that, unless the girl's schedules line up with mine, which is rare these days, I have no one to talk to about my day. About the simple and mundane things.

But JJ looks at me with every ounce of his attention, like my answer matters, and like nothing else does.

"Honestly, I haven't had any time to really work out the details. I want to. But I might just wait until all of this stuff with Grace blows over." He nods but looks me over, assessing, always searching my face.

"And how is she doing?" Another shrug, and this time I can't bear to look him in the eyes. Biting into a bit of my slice, he does the same, settling further into the couch as he does. His attention is all mine, but he doesn't rush me.

"I don't know how to move forward. I don't know how to talk to her. I don't want to upset her, but I don't want to let her hurt me again. I just want to talk, but every time I try, it's like I say the wrong thing." I just want to know what I've done, how to fix it. How to undo it.

He squeezes my foot in, I think, comfort, and I look up to find him looking at me with gentle eyes. By the deep set of his frown and tension in his shoulders, I know he just wants to fix it for me, but he hasn't any idea how. This topic has me losing my appetite, as it has over the last few weeks. I discard my plate to the coffee table, then reach across and do the same with his. I push him so he lays flat on the couch and I climb over him, lying down and resting my head on his chest. He wraps his arms firmly around me as he places soft kisses to my hair and forehead.

The tension leaves my body, and I let him hold me. Let him warm me, protect me, and care for me. We stay huddled together like this for a few minutes, when I breathe deeply and feel myself sink into the comfort of his embrace when he whispers into my hair.

"You are sunlight through a window, which I stand in, warmed. My darling."

I burrow myself further into him, trying desperately to hide my blush but hearing the race of his heart. When I don't respond, but hum comfortably, he speaks, and I hear that gorgeous smile in his delectable voice, "Jessie Burton."

"I hadn't heard that one." I giggle softly.

"Damn. Should have claimed it as my own." He huffs a gentle laugh and his hands rub gentle circles on my back.

"You could make one up."

"I could." He nods, and I feel his lips press gently to my forehead in a few more soft kisses.

"Well, let's hear it." I tilt my head, shifting to rest my hands under my chin and look up into his eyes. His gentle gaze roams my entire face before landing on my lips for a moment.

"I'll work on it." He smiles shyly, and with a touch of vulnerability, he inches forward slightly, his lips hovering just above mine, and I close the final distance, reaching up and sealing his lips with mine. What I had planned to only be a gentle and soft kiss quickly gets away from me when he sweeps his tongue in and caresses mine. A small groan leaves his throat as he shifts my position, my legs straddling him and my hands wrapping around his neck.

"Your lips are my vice. I could kiss you for eternity," he whispers before he takes them again.

"That was pretty good for off the cuff," I pant and then kiss him back, growing desperate, and his hands travel my back and find their way into my yoga tights, gripping my ass, pushing me to his lap.

"That wasn't what I was working on. I can do better." I almost groan at the way he punctuates his words with an upthrust of his hips, and I feel just how much his desire matches mine.

"I'd say you're doing pretty good already." I pull away and bite my lip as I try to catch my breath. His eyes dance with mischief and he sits up so quickly I barely have a chance to hide my squeal before the positions are switched. My back to the couch, he hovers above me.

"Oh, but I love a challenge."

27

the missing piece

Jessie

Casey was up at 6am, pulling herself from my arms, letting me sleep as she snuck around to get ready for another day of taking every single fucking class at the studio. I didn't need to be at the shop to relieve April until 11am, so I made a coffee, locked up, and headed for Karvelas Media. I hadn't been to Noah's office yet, the modern space located on the 13th and 14th floor of a corporate building in Midtown East. Clean lines, exposed brick, with modern-industrial accents. The space looks exactly like what I'd pictured.

The receptionist points me in Noah's office's direction and I head that way, not really paying attention to the people, but rather lost in thoughts of a specific auburn ray of sun and how she smiled at me as she kissed me this morning, the sound of her laugh as I tried and failed to drag her back to the bed, lost in the confusion of how all of this feels. When I lost my mind for a few moments and asked if I was going to see her again tonight, she had informed me she had a date with Rosie Garcia that was non-negotiable unless she was to be fired as a best friend. I was grateful because we agreed to slow, and slow felt like the opposite of how I was traveling. I really need to put some space between her and my heart, but I am also bummed because… well, being with Casey is the only time I feel at peace.

"Jessie? What are you doing here?" Caleb queries, delight being the surprising undertone of the question. I was so busy twisting through my thoughts and staring at the floor, I didn't see him coming.

"Came to have a chat with Noah about the shop."

"Sick! What are you doing later?"

I shrug and continue to walk in Noah's direction, Caleb on my tail. "Come to Bozzelli's with me."

"You are always out. Have you ever just enjoyed a night in?" I question, but without my usual annoyance, and when I glance across at him, I can't work out whether his confusion is at my tone or my question.

"Well… no. But why would I hang out at my house alone when I could be warming someone's bed?" he retorts and winks at me. Rolling my eyes, I come to a stop at an office door and see Noah's large frame hunched over and looking seriously at his computer screen. Where I stop at the door, Caleb strolls in and plants himself in a chair across from Noah.

"Picked up a stray," he states and Noah's gaze lifts to mine, an instant smile hitting his face.

"JJ, what's up, man! To what do we owe the pleasure?" His usual arrogance is firmly in place as he leans back in his chair, an arm thrown over the back, and he gestures to the chair next to Caleb. Doing my best to put on a smile, I make my way over, sitting down in the deceptively comfortable chair.

"Actually, wanted to talk about the café. Maybe look at doing an online store as part of the website?" His eyes light up and he leans forward on the desk.

"Absolutely! When did you want to launch?"

"Sooner the better. How long would it take?"

He rubs at his jaw, the light never leaving his eyes as he looks to his computer a minute before coming back to me.

"Could have it up and running in a couple of weeks. Building the stock in might take a bit at first, but once the base of it is in, it'll be simple to compile."

"Can we have it staff run? Then I can have the girls add in any new stock we get?"

"Easy. You offering shipping?"

"If we can?"

"Done. What brought this on?" he questions, but the excitement never leaves him and I can't help but soak it up, making me buzz with a similar feeling. Excited to grow, excited to try something new and get somewhere with the shop.

I tell him about my chat with Ethan, and both he and Caleb decide to add their two cents in for ideas about new marketing campaigns.

"You could host author spotlights, pair it with a coffee that matches their book, even host it the week of their release and run a special. That's something that'd work even if you don't get the actual authors in," he provides, and for the first time, I see the business-minded Caleb. The focused, driven, and determined guy who runs the sales team for a serious company. Respect settles deep, and I nod at him appreciatively.

Hope.

That's what the buzz is. It's the same sensation I had when Casey smiled at me this morning, and the same feeling I got when Ethan offered to help me. The way Noah soaks up this idea and the way Caleb is bustling with energy has me feeling... hope.

Me: How's your dinner date?

Ace: Almost perfect.

Me: What's missing then?

Ace: You.

I sit in my reading chair, staring at the text. At the one word that threatens to bring down every wall I've tried to keep up around me where Casey is concerned.

I could fall really hard here. I really can't tell if this is the fun Casey just being her usual cheeky self. Or is this Casey falling for me, too?

What are we doing?

My hand raises to rub at the pain in my chest, confused and somehow also feeling lighter. But, I leave the message thread on read to stop myself from saying a whole bunch of shit that would get me into trouble. That will spin us out of control where the only person twisted and bound is me, as I watch the hope I am desperately trying to cling to gallop into the sunset as her Prince Charming sweeps her off her feet.

Pulling my attention back to my laptop, I slip my phone onto do not disturb and get lost in the world of words. The ones trapped in my mind, begging to find their place on a page. The story churning in my mind amongst the pain, madness, and despair.

The only parts of joy within the deepness of my mind these days seem to be the parts taken up by Casey. Casey Moira. The guiding star.

Fitting really, which is what I had barely told her the night I saw that M embossed on her bag. That she is the star in the sky, high above the sea. Meant to guide lost sailors home. In some other forms of the legend, it is a sign of hope that rain will come and free the land from drought. Without even really trying, she has guided me from my misery, helping me find my way back to myself, to start feeling whole again. Giving me hope that there is something out there that could be wholly mine and bring peace and joy. Even if it isn't Casey who ends up being that person, I am suddenly not completely closed off to the idea of letting someone in again.

Maybe.

Of course, I couldn't tell her any of this. So maybe I wouldn't tell her. Maybe I could put all the things I want to say into fiction. Give the characters that live in my mind the happy ever after I would likely never have for myself.

28

denial with sideline support

Casey

"So, what are we doing for your birthday this year?" Rosie questions from her position on the couch. As usual, a blanket over her waist and a wine glass in her hand. Her question pulls me from my text thread, thankfully, distracting me from my idiotic decisions.

You.

I essentially told Jessie that I miss him when I just saw him this morning. The more mortifying detail of that is that he then proceeded to leave me on read.

I am such an idiot. We haven't defined anything. We've slept together twice, and done a variety of other toe curling activities, and I am like a starstruck teen falling in love for the first time.

I am obsessed.

"Case?" Right, Rosie asked a question.

"Hmm?"

"Your birthday. What are we doing this year?" she asks again, twisting on the couch to face me fully.

"Addison's birthday is on Tuesday. Let's just focus on that one," I retort, trying not to think about my birthday.

"And she is going to be in Chicago with Noah until after Thanksgiving. I ask again: what are we doing for your birthday?" I shrug at her question. My birthday still isn't for another month, but with it being on Christmas Eve, I am used to it being overlooked, at least by my family. Now, with everything going on with Grace, I'm really not expecting anything extravagant. The girls and I usually have some kind of date—drinks, movie night, dinner, sometimes even a night out.

"Why don't we go out? We could invite the guys and Stella?"

"Do you see her much?" Rosie shrugs at my question.

"We speak when I'm at the bar, which is rare recently. She's quiet. I've been trying to get her out more because she looks... I can't really put my finger on it, but I think she might need some girls." I nod, finally getting my mind off of the lumberjack. Rosie's instincts never usually miss anything. If she's picked up on something, I'd say there was something to pick up on.

"Well, why don't we go out, just us girls? You, me, Addy, and Stella?" Because if she needs a girls' night, I'd help give her one.

"Casey, you wouldn't be making a plan to dedicate your birthday to save someone else... would you?" Rosie accuses, and I roll my eyes, downing the remaining wine in my glass.

"Give me a break. You're the one who said she needed people."

"Yeah, and you have a habit of forsaking everything for everyone else." I shrug, hating how wine makes me so emotional and tired. I need something harder. Like gin.

"I'm fine, Rosie. I look after myself just fine." I try to pull a playful smile. She narrows her eyes at me for a split second before she shifts her attention to her wine glass.

"So, how's the dull dick going?" I question, turning the conversation to something less morbid. She responds by laughing, her head thrown back to the couch, before her attention is back on me, that playful lightness of hers that makes me feel warm.

"Not so dull, thank fuck. But I bought myself a new companion." She hits me with her wiggly eyebrows, which makes me chuckle.

"Oh?"

"Her name is Vivienne, and she treats me really, really well." This has me giggling, and as I get up to grab another bottle of wine from the kitchen, she clarifies, "She's purple and soft, long enough to please, wide enough to satisfy, and has just the right amount of bumps in all the right places." As I make my way back to the couch, Rosie's head lies on the back of it, a gentle smile as she speaks wistfully. I lean over the back, looking down at her pretty golden face, refilling her wine glass, and her big chocolate eyes open, her trademark playfulness staring straight back at me.

"You named your new vibrator Vivienne?" I say through a chuckle.

"Well, I didn't want to give her the name of someone who I knew in real life. That would be weird. How many Vivienne's do you know?"

"Fair point." I sit back down and pull my knees to my chest as I settle back into the couch. "So Vivienne has replaced the dull dick?"

"Mmm. Sometimes. It's just hard to find anyone good, you know?" I nod and she continues. "Like, someone who just... you know?" She looks out to the window and struggles to find her words, but somehow, I just know exactly what she is talking about

"Someone who can choke you but tell you you're pretty," I whisper—I thought—to myself. Rosie's mouth drops open, and she shoots up to a sitting position as her eyes bug out. I try to shrink under the blanket while chuckling at the embarrassing confession, but Rosie is ripping the blanket away from my face.

"Casey. Moira. Baker." The demand I know that it is. She wants details.

I peek my eyes open to find her agape mouth pulling into a wide opened smile, and she starts slapping my thigh.

"Tell me. Tell me. Tell me!" she shouts excitedly.

"Jessie—" She gasps, covering her mouth before she squeals and giggles, then starts slapping my thigh again.

"We... kinda—"

"Fucked roughly with gentle aftercare?!" she guesses, and a loud laugh bursts from me. When I recover, I nod.

"Literally, exactly that." I close my eyes and mimic her previous position, my head fallen back to the couch and remembering the feel of Jessie's rough hands around my throat. The same rough hands that gently massaged my body in the shower after. That magic mouth that said he wanted me.

But can't tell you what any of it means.

The same Jessie that just left me on read after I said I missed him.

That thought has me sitting up and frowning. Rosie sobers enough from her excited rambling I hadn't paid attention to, to notice my expression and she scooches closer.

"What's the look?" She tilts her head questioning, and I sip my wine, shrugging in response.

"I don't really know what I'm doing," I mumble.

"What's there to know?"

"I'm going to fall for him, Rosie. I think I already am."

"But you love love. What's the problem?"

"I think he is going to pull back. I just feel like he is going to slip through my fingers and I don't know how to make him stay." Rosie assesses my whole face, like she can read every thought, and I nervously sip my wine, trying to shrink from her gaze.

"Addison said, even if he did fall for me, he likely wouldn't let himself and would let go or push me away. I just... everything is amazing when we're together, but then as soon as we have some space, it's like he has regrets, or he doesn't want to go down the path I think we're already on, and I don't know how to tell myself to stop. To make him fall first so I know he'll catch me." Rosie's face shifts to something like sympathy and she rubs my shoulder.

"Okay. What do you want from him?"

"Well... I don't know."

"Then what do you like about spending time with him? You guys are literally joined at the hip lately, so what is it?"

Everything.

"I feel at peace. I... feel taken care of. Like I don't have to anticipate his feelings or what he needs from me. I don't have to worry about what topics to talk about or whether he is bored of my company. I like that we can be in the same room and not speak for hours. I really like when he quotes classic literature, like it's his way of telling me what he wants to say without knowing what words to use. I like that he makes me feel not so lonely, even when I am."

When my eyes make contact with Rosie again, a gentle smile sits on her face and she tilts her head.

"Awh," she says, then her face slowly morphs into disgust. "That was gross. But I think you might be in love, Case." She rubs my arm and pats me gently before getting up from the couch. "I knew I'd lose you both to that disease," she jokes as she heads for the kitchen with her wine glass. But I'm still frozen in my spot on the couch. When she starts making noise in the kitchen, I have to shake myself from my frozen thoughts—because I am most certainly not in love with Jessie Jenkins—and I follow Rosie.

"Excuse me, I am not."

"Mmhmm, kay," she muses as her head searches the fridge. I stand behind her, trying to get her attention.

"Hello! I am not."

"Casey, it's okay." She chuckles. "I know you weren't ready for that... But you are." Her lips pull into a pitying smile, and she turns back to the fridge searching.

"I am... What on earth are you looking for?"

"Well, you just realized you are feeling an emotion you have no control over, and it only benefits you and not someone else, so you're about to spiral. I figured you'd need to bake," she declares then pulls out the block of baking chocolate from the fridge, and I have to blink a number of times so my brain catches up.

"But... but you can't bake."

"No, but you can, and I'm an excellent learner."

"You're terrible at following instructions, Rosie." She rolls her eyes as she hands me the chocolate and walks around to the kitchen island, pulling out a bar stool and plopping her ass onto it.

"You're right, I'm better at side-line support and the cleanup. So you bake, get your control back, then we can get drunk and I can tell you about how Vibey-Viv has changed my life."

A laugh bursts out of me and I flick my best friend a grateful smile as I pull out everything I need for a cookies and cream slice. Rosie sends me over a wink and connects her phone to the speakers.

The music fills the kitchen, Rosie tells me about her self-care adventures, and the apartment fills with the smell of a baking biscuit base and light laughter.

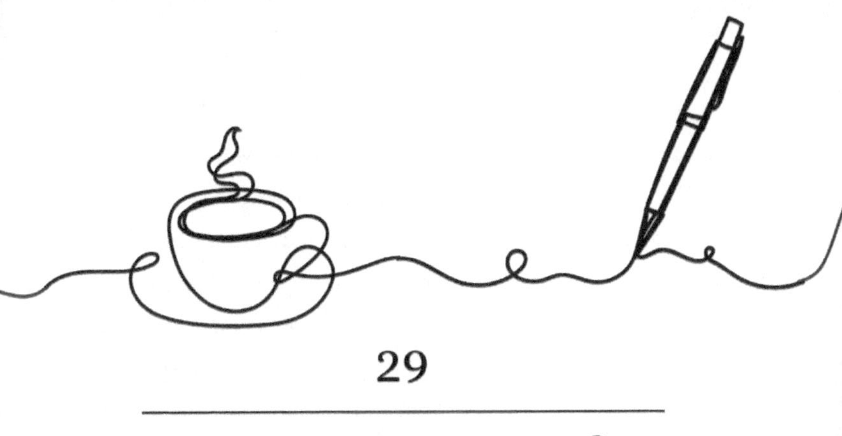

29

---

ace, sunshine, baby?

Jessie

The chorus of Burning by Maggie Rogers fills the girls' apartment as I twist the key and let myself in. Addison will still be in Chicago with Noah for another week, coming back just in time for Thanksgiving, and I am beginning to abuse the apartment key privileges. I'm not ready to admit that the last three weeks of letting myself into Casey's apartment, kissing her hello, and making myself comfortable on her couch has been the best part of my days. Because admitting that would mean labeling us, and doing that feels like tainting something pure. How we are is perfect. It is easy comfort, and I am not ready to complicate anything.

I also wasn't ready to analyze how these last three weeks haven't felt like my life at all. The regular catch ups with the guys at Pucks, seeing Casey almost daily and walking around the cafe with a goddamned smile on my face. None of it felt real. I was waiting for the other shoe to drop. Either they were all going to work out I wasn't worth it, or I was going to fuck it up somehow.

The further I head into the apartment, the louder Casey's gentle singing becomes as I hear her sing select lyrics, *'I'm in love, I'm alive, oh I'm burning.'* I pause at the entrance to the kitchen, leaning on the wall and admiring her from where she stands at the stove. With her back to me, hips swaying to the beat of the song, a light hum of the lyrics and gentle giggles when she realizes she doesn't know the words. In only her tight as fuck yoga leggings–these light purple ones are my favorite–with a white crop top, her auburn hair in a topknot on her head, the lazy strands falling to the back of her delicate neck in invitation. She is delectable. Lord, bring me patience.

The music is loud enough that she wouldn't have heard the door open, which is possibly a measure of safety I'm really going to have to talk to her about. And the incredible smell of whatever she is cooking fills the room. I just take in the sweet sound of her voice, the chuckle that follows, and the way the lyrics wash over me, because I think...

No. I can't.

I shake my head just as she turns toward the counter, but noticing me in the corner of her eye, she snaps her head in my direction, a little squeal and almost slipping, she catches herself on the counter.

"Jesus Christ, Jessie!" I laugh gently, reaching for the speaker volume and turning it down as I make my way to her.

"Maybe you shouldn't play your music so loud," I say smoothly as I stalk in her direction. A cheeky smile pulls at her lips as she watches me with interest.

"Maybe you should announce yourself when you enter my apartment," she teases back, and as I get into her space, she tilts her head back, and my heart bottoms out at the size of the smile she gives me.

"Maybe," I whisper, my lips hovering above hers, and instead of closing the final distance, she just stays there, biting her lip before whispering.

"Hi."

"Hi," I reply.

"Well, are you going to kiss me?" she says, her eyes snatching to my lips. The taunt in her tone makes me chuckle, but I oblige her, sealing my lips gently with hers in a kiss. The kind of kiss that feels like finally.

Finally, I'm home from work.

Finally, Casey is in front of me.

Finally, I can touch her and see her ocean eyes.

I just really want it to also be, finally, Casey is mine.

She hums happily when I pull away, and I'm hit with that gorgeous smile again. I can't even help myself; I grip her hips and lift her to the counter. When she gasps in surprise and holds my shoulders for balance, I steal her lips again, this time a demand. Showing her how badly I need her, even if I can't tell her with my own words.

She tastes of honey and mustard and—

"What are you making?" I practically pant as I pull away from her delicious lips and look to the stove.

She releases a breathless chuckle as she responds, "Honey mustard chicken. Was tossing up between rice or pasta, I hadn't decided." I look back at her, and pure happiness radiates from her.

"Rice," I respond. And she nods, her beaming smile growing even more.

"Okay," she says as her eyes move to mine.

"How long has it got to go?" I question, nodding in the direction of the dinner cooking on the stove, my heart racing in my chest and my desire for Casey growing rapidly in this moment.

"Umm, maybe five minutes, plus however long the rice takes." Her response is breathless as she senses my desire, matching it with hers.

Dammit. I want way more than five minutes. I smile mischievously and kiss her gently, lifting her down from the counter. She huffs and frowns in disappointment.

"Later, sunshine. I want to take my time," I promise before kissing her again and stalking for the fridge.

"Fine," she breathes, then turns back to the stove. "What was your day like?"

"Busy. Had to get stock lists and pictures for Noah. He's building the online store, so I've been tied up doing that." I pull out the vegetables from the fridge and turn to the counter next to the stove.

"You hear from that developer again?" she asks as she hands me a chopping board and knife. Taking it, I respond.

"Nope. I'm hoping I won't." I eye her side on and see her gentle smile as she stirs the sauce, preparing a pot of water for the rice. "How was your day?" I ask as we settle into this easy domestic pattern of the last few weeks. Either in her kitchen or mine.

"Busy." Her shoulders tighten, and the smile I love disappears.

"And?" I push, because she should know better than to shut down on me.

"And nothing, it was just... a big day." Won't be having any of that. I drop the knife, the vegetable prep forgotten, and I crowd behind her, leaning my hands on the edge of the stove, pressing my front to her back and nuzzling her neck.

Trailing delicate kisses up her neck, I feel her relax back into me, and I say softly in her ear, "Talk to me, sunshine."

She releases a big breath. I can feel the way her face is scrunched in pain, even if I can't see her from where I continue to place kisses along the soft line of her neck, encouraging her to talk to me.

"Grace won't answer my calls. I've moved the girls' roster around a bit to give me a bit more time off. I've posted an ad for another trainer, but I really need Grace. I know she is going through a lot, but... this just isn't fair; she was the one that pushed for the new studio. It just feels like she has bailed on me, and I don't know how much longer I can be patient for."

"Have you tried to go over and see her again?" I press gently, pausing my kisses, but remaining behind her, not willing to leave this closeness, the way her floral scent wraps around my lungs and squeezes my chest.

"I went over on Friday, but Evan said she was sleeping, so I went home. I tried to message her, she didn't respond. Tried calling her, she won't answer. I'm avoiding Mom now because I know she wants to talk about Grace, but it feels like a betrayal to talk about Grace when she won't even talk to me." Her head falls back against my shoulder, and this time, I see the pain etched into her scrunched brows, and the way her bottom lip drops, her chin quivering, and pain spears me in the chest.

"Hey, hey, hey, don't cry, Ace. She really doesn't deserve your kind heart, you know that, right?" I say gently, gripping her chin and turning her to face me. Her eyes remain scrunched shut, and the further dip of her bottom lip has me turning her fully and burying her in my embrace. Squeezing her like I can squeeze the pain from her. Take all of it, rid her of it.

"She's my sister," she whispers between a gentle sob and breath.

"I know, baby. I know," I say gently back, and at the realization of the pet name that slipped my lips, she goes rigid, pulling out of the embrace and blinking at me rapidly.

"Um."

"I'm sorry, I didn't..."

"It's fine, really." She gives me an awkward smile. Wiping at her tears, she waves me off, returning to the sauce, adding the rice to the water. I reluctantly return to the chopping board beside her, not really sure what just happened.

"How..." she clears her throat then tries again, "How come you give me so many names?"

"What?"

"Ace, sunshine, baby?" I shrug at the question, not willing to meet her gaze, but feel it on me.

"Ace came to me when we were kids. I don't really know why, you just seemed... so good at everything, you know? Like everything you tried, you aced it. Being a friend to my sister, baking, being happy." My gaze floats to hers, and she only tilts her head to the side in contemplation, so I focus back on the vegetable prep. "Sunshine, well, that one is obvious." I shrug again.

"Obvious?" she queries, and I feel her disappear behind me to grab something from the fridge.

"Yeah, you are sunshine. You glow." When I meet her gaze again, a bright pink blush warms her cheeks, and she blinks self-consciously back at the rice pot, the cream she had grabbed placed gently on the counter. The look makes me chuckle, and then she turns an upturned smirk on me, leaning a hip on the counter, giving me her full attention.

"And then you just called me baby. You haven't called me that one before." Her tone is laced with playful challenge, like she knows exactly why that had slipped my lips but wants to hear me say it.

To tell her I've claimed her as mine and that I'm all in.

Telling her all the feelings that have gripped my chest for the last few weeks, probably longer, that I've been too much of a coward to admit to. But when I look into those deep blues, their depths of hope and joy, memories of watching Jenny walk out on me when I had been ready to give her my all burns a path across my heart. The echo of the pain I held the last time I put my heart on the line causes my words to stick in my throat, and I can't manage to get them out. Instead, I force them back down, swallowing them whole and shrugging.

I say nothing.

And I feel regret cover me, like a blanket of shame.

I feel her retreat. Not physically, but I can feel the way she pulls back. Instead, we continue to prepare dinner in silence.

As she begins to plate it up, I break the silence, like the complete coward that I am. "Where is Rosie tonight?"

"Working late," she responds with clipped words, but because she is Casey and doesn't want to hurt my feelings, she still gives me a gentle smile before digging into her food.

Fuck. I run a frustrated hand down my face, scratching at my beard and trying to force myself to eat. Even though I have lost my appetite entirely. I am such an idiot.

"Casey—"

"It's okay. Anyway, I'm glad you came over tonight." She rests a hand on my arm, but focuses on eating her dinner.

"You are?" She simply nods and hums an agreement as she chews her food.

"It was a hard day. You make it not so bad." She smiles again, but it isn't a real one. It isn't the sunshine I love, it's... appeasing. I grumble and pull my hand from her grip. Feeling her burn through my ice is usually a welcoming feeling, but she's burnt through me almost completely, and every attempt to keep her at any kind of emotional distance only ends with me feeling like a dick. The worst part is that she doesn't even push me back, like I'd expect any sane person to do. Instead, she lets me push, she takes it, and is just... still fucking there.

Smiling at me. Even if it is fake as fuck. And now I'm frustrated, because even with me, she is continuously being what she believes other people need.

She thinks I'm stuck on unrequited love with a woman on the other side of the world. She thinks I'm in pain and that I'm suffering. That she owes me gentle smiles and soft touches. A few kisses and heated moments to help me work through my pain?

Fuck if that doesn't make me want to throw her on that counter and demand her to understand that the only woman that has me fucked up is her. That the only unrequited love is the one for her heart. Her smile. That beaming sunshine when she directs it at me.

I'm a fucking coward. And I'm a mess.

She deserves so much better than me. Than this bullshit.

"How's my little man?" I coo to Ollie as I bounce him in my arms. Matt and Ava's dining room is filled with the smell of the Sunday roast we just finished, my eight-month-old nephew smiling and sucking on his balled up fist.

"Ready for his bath and bed, I think," Ava says, clapping her hands and making baby noises at Ollie as she pulls him from my hands.

"You next, Jessie?"

"For a bath?" Addison and Riley basically choke on their water at my response to Mom's question, but when she scowls at me, I bite back my smile and answer her actual question.

"Not even close. You have a better chance of getting one from Addison," I throw back.

"Hey!" Addison scolds, but her smile beams. What was once a rarity is now common, and the tall, usually happy, currently ashen man sitting next to her is to thank for that. A satisfied smirk pulls at my lips at the way Noah's eyes are bulging and a sheen of sweat builds on his forehead. Addison taps his thigh beneath the table, giggling when she gets a look at his face. "Oh, Romeo, don't worry. I'm not having any of your gigantic babies anytime soon." He nervously chuckles before gulping down his water.

"I think we're just fine with the two silly kids we have," Matt provides as he ruffles Mia's hair, who is perched on his knee. She smacks away his hand and laughs.

"Uncle Noah, don't you want to have kids like me?" She leans on the table, her hands resting on her chin as she stares deeply into his soul. Noah's eyes go to Matt's in pleading, but he just shrugs and lets the big idiot flounder.

Of course, Addison rescues him. "There are no other kids like you, kid." Addy winks at Mia, who giggles and, unfortunately, turns her attention to me. "Are you going to have cousins for me, Uncle Jessie?"

"One day, kiddo. Can't exactly do that on my own." I mimic Matt's gesture of ruffling her hair and she swats me away, that childish giggle filling my cold heart.

"Actually, you can. It's 2024. Anything is possible." Riley smiles at me and I roll my eyes.

"Wouldn't want a child to suffer with just Jessie. They'd need at least one parent who is... nice," Addison says and folds her lips into her mouth, trying to smother her laugh. Matt and Noah hide theirs in their drinks as Mom scolds Addison.

"Don't be so cruel, Addy." Addison just rolls her eyes. I see the very subtle gesture of Noah reaching an arm to Addy's leg under the table.

Mom and Addy have certainly come a long way, but there is some awkwardness between them still. This is our first full family dinner in a few months, one where Mom has attended. Ava came up with the brilliant idea for dinner to celebrate the first day of December. The girls helped Mia decorate the Christmas tree and, now that Addy and Noah are back from Chicago, we had a little moment of giving thanks around a roast turkey as well.

"Golden child," Riley mumbles, taking another swig of her drink.

"You get settled at Lucas's, chaos?" I ask Riley, ignoring her rib.

Riley nods and settles into her chair. "Yeah. Still have some boxes to unpack, but it's good. Huge room. The place is like one big loft. I think it was once an old warehouse. Has this incredible view over the city. You'll have to come see it. I just don't know about living with two dudes." I nod, happy that she seems to be happy with the new digs, but also apprehensive about her living with two guys she barely knows.

"Don't you have girl friends in the city?"

"I do. But living with them was never going to be a good idea. Plus, guys are a lot less drama," she mumbles, and the entire table's attention shifts to her. She looks up and sees everyone staring at her and rears back slightly, her arms wrapping around herself.

Riley has a history of some very shitty friends, but I thought that was just high school. I hadn't realized this had carried over into her adult life.

"What happened with your friends?" I press.

"Nothing. We just aren't those kinds of friends. I don't want to be stuck in a lease if something bad happens. It's no big deal."

I analyze her for a beat and try to be... nicer. I am trying to stop being a dick to my sisters and keeping them at arms' length. I am being... friendly.

"Can we not?" Riley grimaces and rolls her eyes before settling us all with a bored look. "With the loving looks and need to shower me with compliments. I know it's coming and I'll pass. I'm fine. I was only reluctant to live with two guys because it means I can't walk around naked. At least they'll be fun, and I won't have to pretend to enjoy all that girl bullshit and gossiping that comes with living with women." She finishes her drink and heads for the bathroom.

"Okay, Mia, Ollie's down. Your turn." Ava claps her way back into the dining room, breaking the tense silence.

"I got her." Matt lifts Mia into his arms, who is obviously tired enough because she doesn't protest and instead nuzzles into his shoulder. Matt kisses Ava delicately on the cheek as he passes her and Ava joins the table.

"How's Casey?" she asks innocently, as though the way I have a little section of my heart carved out for her is obvious to everyone in this room. I blink at her question but stumble on my words. I open my mouth to say something when the chuckle Noah attempts to hide in his drink turns into him violently choking on it. Karma, fucker.

"Good, I guess." I shrug, but can't seem to make eye contact, focusing on my drink. "Ask Addison." I'm still in obvious denial after over a month of sitting in 'almost' with Casey. I still haven't told her what I'm feeling, but neither has she. We'd get hot and heavy and nearly everything pours from my mouth. In an effort to shut it down, I push her away and she lets me. Just accepting where we are and being persistent in exactly who she is. A solid rock. A reminder that she isn't leaving.

That she isn't Jenny.

She is so much more than that.

"I see," Mom teases from across the table.

"Yes, we're still in denial," Addison informs them.

"Indeed, we are." Riley's smile reminds me of the Cheshire cat as she returns from the bathroom.

"What the fuck are you all talking about?" I grumble and try to fist my hands to stop from fidgeting.

"Oh, please, Jessie. You've been in love with that girl since you were twenty-two." Mom waves her hand and rolls her eyes, sipping her glass of wine.

"Ew." Addison shudders, covering her face.

"I have not. I dated Jenny for years," I retort, but somehow the thought of Jenny feels empty, like a distant memory that makes me feel nothing. No pain at not being enough, no despair for the years of loneliness, of a shattered future.

Well, that's new.

"You existed with Jenny. But with Casey, well, you seem different," Ava provides.

"How so?" I grumble back, the frustration evident in my voice as I try to grasp how the fuck we got into this conversation.

"Well, for one, you're much more pleasant to be around," Riley provides.

"Agreed," Matt chimes in as he enters the dining room.

"You seem happier," Addison provides.

"More... alive," Ava says, her expression contemplative, and the room breaks out into a joint 'mmm' in agreement.

"I don't need to listen to this." I push off from the table and stalk for the bathroom. Some chuckles and tsking reach me from the dining room as I lock myself away.

My mood has nothing to do with Casey. Sure, getting through the day is easier when I know that when I get home, she'll be there snuggled on my couch, or she's either dancing in the living room, baking in the kitchen, concentrating on a re-bind project on the couch, or sometimes napping in her bed. And each time, it's a gentle smile, a quiet, 'hi,' and a kiss that whispers, *finally*, every time.

Okay, fine, so maybe my mood has everything to do with Casey.

When I look up, I have to blink to bring my brain back to the present. Startled by my reflection because a smile is plastered to my face, my heart is calm, and it feels like it's easier to breathe. Because I was thinking about the way her lips feel soft on mine, and how my head empties of every stress or worry when we lie together on the couch reading. When I question her about her plans for the studio, when she tells me about a horrible new coffee flavor she tried.

A chuckle works its way up my throat over a particularly fun evening with her only a couple days ago. We were at my apartment, ordered pizza, because she was too exhausted to be cooking, and she goaded me into trying some new acro-yoga poses. It had involved a few partner poses, and she had laughed her head off at my lack of flexibility and coordination, but when I finally got her upside down, her delicate hands squeezed in mine, I deliberately lowered my legs that held her hips, so I could steal that smile in a kiss.

Without meaning to, and without even noticing, all my good days had become hers. Every bad day had ended up with Casey wrapped up with me, under me, or on top of me, and I couldn't see a part of my future where it wouldn't always be her that I wanted there.

The slow realization has me blinking again and shaking my head, rubbing a hand on the pain in my chest, but more so, a pain of regret. Regretting making Casey exist in the unknown, not understanding what we are. She stuck by me even when I was a coward, and she deserves to know exactly what I was feeling. She deserves to have someone fight for her.

I throw the bathroom door open and roll my eyes so hard they nearly fall out of my head. The pack of hormones stands before me, Addison and Riley, in matching stances, with their arms crossed, while Ava stares knowingly up at me. Riley is closer to my height at five-seven, so she towers over the other girls, and I catch the waggling of her eyebrows as she hits me with a knowing look.

"I need to leave," I mumble and try to push past them.

"To go and confess love?"

"To run away from your feelings?"

"To hide in your hovel and pretend no one exists?"

"Jesus Christ." I run a hand down my face as they each throw me their thoughts. But after how long I've made Casey wait, I'll be damned if I am telling them how I feel before telling her.

"Beat it." I nod my head in the direction of the dining room, trying to rid myself of these buzzards. Riley and Ava scoff but file off back down the hallway. As I turn to head for the front door and slip out, Addison grabs my elbow.

"What?" I scold her, and she pulls back, but her fury holds her strong. She is barely at my shoulder height, but when she levels me with that look, it feels a lot like she stares down her nose at me.

"Are you going to hurt my friend?"

"Why the fuck would I do that, Addison?"

"I am just making sure that in your attempt to bury your feelings, to rip out your own heart and refuse yourself the opportunity to feel something, that you're not going to destroy my friend right along with you."

"I'm in love with her!" I roar at her, my heart racing, and when her satisfied smile spreads across her face, my mouth opens and closes again. To take it back, to lie and say I'm not, but I am.

She holds her smirk and nods. "I know." She closes her eyes and drops her head. Her hands on her hips like she is finding patience to deal with me.

"I know you are, Jessie, and I'm really hoping that you're about to leave here and tell her exactly that." She points at me. "Because if you're going over there to pull away because all of our talk has scared you off, you better fucking stay gone. You'll rip her heart out and she deserves better than that." Burning green anger levels me, and I feel my heart bottom out. Pride burns deep inside, both at Addy's strength and her unwavering support and love for her friend.

I had convinced myself that Casey wouldn't have me if I went over there and tried to convince her to give us a chance. I am broken, but

I am healing, and I want her to be the one that sat by me as I help her grow strong, too. I want to take care of her, give her what she needs when no one else does. When everyone else takes, I want to give, and I want to give until there is nothing left.

I just nod slowly at Addison, heeding the warning, but knowing, deeply, that if I have any control over this thing between Casey and me, it wouldn't be to pull away or shatter her. It would be to steal her for just myself. To make her mine and never look back.

Addison nods back, and a wide smile spreads across her face as she whispers, "Go get her, then."

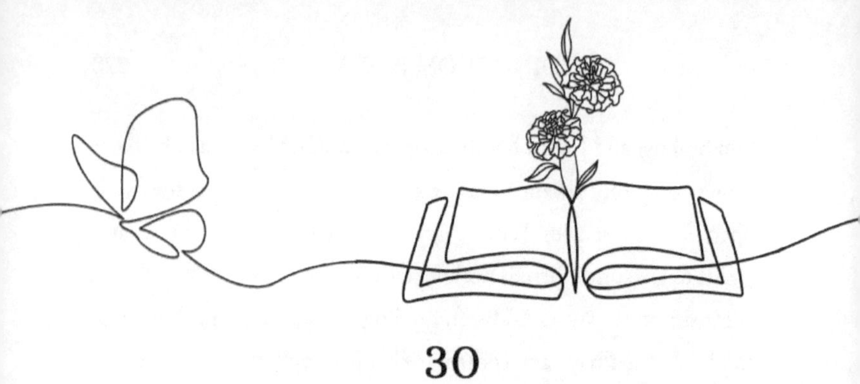

30

little bubble of peace

Casey

I think the fumes of the glue are going to my head. I blink and shake my head, not realizing I've been hobbled over this re-bind for a few hours now, the ache in my knees evidence enough.

"You're still at it? It's 10pm, Casey," Rosie chuckles as she drags her body from the entryway and falls to the couch.

"You're home late." I turn to her and give her the eyebrows.

"Ugh, it's not what you think. Unless you're thinking that I was held captive in my cubicle as Dickbag-Daniel mansplained why his general fiction pitch was more deserving of the editors' pick than my 'pathetic porno piece'. Then, yes. It is exactly what you think." She heaves a huge sigh. "I need alcohol." She groans and I chuckle, returning my attention to the book press, tightening the clamps to hold the glue in place, and then repositioning myself on the couch while I let it dry.

"That bad, huh?" I question her, and she tilts her head in my direction.

"I'm so sick of working at this huge company. It's such a penis fest. My ideas are always shoved at the bottom of the pile and simply because a lot of my suggestions happen to be romance books with smut. It's not like they are terribly written. These are heartbreaking tales with incredible love stories, and then we are gifted with what usually happens behind closed doors." She throws her hands up as her voice raises, her passionate explanation getting progressively louder. "And you know what? Some don't have any smut! Some are poetic pieces of literature in the modern form, written by extremely talented nobodies." Her voice grows louder, my enjoyment at her animated venting growing with it.

"Might I add, I'm almost certain these idiots watch porn more often than I read it, but they are suddenly children of the church when I pitch a female written romance that describes how a man really should be loving on a woman." She scoffs and sits up, her anger too much for lying down, apparently. A chuckle works its way up my throat as she aggressively grabs a pillow to her lap. "I wish I could just publish these books on my own."

"Why don't you, then?" She scoffs at my suggestion but, seriously?

"Rosie? Why the hell not? Actually, that is an excellent idea. Why don't you go out on your own?"

"Please." She waves me off, then heads for the kitchen

"Okay, no I'm actually serious, why don't you? You'd be amazing at it!"

"Casey, I can't just start my own publishing company! That's... that's just..." She trails off, looking at me, but not really looking at me, like she is actually finally considering the idea.

"Genius?" I try to finish her conversation for her and she stutters. Opening her mouth, closing it, then opening it again, and for the first time in history, Rosie is speechless.

"I hadn't really considered that," she mumbles. "Anyway, what book are you working on?" She maneuvers the conversation in a new direction, but I let her, all too excited about this project.

"I'm doing the *Odyssey* by Homer. It's a gift." I smile to myself and return my attention to the book currently drying, clamped to the coffee table.

"Ooo la la," she teases from where she pours two glasses of wine.

Rolling my eyes, I shake my head, but don't dignify the taunt with an answer. She is quiet for a beat, a loaded silence, and I can almost feel the words she is about to level me with.

"Have you talked to him about how you're feeling?" she asks, and I'm grateful for how gently she does it.

I shake my head and look at my thumb, fidgeting with the ring that sits there. "He isn't ready, Rosie." She sips her wine and settles deeper into the couch, so I do the same. "We have so many amazing quiet moments, and I think I'll get the courage to tell him. But then, it's like he picks up on the energy and he shuts it down before I can even say anything. Sometimes I try to lead him there, try to gauge what he is feeling, and again, like he knows exactly what I'm doing, he either pushes me away or shuts it down."

"Why put yourself through it, Case?" She almost frowns, but rubs a soft hand on my leg.

"Because he has this incredible heart. And without even meaning to, he just wormed his way in completely. I can't bear to be the one to leave, because it's the whole reason he is this way. He is terrified. I can see it. Jenny abandoned him when he was planning for their future. I mean, his heart is scared." My chest aches as I give Rosie what's been stuck in my head for weeks. Jessie and I dancing around our hearts. Giving into our lust, the fiery passion that buzzes around us every time we're alone together. We've barely spent a night apart in over a month, and it all just feels so normal. So easy and perfect. Like how we are is exactly the way it's meant to be. So much so that there have been countless times the words I feel nearly fall from my tongue, but I have to stop. Because I know he isn't ready for them, and I don't want to risk losing my little bubble of peace because my heart couldn't keep to itself.

Rosie blows out a huge breath, sipping her wine, and opens her mouth to say something when a knock at the door startles us both.

"You expecting someone?" I ask her. She never brings her dates here, but it was at least worth asking. She shakes her head. "Me, neither." We look concerned and then Rosie nods at the book. Oh shit. It's probably Jessie! "Crap, cover it with a blanket. I'll just take him straight to my room." I quickly leap from the couch.

"Yeah, you will," Rosie teases, poking her tongue to her cheek and making a vulgar gesture with her fist. I scoff a laugh at her and quickly check the book is covered before I swing the door open.

My smile dies as quickly as it appeared when I see who stands at my door.

"Connor?"

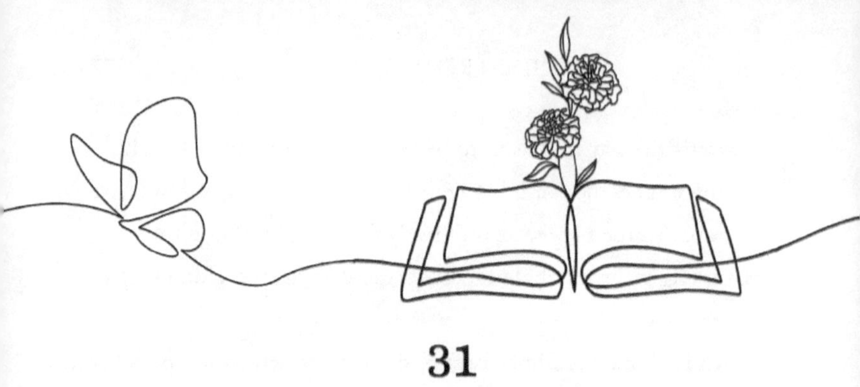

31

the goodbye we needed

Casey

"Connor, what are you doing here?" I ask, stepping out into the hall and closing the door behind me. It was an attempt to stop Rosie from eavesdropping, but I know she skidded up behind this door immediately and has her ear pressed firmly against it so she misses nothing.

"I came to see you," he says gently. He is so different from the last time I saw him. Polished and looking every bit the grown up I had begged him to be for the better part of our relationship. Wearing a tailored suit, his hair coiffed and combed, the dark shiny strands look like they were each individually placed on his head. Connor was always private-school-boy-handsome. He is tall, has a muscular build, slender, but nicely toned and high cheekbones that meant he had small dimples when he smiled.

But the Connor I broke up with was not the Connor I originally fell in love with. Over time, it felt like I was begging him to care. To notice me, to breathe life into me. I wanted passion, desire, an all-consuming love. I wanted him to want me so badly he couldn't be in the same room as me without needing to tear our clothes off. I wanted him to get so worked up and passionate that we fought, that we challenged each other. I wanted to never run out of things to say and simultaneously enjoy the quiet moments where we held each other. Connor was never that person, and it was wrong of me to want him to be that. I knew then, that morning we broke up, that we had outgrown each other, simply because we were growing in different directions. I think our end was always inevitable, and seeing him standing here in front of me, nothing but the nostalgic twinge of seeing an old friend hits me, confirming all that I knew.

"Okay." I nod at him, not really understanding. "Is everything okay?"

"Perfect, in fact." He steps forward, his gentle smile tipping to the side as he appraises me. I hadn't been expecting company, so I am wearing my apartment clothes–comfy blue cotton overalls with a white sweater underneath–my hair in a topknot and absolutely not a lick of makeup on. "You look cute," he muses, pushing a hair behind my ear. "I missed you," he whispers.

"Connor... Why did you come here?" I say back, and my tone gives away my lack of interest. I know why he is here, and the only pain I feel is at how I know I'm about to hurt him, again.

"I want you back, Casey. I am so sorry for how I acted. How I ignored your requests for my attention and how badly you needed me." He rushes it out while stepping forward, and I raise a hand, gently pushing him back.

"First of all, Connor, I didn't badly need you. I just asked you to care about our relationship."

"I know. That's what I meant... I-I want to try again. I know I can be what you need. I've changed. I'm working at Dad's shop, doing mostly the office stuff. He is going to teach me how to run it one day." He puffs his chest in pride, and I smile up at him.

"That really is great. I'm proud of you." He nods and beams an even bigger smile at me. "But, I'm not coming back." I let him down as gently as I can, reaching a hand forward to rub his arm.

"B-but we're it, you and me, we're college sweethearts. We could tell our kids all about how hard we fought for each other." He has so much hope in his face, and try as I might, I can't even help the chuckle that comes up my throat. He looks like a damn puppy, and I hate having to let him down like this.

"Connor, I care about you. I do, really. I hope that you find someone who makes you happy, someone who is worth all that fight you've found. But it isn't me." He swallows, and my heart sinks when his face does.

"It's not you," he repeats in a low voice, and I shake my head. "You... Is there someone else?" I bite my lip and contemplate how honest I'm going to be.

My long-term college sweetheart is dressed in a suit, looking like a puppy being praised, and I settle with the fact that he deserves the truth. He deserves my complete honesty if he is ever going to put us behind him.

"There is. I...I care about you, Connor. I probably always will. But, I don't love you, and I haven't for a long while. There is someone else, and I really do love him." He drops his head and takes a few steps back. Rolling his shoulders, he looks up at me with so much longing in his eyes, and I step forward to grip both his arms. "I'm sorry I couldn't be what you were hoping to have, but I know your forever is out there somewhere. It's okay that it isn't us. You deserve someone who loves you deeply, Connor. Don't settle for what's comfortable." A little tip to the corner of his lips showing off those cute dimples, and I see it, the realization that he probably wasn't even in love with me, not right now. It was just comfy, the thought of us. I know the feeling of not wanting to be alone and missing something familiar, but that's all this was. He doesn't love me like how he thought, and he is just starting to understand that.

"I hope you're happy, Case." He nods and smiles. He steps forward cautiously, and I roll my eyes, giving him one of my big smiles to let him know there are no hard feelings. "Come here, you goon." I chuckle at him and let him hold me in a hug. Nothing but platonic love for him fills my chest. I think we'd be friends in another life. He wraps his tall frame around me and squeezes. It's the goodbye we both need, the closure.

Pulling back, he tucks a hair behind my ear again and says quietly, "Well, this is embarrassing." It makes us both chuckle and I step out of his reach, but before I can respond, movement hits the corner of my eye and my head snaps in that direction.

"Jess?" For a moment my chest inflates with happiness as it always does the second I lay eyes on him, but... but he takes a few steps back and I realize what I see in his face.

Pain.

So much pain and anger, I think also shock.

"Sorry. I... I didn't mean to..." He doesn't even finish his sentence before he spins and bails around the corner.

Seriously!? He just bailed.

"Wait, Jessie!"

I look back up to Connor, who has the right mind to look guilty. He scratches the back of his head and says sheepishly, "I assume that was him?" My joy is immediately gone, and I level Connor with an unimpressed look.

Jessie looked like he was ready to murder Connor, and the only reason he would be doing that while turning up unannounced was because he was going to hit me with some truth. Truth I think I've been waiting for. But the big dumb idiot jumped to conclusions and didn't even give me a single chance to clarify.

Well, I was done with that.

"I have to go," I say to Connor and he nods, waving a last goodbye and leaving. I quickly duck back inside the apartment to change and explain everything to Rosie, who is relentless in chasing me around my room for details while I change.

I think it's about time I set this brooding lumberjack straight.

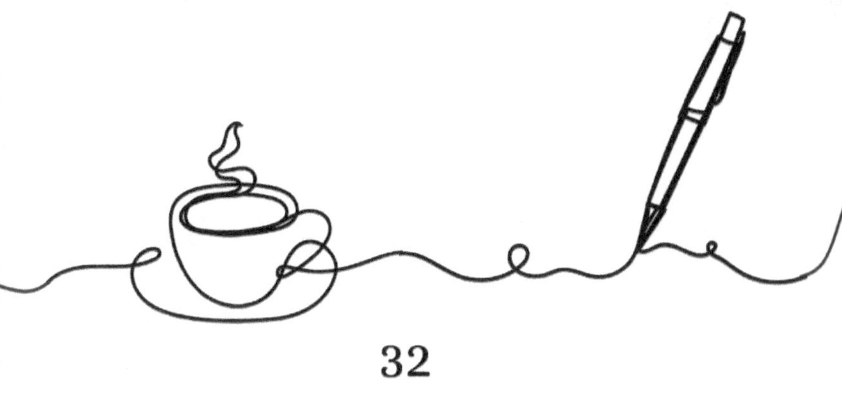

32

you are my guiding star

Jessie

"Wait, Jessie!" Casey's voice calls after me, but the elevator doors close and I fall back against the wall as it takes me down. Rubbing the heel of my palms into my eyes and cursing myself.

"Fucking idiot!" Addison hasn't a clue what she's talking about. It sure as fuck wasn't Casey's heart torn from her chest. It was mine.

I know we hadn't planned to see each other tonight. I just didn't realize I was sharing her attention.

If I wasn't enough for Jenny, why would I be enough for Casey?

Fucking. Idiot.

The Uber to my apartment was quick and a complete blur. I don't remember what the driver looked like or really how I even got inside my apartment, but the walls feel entirely too close and the breath is scant in my lungs.

I pace the floor, not at all worried about the hole I'm possibly wearing into the boards, but ready to flip a table as rage and shame threaten to overtake me.

Anger at myself. I was such an idiot. I took too long. I pushed her away. Away and right into the arms of another man.

I might be a fool, but I was also delusional, like she was ever going to settle with the likes of me.

A normal man would have stayed and fought for her, told flashy-suit-guy to fuck off, that Casey was mine. But the way she looked up at him? The way she hugged him, the delicate smile she gave him, like his presence was precious. I couldn't... pull her down into my darkness. If she shines brightly, is smiling and glowing, does it really matter whether it is for me or someone else? It should be enough that she is happy and taken care of.

But I'm a selfish bastard, and instead of being happy that she found someone to make her smile, I am fucking pissed! Livid that the future I was only just finally letting myself believe I deserved was snatched out of my hands. And I have no one to blame but myself.

Hope. Hope did this.

Well, hope can fuck right off.

A loud pounding on my door snaps me from pacing and the deep dive my thoughts are taking. I stare at the door, like I could suddenly gain x-ray vision and burn whoever stands there.

I'd rather fray my flesh alive than see a human right now. No doubt it is Addison, ready to berate me for not being at the house, but it is almost fucking midnight, and I am ready to fall into a fitful sleep before I drag my body to the cafe in the morning, make Betty her usual, and forget that these last couple of months ever happened.

The pounding comes again, but this time, the sweet-sounding voice that usually brings me calm shouts back at me, "Open up this damn door, Jessie Jenkins." Like a pirate to his siren, I'm at the door and aggressively swinging it open to be met with eyes as angry as an ocean during a storm, the deep blue smoldering with a million unspoken words. I push away the feeling of the peace her presence brings me, that she is here, and instead embrace the fury, latching on to the only thing that is keeping me breathing in this moment.

"What the hell was that!?" she seethes. But I can't find my words. Something like a grunt or a growl leaves my throat, and I just cross my arms.

She shakes her head, and her anger softens. Letting go of a breath, she drops her head before her rageful eyes turn sad and she looks up at me. "Why were you at my apartment, Jessie?" she whispers. I try to read her emotions. Try to find guilt or something, but I can't. I only see sadness, and it aches. The pain of her misery feels like a heavy weight on my shoulders, and it makes me let go of the anger, allowing it to recede, and I drop my arms.

"I was there to see you," I manage to croak out.

"And?" she pushes.

"What does it matter, Casey? You're with Mr. Suit, right?" I couldn't hide the pain from that statement if I tried.

"What—"

"Look, it doesn't matter. I didn't mean to interrupt. I'm sorry if that caused a problem or something." I wave a hand at her and look past her face because I can't bear to look into those blue eyes as she finally says goodbye to me. "I understand, really. But I don't think we should keep doing whatever it is we're doing here." I claw back at my anger. Holding tight because my chest feels like it's caving in, and when I finally look back at her face, she has a look I can't quite make out. Confusion? Anger? Maybe it's both.

"Hang on..." She holds up a finger, shaking her head. Then she does what I really had not expected. She buckles over, her hands landing on her knees. She is... laughing at me.

"Nicely done. I'm glad you stopped by. Have a nice night." If she wanted to tear me to shreds, she didn't have to also laugh at me.

"You wait a damn minute!" she shouts as she slams a hand to the door, stopping it from closing, and I seethe down at her.

"What now? Are you not done?" I growl.

"No! In fact, I'm only just getting started, you fucking caveman!" The fact Casey swore in anger is enough to shut me up. She mostly did that to stick a joke... or when I made her come.

She shoves at my chest, pushing me back into the apartment as she slams the door closed, stalking toward me.

"That was Connor at my door," she clarifies, and my snarl only intensifies. "We are not back together, and you would have learned that had you not cracked a tantrum like a stupid child and stormed off!" Her tone vibrates with rage, and I try desperately not to rip the clothes from her body. Casey is soft, delicate, and so incredibly sexy in her femininity. But when she is flushed from her anger, growling and shouting her words at me with venom? She is something else entirely. She is... fucking otherworldly.

"Tell me, right now, what were you coming over for?" She thrusts a finger to my chest, churning in her anger with her jaw clenched tight, fists balled at her side.

Fuck, I like this side of Casey.

"What does it matter?" I throw back at her, a sneer on my face, as I try to get her to run back to Connor.

"You're such an idiot, you know that?" she breathes, shaking her head again. "Do you know how tiring it is to be the one to give every fucking day?" Pain shoots up my spine at the accusation.

"Don't give me that bullshit, Ace. It was never like that with us, not once, and you know that."

"You're right. To a point, it was never like that. Except then you'd go to tell me your feelings and push me away instead. But I never left you. I never walked away. I stayed. I gave you everything else instead, so you'd know that I was still here and that I was never fucking leaving you!" A stray tear races down her cheek and it has me dropping all defenses. I never like seeing her cry, and I hate it even more now that it is because of me.

"Well, stop dancing around my fucking feelings, Casey, and tell me something real. Stop pulling back, stop coddling me and behaving in a way you think is for me! Give me you! Tell me the things you want to say without thinking about my fucking feelings or my stupid head!" I punctuate with a fist to my chest, challenging her, staring down at her, encouraging her.

"You want something real?" she challenges back, as she leans in, her eyes brimming with tears full of passion and anger and pain.

"I'm in love with you." She speaks clearly, and I feel my breath leave without returning.

"I've been in love with you since I was sixteen. I might have had boyfriends to fill the hole of loneliness, but it's always been you. And these last few months I've been waiting." She ends on a huge breath, her fire burning out as each word leaves those pretty pink lips. But my heart races. Rational thought evacuates my brain.

"Waiting for what?" I breathe.

"For you to let yourself finally feel something real. To see me! To want me! I told you, I'm tired, Jessie, and I am. I am so fucking tired of doing the fighting and never being fought for." I really am a fucking idiot.

I take a step toward her and grip her chin, holding her in place as she tries to take a step away from me. She squeezes her eyes closed and a sob levels my soul as I wipe a tear from her cheeks.

"You want me to be real, too, sunshine?" She sobs, nodding, but her eyes still squeezed closed, leaking the evidence of her pain.

"I'm in love with you," I whisper in her ear, and when I pull back, she snaps open her eyes, that little mouth open in an adorable look of shock.

My sunshine.

"You... love me?"

"I do. Have since you were twenty-one." And will forever.

"Why'd you come to my apartment?" she questions again, but steps closer to me, our bodies now touching, and her gaze goes to my lips.

"To tell you those words, and a bunch of other things. To apologize for being a fucking fool. For taking so long, for pushing you away, for not claiming you sooner."

"Tell me the other things. I want to hear all of them."

"Casey Baker, you are my guiding star. You burn bright and have thawed my soul. You're mine. I love you."

She answers with another tear, but leaps at me, her arms wrapping tightly around my neck and legs wrapping around my waist as I grip her hips.

"Say it again," she whispers against my lips.

"I love you," I comply.

"No." She pulls back, panting. "Not that part, the other part." She bites her lip, and I tilt my head in confusion.

"I'm yours, Jess. Say it again." It feels like my heart explodes out of my chest. I am so gone for this woman.

"You're mine." This time it comes out as a growl, and I fist her hair to slam her lips back on mine, turning to walk us to the bedroom. To claim her properly, make love to her, tell her all the things I'm finally ready to say, to make up for all the ways I've been a fucking coward when it comes to her. But before I can completely close the door, she pulls away and wriggles down my body.

"Wait." She barely speaks as she runs from the room.

"Ace, what's wrong?" Confused as to what is happening, I follow after her, a painful boner straining my pants, but my anxiety is eased as she turns and hits me with that stunning smile.

"I have a song for this moment." Of course she does.

I playfully roll my eyes at her, and she bites her lip, pressing play on her phone connected to the speaker and then runs and leaps into my arms. The caveman in me growls at the image of Casey jumping into my arms like a starved animal. I catch her and hold her wrapped around my body as we wait for the song to play, and the moment it does, I throw my head back in a laugh. My chest grows three times its size, making even more room for Casey inside my heart.

"What do you think?" she teases and spears her fingers through my hair playfully as the beginning verse of Jessie's Girl by Rick Springfield plays around us, my chest lighter and my smile easy.

"Jessie does have himself a girl, but no one is stealing you from me now, sunshine." I pinch her ass and she giggles. I turn back and head straight for my room, and the song continues to play throughout the apartment.

When I take her lips again, she moans into the kiss, her lithe body searching for friction. Friction I'm desperate to deliver, but first...

"Why was Connor there?" I demand because while I hadn't allowed myself to act jealous before, I sure as fuck am feeling it now. Her smile. Her embrace. At him.

Fuck, I'll rip him apart.

She pulls back from the kiss and says, "He wanted me back." She whispers it like its nothing and goes in for another kiss, but I throw her to the bed instead.

"What—"

"Talk. Now," I demand and crawl over her. Pinning her hands above her head–Oh, would you look at that, her pony is tied with that pretty blue bow, how convenient. Reaching to tug the ribbon loose, I kiss down her neck and proceed to bind her wrists together with the delicate satin. "I'm waiting, Casey."

"He... oh, god... He came to tell me he missed me." I bite her collarbone, and her hips lift toward mine. I continue lower until my hands are pulling down her jeans.

"And?" The pants are discarded, and I focus my attention on her top, slowly lifting it up her torso.

"And that he had pulled himself together," she breathes, practically panting. I wiggle her top over her head along with her bra, and she lay beneath me in a pair of black panties and nothing else. Fucking exquisite.

"Keep going, Casey," I taunt her and she growls in protest.

"Later. Please. Touch me," she begs, and I bite her hipbone in response.

"No answers, no orgasm." Her head snaps up at me, her mouth agape, and I can't help but steal it in a kiss. My tongue dancing with hers, her taste of wine and chocolate. Her moans that I swallow and the feel of her body beneath me. It takes every ounce of control to not forget my demand and just have my way with her. I pull away before I head down that road and move down her body, letting go of my grip on her still bound hands.

"Keep talking, sunshine."

"Fine." She moans. "He said he had spent this time, oh my god... cleaning himself up. Getting a job. God." She struggles to string a sentence together as I leave delicate kisses on her inner thigh, breathing gently over the wet spot of her panties and biting the flesh only centimeters from where I'm dying to be buried.

"He... he said he knew I deserved better... ohmygodohmygod." She pants harder as I slowly drag her panties down her thighs and discard them.

"That he wanted me back. He was ready to show me he could be a good boyfriend. Oh my god! Jessie. Please," she begs, her sentences increasing in pace as she writhes below me.

"If only you could see how desperate you are for me right now, Ace." I demonstrate by gently running a finger up her center, spreading her need everywhere, the sound of her bare and soaking pussy music to my ears as I bite down on the growl rising up my throat.

"You want to come, sunshine?" I taunt with a quick swipe of my tongue on her pussy. She nods frantically. "Then hurry up with the details." She gasps when I bite her clit and lick her again, trying like hell to hold on to my control, get the answer I am looking for before I devour her.

"Okay, okay..." she breathes. "I told him I appreciated his effort—" She gasps as I slap her pussy. Not the answer I am looking for.

"Try again," I growl.

"I said I wasn't coming back. There was someone else, and we weren't meant to be." I reward her and myself by finally letting go. My mouth descends on her in a second, my tongue devouring her center and teasing that delicate bundle at her apex, feeling her squirm below me. She moans and tightens her thighs around my head.

Stuck between her thighs and unable to drag myself out, I mumble into her, "More, keep going."

"I told him goodbye. That we were done. I hoped he found happiness, but I already had mine. That was why I hugged him." She grips my hair to a point of pain and yanks me up from between her legs. Her eyes are misty, but full of desire, as she searches mine and pants, lips only inches from mine.

"I hugged him goodbye. I told him I was already in love with someone else and that I wasn't coming back to him. My heart isn't his. It never was. Jessie, I love you." She drops a tear, but I seal her words with my lips, my pants gone, and my fingers find her center.

"I love you, sunshine. I'm never letting you go now. I can't quit you."

"You better not," she teases as she kisses me again, her bound hands looping my neck, pulling at my hair, and snapping the last of my control.

"Do you want to come on my fingers, my tongue, or my cock?" I bite her jaw before pulling back to remove my shirt. When I look back down at her face, she pants, a mix of excitement and passion floods her eyes as she bites her lip.

"All three."

33

we don't have to wait anymore

Casey

I gasp as Jessie spears me with his fingers and he seals his lips on mine.

'You are my guiding star, you burn bright and have thawed my soul. You're mine. I love you.'

Finally.

I could breathe. It felt like a weight lifted from my chest because Jessie had finally taken what he wanted, and like I had been longing for, what he wanted was me.

Connor was a big part of my life and I, his. He wasn't a bad guy, we both just had different futures now. And I was currently having a sexual awakening with mine.

"Jess," I grind out through a clenched jaw, barely holding a foot to my sanity as he edges and teases me right on the threshold. "Please." I beg for the release, my body pulled so tight, and the way he trails his kisses down my neck, across my collarbone, while his fingers play me like his favorite instrument, I'm on the cusp of ecstasy.

"I love when you beg for me," he murmurs into my neck, his fingers curling and diving deeper as he pushes me over the edge. The waves of euphoria have me crying out for him and barely able to catch my breath when he kisses me. Hooking his arms around my knees, he flips us, so he lays under me, his back now to the bed. "That's one," he hisses, smacking a hand to my ass, and I gasp. "Now get up here and hold on tight." He points to the headboard. I waste no time climbing over him, anticipation and a sudden wave of wariness hits me. I haven't done this before.

I look down at his glittering eyes and bite my lip.

"Sit, sunshine," he coaxes, his hot breath teasing my center. "I won't ask again," he orders. But I'm still frozen. I haven't been seen from this angle, and what if I suffocate him?

My thoughts are cut off when he grabs my hips and firmly pulls, his tongue spearing me, and I almost squeal.

"Oh, God!" My vision blackens, and I see stars as he devours me.

"Ride my face. Take what you need from me, Casey." He lays beneath me, but right now, holds all the power as he clutches me firmly to his mouth. "I love tasting your tight little cunt." He smacks my ass again and reaches a hand around to tease and pinch my clit.

"Yes," I encourage and beg, while my hips roll with a mind of their own.

With barely a breath being caught, he spears his tongue into me, pinches my sensitive peak once more, and I'm hurtling over the edge, screaming his name as it hits me harder than the last.

"Fucking hell. Jess." I reach down the best I can to pull him up with my hands bound by my ribbon—who knew I had a kink for that? His licks start to slow. "I need you. God, I need you now!" I'm a panting mess and I think I'm crying. I've never felt need like this. Never felt claimed and taken so thoroughly, not like Jessie does.

"That's two. And the sweetest dessert I've ever tasted," he rasps as he sits up, my legs still over his shoulders, and I'm on my back as he maneuvers himself between my legs.

"I'm going to take you hard and fast, Ace. Because I need you. So fucking bad." He punctuates his words with a deep kiss, and gently removes the ribbon from my wrists. He pauses, the intensity of his eyes makes my breath catch as he peruses me. "But now that you're mine, I'm also going to spend every day loving you. In every way I can. Gently, quietly, extravagantly—" he kisses me again, his smile turning down right feral, "possessively, aggressively, and any other way that you need. Loving you is going to be the easiest and best thing I've ever done. And I'm going to make up for all the lost time. I'll make you forget everyone from your past and give you the future you've dreamed of." His vulnerability stares back at me and my chest aches. I love this man with everything in me.

"I promise," he whispers, and I feel the pain of regret, for how long he took, for not making a move, for not saying everything sooner. But I really don't care. I want him now. Screw the past. If he's my future, I only want to look forward.

"I'm on the pill," I whisper, and his gaze darkens, the hunger deepening.

"Are you sure?" he whispers back, but I don't hesitate. I'm done with all the barriers between us. I just want him.

I nod and pull him into a kiss as he shifts a pillow beneath my hips, spanking my ass and making good on his promise.

With one single hard thrust, he sinks inside me completely. Feeling myself adjust to him, I take a few breaths, if you can call them that. They feel like groans, as the desire takes over my mind, body, and soul. He pulls out slowly, then thrusts back in.

"Jesus fuck. Casey, you feel so fucking good," he says into my ear, his warm breath has a moan escaping, and I wrap my legs around him, tightening and pulling him closer, needing more.

"More, Jessie. Fuck me!"

Any control he was trying to retain evaporates, and he sits up on his knees, taking my hips with him as he drives into me, his hips snapping at speed.

"You're going to be the fucking death of me, sunshine," he grinds out.

My cries of pleasure and his growl of need mix with the sounds of our bodies coming together. He leans forward to trail wet kisses down my neck, sucking a nipple into his mouth as he brings me closer to that third orgasm.

"You're close. I can feel you." His contented smile smacks me in the chest as he reaches a hand between us. "Let go for me, Ace. Be a good girl and come all over my cock." He drives even harder. So deep, I feel him everywhere. Every nerve-ending on fire, and the black spots start to cover my vision. With a few firm circles of his thumb on my clit, I come for the third time. The waves drag on, and in a few more thrusts, he is right there with me, moaning my name into my neck.

"Beautiful. It's insane how fucking beautiful you are. So perfect. And all mine," he breathes before he steals my lips in a claiming kiss.

"I think you wrecked me," I pant between a laugh and utter exhaustion.

"Good." He's smug as he rolls off me, ducking into his bathroom. Returning with a washcloth, but pausing as he stands at the end of the bed, staring into my center. A hungry look takes over his devastatingly handsome face, and he crawls toward me like a predator.

"Fuck, you're even more beautiful when you're dripping with my come." He drags a lazy finger through my slit, poking him back inside me, and a stray cry leaves my throat.

"Jessie, please." Please stop, please keep going. Fuck. I am utterly destroyed by this man.

He hums knowingly, and then his finger is gone. Feeling more empty than ever before, he wipes the warm cloth over me, cleaning me up before it's discarded and I'm pulled between his arms.

"You need to rest," he whispers as he kisses my forehead, gently pushing the hair from my face. "And you need to rest right now, because if we stay awake, we're doing that again. And not only will you have no sleep before tomorrow, you also won't be able to walk." Chuckling, I run a hand over his warm chest.

"I love you," I whisper into his skin. His lips press gently to my forehead as he says it back.

"I love you." His voice sounds pained, and I hold him tighter. "Fuck. I just... I really love you, more than I ever thought was possible." He hooks a finger under my chin and pulls my gaze to his. "You're my best friend, Ace. I can't wait for our forever." A tear leaks down my cheek.

"We don't have to wait anymore, Jess. Our forever has already started." I kiss him deeply and he holds me tighter.

Sixteen-year-old Casey would positively die if she could see me now.

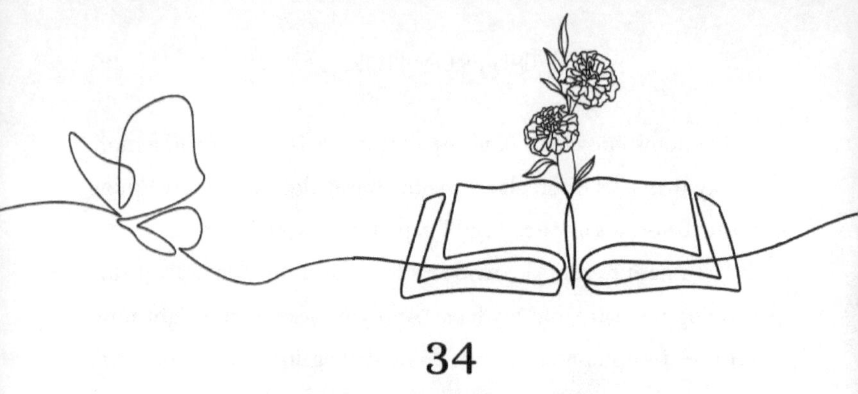

34

why am i such a mess?

Casey

"What are you reading?" Jessie asks quizzically, looking down at me, my head resting on his lap as he reads the paperback in his hand.

"Just a book." I can't help the giggle. I know he is only asking because I've been gasping, chuckling, and cooing at this book for the last twenty minutes.

"One of your dirty books?" he pushes, humor lighting his tone as he discards the book he seems no longer interested in.

"How dare you!" I gasp, feigning offense, slapping the book to my chest and looking up at those gorgeous eyes. A hand combing smoothly through my unbound hair as he holds my gaze. He truly is so perfect, with his gentle smile and handsome features. This afternoon we have spent peacefully together, my heart has never felt so full.

"Read me something."

"Oh, no. God no. Jess, this isn't some heart-breaking classic piece. I don't think you want to hear it." I laugh at him, picking the book up to continue when he snatches it from my hands.

"Hey!" I squeal, and he holds it above his head, a hand wrapping around my hips to hold me down and stop me from stealing it back.

His deep chuckle vibrates my body, and like it always seems to do, heat and desire pool in my lower belly, making me ache between my legs. When I have stopped squirming, he looks to the open pages where he holds the book above us and reads aloud, "'*Well, it doesn't matter if you see me or not. You're going to feel every in—*'Jesus Christ, Ace, what are you reading?" His smile contradicts his scolding, and he starts to laugh as my cheeks heat and I raise my hands to cover my face, completely mortified, but still, he continues, "'*...inch of me. I'll be so deep, you'll be able to feel me in your fucking throat...*'" When he pauses, I spread the fingers that cover my eyes to peek up at him and catch him still reading, his lips folded inside his mouth as he tries to smother a laugh, those stunning eyes sparkling with humor.

"Well, well, well. Casey Baker, you're a dirty fucking girl." He chuckles but continues to hold my book hostage. When I groan in protest and roll into his body, trying desperately to hide my mortification, I feel his arm drop the book and wrap around me, still trying his best not to laugh at my expense.

"Don't go shy on me now, Ace. We've done things dirtier than these books." He runs a finger across my cheek, and when I finally look back up at him, that devastating smile hits me in the chest again. Remembering said dirty things over the last week, spending that time practically hiding out at his apartment. I don't want to hide what we are, but it all seems very new and I really love this new bubble of us.

Wanting to be closer, to get lost in those stunning eyes of his, I climb to a seated position and let him pull me into his lap, straddling him as we sit on the couch and scratching at the back of his neck.

"It doesn't like... weird you out? Me reading that stuff?" I can't help but admire the strong line of his neck as he throws his head back in a laugh. When he comes back to me, there is nothing but love in those eyes.

"Not in the slightest. Although, if you do need me to demonstrate my superiority over..." He trails off, raising an eyebrow,

"Baseball Daddy Kai," I clarify with a wink and bite my lip.

He just rolls his eyes and continues, "If you need me to demonstrate my superiority over *Baseball Daddy Kai,* I have absolutely no trouble doing so." He leans forward, both his hands palming my ass and grinding me into him, his lips hovering just above mine. "And I bet I could make you come way harder than he could." He sucks my bottom lip into his mouth and bites before he releases me. The moan from my throat is pure animal as I try to wrap my head around that offer.

"Umm..." I pant. "I also have no trouble with you doing so." My words are barely louder than a whisper. His responding chuckle has warmth spreading low and the coil of desire twisting tighter.

"I guess it's too bad, then," he whispers just above my lips, his hands still massaging my ass, as I practically whimper and grind on him. Too distracted by his raw sex appeal to understand what he is saying.

"Hmm?"

"Well, you have work, and so do I." He spanks me and lifts me off his lap.

"No fair!" I smack his chest as I climb off the couch, completely appalled by his audacity. I go to storm off to my room, but he grabs my elbow and pulls me against him, his fingers immediately down the front of my yoga pants, finding themselves inside my panties, as though the barriers of my clothing mean nothing.

"You really are a needy girl," he states, leaning in to bite my neck. But the only thing I can do is pant as the evidence of my need soaks Jessie's fingers.

"Fucking hell, Case, you're right there, aren't you? You're going to come on my fingers right now." He spears me, his palm aggressively rubbing me as his free hand spears into my hair, gripping me.

"Oh god, oh god, *oh god!*" I can barely catch my breath, not caring that I'm standing in my living room–thankfully with no roommates home–about to come on Jessie's fingers.

"Good girl. *Fuck,* you're so pretty when you come apart, just for me." My head falls back, my knees buckling. Jessie's strong arms wrap around me in time for the orgasm to hit me, and I practically scream his name as he finishes me off. "Nothing I love more than taking care of you, sunshine." His gentle words and the caressing kiss he leaves on my lips in contradiction to the way he had me like putty in his hands. When he's finished rubbing me through the waves of my orgasm, still holding me up, he pulls his hands from my tights, makes a show of licking his fingers, before he spanks me and whispers, "Now go get ready for work, we can finish this later." Pulling away, he winks and heads for the bathroom, leaving me a gaping, boneless mess in the living room.

"Deep breath and relax," I instruct my last class of the day. Thankfully, Elle offered to take my last two, so I will be able to leave just before dinnertime. Addy had messaged that she and Noah are coming to Pucks this time, and because it has been ages since I've had any sort of time with her, I'm excited to get the rest of the night off to hang out with our friends.

"Settle into your mind, allow yourself to track everywhere that your body is touching the ground, feel the sensation, exist in it, but then move to the next." I walk them through the usual meditation for the end of the class, and just as I'm about to begin the individual muscle relaxation, a door to one of the studios–that I thought was empty–closes with a bang. I sit up quietly, trying desperately not to disturb the meditation. Making eyes with Elle, she nods, taking over the meditation as I head for the door.

Quietly closing the door to the studio, I head in the direction of the noise, but before I can round the corner, someone comes around and we run into each other.

"Grace?" I shake my head and look her up and down, confused, and... "What are you doing here?" She rolls her eyes at me, and that same anger that has been bubbling under my skin where she is concerned returns with a vengeance.

"It's my studio, too, remember?" she throws back at me before she attempts to sidestep me, heading for the door.

I'm so goddamned sick of this.

I grip her elbow and turn her to face me. "I asked you a damn question. You don't get to ignore all of my messages, calls, and visit attempts and then just show up."

"My name is on the building. I can do whatever I please."

"What the hell is your problem?" I shout the question back at her, embracing the anger, no longer able to bury the feelings she brings out of me. Not the first time I've stood my ground recently. The first time, it got me Jessie. Maybe this time, I'll finally get my sister.

She rips her arm from my grip, but, to her credit, doesn't shrink away from my burning gaze.

"None of your fucking business, Casey! God, get your nose out of my ass and leave me the hell alone," she shouts back. Thinking I'm not going to have the balls to retort, she spins. To hell with her stupid feelings. If she isn't going to love me, I'm sure as hell done loving her.

"I'm meeting with the accountant and my lawyer next week. I want this partnership dissolved," I snap at her. That has her rooted in place before she slowly turns in my direction.

"What?" she whispers, except there is nothing but rage in her tone.

"You heard me. You want to throw away our relationship? Fine. You want me to leave you alone? Done. But you know what I won't do, Grace? I'm not going to just sit by while you let the business we've spent years building–that *I've* spent my life on–be run into the ground. I can't afford to run both studios on my own. Since you're hellbent on feeling sorry for yourself and not communicating with me as your business partner, I'm making the economical decision for myself. I want the Upper West Side Studio to myself. The East is yours." I cross my arms, feeling my heart pound aggressively in my chest. I am so lost in my anger, in feeling it all, I hadn't realized we now have an audience. Grace's gaze flits over my shoulder and a blush hits her cheeks. She stews there, in the wake of my words for a minute, maybe two, and I let her. Refusing to be the one to fix anything this time. There is only so much I can give a person who refuses to take or give back.

I'm done.

She purses her lips in indignation before she nods her head and smiles in defiance. "Fine."

One single word, barely any pain in that delicate face of hers, and she spins on a heel and is out of the studio without another.

I just stand there, staring at the spot she just vacated, my heart still racing, my neck hot and flushed, my bones aching. The need to scream burns through my lungs.

"Casey?" Elle's gentle touch to my shoulder makes me flinch, and when I turn, there is sadness on her face. *Shit.* I just told a room full of staff and clients that I'm closing one studio, or at the very least removing myself from it. Not that I actually *am* planning to do that next week. The idea came to me in the moment, and I just spoke without thinking.

"Can I call you later? I need to go," I whisper to her, blinking back the sting in my eyes.

Elle nods. "Of course, go. I have the rest of the night, anyway. I'll call you tomorrow." I nod in thanks, and her pitying stare follows me as I grab my things and head for the door.

The air is crisp now, completely in the thick of winter, a bite to the stiff breeze and light snow dusting the streets as I make my way to Pucks. It sits between the West studio and our apartment, so there really is no point in heading home first. I'm stuck in a daze, running over the things I had said, the things I *should* have said. That I still love her, and I'm not giving up. I'm just stepping back. But I couldn't, the rage it just, overtook me.

God, I feel sick. I don't even know what just happened.

"Hey, sunshine." That deliciously smooth voice has me sighing both internally and externally. Jessie is standing in front of Pucks. From the looks of things, just stepping out of his Uber, and briskly making his way to me. "I tried to call you. You walked? It's freezing!" His tone is similar to a parent scolding a child, but lovingly. I know he just cares for me, but my skin feels too hot to be worried about the frost in the air. I shrug, still not having greeted him or met his eyeline. He doesn't seem to mind, and instead, wraps his arms around me and kisses my forehead.

"Hey." He hooks a finger under my chin and directs my eyes to him. "You good?" A knowing look and a loaded question. Because I see in his eyes the real questions. *'Do I need to hurt someone? Do you want to go home? Can I fix this for you?'* All the questions I don't have the capacity to handle right now, so I smile at him, small but sincere, and nod at him. Giving him a quick kiss and diving back into the warmth of his arms.

"I think I need gin."

He chuckles lightly. "That, I can arrange." Keeping an arm hooked around my shoulders, he directs us to the entry of the bar. As we make our way through the tables, Riley's head snaps in our direction, which prompts the rest of the table to look and gawk. *Oh boy, we're hard-launching our–whatever this is–right now.*

Matching looks of shock and smugness plaster over all of them. Well, all except Stella. She just winks, giving me her usual sad, dark smile, and then returns her gaze to the TVs and her whiskey.

Despite my rigid posture and frozen steps, Jessie remains warm and calm at my side. He pulls me tighter and leans down to whisper in my ear, "If it's too much for tonight, we can pretend. But I'm not looking to hide anything from anyone, Ace. I love you, and I'd happily shout it to the world."

My eyes squeeze shut for a moment, taking in his words and feeling my anger recede, and when I look up into those eyes, I let myself smile fully this time.

"Nothing with you is too much." His eyes sparkle with a touch of shock at my words, but I just squeeze an arm around his waist and use the calmness and joy he breathes into me, to hold me through the rest of the night. The knowledge that this night will end with my big, burly lumberjack holding me as I sleep, making it all the more bearable.

"What's this, then?" Rosie questions, except she knows exactly what it is, and by the cheeky look on her face, she is just getting me to admit it.

"I don't know what you're talking about?" I muse, not meeting her eyes, if only to get a reaction from her. Addison scoffs at her, but meets me before the table and pulls me into a hug.

Her small frame nestles into mine in comfort, and I squeeze her shoulders when she whispers, "I'm happy for you both." Pulling away, she winks, levels her brother with a scary look, before she turns back to her seat.

As Jessie and I pull out a chair each and sit, we seem to be in agreement that we aren't hiding, but also not broadcasting, and Caleb lets go of a humorless laugh before staring at his beer. "Another one bites the dust."

Rosie raises her drink to him in agreement, and they both down what's left. Everyone else seems to be on board with not mentioning anything. Riley is just staring wide-eyed and smiling large, obviously ecstatic with her big brother's lack of comfort right now. But after a few minutes, the silence becomes awkward. Everyone is shifting and not making eye contact, and I can practically feel the tension roiling off Caleb's and Noah's shoulders from trying so hard not to laugh.

"For goodness' sake, you're all a bunch of children," I mumble and turn to Jessie. "You need a drink? Because I do." He nods, also trying not to laugh but shaking his head at our stupid friends.

"I'll get it," he says, and gives me a pointed look that I know translates to something like, *'sort out these fuckers before I get back.'*

He heads for the bar, and I level the group with a look and deliver the warning, "Yes, Jessie and I are together. No, it hasn't been going on this whole time. No, we haven't really discussed what any of it means. Yes, it is serious." I take a breath and then, rolling my shoulders, I breathe out, "Any questions? This is your one and—"

"So many questions," Rosie gasps as she slaps the table in front of her.

"How did it happen?" Caleb questions.

"Also, dick size—"

"Rosie!?" Addison scolds, followed by a mumbled, "For fuck's sake, gross." From Riley.

"You were the one that asked if they had any questions," Ethan provides and gives me a look that says this was my own doing.

"Okay, I take it back. No questions. It is only new, the finer details are for Jessie and I. Grow up and deal with it." As my gaze flits around the table at each person, they all seem to nod in agreement. Not sure that Lucas and Ethan could care less, Rosie and Caleb are the most disappointed with the lack of details, but I get a weird look from Stella, something that hits like respect, and I think that is also almost a smile.

"Sorted?" Jessie asks as he comes back to the table and places the drink in front of me. I nod and level the entire table with a glare, to which they shrink from. I internally pat myself on the back because I think I *finally* nailed the Rosie look.

"How's the online store coming?" Ethan asks Jessie, and the conversation between him, Jessie, and Noah breaks off, Lucas and Stella in their own discussion as Riley, Rosie, and Addison turn to me.

"So, Casey's birthday celebrations. Ideas?"

"This isn't some big party. We don't have to do anything, really." I wave Rosie off and sip my drink.

"You've had a big few months, though, so—"

"But we're still waiting to hear exactly *how* big," Rosie interrupts Addison and looks at me pointedly through her thick lashes as she raises her hands under the height of the table, like she is *again* asking for indication on the size of Jessie's dick.

"Rosie, yuck, stop!" Addison hisses at her, trying not to get Jessie's attention.

Honestly, at this point, I might as well tell her, just to shut her up.

I make a point to look at her hands, tilting my head and smiling mischievously. "Much bigger."

"I KNEW it!" Rosie screeches, slaps the table and throws her head back in a laugh that sounds almost like a hyena. She takes a few minutes to gather herself, the entire table now staring at us, and Addison just covers her head.

"What did we miss?" Noah questions.

"Absolutely nothing," I assure him with wide eyes, but when my eyes dart to Jessie, the blue in them glows and his tongue-in-cheek smugness tells me he knows *exactly* what Noah and the rest missed.

I swear to god, Rosie is going to burst a blood vessel from restraining her laugh so much.

How mortifying. The guy only just started to admit his feelings for me, and here I am telling people he has a huge cock.

I mean, he does. A really, really nice one, too.

I have to shake my head to clear the haze of desire. But my gaze remains on Jessie as he and the guys return to their conversations. He sits relaxed, nodding at them, wearing the biggest smile they would ever get out of him—which is to say, it's barely there. But I secretly love that he saves his showstopper just for me. He seems a lot more at peace of late than I had ever seen him and, like his strength and solidity, are infectious; I feel the tension inside me slowly evaporate. Forgetting the words, both said and unsaid between Grace and I. Letting it go because as of right now, there is nothing I can do to change her, fix her, or make anything different from what it is right now. So why let it take hold and ruin a night of joy?

"Oh Case! I have amazing news. You remember that manuscri—"

"I need to pee!" I scream in a panic. *That fucking manuscript is going to ruin me.* The entire table freezes. Jessie's eyes are on me with concern, but I pretend I can't feel it as I stand abruptly, my chair nearly falling to the ground. "Rosie, come with me?" I ask with eyes that basically say, '*Stand the fuck up right now and follow me, or you die.*' Thankfully, she gets the message. Her stunned face at my outburst and raised hands in disbelief follow her the entire way to the bathroom.

When we make it into the bathrooms, she yanks on my elbow to make me face her. "What the hell was that?"

"You can't talk about the manuscript I gave you, okay, I told you, it was confidential and anonymous."

"Well yeah, but...it's anonymous, no one on that illiterate table is going to know someone who writes an incredible piece of literature." She waves at me before she gets bored and heads for the mirror, fixing her face. I throw my arms up in frustration and just head to the stall, suddenly actually needing to pee. I lock the door and sit down, talking to Rosie through the charming sound of my stream.

"Can you just, like, talk to me in private about it, or text me or something? Just don't mention it in front of people."

"Okay, okay. Whatever." She sighs. Wait... did she say—

"Is it really that incredible?" I ask, even though I know it's amazing, I read just over half of it, and knew it was going to be beautiful. I just wasn't sure if I was biased. "Well... we're in private *now!* Answer me." This woman, I tell you.

"Oh, right, well—"

"You guys ran off in the most suss way possible. Who is pregnant!?" Riley announces as she enters the bathroom. I mutter profanity while I finish up and meet the girls at the sink, Addison and Stella also now in tow. *Freaking gossip patrol.*

"No one is pregnant," I mutter.

"There are way too many women in this bathroom for you to make that kind of assumption," Rosie points out. Addison matches my eye roll with hers.

Stella's gentle laugh lightens the mood slightly, but it is out of the ordinary to hear from her. When we all snap our gazes in her direction, she waves us off and heads to the mirror next to Rosie.

"Nice color." She lifts the corner of her smile, her onyx eyes painted with a delicate wing analyzing Rosie from head to toe, nothing but fellow female appreciation in her appraisal.

"Nice wing. Wish I could do that," Rosie admires Stella.

"I'll teach you." She shrugs in return and Rosie nods in thanks.

"Anyway, what was the drama?" Riley refocuses everyone.

"Nothing. Rosie just..." Oh, I am terrible at lies.

"Was updating her on this work drama stuff. Nothing interesting." And Rosie lies fabulously. If I wasn't aware of the real topic, I wouldn't even know it was a lie. But I know Addy can see right through her. She most definitely sees right through me.

"Ugh, I thought we came in here for fun gossip." Thankfully, she reads the room and only hits us with narrowed eyes before she joins in.

"Boring." Riley rolls her eyes and leaves. Stella fixes her hair, smiles at Rosie, and then heads out, too.

"You lying bitches. Tell me." Addison wastes no time, but... this is her *brother*. I really hate keeping something from her, but telling her to keep this from her brother would be so much worse than her not knowing. I just have to find a way to get the manuscript back and return it to his apartment without him noticing. No biggie.

"It's nothing, really." Rosie, bless her soul, is sticking to her guns.

"I did a thing." And again... I'm horrific at this lying game.

"Oh, Jesus, you need a backbone, Case." Rosie sighs as she shakes her head at me.

"I knew it!" Addison's smile grows. "What's the goss?"

"I can't tell you." I wince at the way her head jerks back. Her eyes flit between me and Rosie, and my stomach threatens to empty on this very floor. Because I know that look. All the hard work Addy has gone through these last twelve months feels like it is being completely undone right now.

"Honestly, it's not even that big of a deal." *Lies.* "Well, like, to you,

you probably wouldn't even be interested." So many lies my mouth is dry. "Really. But I can't say anything. I really, really can't. I wish I could." Rosie smacks my arm in an attempt to shut me up from my rambling. Each of Addy's walls slams down behind her eyes, and I watch as she pulls back. Rosie's heartbreak matches mine as Addison speaks.

"Right. But you could tell Rosie?"

"It's just about her work, is all," I try to clarify. She purses her lips, analyzing and seeing all too much of me. I know my guilt is written all over my face and she can see it. Eventually, she nods.

"Okay. Guess you'll tell me when you're ready." She forces a smile and turns to leave. I let go of a huge breath and slump against the sink as my head drops and I cover my eyes.

"You need to sort that out, and fast. I hated lying to her, as much as I would hate lying to you." I look up to see Rosie with hurt and anger in her eyes. A sprinkle of pity in there, too.

"What the hell is going on, Casey? It's one thing to keep it quiet, but it's a whole other ball game to outright lie to our best friend."

"I know, I know. I'm so sorry," I whisper and squeeze my eyes closed so I don't drop any of the tears that want to leave.

"Don't be sorry. Just be better." She punctuates with a little pat on the shoulder and her stupid line has me almost chuckling.

She waits a beat, but leaves me alone. In the bathroom. Staring at myself in the mirror, I shake my head slowly. "What a mess."

I leave the bathroom and make my way back to the table. Seeing them all sitting there laughing and talking, the exhaustion sits heavy in my bones. I just want to go home. I grab my coat and bag when I make it to the table and push my chair back in, noting that Noah and Addison have already left.

"I think I'm going to head out. I'm beat." I give my best smile, but before I can turn, Jessie is out of his chair and grabbing his coat.

"Oh, you don't have to leave. You can stay." Because he looked like he was finally relaxed and enjoying himself, I don't want to take that away from him. Instead of answering, he levels me with a, *'yeah right,'* kind of look which makes me smirk and relent. I was super looking forward to his big snuggles, anyway.

He helps me into my coat and grabs my hand, interlacing his fingers with mine, and waves goodbye to our friends. Rosie gives me a pitying smile, her eyes all the warning I need. Fix it, and fast.

What the hell am I going to do?

35

Jessie

"You have to add it in gradually and mix slowly, otherwise it'll curdle the mixture." Casey's gentle voice fills my small kitchen as she walks me through the recipe.

"I *am* mixing it slowly."

"You are not. You're mixing like a caveman." Laughter lightens her tone. The melody of it has the blood humming through my veins, my lungs inflating with the way she breathes life into me.

The last few weeks have gone past in a blur, but they have been by far the best few weeks of my life. I knew loving Casey was going to be the best and easiest thing I had ever done. Seeing her smile, hearing her laugh, listening to the gasps she makes when she reads, the look of concentration when she bakes, and the way her brows furrow slightly as she sleeps, those perfect pink lips pouted. How I know she's had a hard day from the way she walks through the front door and falls into my arms without greeting. When she cries in the shower like I'm not going to climb in there and hold her. How she can sense my frustration, anger and insecurity, and can ease it through touch, a small scratch at the back of my neck, baking something sweet, or reading me something from my classics collection. Casey and I feel like a puzzle that has had a missing piece, and it's finally slid into place. I realized that whatever I had felt for Jenny pales in comparison to the way I feel for Casey. Love doesn't even quite fit it. That word feels too small.

"You usually like my caveman skills," I retort, forgetting about the mixture in the bowl and turning to lift Casey onto the counter, baking mess be damned. She squeals at the unexpected movement, but promptly wraps her legs around my waist from where she sits on the counter and giggles as I pull her top over her head, unclasping her bra, and descending my mouth on her perfectly perky tits.

"I fucking love these." I bite her nipple and she gasps, arching up into me.

"*Jess.*"

I groan, rapidly turning into the caveman she accused me of being at the sound of her moan mixed with her light giggles and gasps for air.

"The... flour, it's, *oh god*...everywhere," she breathes as my hands roam her back, torso, finding their way to her hair, her neck, and I take her lips in a demanding kiss.

"Jessie," she whispers.

"Sunshine," I whisper back, and I can feel her smile into our kiss, her tongue dancing with mine in a loving caress. Her breath deepens, her hips searching as she grips my hair.

"I wan—"

The sound of Casey's phone ringing interrupts us, and I nearly growl at the fucking thing. I was very much interested in where this was headed. Casey pulls back, panting and chuckling.

"It's Rosie, and she is anti phone calls. I really should take it," she breathes and bites her lip because she knows I'm about ready to bust a nut right fucking now. I let go of a breath and my forehead hits her collarbone as she reaches over and grabs her phone.

Not letting her go from where she is trapped on the counter, I continue to pepper light kisses across her delicate skin, leaving little licks and bites, my left hand combing through the soft curls of her auburn hair, the other roaming the expanse of her bare chest and stomach.

I fucking love this woman. Every. Single. Inch.

"Hey, Rosie. What... uh, what are you—want?" Casey tries to ask between breaths, distracted by my tour of her body.

"Huh? They... wait, what?" She sits up straighter and manages to shove a hand at my chest to push me back. I oblige reluctantly and release a light chuckle at the exasperated look she gives me, trying to get me to stop so she can focus, but then her face drops in shock. I drop the pursuit of my desire, and instead move toward her in concern, handing her back her top and bra as she continues to listen to Rosie.

"Okay. Yep, I'm on my way." She hangs up and rushes around the apartment the moment she jumps from the counter. As she storms past me again, I have to grab her elbow, pulling her back into the safety of my arms. Feeling her heart race, I frame her face with my hands so I have a moment to drown in those blue eyes.

"What is it, Ace?"

"Oh, um... my parents. They turned up at our apartment." She pulls a tight smile, eyes searching mine.

"Oh." *Why am I nervous-sweating right now?*

"Yeah. Um... so I should probably go." She shrugs, biting her lip, which is kind of pouted from where my hands grip her face. It's super adorable, so I can't help myself but give her a quick kiss, finally letting her go and grabbing my coat.

"What are you doing?"

"I'm coming with you, obviously."

"Why?"

"Well, I haven't seen Bev in over a decade. Maybe she brought treats?" I flick her a wink, trying to swallow my nervous energy, because Casey is about to be nervous enough for the both of us. I quickly move to put the cold ingredients we have out back in the fridge. Remembering those containers of delicious pastries Casey's mom used to give her any time she came over to see Addison. Poor girls never had enough because I had polished them off every time. I definitely knew where Case got her cooking and baking skills from.

"Oh, you don't have to come. Really, you should stay." I tilt my head, assessing her from where she fusses with her scarf and boots.

"Ace, you wouldn't be avoiding introducing me to your parents as your boyfriend, would you?" I'm not offended, it's actually slightly amusing seeing her anxious about us, but my heart does beat a little faster when I see her go rigid at the mention of the b-word and even more so when she avoids making eye contact.

"Casey." The demand in my voice a little deeper this time. I don't want to invade her personal space if she is freaking out, but I need her to focus on me so that we can work this out together. Like we always do.

"Uhh, we hadn't said anything about labels." Her voice is nervous, the insecurity in her voice refreshing, and it gets me to take a step forward. When I'm just before her, our toes nearly touching, her chin tipped back and those pretty eyes sparkling up at me, I let an easy smile show. I reach a hand forward to tangle a finger with her thumb and twist my ring that sits there, in an effort to comfort her. I've seen her fidget with it when she is anxious, and every time, the tips of her lips curl as they do now, and she takes a big breath.

"Are you okay with labels?" I ask gently, and she shrugs slightly, biting her cheek nervously.

I search her face and try to read her thoughts, the mind that tries to figure out what everyone wants and needs and very rarely makes her own known. I've gotten especially good at reading her, so when I see the small pull of her eyebrows, that little crease in her chin, I can see everything she is trying to hide from me.

"I'm not going anywhere, Casey. You can call me boyfriend, or you can call me Jessie. You can call me JJ, Jay, Jess, caveman, whatever. The name or label or tease doesn't matter, the only thing that does is that every one of them is yours. I am yours." With my fingers twisting her ring, I use my other hand to tuck an errant hair behind her ear and give her the smile I know makes her wild. She heaves a sigh and leans into me, dropping her head to my chest, and I wrap my arms around her tightly.

"What's scaring you?" I ask quietly, leaving little kisses in her floral scented hair.

"That you couldn't possibly love me like I love you. That I am too much to take care of and you'll resent me. That you'll leave for something bigger and better when it comes along."

I feel my heart drop and my stomach bottom out.

"This all just feels way too good to be true. Too easy. I... I'm scared to go deeper, because I won't survive you, Jessie." Her voice feels so quiet and so contradictory to the strong version of Casey that I know so well. When I pull back, I see that worry lining her eyes, and even though I know smiling is probably inappropriate, it just warms me slightly that she feels as scared to lose me as I do her.

"I wouldn't survive you either, sunshine." I kiss the tip of her petite nose. "Love seems too small a word for what I feel for you." I kiss her pretty pink cheek. "You'll never be too much for me. Caring for you is one of my favorite things to do." I kiss her other cheek. "And if you fall deeper, I promise I'll already be there waiting to catch you." I wait for her eyes to meet mine so she can see it in my eyes, the way she has my heart entirely in her hand. It's hers to do what she pleases with.

The corners of her lips tip up again, and gradually, it grows into a stunning smile, and she reaches up on the tips of her toes, giving me her soft lips, which I take immediately. Sealing the promises.

"So, you're... my boyfriend?" she asks, scrunching up her face. The look causing a chuckle to release from me.

I nod gently but ask, "Do you want me to be?"

"Yeah, I think I do," she responds. "Because that makes me your girlfriend, and I like the sound of that. Jessie's girlfriend." She bites her lip and my desire from before comes roaring back.

She could be my girlfriend for right now.

But, in this moment, I knew, one day, Casey Baker was going to be my wife.

36

seriously, who says 'item' these days

Casey

"Okay, just breathe, and relax, and everything will be fine. There is *nothing* to worry about at all. Because this is normal. It's totally normal to start dating your best friend's older brother. My dad met you when I was fourteen and you were twenty, so I'm sure he isn't going to care about that *at all*. I am—"

"Baby, just breathe." He wraps his arms around my shoulders from where he stands behind me on the outside of my apartment door. Because I am a huge chicken, who is now a rambling bunch of nerves. I am never scared of my parents. But for some reason, I just really, really want them to love Jessie, and I really don't want them to judge or hate. It's not like anything ever happened when we were kids. I was just a hormonal teen and Jessie was–*is*–so fucking gorgeous. It was impossible not to crush on him. And now that I know his soul, it would be literally impossible not to fall in love with him. Like I already have.

This nickname, though? I could love that, too. Ace? Panty melter. Sunshine? Swoons and internally sighs. But, *baby?* Dies as heart explodes.

"You forget, they already love me, anyway. I know Bev packed extra pastries in there for me every time." He gives me a delicate kiss on the neck, then reaches ahead of me and opens the front door, not giving me the time to spiral further.

We enter the apartment, and I speed walk into the kitchen.

"Hi, Mom," I call to her from where she sits on the couch with the girls, and she leaps up and jogs over to me, wrapping me into a tight hug. "My baby girl! Oh, I missed you," she says as she squeezes the life out of me. I pat her back, chuckling.

"I missed you, too, Mom."

"There's my angel." Dad's deep baritone hits me from the hall and wastes no time in circling us in a group hug, his height being where I got mine from, and he towers over us in a tight, loving hug, the familiar smell of them both giving me a pang of nostalgia in the chest.

"Oh, hey, Jessie. I didn't know you were joining us, too?" Mom asks from over my shoulder, and my palms are instantly sweaty.

"Hey, Bev, lovely to see you again." He leans in from behind me, leaving a polite kiss on her cheek. "I knew there'd be delicious treats if you were in town." His smile is *devastating,* and Mom is no more immune to his charm than I am, and she hits his shoulder. Pulling on his trademark smile, Jessie turns his attention to dad.

"Tony, long time." He shakes my dad's hand, who pulls him in for one of those bro-hug pat on the backs that young people do, and I think this is his attempt at being '*up with the kids*', but Jessie lets him, the same comfortable smile they give each other, still there.

"Good to see you, Jessie." Dad nods at him. "How's the café?" Hands are now on the hip and he is ready to settle into a deep discussion about business. *Ugh.*

"The café is great," I finish, ready to just rip the band-aid off this so I can stop freaking out like a child. "Anyway, we have to tell you something." Addison and Rosie are standing from the couch so fast. Addison has wide eyes, and Rosie looks like she does on Christmas morning: mouth agape, heart eyes, and brimming with energy as she physically restrains herself from jumping on the spot.

"Jessie and I are together." I don't know *why* that sounded like a business announcement. And why my arms are crossed this way?

I move my arms to hang by my side, but then that feels too weird. I move them to rest on my hips. But now I look like mom when she is lecturing me. I cross my arms again. *What the hell? Why am I so weird right now?*

Jessie's snort chuckle from behind me has me spinning and pinning him with a stern look, and I make a mental note to punish him later. Something creative. Like reading about Baseball Daddy while I'm naked, with a no-touching rule in place. I'm sure he won't be laughing *then.* Jessie has his hands tucked into the pockets of his jeans, his lips pulled into a smug smile, as he quickly squeezes his eyes shut. Laughter sputters from where Addison and Rosie are now hiding behind the couch, and Jessie finally breaks the awkward silence.

"Uhh... not how I thought that was going to come out." He steps up next to me, and returning my attention back to my parents, I see Mom with a pout, trying to suppress a smile, but Dad's face is unreadable.

"You guys are an item?" Dad questions, looking only at Jessie. *Who the hell says 'item' these days?*

To Jessie's credit, he doesn't falter. He stands up straight, matching Dad's energy, and nods. "We are."

"Since when?" Dad pushes, and I nervously bite my lip. Before I can intervene, Jessie continues.

"A month or so." *Liar.*

"How?" At Dad's question, Jessie smiles easily and looks at me for a moment before he looks back to my dad, that smile stuck in place.

"How could I not?" he responds, and Mom covers her mouth, her eyes failing to hide the size of her smile.

Dad nods, and his smile grows slowly. "Good answer, son." He shakes Jessie's hand again and then heads for the fridge. "Beer?"

"Love one," Jessie responds, leaning in to give me a kiss on the forehead, then follows my dad to the kitchen.

Mouth agape, brain traveling one hundred miles an hour, I return my attention to mom, the girls now coming our way from the couch.

"I knew you two would find a way," Mom coos.

"They're adorable, aren't they?" Rosie says as she slings an arm around Mom's shoulders.

"Disgusting, sure. But I'm happy for them." Addison winks at me with a sad smile. We still haven't smoothed over everything that went down in the bathroom of Pucks, and I can feel the tension and irritation radiating from where she stands, arms crossed and leaning against the wall of the entryway.

"Yeah, it's only new, though. And I don't really know how it all happened, but I—"

I stop, freezing, realizing this will be the first time saying it to someone that isn't Jessie. The realization that we aren't in our bubble anymore, that it isn't just us. It makes it real.

"I really love him," I whisper quietly, and Mom leaps in to hug me while Rosie screws up her nose while smiling and Addison fights away tears.

"Okay, so tomorrow night, I say we meet at Lucas's, because he is closer to the bar. We start out at Bozzelli's, and then see where the night takes us," Rosie plots from her spot on the couch. We ended up ordering pizza, having a few drinks, and are now all snuggled on the couch with the heater blasting. Jessie kept a respectful distance most of the night until we moved to the couch. Like he was done with the *'above the waist'* only touching. The moment we moved to the couch, he had me tucked into his side, my legs swung over his lap as he massaged my calves.

"What is this for?" I question.

"Your birthday, obviously," Addison clarifies.

"Oh, that's lovely! We were hoping we could take you and Grace out for dinner on Sunday? I know everyone will be busy on the 24th, so I don't want to make any plans on that day," Mom suggests. No, of course, no one would risk ruining their Christmas Eve to celebrate me on my actual birthday.

I give Mom a tight smile and nod. "Sure, sounds good."

"You're welcome to come, too, Jessie."

"Thanks, Bev, I'd love to come," he replies. "I'm also stealing Casey on Christmas Eve, too," he says to everyone except me.

"What for?" I look up at him, and he returns the look below hooded eyes, his bluey-greens shimmering with desire as his hands continue their delicious torture on my legs.

"Birthday surprise." He punctuates with a wink, and I fold my lips into my mouth to stop myself from pouncing on him in front of everyone.

"Anyway!" Rosie almost shouts, getting the attention back on her, Addison and I chuckling at her look of indignation. "Tomorrow night?"

"Sure, sounds fun." I shrug, and my head falls to Jessie's chest.

Rosie sees the gesture, so she makes sure to clarify. "This is a girls' night, though. We don't need men out here ruining our fun."

"Noah is going to rock up, anyway," Addison says with a sigh as her head hits the couch. "Wouldn't matter that I said no guys, he'd pretend to be there for Caleb." Her smile tells me she secretly loves that, and I have a feeling there will be another caveman there, doing exactly the same thing.

"You good with not being invited?" I ask up at Jessie with a knowing smirk, reveling in the dirty look he is giving Rosie. As expected, he avoids actual words and grunts instead.

"Probably hang out with Noah." *There it is.* We all end up in a fit of giggles and Rosie just rolls her eyes.

"Bunch of insecure pussies," she mutters.

"Don't judge yet Rosie. Wait until you have your very own drooling idiot worshiping the ground you walk on. You'll understand one day," I clarify, and it earns me a pinch that has me smacking Jessie's chest.

"In my defense, you're also completely unaware of your surroundings," he accuses, but a smirk hides under that look.

"I am not! I know exactly what is going on."

"Oh, Casey." My dad sighs, shaking his head and chuckling.

"Excuse me!" I pull my legs from Jessie's lap to cross them and nudge his shoulder while he laughs. "I am very aware. Thank you."

"I've seen you out and watched as you made your way around. You're oblivious to the way people watch you. Noah's birthday is a prime example, and you *know* I was right about the bartender." He bops a finger on the top of my nose. *Ugh,* I hate when he's right. Might have to up that punishment later.

"I don't care what you men do, but if I see you trying to steal the women away, I will end you." Rosie levels at Jessie, and Addison and I chuckle. "Tomorrow night is for the girls, and I don't even want to smell your stupid cologne." That makes mom snort, and Dad's chuckle rumbles through the room.

Jessie raises his hands in surrender, smiling at Rosie, before looking back at me and pulling me back into his arms. "You just let me know when you're done and I'll come get you."

"We'll Uber, it'll be late." Rosie waves him off, sipping her wine, and it makes me smile because I know his response before he says it.

"I don't care what time it is, I'll be there." She just rolls her eyes at him, but I can see Dad's small nod of approval. I do love my independence, but I'd be lying if I said I don't love how Jessie is slightly overprotective of me.

"Well, we'll get out of your hair," Mom states as she stands, Dad following.

"Where are you guys staying?" I ask. I had assumed they would stay in my bed and I'd crash with Addison or Rosie, like usual.

"We have a hotel a few blocks down, we'll catch an Uber," Dad clarifies. "We didn't want to intrude," he says, giving me a pointed look before his eyes dart from me to Jessie, then back again.

"How did you know there was anything to intrude on?" I ask, head tilted to the side.

He doesn't respond, just turns and looks at Mom.

"Mom?"

"Well, you mentioned something about a boy back in November. I didn't know who or how serious, so I thought we'd be safer if we got our own room." She winks at me and grabs her coat, Dad following.

"You brag about me to your mom, then about my cock to the girls? I think you're obsessed with me, sunshine," Jessie whispers in my ear, and I feel my cheeks heat.

"Maybe I was bragging about my other boyfriend." I raise my eyebrows at him as I turn and see his face drop into a dark look at the challenge. He just grunts in response, and I pat myself on the back. *Punishment is underway.*

Jessie, the gentleman he is, helps Mom into her coat, opens the door, and walks them down to the front of the building. I hang back with Rosie and Addison, no longer able to handle the tension that is practically flooding from Addison. I turn and try to communicate just how sorry I really am.

"I know you are mad at me right now, and I'm so sorry for how things went down at Pucks. I—"

"It's exhausting being angry, and I have enough of that for things that deserve it," she says with a gentle smile while rolling her eyes.

"Well... thank you for tonight and for... being so cool about all of this," I say through a tight smile to Addison.

"I spoke to my therapist. I don't know what your secret is, but you can have it. I know you'll tell me when you're ready, or maybe it's even better. I don't know. I know you wouldn't keep something from me that would hurt me and I'm choosing to just love you, anyway."

"Aw, Ads, that was cute." Rosie wraps an arm around Addison, who just chuckles and wipes a tear from under her eye. "I'm still working on the anger thing, so just bear with me if I snap at you or just randomly start crying." She laughs and I go in for another hug, grateful to be back on some semi-normal ground with her.

Jessie makes it back into the apartment and manages to pull me away from the girls, hiding us away in my room.

"Wasn't so bad, was it?" he asks, circling his arms around my waist and backing me up to the bed. My arms find the back of his neck, and when my knees hit the mattress, we stop, not yet falling, content in peering at each other.

"I guess it wasn't," I whisper.

He just shakes his head, a ghost of a smile on his face as his eyes search my entire face.

"What?" I prompt, matching his smile and drawing my bottom lip through my teeth. My stomach does that thing with the butterflies when I see the way the lines of his eyes crease with his smile, the way his jaw clenches and eyes hood when his eyes latch on my lips.

"It's just... I don't know how to say it," he says quietly, self-consciousness knots his words, so I pull him closer.

"Close your eyes," I whisper and pull his head toward mine, so our foreheads touch. Standing on the tips of my toes, we stay there for a breath. "Tell me in the way that you can. Tell me through great poets or classic literature. Let them tell me." I can feel his smile as we stay embraced with each other. I feel his heart race from where our chests touch. I feel his desire where his hands roam my lower back, and every so often, my ass. I scratch the back of his neck delicately and comb my fingers through the hair there, and after a few breaths, he speaks.

"*'And it was only when I began to feel actual, physical pain every time you left the room that it finally dawned on me: I was in love, for the first time in my life.'*" My eyes snap open, and I watch him whisper the words of his heart, his eyes gently closed, his smile bright and cheeks flushed with vulnerability. Unable to keep my eyes closed, unable to miss this, I watch him as he continues. "*'I knew it was hopeless, but that didn't matter to me. And it's not that I want to have you. All I want is to deserve you. Tell me what to do. Show me how to behave. I'll do anything you say.'*"

I take a steadying breath, basking in the silence for a few heartbeats, and watch as the man I love bares his entire soul to me.

"Choderlos de Laclos, *Dangerous Liaisons*," I whisper as a tear drops from my eye. Feeling the weight of his words, the insurmountable pressure of holding his delicate heart in my hands. This man, who has spent so much time closed off to everything in life, is finally opening up to everything he'd denied himself. And it's all for me, all mine. I have to breathe deeply to settle my heart, to tell myself we can do this, that I can handle that, because that's what love is.

Jessie catches my lone tear the moment his eyes open and lock with mine.

"Why are you crying, baby?" His eyebrows pull in tighter.

"Because it still doesn't feel real. That you could love me like this."

"You don't believe you are deserving?" I shake my head at his question, and he tilts his in confusion.

"It's not the deserving, it's you. That *you* could see me and want me. To feel so deeply, for *me*. I used to dream about you just being *interested* in me. It just... feels like a fantasy," I whisper back, my heart ricocheting in my chest at the emotions flooding this room, the way it feels like Jessie has completely intertwined himself in my heart. I couldn't possibly get him out now, even if I tried my darndest. He is stuck with me.

"The way you have my heart and soul, sunshine, is the realest thing I've ever felt." He leans down and kisses me gently, whispering his next words to my lips. "I was frozen, moving through time just existing. But with you beside me, burning, glowing, you melted right through all my ice and made me feel again. You brought me back to life. I never cared much about fighting for a future, but when that looks like you, I'll fight as hard as I need to keep you." My nails dig into his scalp as I pull him down to my lips, sealing his words the only other way I know to tell him how I feel. That my heart is his, he is in me, under my skin, surrounding me completely, and I never want to be without him ever again.

"Jessie—"

He reaches the back of my thighs and lifts me, my legs wrapping around his waist, and he gently lowers me to the bed.

He looks down at me, our bodies completely touching, burning, my breathing matching the pounding of his heart against my chest as he takes my lips in a demanding kiss. His hand trails up my outer thigh as the other finds a circle around my neck.

"I'd spent so long hiding from hope." He kisses each of my cheeks, gently scraping his teeth across my jaw before he rises up to hover his lips above mine. "I hadn't realized I had been hiding from you. I'm done hiding, Casey. I want this, all of it. I only want it with you, and I want it forever." I can't pinpoint the reason, but there is pain in his words, so much longing and pain, and my heart catches when I spot the moisture welling in his eyes. Unable to bear it any longer, I frame his sharp jaw with my hands and pull him closer so I can whisper the words against his lips. "It's like I said. Our forever has already started." And then I take him in a kiss. He kisses me with such skill, his tongue tangling with mine, his taste of the dessert mom had baked, the sweet cream and just *him*. A moan leaves my lips, and it undoes his composure just that little bit more as he pulls back and rips his shirt from his back. He sits on his knees and raises one of my feet.

"You have cute little toes." He points out and I laugh self-consciously. But his eyes never leave mine as he pulls at the cuff of my tights, raising my other foot to do the same and when they are both loose, he lazily drags them down my legs, his gaze burning through mine, the blue of them glowing in the low light of my room.

"Your thighs are the sexiest I've ever seen," he states as he leans forward, tights discarded on the floor and kisses a path slowly up the inside of my right thigh. I gasp the closer he gets to my center, reaching a hand under my shirt, massaging a breast as he continues his trail up my left thigh. Dodging the one place where I want him most, I can feel the smile of satisfaction on his face and the hard bulge nudging my leg. When he looks up at me through hooded eyes, his devastatingly handsome smile hits me as his teeth latch onto the strap of my panties. He starts to pull them down, slowly, warm breath leaving a trail of need in its wake, the scratch of his beard a painful tease making my back arch, searching for friction.

I feel hot all over, like a live wire loaded with energy. When I feel my panties leave my legs, I manage to look down and see him staring hungrily between my legs.

"But this? Fuck, Casey. I fucking *love* your pussy." He drags a lazy finger through the middle of me. The sound of how badly I want him is almost embarrassing, but I am so taken by my need for him I can't find it in me to care.

"Please, *Jessie,*" I beg.

"Please, what?" he challenges, a dirty smile on his face as he sits smugly between my legs, his fingers playing with me like it's nothing, like I'm not about to come apart after a few small touches and dirty words.

"Make love to me?" I ask on a gentle whisper, for some reason overcome with emotion. Not feeling the animalistic desire, but something completely new. It's deep and raw. It hurts, but in a way where I never want it to stop hurting.

He sees everything running through my head. Peeling his pants and boxers from his body, he leans forward, pulling my top and bra from me and hovers over me.

"*Stella mea,*" he whispers the language I haven't heard before, as he lines himself up and gives one gentle push, stealing the gasp from my lips with the seal of his. The moment he fills me completely, he moves his hips out slightly, rotating and circling to make room and picking up the pace.

"You somehow end me and breathe life into me all at once." He kisses me gently, his tongue dancing at the seam of my lips until it finds mine. He kisses me fervently, and I feel every word he says right to my bones. It feels like he too has brought me back to life, like breaching the surface in the ocean, finally able to breathe again.

The delicate passion of his kiss turns into a desperate need, his gentle caressing hands gripping my hips and growling as he slams into me harder, faster.

"My." *Thrust.* "Fucking." *Thrust.* "Woman." *Thrust.*

"Yours," I all but moan. "I'm yours, *Jess.* Always."

He thrusts harder again as I hook my legs around his waist tightly and pushing up with all my weight, throwing him to his back, never letting him leave me, and when I settle on top of him, impaled completely my head drops back on a moan as I guide myself up and down a few times.

"So fucking beautiful," he whispers as I rotate my hips, looking down to see those magnificent blue-green eyes. I feel the rapid beat of his heart, my own personal love song.

"You feel so fucking good," I whisper back.

His fingers dig into my hips as he encourages my movements, his eyes tracing my entire body, from my lips to my breasts that bounce slightly, to where we are joined, and then he places a finger to my clit, massaging me gently. Edging me even closer to the precipice.

A strangled moan leaves my lips as he sits up, taking a breast into his mouth and pulling it gently with his teeth. His hands firmly on my ass and bouncing me on his cock. "*Fuck* Case."

His hands fist my hair and pull my lips to him, and before I know it, I'm on my back again. Jessie's arms wrapped firmly around my hips as he sits on his knees and pistons into me at speed.

"I fucking love you. If you ever leave, I hope you're ready for a stalker, because I'll chase you to the ends of the earth." He thrusts hard again, my mind losing all sensibility, and I claw at his back.

"*Oh, shit!* Jess!"

"Yes, that's it. *Fuck,* you feel so good." He trails his teeth down my neck, leaving light kisses in their wake.

"Come with me, Jess." I pant in his ear as I squeeze my eyes shut, feeling the tingles travel my spine and my toes going numb. I trail my hand down his back and find his ass, pushing him deeper. "Harder. *Fuck,* harder, please!" I beg.

He delivers on a growl, lifting my hips from the mattress and fucking into me. I love him. I feel it like an ache in my chest, but *fuck,* I love his cock.

He adjusts his hips to hit upward, and the orgasm hits me like a bomb detonating. Cursing on a scream he slams a hand over my lips to smother it, and when I manage to peel open an eyelid, I see his head tipped back, his bottom lip pulled in to smother his own roar and I feel him come apart inside me.

Jessie's firm torso collapses forward, his weight caught on the arm above my head, and he gently kisses my shoulders.

"*Stella mea,*" he whispers again.

"What is that?" I ask quietly, still trying to catch my breath. Without withdrawing, he rolls on to his back, pulling me with him. A little moan at the friction while he's still seated inside me. Not wanting to sever the connection, I leave him there and let myself fall onto his chest and nuzzle into the gap between his chin and collarbone. He wraps his arms around me firmly, and when he catches his breath, he answers.

"My star."

the caveman gives an epic orgasm

Casey

Sound in the kitchen stirs me awake, the heavy arm thrown over me, pulling me back in has a sigh of contentment leaving my lips. I roll over and let Jessie's arms hold me firmly.

"You're holding me like I might escape," I say quietly to him, not hiding the gigantic smile spreading across my face.

"You might." His voice rough with sleep, eyes still closed with his face held in his usual sleepy frown, and still, even without seeing, he knows where to find my lips and leans down to steal them in a kiss.

"Why would I ever leave when you kiss me like that?" I tease as his hands find my ass in a gentle slap.

"I thought it was my big muscles and winning personality that kept you around?" His eyes start to open and the light in them is unmistakable. I hum lightly as he pulls me in tighter. "Yeah, that helps, too," I respond, scrunching my nose and quickly kissing him again before untangling myself from said strong muscles.

"Why on earth are you leaving this perfectly comfortable bed right now?" He groans, his eyes traveling my body, still naked from last night's escapades. With a smug tilt of his lips, he sits up and rests his head on his hand, watching as I pull on his shirt.

"And why are you putting clothes on that incredible body? I much prefer you naked." I leap onto the bed and smack his chest.

"You're naughty." I giggle as he takes the opportunity to wrap me up and flip me over, pinned under him.

"So naughty. What's my punishment?" He winks and bites my neck gently before licking away the sting and trailing my skin with kisses. I struggle to fight the moan and remind myself I was getting out of bed.

"It's about to be a sex ban if you don't let me go make a coffee." I giggle and manage to shove him off me. He grunts disapprovingly, but smacks my ass as he rolls over and pulls on a pair of his boxers.

Shaking my head and still laughing at the caveman lingering in my bedroom, I head into the kitchen and find Rosie attempting another bowl of cereal. The source of my wake-up call now discovered.

"Morning. Bet you slept well," she says over her shoulder, her attention leaving the milk, which is a bad decision.

"What are you talking about?" I ask, practically skipping into the kitchen, feeling light, happy, and altogether like myself again. "Also, watch what you're doing. We don't need another spilt milk situation."

She rolls her eyes and focuses back on the milk carton she now has unscrewed and I reach into the fridge to find the fruit and batter mix for pancakes, flicking on the coffee machine to heat a pot.

"Please, I think the concierge heard you and Jessie last night," she accuses, disgust lining her tone, and I nearly drop all the fruit as I place them on the counter and spin to look at Rosie.

"What!?" I whisper-shout.

"*Fuck, harder, oh, Jessie, you're so BIG!*" Rosie starts making sex noises, and I have to loudly slap a hand over her mouth and shoosh her.

"Oh my god! For a start, I never said that last bit," I scold, my cheeks feeling very hot even in the dead of winter.

"May as well have," she says under her breath.

"Oh, god, how embarrassing." I cover my face.

"The only thing embarrassing about it is that it sounds like you're having better sex than me. And that is not okay." She shakes her head, her tight curls bouncing around her shoulders, and it makes me giggle.

"Well, don't say anything when he comes out here because I'd like to keep having great sex, and he won't do that here if he thinks you can hear him."

"I'm sure the caveman loves everyone knowing he can deliver epic orgasms with his huge cock."

"He does." Jessie's amused response has me choking on air and my cheeks turning a shade of red that'd give Rosie's favorite lipstick a run for its money.

"Oh my god." I cover my face with my hands, and Rosie just starts giggling under her breath.

"Good job, Jenkins. You might be alright after all," she says in his direction. I can hear his amused laugh but refuse to look up from my hands. I feel his entire body surround me, like I always do when he is near me. His scent, his warmth, the desire and lust that radiates from him send shivers over my whole body.

"I more so love everyone knowing that you're mine," he whispers in my ear.

"Ugh, see? Caveman." Rosie rolls her eyes and takes her cereal to the counter, where she sits on a bar stool.

"Coffee?" he asks, after thoroughly satisfying himself with my mortification. I nod and go to make the pancakes.

"None for me, Ace. I have to head to the café." He kisses my cheek and pulls out two mugs.

"Oh, you're not staying for breakfast?" I hate how pathetically sad it makes me to miss him, and he hasn't even left yet. It just reminds me of the quote he had used when he couldn't find the words; *I began to feel physical pain every time you left the room.* A little kernel of warmth replaces the sad, knowing that he feels this as deeply as I do. That it isn't one sided. He won't abandon me or resent me. We're in this together. On the same page and *finally* my future is something I can't wait for.

"I'll grab something on the way, or I'll eat at the café. Need to get the stock sorted before we close over Christmas, and the online store goes live today."

"Oh, that is so exciting!" I jump up and down. I hug him from behind from where he stands at the coffee machine, and he finishes pouring the two cups. He turns, a light smile on his lips, and places a cup in my hands. His eyes trail hungrily down my body, and I feel it tingle all over my skin. I have to sip my coffee to hide the blush on my cheeks.

"Mmm. I like you in my shirt," he says deeply, reaching out to fist the shirt, pulling me into him and leaning forward for a kiss. He manages a swift slap to my ass before he heads back to my bedroom. *Sighs.*

I watch him, and when his back disappears behind the closed door of my bedroom, I have to bite my lip to suppress the squeal that wants to leave. The overwhelming excitement, the way my heart sings with joy, it really does feel unbelievable that this is my life. That Jessie is mine.

"Good lord. You two are worse than Noah and Addison."

"What is that supposed to mean?" I giggle at her and round the corner to sit next to her at the counter.

"So romantic, so swoony, so yuck and all in love." She rolls her shoulders. "Don't you get sick of each other? Like all the cuddling and the cliché declarations, being in each other's space all the time?" she questions, and when I look at her properly, her face is pulled into disgust. *She might be serious?*

"Of course not." I chuckle at her. "I think of it like everyone's soul speaks a unique language, and Jessie learnt how to speak to mine with his. I've never been known by someone like how he knows me. It feels—"

"Yeah, that will do." Rosie holds her hand up. "I have enough romances on my plate at the moment, and you're ruining my running story dialogue." I tilt my head in confusion and she waves a hand around as she clarifies. "You know? Like, if I'm stuck in a hard part of a story that has some developmental holes, and I'm trying to help the writer, I carry it in my head. I work through it, talk through the dialogue, try to come up with the fix, try to picture it organically."

"Why don't you write books, Rosie? you sound like you'd be very good at it." I shake my head in amazement at her.

"Absolutely not. I like to pick at people's work, not create my own. That's too much." I just roll my eyes and finish my coffee as Rosie dives back into her cereal.

"Oh, while I'm thinking of it, that manuscript you gave me, I have excellent news. The editor picked it! They want to make an offer to the writer, talk about some developmental things and all that. You need to give me a name and some contact info!" Her smile grows, and I feel the blood rush from my face.

"Oh, uhh, I'll come back to you on that. Just forget it for now." I wave her off, praying to god she drops it, because I really needed to find a way to tell Jessie about my moment of stupidity without ruining our little bubble of perfection.

"You're kidding?" She pulls back, her eyes searching mine. "Wait, did you write it?"

"What?! No way. How could I write a book?"

"But it would make sense. All the secrecy, the love, the hurt, the pain, and the pining for something bigger, deeper." She pretend-coughs to clear her throat and puts on her best actress voice as she recites a line, "'*Feeling vacant internally only to realize the person you held space for wasn't what you had been waiting for at all. But another heart was out there, whispering your name. A heart you couldn't find nor claim—*'"

"Shh! Those aren't my words, Rosie," I assure her.

"Those are my words."

My head snaps in Jessie's direction, and Rosie chokes on the spoonful of cereal she is shoving into her mouth. You could hear a pin drop in the deathly silence that takes over our apartment.

My feet find the floor, but it feels like I'm walking on clouds. I can't feel my face, can't hear anything other than the sound of the blood rushing in my ears. Jessie's face–shock and pain.

"Jessie," I urge, heading toward him, but he doesn't reach for me. He just stands there, letting me grab his arms, trying to force him to look at me, touch me, hold me. Something.

He looks at Rosie, and I have no idea what look she gives him, but he looks down at me.

"You found my manuscript?" he says, a world of hurt behind those words.

I nod and a tear escapes. He doesn't stop it or wipe it, like he normally would. He watches it trail my cheek and his brows furrow deeper.

"You gave my manuscript to Rosie?" he asks and, *God* if his voice isn't ripping my heart out of my chest.

"Jessie, I'm so sorry. Please, just let me explain. I'm so incredibly sorry. I didn't mean for this to happen—"

"What else did you think would happen?" His voice deepens, rising slightly with the anger that vibrates around him.

"I just found it." I can't stop the sob that leaves my lips. "I read it, Jess, it's so incr—"

"Don't do that right now." He pulls back from my arms and steps back, his face curling in anger. "Don't call me Jess. Don't use that name, you know what that does. That isn't fair." His chest rises and falls as fast as my heart beats out of my chest.

"Jessie, *please*," I beg, now properly sobbing. I can see him watch as each tear leaves my eyes. It feels like I'm suffocating. Like someone is sitting on my chest and I need... *oh, god.* I need Jessie to help me breathe. I reach for him again, but he steps back, his eyes vacantly looking at me. "I have to get to the shop," he says quietly. "I'll see you." Without a goodbye, a kiss, even the twist of my thumb ring to ease my mind, he leaves through the front door and I can't stop my knees as they buckle, and I hit the ground.

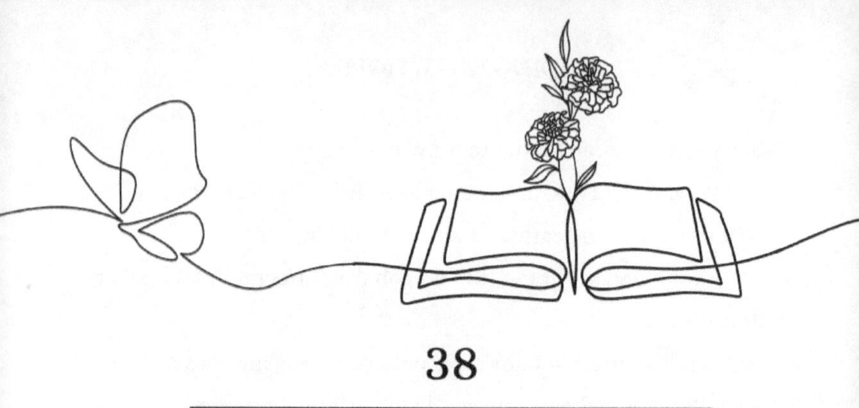

38

sixteen-year-old casey would murder me

Casey

My body shudders as I sob. It feels like I just ripped out my own heart. I can't breathe, I can't organize a thought. It hurts more than the fight with Grace. It hurts more than the words she said, than my parents avoiding celebrating my birthday because it's a day meant for everyone. It hurts more than Connor not giving me the effort I deserved.

"Breathe Casey. Just Breathe," Rosie whispers. "I'm so sorry. I had no idea. No wonder you wanted me to keep my big ass mouth closed." She pulls my hair from my shoulders and lets it fall down my back as I hunch over my knees.

"At least that explains the secret with Addy. She might thump you when she finds out." I don't even have the mental capacity to consider those consequences right now. It simply feels like there is a hole in my chest. "C'mon, let's go get freshened up and we can find a delicious hot coffee down the street," she suggests, but I just shake my head, trying to clear the fog and tears.

"I need to go after him. I need to explain." I go to stand, but Rosie grips my arm.

"That isn't a good idea, Case. He is pissed. He has rage like Addison with the pain of a heartbroken man. Give him space to calm down." I know she is right, but *I* can't breathe.

"But... what if that wasn't... he said he loves me. So, does that mean..." I can't even speak the words. I feel like I'm going to throw up. "We're still together... right?" I ask through a sob, and the sympathetic look on Rosie's face as she shrugs has the nausea rising with a vengeance.

The sobs continue to wrack my body, and I angrily wipe at my tears. How did this go so wrong so quickly? I should have stopped Rosie. I should have taken the manuscript back.

"Do you have it with you?"

She shakes her head. "I wasn't kidding before. The editor-in-chief loved it. He said it was what they needed to add to the romance genre. The heartbreak was pure and painful. It was relatable, with equal amounts of misery and hope. He wanted to make the author an offer. For publishing and for another book. He wants to take them on fully. Assign an editor, a PR team. Casey, Jessie could be a big name in literature. You need to get him to consider it."

"Rosie, this piece is so personal to him. There is no way he will want other people reading it. *God,* I don't know why I thought this would ever be a good idea. He is the most private person I know!" I am *such* an idiot.

"Who's the most private person you know?" Addison's husky morning voice fills the room, and I look over to find her tightening her robe around her waist and rubbing sleep from her eyes.

"Your brother," Rosie says gently, and when Addy looks at me and notices the tears, her eyes heat, her breaths coming in quicker.

"What did he do?" Her question is down right lethal.

"It wasn't him, Ads, it was me," I sob and wipe my tears, trying to pull my shit together. I owe her a proper explanation, not this half-assed crying mess. "The secret. It was me. It was about Jessie." I watch her face change, trying to understand. Her eyes are so intense, the green of them flares, her breathing intensifies, and she promptly strips her robe off, rubbing a frustrated hand down her face before silently waiting for an explanation.

I take a centering breath and explain everything. The existence of the manuscript, the night I found it, the idiotic decision to steal it and give it to Rosie to see if her publisher was interested. I tell her how I read it, explain how incredible it is. I try to move on to explain this morning, but the sobbing won't stop. I am now hiccupping and trying to control my breathing and instead, crying a mess into the sleeve of Jessie's shirt.

I note it still smells like him, and it just makes me cry harder.

Rosie proceeds to fill Addy in on this morning's events. To my shock, Addy's shoulders just drop, her brows falling, and a gentle smile hits her face before she quickly pads across the room and swings her arms around me. I instantly wrap mine around her, and she shooshes my wailing while rubbing circles on my back.

"It's going to be okay, Casey," she whispers.

"You don't know that. You didn't see his face," I sob in return. She pulls back and a pitying but humorous smile sits on her face before she squeezes my shoulders and steps back, nodding.

"But I do. I know him. It's going to be okay." Then she just turns and heads straight back into her room, leaving both Rosie and me completely dumbfounded. I look at Rosie and she shrugs.

"Well, at least you stopped crying?" I stare at her for a beat and then burst out with a laugh. She does the same and then brings me into her arms in a firm embrace.

Once again, a crying mess.

Oh, sixteen-year-old Casey would murder me if she could see me now.

"Hey, April, Jessie in?" I don't bother with the pleasantries. I could barely stop crying enough to be presentable in public, let alone ask someone how their day was. April turns to me from behind the counter and smiles.

"No, he took the day off." She shrugs and goes back to whatever she is doing behind the counter. I look around the shop, and they are slammed. April seems less than worried about the line of people waiting for their coffee or the stacks of boxes with stock needing to be put away, the pinging from the retail computer I assume are orders from the launch of the store that aren't being filled, but instead, she is twirling her hair and chatting to the person I *assume* she is making that coffee for.

"He just took the day off?" April looks at me again and shrugs. Wasn't he worried about the developer? About bringing in more money? It's freaking launch day?!

Heaviness sinks low in my stomach. I did this. This was my fault. I ruined him. I blew up his day, wrecked his heart, betrayed his trust. *Fuck.*

What if he loses the store because of *me?*

What if the online store is a massive flop all because I am the biggest idiot of them all?!

"Okay, throw me an apron." I gesture to April, making quick work of heading for the back room and swinging my hair into a topknot.

As I start to head for the counter, April tilts her head and looks at me funny. "What? You... you're working here?"

"April, I'm sure you're a lovely girl, but cute and ditzy aren't adorable anymore." Her spine straightens, and she drops the hair she was twirling. A light blush hits her cheeks. Glad to know my assumption was right; she was flirting instead of working. I level the other instigator with a look and he scurries off. Freaking kids these days.

"I know you're intelligent, so use that brain of yours and get back to work. We don't have time for this. Those three boxes over there have stock that needs to go up." I point to the boxes, and I see her work mode finally click into place, reading my tone and understanding that I mean business right now. "Have you filled any of those orders yet?" I ask, pointing to the register that has receipts printing like a madman. Reading the stern look on my face, she wastes no time answering and shaking her head. "Right, start there, collections first, then get the ones for shipping done before 4pm. Stock can be done after the rush."

"What about the coffee?"

"I could make coffee in my sleep," I mutter and pick the notepad and pen from her apron, shoving it to the front pocket of mine. I watch her dart behind the counter and head for the back, where I assume the packing and collection bags are. When I'm satisfied she has actually followed my instructions, I dig deep into my college days and all that time I spent at Oliver's Bean Roasters mastering those incredible latte flavors. I plaster my best anti-Addison sunshine smile on and turn to the line of customers.

"Thanks for waiting! What can I get you?"

"Coffee for Dave?" I shout and smile at the guy who collects the to-go order. Nodding, I clear behind the counter and head for the tables. The line has disappeared, the lunch rush now having ended, so I busy myself wiping tables.

"The orders are packed, and Jessie messaged me to flick it off for the rest of the afternoon."

My heart sinks that he has managed to message April but hasn't returned a single one of my texts or calls. It makes sense, though. I did this. It was my fault. I spent so long building him up, getting him to open up and trust people again, only to be the one who pulled the rug out from under him. *God.* I am the worst person in history.

He deserves so much better than me.

I continue wiping the table with my back to April, trying my best to rest my racing heart and not break down while on the clock. He has every right to be pissed at me, and I know this will likely be the end. How could he ever trust me again? Why would he even want to? I am a rotten human.

Even if it feels like my heart has broken into a million pieces, like my chest is caving in and I can't suck in a breath, I will at least make sure he has a business to come back to when he recovers from the tornado of Casey Baker. I am on a real destruction streak at the moment. Making Grace blow up, lying to Addison, making Rosie lie to Addison. Now this, with the manuscript.

I deserve this, this pain. I deserve so much of it.

"It's 3pm, why don't you finish up? I'll lock up and take the shipping orders at four," I say to April.

"Oh, it's fine. Jessie said he'd pay me double for the double shift and lock up. I kind of need the money right now." She shrugs, and when I flick my eyes over my shoulder at her, I relent. I've done enough bossing around, and I know what it's like to be a broke student living in a big city.

"Okay. Call me if you need anything." I write my number on a ripped piece of paper from my apron and hand it to her. "Seriously, anything. Jessie... well, he is just having a day. So I'm here if you need." She takes the paper from my hand and nods before turning back to the stock, packing away each of the orders that are to be collected later and heading for the back.

Looking at the pile, it seems like it was a super successful online launch. He would have been so proud of himself if he'd been here today. I could have met him here. We could have gone home and celebrated before my birthday drinks tonight. It could have been perfect.

But I ruined it.

I ruined us.

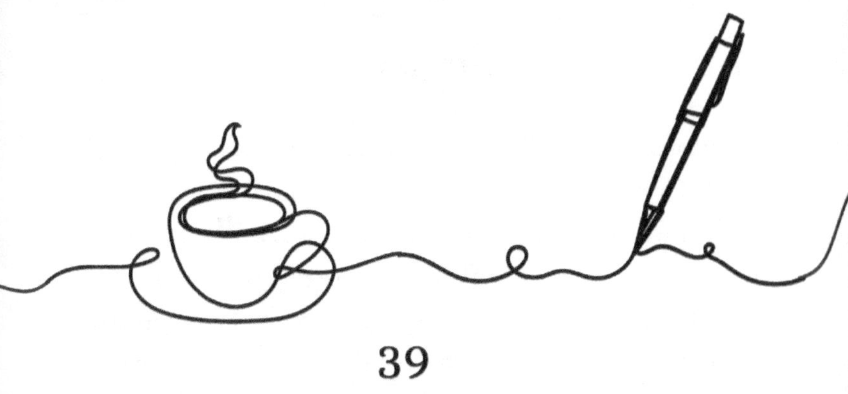

39

our sunshine is a super dark gray cloud of doom

Jessie

"I know you're in there."

"You know nothing," I shout back, like a petulant child, at Addison through my apartment door. The apartment that smells like flowers and cinnamon apple pastry. Because that's all I've been making since I bailed on my shift at the shop before I fell into my reading chair an hour ago.

"I'm just going to stand here until you open this door and let me in." I snap the book I was not really reading closed and head for the door. Tearing it open, Addison stands there with a bottle of tequila in her hand and raises it.

"Drink?" I roll my eyes, but snatch the bottle and turn back into the apartment.

"Thought having that tall idiot you hang around with all the time meant you didn't drink away your feelings anymore." She rolls her eyes at me.

"This one time when that tall idiot was an ass, I had a complete rage spiral and some grumpy bastard inserted his nose into my business," she prattles on as she follows behind, heading for the sofa in my living area. "He paid for a few shots of tequila, let me cry, and then we became besties after. Turns out it was just the healing I needed. Or the start of it." Again, I'm rolling my eyes because I know what she is referring to. Back then, though, I was just trying to get to the bottom of her and Noah. Trying to work out whether I needed to kill him or help him.

"You're reading *The Notebook*?" she sounds shocked, but I ignore the question.

Snagging two whiskey glasses from the cupboard above the stove, I drop a couple fingers of tequila into them and take them down to meet Addy on the sofa.

"So, what do you want?" I ask, sipping the drink and letting it burn its way down my throat. She sits sideways on the couch, nursing the drink and narrowing her gaze at me.

"Casey and Rosie explained everything to me," she says gently.

"You wrote a book? A good one?" That has me scoffing and throwing back the rest of the tequila. Should have brought the bottle down.

"Sure." I nod, not meeting her eyes.

"And Casey stole the manuscript from you?" The confirmation of the betrayal stings now that it's spoken out loud. I felt such severe rage this morning I had to leave. I was going to say or do something that I was going to regret, that was going to blow back up in my face. Even now, I am barely back to simmering. At least that much I knew Addison would understand.

"She did."

"And you're mad?"

"Livid." I look up to her and she must see it there. She nods and downs the rest of her drink.

"So, what are you doing about it?"

"What the fuck do you want me to say right now, Addison?" I stand

and steal her glass, going to pour us both another one. I'm not nearly drunk enough for this conversation.

"Well, I'm going out with her tonight. She is going to ask me a hundred million questions because you're ignoring her texts and phone calls. So I need to know how to handle this." The reminder of Casey being out has me putting the bottle of tequila down. I want to be sober enough to pick her up, meet her there, or, I don't fucking know, just be sober in case she needs me.

"It's none of your business," I say under my breath and come to sit back on the sofa with glasses of water instead.

"But it is. I need to know whether I try to protect her heart or help her give up? Do I make sure she holds on so you have a fucking girlfriend when your rage lets go of you? I need to know how to help you. She's my best friend, but you're my brother. Tell me what you need." Her voice doesn't skip, doesn't falter or strain. Pure power, assuredness, and strength radiate from her, and I have never been prouder of my little rogue.

"I appreciate it, Addison, really." I look up to her and let her see my genuine gratitude, but clarify, "You don't need to do anything. I'm just here to simmer. I'll be at Bozzelli's for her birthday, and I'll be there to take her home." She releases a huge breath and falls to the back of the couch.

"Oh, thank god." She sighs.

"What's that supposed to mean?" I feel the tightness in my chest release slightly at the small smile she pastes on her face.

"Well, you're mad, but you're not like *we're breaking up* kind of mad."

"Fuck no." Breaking up with Casey? I almost laugh at the absurdity.

"That's good. Except if you're going to make this work with her, you're going to have to find a way to exist in the madness without running away. She is a fucking mess right now, Jessie. I've never seen her like this. She is our sunshine person, and right now, she is like one of those super stormy dark gray clouds of doom." Her eyes grow wider and more sad as she explains. Pain and frustration pin me right in the chest. I didn't want that. I didn't want to hurt her or make her feel pain. I just couldn't explode and let it go right there. I was worried I'd do even more damage. But I can't cut Casey out of my heart just like that, not even if I wanted to. Which I don't. Casey is still very much mine. I just needed to breathe for a moment. I knew it was going to be our first fight, and I didn't want to lose my cool and risk blowing up the best thing in my life.

"I had to run. I couldn't explode right there in front of her. She doesn't need to see that." Addison nods. If anyone understands, it's her. But it's the way she smirks knowingly at me.

"You know what being with Noah has taught me? That the right people aren't scared by our intensity, they just love us more because of it. Casey is the right person, Jessie, and I know you know that. Give her a chance to not be scared and to show you how you should have been loved. She'll do it properly." I know. I know all of this already. But it's easier said than done.

"Oh, and do me a favor and stop fucking ignoring her, you jerk. I know she fucked up, but c'mon, don't make her sweat like this." She slaps my knee and stands.

"You know what she did for you today. You at least owe her a thank you text."

"What did she do today?" That has me standing to match Addison's pace to the door, my stomach dropping.

Addison spins on me, pinning me with an assessing look before shock and something else hit her face and she giggles.

"You fucking dick head, she ran your café for you because you bailed on your launch day!" *She what?!*

My mouth does something that mimics a fish out of water as I try to understand what Addison just said. "I... I—"

"April is basically a child, and you just left her in charge of your business on a major milestone day?! Are you that much of an idiot?" Her words are venomous, but light, as she smiles and laughs at my expense. I think on some level she knew I hadn't thought it through, hadn't been capable of thinking much through. I run a frustrated hand down my face, reprimanding myself for being such a colossal moron.

"I didn't bail on the launch." I sigh heavily, and she levels me with a knowing look. "Well, I didn't completely bail. I was watching it from home." I point to the laptop on my coffee table. Addison looks at it and shrugs her shoulders, finding me again.

"Well, she went looking for you about half an hour after you skipped out, according to Rosie. She only got back to the apartment after I left to come here." My head snaps to the clock hanging near my fridge. Six hours. Casey went and worked in my fucking shop for six fucking hours?!

I really don't deserve this woman.

I look back to Addison, and she is barely containing her laughter at my confusion and anger, the way the emotions are fighting each other.

"So you know," she continues, "Rosie and I plan on getting Casey extremely drunk. She plans on wearing a tiny scrap of material us women call a dress. Those long legs will be on display, her tits will be pushed up to her eye sockets, and would you look at that," she gestures out the window, "it's snowing. She'll be cold, might need a big, strong man to wrap her up and make sure she is warm." She is doing nothing for my rage levels as she continues to taunt me, my fists balled by my sides. "I wonder if there will be enough men at Bozzelli's to take one for the team and get Casey all warmed up." She winks at me, opening my apartment door to leave.

"Rosie does the teasing better," I throw at her before the door slams behind her. "And you keep those fuckers away until I get there!" I shout louder, to make sure she hears me.

"Don't be late, then, or I'll tell Rosie she is single and needs a rebound!" she shouts back.

Dammit.

Like fuck was I going to be late. I ripped my clothes off and headed to the shower. I really needed to blow off some steam and then go fix this shit with my woman.

40

feminism has left the building

Casey

"I really don't want to be here tonight. Can't we just spend it at home with movies and wine? That sounds like a much better birthday," I complain to the girls as we wait to have our coats checked. It is literally snowing, days out from Christmas, and they've put me in this tiny blue dress. It has a modest neckline, but the back of it doesn't exist, and like it wasn't already short enough, one of the legs has a slit in it. The heels Rosie bought for me are a gorgeous pearly white. They shimmer like they have sparkles sprayed on them, with two giant tulle bows on the back. Really, my outfit just screams, 'I'm the birthday girl', without me even trying. I felt sexy leaving the apartment. Sad, but sexy.

Now I'm sad and cold. Freezing, in fact.

"You'll be warmer with a few drinks and a pit stop on the dance floor," Rosie assures me. She and Addison agreed to dress up similarly, While not as sparkly, they were still in tiny dresses, heels, hair and make-up done to the nines. We were meeting Stella inside, apparently, and I expect the guys will also be inside or on their way.

We never ended up meeting at Lucas's first, the mess of my emotions meant it took every bit of cajoling and finesse for Rosie and Addison to pull me out of the shower, force me into this skimpy bit of clothing, wrangle my hair into something of a wave, and apply some mascara. They are lucky I let them drag me into that Uber. All I wanted to do was curl up with my Special Edition of *Age of Innocence,* watch *The Notebook,* and cry into the hoodie Jessie left in my room. The real gut punch was the quick sniff I took of it before we left–because yes, I'm pathetic–and in case you're wondering, yes, it still smells like him, and yes, Rosie scolded me for being tragic and had to re-apply my mascara.

My heart beats a little faster at the memory of Jessie saying he would be here, but I have to shove that hopeful little sucker back down. There is no hope in hell Jessie is coming out to see me–the destroyer of worlds. I'm not above begging, though. I would beg for Jessie to be with the guys when they rocked up. I know he is probably done with me, God knows I don't deserve his forgiveness, let alone his attention, but I want to apologize one more time, not just for the mistake, but for pulling him in only to drop his heart on its face.

I know he deserves better. I just want one more goodbye.

We make it into the main bar, which is already packed, and we spot Stella with Lucas and Ethan. I can't help the way my eyes are immediately searching the perimeter of the room, but I know he isn't here yet. Because I would know, I'd feel him. I'd sense his gaze on me like a brand. It was always that way with us.

Not anymore. I ruined us.

"Alright, drinks, first round's on me!" Rosie calls, and we spill our orders as we take a seat at the high bar.

"Happy birthday, Case!" Lucas says with a large smile. Ethan's enthusiasm is at a two in comparison, but he gives me a half smile and wishes me the same, along with Stella.

"Thank you," I reply, not feeling any of the '*happy*' for this birthday.

"What did you wish for?" Lucas asks. But, because I can't say, *a big burly lumberjack to sweep me off my feet, kiss the shit out of me, and remind me how much he loves me,* instead I say, "For winter to be over." A small round of chuckles hits the table, and Rosie makes it back with the drinks.

"To our eternally sunny girl, happy birthday, Casey!" Rosie raises her drink in the center of the table. Everyone follows suit in a *woo*, before we drink and settle into the table. I feel anything but sunny right now.

"So, how's the studio?" Stella asks, leaning her chin on her palm and looking at me. I can't really read her facial expression. All I know is that her eyes are terrifyingly dark, and I really wish I could do a wing on my eyeliner like that.

"Great, I have a couple interviews coming up with some new trainers, so that should be good. Free me up a bit. Might actually be able to pursue the self-defense classes I wanted to hold."

"You do self-defense?" She sits up straighter, her eyes now sucking in all my attention. I couldn't look away if I tried.

"Yeah, I want to. I held a demo class a few months ago, and it was a hit. I just need permanent instructors. My goal is to have at least two. Then I have someone to teach it and the other to assist in the demonstration."

"What do you need from the instructor or person demonstrating?" This comes from Ethan, who is also just as perked up. I shrug, a little taken aback by his interest in the topic.

"Oh, um, I guess, the demonstrating person just needs to be a guy. I kind of want to help teach women to defend against the actual threat. You know, against someone bigger, taller, stronger, more intimidating. Teaching people to defend against someone like Addison, for example, might be futile when the people more likely to attack them look like you and Lucas." Both guys nod in understanding, but Addison slaps my arm. "Hey, I might be small, but I am mighty." Rosie chuckles.

"We know, Addy, don't worry. Noah has sent footage of you at that Rage place. It's terrifying." Addison's smile is borderline feline.

"I fucking love that place." She hums and sips her drink.

"Well, I'm happy to be a permanent volunteer if you need," Ethan suggests, and my head snaps back in his direction.

"Really?" A touch of excitement buzzes through the sadness that swims in my veins.

"Yeah, for sure." He shrugs. His eyes land on Stella for a brief moment before they come back to me. "I've always been interested in helping women stuck in those kinds of situations." Lucas moves uneasily next to him and downs his drink, gesturing that he is getting another. Ethan follows the movement before he comes back to me. "I want to help where I can, so just hit me up. I have a black belt, but I'm no instructor. I'd be happy to just demonstrate." Ethan gives me an easy smile, but before I can query further, Rosie interrupts.

"You're a black belt?!" He smiles larger and nods at her, sipping his beer. Stella only manages a side eye and shifts slightly away from Ethan as Rosie continues.

"My guy, you should lead with that. You just went from like a seven to a nine-and-a-half."

"Liar, he is at least a nine without the karate." Addison shakes her head at Rosie.

"Not a ten?" I ask while chuckling, and Addison joins me. Ethan can't stop his shy smile, but he just looks down at his drink, shaking his head in a chuckle.

"Ten is a very big call. You have to have, like, no flaws to be a ten in my books," she clarifies. "No offense."

"So, I'm a ten, then?" Caleb's teasing hits us from behind and when I look over my shoulder, he and Noah are making their way to us, Caleb having overheard the conversation.

"Hey, shortcake," Noah coos and leans in for a kiss with Ads. About seven hundred tons of jealousy lands on my chest, and I have to pinch my eyes closed and skull my drink.

He didn't come. *Of course he didn't come!* I betrayed his trust and broke his heart into a bajillion pieces. He isn't going to want anything to do with me.

"Pest, you are so far below a ten, you're barely on the scale." Rosie rolls her eyes at Caleb. She's wrong, of course. Caleb is just as stupidly attractive as the rest of this group of guys. With all of his arrogance, the insult doesn't even register, instead he feigns offense, hitting a hand to his chest before leaning in to whisper something in Rosie's ear with a grin. It appears Rosie had been keeping their one-time romp a secret, and by the way she is blushing and trying to hide the lust from her eyes at whatever he said, she is struggling to keep a lid on that secret. Rosie pushes back her chair, interrupting Caleb's whispering, and demands, "Ladies, dance floor, now." Stella and I stand. Addison goes to stand, but Noah lifts her from the chair and appraises her outfit with a frown.

"I really don't want to get into a fight," he tells her and she just rolls her eyes.

"Like I can't fight my own battles," she deadpans at him, which earns her an intense look.

"I'd like it if you didn't fight anyone, Addison. It's my night off," Lucas clarifies as he makes it back to the table. Noah hits him with a deadpan and I turn, following Rosie and Stella into the throng of people. Not all that interested in coveting Noah and Addison right now.

When I look over my shoulder to see if Addy is following, she is skipping up to me and looping an arm around mine.

"Is the caveman going to be okay while you dance?" I ask. She giggles in return.

"I promised him lots of private shows later in exchange. He reluctantly agreed." I flick my eyes to where Noah stands and can see his eyes glued to the back of Addy, his gaze never faltering.

"You snagged a good one there, Ads," I tell her, and when she looks up at me, she smiles gently.

"So did you, Case. Don't quit him yet." She winks.

She's nuts, because quitting him would mean cutting my heart from my chest. I just don't know how to tell her that I think he's the one that quit me.

You know why I like gin? Because it makes my head feel like it floats on clouds. Wine makes me feel heavy and tired. Vodka makes me want to run a mile after two drinks and then violently throw up every drink after. But gin makes me laugh. It makes me feel like my skin is buzzing and my heart is wrapped up in joy. It was exactly what I had needed after today, and with everything that happened with Jessie, I want to let go of the shame and the guilt. I just want to forget how much my chest aches and to take this time for myself.

I dance with Rosie, Stella, and Addison in the middle of the dance floor. The guys joined us at a distance, at one of the high bar tables that had dance floor viewing, and we stayed there for a good hour. We all had our fair share of gropers to shoo. Stella has artfully managed the death stare of the century, and most have steered clear of her. Rosie embraces most, but seems overall uninterested. Addison just gestures to where Noah stands at the edge of the dance floor, and after a number of seconds, the perpetrator disappears while she remains smiling and dancing. I've been lucky so far. Most are just friendly and looking to dance, which is fine. Stella did scare the living shit out of one when she said she'd flay his flesh if he touched me without permission again. That was fun to watch. But the more the night went on, the more I wanted to be rescued by someone much taller, bigger, scarier.

From the corner of my eye, I feel another confident idiot slink on through the pack and shimmy his way up to me. His chest to my back. I take a small step away from him and he follows. The guy's hand lands on my hip, and as I go to spin around and scold him, he's pulled back by the neck of his shirt.

Both surprise and desire rip through me at the same time. Because I really hadn't expected Jessie to show up, looking downright edible, by the way, and I certainly hadn't expected him to care about some random guy. I honestly hadn't expected his attention on me ever again.

Jessie has Mr. Confidence's shirt fisted in his hand, the guy almost hovering off the ground as Jessie brings his raging snarl into his face. "*Mine,*" he growls, coating my skin in awareness, my whole body lighting up at the sight and sound of him. *I guess he is still working off that rage.*

He drops Mr. Confidence on shaky feet, who scurries away like a mouse running from a lion. When his attention lands on me, the look I see sends a shiver over my whole body. I become a stupid panting mess, feeling my desire pool between my legs. I want him to take me here and now, public indecency be damned. I have so many things to say, so many apologies to make, so many questions about what he is doing here, because seriously, *what is he doing here?* Are we actually okay? What does this mean?

But those blue-green eyes with flecks of gold are pure ice. Where he'd usually soften or curl the corners of his lips, he only glares. The only difference between me and Mr. Confidence is that the ice is of the hottest fire and they burn with desire, aimed solely at me.

His eyes trail down my body, and I feel it everywhere. He takes a few assured steps forward until he is standing right in front of me. The anticipation alone almost makes me sick, but then, with his magic barista hands, he grips my jaw, pulls me forward, and plants a kiss to my lips. Quick, demanding, and aggressive, with a possessive swipe of his tongue, he holds me in place, and I let him. Open for him and yielding all control to him, begging him to take it. Take me.

A little moan leaves my throat, and when he pulls back, his grip still firm, lips hovering so close to mine, his deep gravel voice hums through my body. "I don't like people touching my things." Feminism gone.

Shivers race over my back, and I shudder. Hit with desire and a little touch of fear from his words. Both a declaration and a threat. He was still very mad about the manuscript, but that was a reminder that I am still his. While the sour pit of shame still stirs with guilt over that manuscript I stole and the trust I broke, a little bit of the tension I've held all night dissipates at the recognition that he still burns for me and still sees me as his. I am praying he meant it.

The moment doesn't linger, though. In a few blinks, the domineering show is over and, without another look, he turns. Walking toward Noah and the guys, I watch him go. Like a lovesick puppy under a spell, I stand there, gazing after him, before turning to Rosie, Addy, and Stella.

I haven't managed to catch my breath, but the whole interaction has me feeling hollow. Every part of me aches for him, and the sudden need to cry stings the back of my eyes.

When I'm quiet for a moment, it's Stella who breaks the silence.

"You good?" She raises a brow and I have to shake my head.

"I mean, yeah... but... he just... What does that mean? Why did he..." I trail off looking over at him again, only to find him and Noah in conversation, every now and then both looking this way before sipping their drinks, the rest of the guys floating around and engaging in conversation around them.

"He just needs to simmer down, give him a beat to catch his breath. He can't cool his jets like you can," Addison confirms. I just nod, but still look over at him, not feeling all that secure about where I stand, not sure what any of this means. But he did at least give me part of my birthday wish. He kissed the ever loving shit out of me.

"I think I need to go to the bathroom," I tell the girls as I try to blink back tears.

"Oh, we'll come with." Rosie shrugs.

"No, I just need to go by myself for a second." Because the gin was winning, and I might cry. They seem to get it and back off as I turn to head for the bathroom.

When the door swings closed behind me, I'm relieved to find it empty, heading straight for the sink to run my hands under cold water.

I splash the cold water on the back of my neck, cupping some to sip and then making my fingers damp to cool down my chest. With my head back and my hand stuck down the front of my dress, the bathroom door opens and I jump back, trying to pull my hand from my dress so fast I smack myself in the jaw.

"*Fuck!*" I shout, and the tears I had been trying to bury start to escape.

"Sorry, sorry, just ignore me. I'm just cooling down." I wave at whoever entered as I try to find some paper towels. When I get no response, I turn, "Sorry, I—Jessie?! What are you doing? This is the women's—"

His lips crash onto mine, cutting me off. I hadn't even felt him approaching. I turned, and he was there. Now, he is backing me against the bathroom sink, his jacket peeled off, thrown to the counter, and he lifts me on top of it.

"What are you doing?" I pant between his tongue dancing with mine.

"Didn't want your ass to get wet."

"I meant in here, Jess. We could get caught."

"I locked the door," he grunts. His tone, those dark eyes, and deep frown, so at odds with the soft soul I've spent the last few months learning and loving. He's all animal, the darkness, madness, and rage. I'm sure a therapist would have some things to say about the way I find this so incredibly hot, but I don't much care.

"You drive me fucking mental, *stella mea,*" he grinds out as he trails his teeth down my neck. My fingers grip in his hair and I moan as he latches on to my shoulder with his teeth.

"Jessie," I breathe.

"I'm fucking pissed at you," he says, his face furious when he pulls back but slams his lips to mine. An embarrassingly weak whimper leaves my lips, and his fingers have the hem of my dress pushed up to my hips and teasing the inside of my thighs. "But I also want to thank you. For today. For the shop."

That's what this is. It suddenly makes sense. He isn't here to have me back. He is here to thank me for today, despite the fact it was the least I could do, that is all this means. And right now, in this bathroom? It's just attraction. Maybe he couldn't fight that, but he is still mad and this is probably going to be the end.

"You don't have to thank me for anything, I'm so sor—"

"No." He shuts me up with lips, his tongue and his teeth, dragging my bottom lip as he moves to my jaw, behind my ear, my neck, and my collarbone. "We can talk about that later. Right now, I just want to devour you." His fingers find the edge of my thong, slipping it to the side, and I gasp as his thumb finds my peak in less than a second. "This. Fucking. Dress," he grinds out, trailing a delicate finger through my middle.

"Jessie, *please*," I beg, so desperate for him to surround me, fill me. Exist nowhere but right here with me.

"So fucking wet for me." He slides one finger in and mutters a curse, using his free hand to lower the straps of my dress. "And this blue? My new favorite color." My breasts slip out with ease, and he takes one into his mouth, letting it go with a pop while slipping his finger deeper inside me. "We have one fight, and you think I'd let someone else touch what's mine?" he growls, his finger curling upward, spearing me at a dizzyingly slow pace. I can barely hold it together to keep my eyes open, let alone understand any of his words.

"I'm so sorry," I whimper, and I almost squeal when he adds a second finger, his pace picking up to an almost punishing speed, and he has to steal the moan from my lips. His tongue demands entrance, and when I open for him, his free hand grips the front of my neck and lightly squeezes to hold me in place. His fingers work me until I'm barely able to tell what year it is. The edges of my vision blur as his grip tightens, and I feel myself become impossibly wetter.

"*Jessie, please, holy fuck,*" I whisper through his grip on my throat.

"I'm not done with you yet," he grumbles and kisses me again, his tongue drags the length of my neck to the tips of each of my breasts, and when I feel myself grip his fingers ready to fall off the edge, they pause.

He burns me with the intensity of his eyes. They swim with so many unspoken words, so much ice-blue rage, and I can't help but drop a tear. I feel my heart fill with so much love for every facet of Jessie, all the while it falls into pieces at the meaning of us right now. This feels painfully like... *goodbye.*

"You seem to have forgotten whose pretty little cunt this is." The taunt is downright demeaning and also, somehow, the single hottest thing he's ever said.

My body hums with need, between the heartache, the orgasm on the precipice, and the way I feel him so deep, I can confidently say there isn't a single person in this world who owns every part of me the way Jessie Jenkins does. "It's always been yours." I struggle to hold back the sob.

In a single breath, his fingers leave me, the button of his jeans is flicked, and he pulls them down enough to unsheathe himself from his boxers. In the next breath, he grips his coat under my ass and yanks me forward, his cock landing perfectly between my legs, stealing the gasp from my mouth with his.

He drives into me with haste, not missing a beat, and when my head falls back from the intensity of the orgasm curling inside me, he grips the back of my head, forcing my eyes on him. The blue of them shines as they bleed his pain, the pain I put there.

"*Fuck,*" I breathe, and his lips tip up in the corners. A smirk of satisfaction has tears welling up in my eyes. I wrap my arms around his neck and pull my chest flush with his, completely unable to bear the distance between us any longer. I need to feel the firmness of his body and the warmth of his skin just one more time. I need him to know, "I love you so much, Jessie," I state breathlessly, feeling his grip move to my ass, holding me in place while he fucks. Turning into the savage I asked for that first time. I lose the battle on my tears, and then my orgasm, as it rips through at the increase in his pace.

"Yes, shit. Fuck! *Ace.* Your pussy is fucking magic," he growls, and with a few more punishing thrusts, he comes right along with me.

Like he has done every time, Jessie leaves little kisses across my shoulder, up my neck, and eventually finding my lips, as he pulls out of me silently. When I find the nerve to meet his gaze, his dark eyes scan every inch of me as he fixes himself in his pants. He helps me to my feet, fixes my dress, and pats down my hair, leaning in to leave a longing kiss to my forehead. The final punch to the gut. The seal to our ending. I can't help but drop another tear and feel as though my heart is being removed from my body. He may have claimed me as his in the most primal way, but I know in my heart and in his eyes, I am no longer his in the way that matters I don't deserve him and I am certainly not going to make him suffer by staying.

41

stella mea

Jessie

Casey is a giggling mess as I haul her into my apartment. My arm around her to keep her upright as her ankles battle against gravity in those fucking heels. But fuck, did they look good wrapped around me in that bathroom.

I can't deny she wore the shit out of her baby-blue dress. I found her immediately, and at the same time, found my new favorite color. Did I mention that my woman is hot? Because fuck me sideways, I nearly passed out from how quickly the blood left one head, going straight to the other.

That dress hugs each of her small curves with perfection, those legs leading to heaven, and all I wanted to do was sink my teeth into her delectable thighs. It was when that piece of shit shimmied up behind her that I realized I hadn't managed to simmer any of my rage, and I just saw red at his hand on her hip. In that single moment, all I knew was that the fucker needed to remove his grubby hands from her, and I was happy to do the removing for him. I had barely blinked before I had him clutched by the neck of his shirt, ready to tear him apart, but the floral scent of Casey's hair and the way her proximity set my entire being on fire, paired with that incredible dress, I managed to turn my attention to what mattered.

Casey was thoroughly wasted now, though.

"Ohhh, this is like déjà vu!" she whispers.

After fucking the rage out of my system in the bathroom of Bozzelli's, we went back out and joined our friends. I tried to pull her away to talk after, but she had simply shaken her head and said it was fine. I couldn't help the guilt eating away at me, though. I loved that Casey could take it rough. That my need for rage and control has never once scared her. But anytime I got *that* rough, I liked to be able to smooth it over after. A bath, a massage, something that allowed me to love on her or care for her, counteract the animal with a touch of chivalry. We didn't get that tonight, and it was *killing* me.

I couldn't swipe her tears before she did, and when I tried to get her alone again, she just shook her head at me. I couldn't get a read on her for the rest of the night. She danced and drank—more than I'd ever seen her drink—and it had forced me to stop so I could keep an eye on her. I didn't see a single smile, didn't hear even a trill of her laughter. Casey was a shell, and I had never seen her so lost behind those ocean blue eyes. I eventually dragged her into an Uber to take her home when she started to forget what walking was.

"What's déjà vu, Ace?"

"Remember? I tucked you in when you were a little drunk. You said my nose was cute. But you probably don't like my nose anymore," she mumbles, and I frown in confusion. When I turn to look down at her and ask further, I note the sadness in her expression. I maneuver us toward the bedroom and hold her against me.

"What's that look for, baby?" I say quietly, tucking her now messy wind-blown hair behind her ears, and she drops her forehead to my chest, hands fisted tightly in my sweater.

"That was the night I stole your manuscript." She has little tears on her cheeks when she looks up at me, and I quickly wipe them. The pain and anger of what happened, of what we haven't talked about, sits heavy in my stomach. Despite how confused I am at why she did that, how dirty it felt to have that secret hidden from me for so long, she's far too wasted to hash this out right now.

"C'mon, sunshine, let's get you into bed and we can talk about everything tomorrow."

She crawls into the bed and I sit beside her, removing her heels and lightly massaging her feet as she wriggles out of her clothes, lying almost naked, her flimsy thong the only scrap of material on her body, and I have to physically restrain myself from joining her with *my* naked body.

Too drunk for a conversation means she is definitely too drunk to be fucked into the mattress.

I drag a frustrated hand through my beard and grab a shirt from a pile of laundry I hadn't put away from the dryer, and throw it at her. "Put this on."

She drags it across her body, and I have to turn and look away to stop myself.

"It smells like you," she whispers. "Your sweater at home smells like you. I wore it today. My sheets smell like you, too. Today, I decided I'm never washing them." Her words are little breaths of slurred sounds, but in the quietness of my small apartment, I hear every single one. And each of them makes my chest ache.

Confusion, anger, and frustration grip me all at once, and I have to shake my head, knowing she is too drunk to hear anything I say, but I mumble anyway, "I'm not going anywhere, sunshine."

"I hope I forget," she whispers, dropping more tears from where she lies on my bed curled up and eyes sealed shut.

"Forget what?"

"You. Because it'll hurt too damn much to remember." She sniffles, and I have to rub my face aggressively to fight off the spike in my anger. I had thought turning up, declaring her as mine, railing her like an animal in the bathroom, had been enough to clear up any doubt about where I stood, but my Casey is a gentle soul, and I knew she had beat herself up. I hadn't realized she was beating herself to the point she was becoming delusional as to how much I loved her.

Resigned to the fact that having this conversation with a drunk Casey wouldn't get me very far, I don't say anything. Instead, I peel my clothes off now that she is covered under the blankets, and one percent less of a temptation–let's be real, she could wear a fucking burlap sack and she'd still be the only woman on the planet worth looking at.

I know I should be a gentleman and sleep on the couch, but I can only put my heart through so much in one day. Knowing that she thinks we're done is painful enough without being able to clear any of it up in her current state. So, I lie down behind her and pull her into me, a tense breath leaving me at the comfort of finally holding her in my arms and feeling her settle into me. That final piece to my puzzle.

Despite the pain in my chest, the way I'm twisted up, a little unsure and a lot mad. I know that Casey and I could beat anything. Whatever comes tomorrow, it will always be me and her at the end of it.

Morning sun has me stirring awake, but the usual comfort of feeling a small frame, soft skin, and a delicate trace of flowers under my nose is missing. My eyes snap open, trying to clear the sleep quicker than usual. Sitting up, I see the bed is empty, feeling the side Casey had slept on is cold has my heart in my throat.

She left?

The covers are tossed, I'm bolting out of bed, and my bedroom door is thrown open. My knees nearly buckle with relief when I see her standing in the living room. Looking out the window, heavy snow covers the city in a white blanket. She turns her head just so, acknowledging my presence, but returning her attention back to the window, her shoulders inching up ever so slightly.

"You feeling okay, sunshine?" I ask gently, cautious to the fact she'd have a killer hangover this morning.

"Had some Advil and water a couple hours ago." My heart races at the uncertainty that sits around her, and when my eyes dart to the oven clock in my kitchen, I note the time. 8am. She's barely slept.

I steal a hoodie from the couch and tug it on, ducking back into the bedroom to tug on a pair of sweats before heading back out to the main area.

"Sleep okay?" I test the waters, and she turns to give me a sad smile.

"I think we should have that conversation." She angrily wipes at a tear and I frown deeply, unable to stop it, but nod at her. Grateful I was able to postpone this as long as I had. I am no longer livid at what she did... just confused.

Heading to the couch, I sit while she remains standing and pacing, so I stand again. I need to comfort her in some way. At this point, it felt like a basic need. Reaching out, I grab her thumb, twisting the ring that rests there, attempting to stop her racing heart and manic thoughts.

"Breathe, Ace." She rips her hand from my grip like I burned her.

"You have to stop," she breathes, her eyebrows drawn in, little frown lines forming on her pink cheeks, and I *hate* it.

"Stop what?"

"All this kindness. Why aren't you shouting or something? Why aren't you angrier? It's confusing!" My hands make their way to my hips, looking for something to do with them as I feel my skin start to itch with the way fury burns my veins.

"Why is it confusing?"

"Because you're mad at me." She spins with hands in the air, her voice raised.

"I am."

"Okay, so act like it." I shake my head at her, utterly lost with this woman right now.

"What do you want from me, Casey?"

"I don't know, not this!" She throws her hands up again and is now borderline yelling. "You're supposed to act mad!"

"What are you talking about? I can't care for you and worry about you while I'm also mad at you?" My tone rises to match hers as I work to shove the anger back down. Back in its box. I *can't* do this here with her. I can't show the monster. I won't be him. *I can't become him.*

I breathe deeply through my nose and watch as her intelligent eyes assess me.

"You're being calm. Loving and kind. You're attentive and assuring me. You're acting like I didn't fuck everything up!"

"Because you didn't fuck everything up," I remind her, because she fucked up, but everything is *not* fucked.

"I lied to you for *months*. I stole from you, I shared your secrets, I pimped out your fucking soul to a publishing company," she starts pacing, her adorable angry eyes are everywhere–between me, the window, the ground then back to me–as she talks animatedly with her hands, "and you're just here like, '*Oh, stella mea, you drive me crazy, I'm gonna fuck your brains out in a public bathroom.*' Like, what the fuck is that, Jessie?"

I have to tuck my chin to my chest and bite my tongue to smother the laugh that almost bursts at the seams. Listening to Casey attempt a deep voice impersonation with her very adorable angry face is the most entertainment I've had in a long time. If this is how our fights are going to go, I can't fucking wait to marry this woman.

"Jessie Jenkins, you better stop fucking laughing at me and get serious." When I look up at her, she levels a pointed finger at me and narrows her big blue eyes. I take a step forward, letting her raised finger jab me in the chest, tucking my hands into my pockets.

"I haven't ever heard you swear like this without my cock inside you. A new side to you, sunshine. I think I like it." I tap her adorable nose and she swats me away. I see the exhaustion weigh heavily on her, and when she looks back up at me, there is a sadness in her eyes.

"Jessie, *please.*" I nod at her, understanding her need for this.

"Okay, then. We're doing this," I say, settling back into my anger. After all this time, it's become easy to tap into it; it's burying it that is hard.

"Why?" I question and she straightens, swallowing deeply, but settles in.

"I didn't really know what I was doing. I tripped on it, kind of... Anyway, I found it, read it... Jessie, it truly is a masterp—"

"You lied to me for months. You stole from me, shared my secrets, *'pimped out my fucking soul'.* I don't really care about your opinion on the writing, Case. I care about why you would do this to me, how you could lie to me like that," I interrupt her and level her with a look, focusing on keeping a level tone. I appreciate her need for a fight, but I refuse to disrespect her by losing my cool and becoming my father.

"I knew you wouldn't do anything with it. I knew you wouldn't see the beauty and the incredible story in that writing."

"So, I was your pity project, then? Something to fix?"

"No, it wasn't that. You would have sat there and thought that no one cared what you had to say. That no one would support you and be excited for you. I thought..." She pauses and mulls on her words, each of her previous ones feeling like little slaps to the face. But I deserve them... she isn't wrong.

"You thought what?" I ask through gritted teeth. Pain sears me as she looks up at me, those incredible blue eyes swimming in tears.

"I thought that if you could see that people do care, that people felt something when they read your writing, that maybe you'd have faith in yourself, too, that maybe you'd start to believe that you deserved more. It was a mistake, I know that. You have no idea how sorry I am. I am so sorry, Jessie. I didn't mean to betray you." Her voice is dripping with self-loathing and pain. She lowers her head and sobs, but she doesn't let me go to her, instead she backs away.

"I know how much you probably hate me—"

"Casey—" I try to stop her, but she holds up a hand. And I'm still reeling from everything she's said, the way she had perceived me as something to fix. It's humiliating, and shame covers me like a wet blanket. But what she doesn't understand is that I know this. I *was* hiding, but I was learning and healing, and she was the reason for that. I know she can't help herself. She saw a way to help someone she cared about, and she took it. I *know* her intentions were pure. What I don't know is why we are talking like this is the end, how she could ever think I hated her.

"I don't want to be a point of pain for you. I only ever wanted to help you." She covers her face, and everything she feels surrounds her like an aura. I want to take it all away, but I'm... stuck. Struggling to wrap my head around any of it. Before I can say anything to smother her fear that this is the end, my phone rings. I pull it from my pocket to stop it when I see the café's number pop up.

"*Fuck,*" I mutter and run a frustrated hand down my face. They would only call if it is urgent because they are under strict instructions not to fucking call unless it is.

"You should take that. I'll get going."

"What? No, Casey. just let me get this. But don't leave."

She doesn't listen, instead she heads for the door. I shut the phone off and head toward her. Fuck the shop. I need to fix this first.

"Case—"

The phone rings again. "*Goddammit!*" I hiss in frustration under my breath again and feel the rage boil up. Casey flinches and I scold myself.

"Just wait here, baby, please, okay? We're not finished," I urge before quickly turning and heading for my room, answering the phone with a bark at whoever was choosing today to piss me the fuck off. "What!?"

"Oh, sorry, boss. Umm, there is a guy here who said he needs to talk to you?"

I swear to all that is holy, if it's not the fire department because the shop is burning down, Eugene was going to be fired so fucking fast. "Who?" I growl.

"Uhh, I don't know someone from a development pla—"

"Tell him to fuck off. I'll be at the shop later, but unless the place is on fire, don't fucking call." I hang up without waiting for an answer, making a mental note to apologize for that later as I turn around and head back into the living room. Completely unable to control my shit right now because my woman wasn't making any sense, and I needed to fix—

The room is empty. "Casey?" I call out, which is fucking stupid because I can see her purse is gone from the counter and in its place is the key I had cut for her. My apartment is small enough to know she isn't here at all. I practically run to the door and rip it open. "Casey!" I shout, and when there is no response, I slam the door again, pacing the apartment and almost ripping the hair from my head.

"Fuck!" I scream at no one but myself. This is my fucking fault. She is gone because I couldn't handle my shit quickly enough to clear up any of her concerns. I couldn't tell her all the shit I am feeling and bury all the stupid emotions.

For the second time in my life, the future I had mapped out feels like it is slipping through my fingers. The difference is, this time, I know exactly what the fuck to do about it.

I'm going to go get her the fuck back.

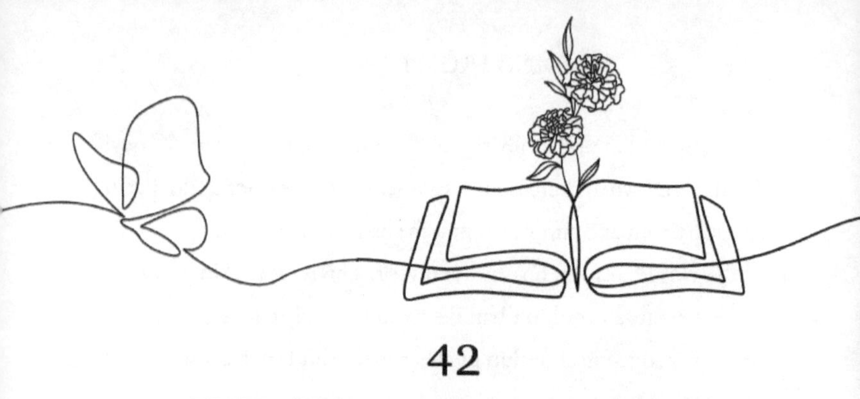

42

---

promise me

Casey

"Are you sure, sweetie?" Mom's gentle voice floats through the phone where I have it propped on my side table. I sniffle–because apparently all I do now is cry–but I push through the tears and respond to Mom.

"Yeah. I'm not feeling like dinner. Just super hungover from last night." And also currently suffering from having open heart surgery, where it was removed from my chest and replaced with a deep black hole of nothingness.

Why am I such a stupid idiot? Why do I have to butt my nose in everyone's business? God knows it's why Grace hates me. And now I've lost Jessie because of it, too. It is any wonder Rosie and Addison have stuck around.

"Okay, honey, well, we're going to go see Evan and Grace. We'll catch you on Christmas day, then?" Because I told them I was spending Christmas Eve–my birthday–with my boyfriend. I hadn't been able to tell them that was no longer happening. I was instead making a mental plan to cry until there was no moisture left in my body.

"Sure. See you then. Love you," I say and quickly end the call, not able to hold the sobs in any longer. I roll onto my side, ready to just fall into the abyss, let it swallow me whole. I had collapsed on my bed, not able to spare Addison or Rosie a single look or word when I had run back to our apartment after my breakup with Jessie this morning.

It hurt like hell to wake up hungover and surrounded by his scent. It made it so much worse that while he was mad at me, he was still the gentleman he always was. Making sure I was home safe, looked after and cherished. Even in the end, he loved me better than anyone ever had.

Noise from deeper in the apartment has my ears perking up, and my heart skips in my chest when I hear his deep voice.

"Where is she?"

"In her room, but this isn't a good time, JJ." Addison's commanding voice hits my ears next, and it sounds like they are right outside my door.

Shit. He probably wants his manuscript back. Rosie had given it back to me under the premise that I would return it to her with a deal ready to be made when Jessie agrees to sign with her publisher, but I know that is never going to happen. I just want to fix this. I want to give it back and pretend it never happened. That we never happened, because it hurt too damn much to think we had just made it, only for it to end.

"Move, Addison." Jessie's growl is unmistakable, and despite everything that happened, the deep timbre of it still sends shivers down my spine.

"Easy, JJ." Noah's usually charmed voice has a menacing air to it.

"Ease off, Karvelas. She's my sister. What the fuck do you think I'm going to do?" Jessie bites back.

"You can watch your mouth when you speak to her." Noah's retort deepens to an octave rare for him, and it's when Addison tries to calm them both down that I realize I need to intervene before the two alpha-males make fools of themselves.

I scramble from the bed, pull the book from my bag, and swing open my bedroom door, interrupting the siblings from their bickering.

I'm stunned for a moment looking up at Jessie's incredibly handsome face, slightly blushed from his anger, which has guilt forming again because I know this is all my fault. The moment I'm in the doorway, it's like the air is sucked from my lungs with his dominating presence. His eyes find mine and lock, never blinking or wavering. He just holds my gaze hostage.

I clear my throat and try to wipe the sticky tears from my face. Bolstering my confidence and trying my best to be unaffected by any of this. From behind Jessie's frame, I can see Noah and Rosie standing by, looks of concern and pity marking their faces, but it's Addison's momma-bear rage I feel vibrating next to me. I rest a hand on her shoulder to let her know I'm okay. I'm incredibly appreciative that she is protecting me right now, when really, I'm the one that ruined her brother. If she should be mad at anyone, it's me.

"Sorry, I should have given this back already." Jessie looks down at the manuscript in my hand.

"What?" he breathes, his eyebrows furrowing, his eyes finally leaving my face and bouncing between me and the book in my hand.

"It's yours. You can have it back." I step forward and give Addison a sideways glance. Taking the hint, she and Noah leave. I feel Rosie's stare on me like a brand, her wide eyes pained as she looks at the manuscript, then at me. She runs a hand down her face, squeaking a sound that is probably frustration and anger in one, before she spins and heads back down the hall.

"Are you going to take it?" I ask again, trying my best not to cry now that we are alone.

"Umm... okay, sure." He takes it, but stands there.

"I could have dropped it off. I'm sorry you came all the way here."

"Hang on, I didn't come back here for the manuscript," he says and makes a point of dropping it to the floor and taking a step toward me. It takes me a moment, but then I remember.

"Oh... *sorry,*" I whisper and turn back into my room, grabbing Jessie's sweater from where it lays across my desk chair. I was hoping he'd forget and that I could keep it, curl up in it and sniff it when I was desperate for a reminder of him. I hand it to him, not able to look at his eyes when he takes it. Instead, he snatches it from my hands.

"Fuck's sake, stop apologising, Casey. Look at me." He throws the sweater to the bed and kicks my bedroom door closed behind him. His tone has me doing as he says, and I inch backward.

"You are making me insane."

"I'm so sorry, Jess—"

"No! It's not about that!" He is shouting in frustration, his hands scraping through his hair before he drags them down his face, making a noise that sounds similar to a growl. Before I can blink, his hand is wrapped around my wrist and he has me spinning, my back pressed against my wall, his body caging me in.

"I don't give a fuck about that manuscript right now. Or the stupid sweater. It's yours. In fact, take all my fucking clothes. I don't care." My heart beats rapidly out of my chest, and my breaths come in quick. His deep scolding voice is no longer shouting, instead he speaks level, his lips inches from mine while his intense eyes burn through me.

"What?"

"I am not angry about the manuscript right now," he clarifies.

"You're not?"

"No. I'm not. I'm angry because you thought I'd quit. That I'd be done, just like that," he emphasizes with a click of his fingers. "That I could possibly leave you, or be done with you, over something like *this*." His words are severe, but I can't quite wrap my head around what he means.

"But—" I try to clear my head, shaking it.

"We're in this forever, sunshine." His expression softens slightly, but his words hold every bit of authority they had when he stormed in here. "You said so yourself. I need you to stop running away. Don't turn and leave when we're in it." I try to say something, but nothing comes out. I'm literally stunned into silence. Thankfully, my tears also appear to be stunned and have stopped. That, or I just ran out.

"I betrayed your trust." The words are a strangled whisper as I struggle to get them out. A menacing look crosses his face as he slowly shakes his head.

"You lied, you stole, but you did something you thought would help me. Am I angry that you didn't tell me? Yes." Shame hits me, and when I drop my head to hide from the way it overtakes me, his calloused hand grips my chin and raises my eyes, forcing me to stare into his heated gaze. I don't think I've ever held anyone's attention the way I hold his.

"Am I angry that you showed people something that was private, a sore spot for me? Yes. Am I a little embarrassed that people have read it, that you thought I was something you could fix? Like you wouldn't fucking believe." I drop a tear and squeeze my eyes closed, trying to hold in the sob. Trying to understand why he is doing this, forcing me to look into his eyes while he tears me apart.

"But I am so much angrier, livid in fact, that you thought I could ever leave you over something like this." His grip on my chin turns into a caress along my cheekbone, tucking a hair behind my ears.

"We've only just begun, sunshine. We're going to make mistakes.

We can't go on thinking that we're done after each one of them." His words have my eyes opening again, trying to make sure I am actually hearing this correctly, and he leans in to kiss my cheek. His one hand framing my face while the other comes to wrap around my lower back and pull me against him. "You have to know that forever is a long time. That means there are going to be times when we're going to piss each other off." His eyes search mine, my breath lodged firmly in my throat, along with my heart.

"You're going to giggle out loud to your books while I try to focus on work, and I'm going to cook your dinner with the wrong ingredients. You're going to forget to eat your lunch, and I'm going to storm into that studio with some pathetic excuse of a sandwich and sit there while you eat it." He did do that once and the memory almost makes me smile. But I'm still stunned into a catatonic state as he continues to list the ways we're apparently going to piss each other off in our apparent future together.

"I'm going to work until you have to come to the café, scold me, and demand that I take a day off. You're going to forever sacrifice pieces of yourself for the people you love, and I'm probably going to overreact like a caveman anytime you want to leave the house in that blue fucking dress." A laugh slips through a sob and his thumb swipes a tear. "I might make a mess in our kitchen, and you might forget to restock the creamer in our fridge." For the briefest of moments, his eyes take on a faraway look before he blinks and sears me with his baby-blues. "One day, you're going to have to yell at me for the potty mouth our kids will no doubt run around with. I'll come in from the lake and leave mud all over the floor. You'll get our daughter hooked on silly romance movies, and I'll have our son in Ice Hockey lessons instead of basketball." I can't stop it, my sobbing turns into a proper cry at the way he tells me of our future in the same way I had dreamed it would be. "But, at the end of all of it, there is you and there is me. We'll still end up on that porch with a cotton-candy or chocolate banana latte, watch the sun set over our bit of land, and breathe in the peace that having our potty-mouthed-ice-skating children finally asleep will bring." I can't stop looking into his incredible eyes and getting lost in that *devastatingly* handsome smile. "I'm fucking in love with you, and there is nothing in this world that you could do that would make me want to quit you." His grip on my chin remains firm, and after a deep breath, I squeeze my eyes shut, letting the tears spill out, and I nod. When I manage to pull my shit a little bit together, I peel my eyes open and see him still gazing at me with all the longing and love in the world.

"So... you s-still want to be with me?" I feel hope lodge itself firmly in my chest and I almost burst out crying *again* from the way my chest inflates.

His smile is extraordinary as he continues analyzing every inch of my face.

"You're the finale, the spectacular, the reward. You're everything that makes being alive worth it. So next time, when I need a moment, while I'm learning to share all my ugly parts with you, don't, even for a second, think that it could be over. I'm never leaving you. You're mine and I'm yours. Got it?" Both his eyes bounce between mine as he holds me to him. I can feel his heart beat rapidly against mine. Not having anything to say in response, no words that can comprehend the relief I feel, the way I ache for him, I leap and wrap my arms around him.

Just as he had promised, he catches me as I fall deeper for the man I think I've loved forever. His arms hold me tightly across my back as he buries his face in the crook of my neck. He kisses a line up my neck to my jaw as I cry and let his words sow my heart back together.

"So... we're going to have a big house on a lake with a wraparound porch?"

"Build it myself if I have to."

I couldn't stop the giggle if I tried. "I knew you had '*I could build you a house*' kind of muscles." Jessie's booming laugh almost makes me cry again as I bury myself back in the comfort of his chest.

"I really thought it was over. I didn't think you—" He shuts me up with a firm kiss and shakes his head, pulling back to lean his forehead against mine.

"Don't say it. You'll break my heart, and holding you is the only thing keeping me together right now." he says quietly and then whispers against my lips, "Promise me."

"Promise what, Jess?" I whisper back through my stuttering breath as I try to slow my crying. Brushing the pieces of stray hair off his forehead, I admire all of his handsome features.

"Promise me forever. No matter how complicated or messy it gets. Promise to stay, and I promise to make it worth it."

When he refuses to open his eyes, I pull his face to mine, placing a delicate kiss to each of his eyelids, then the strong line of his nose, then his lips. Lingering for a moment, I whisper back, "I promise."

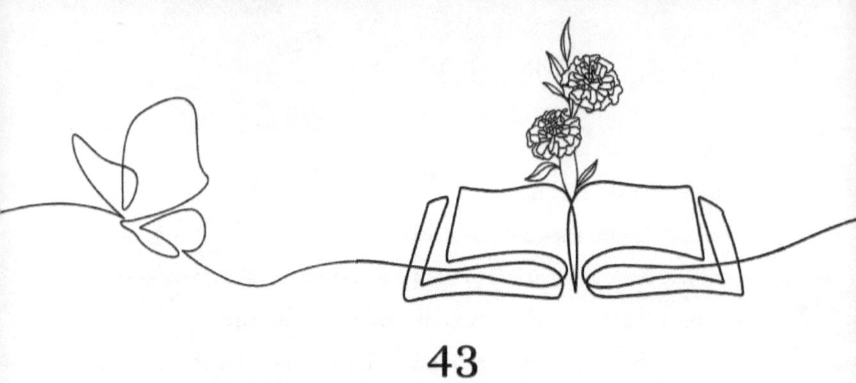

43

lumberjack lunch reminders

Casey

"Thank you so much, ladies! That was a great session, and you should all be so proud of yourselves," I say gently to my last class before Christmas. It is officially my birthday, too, and a happy buzz is keeping my smile firmly in place as I count down the minutes to tonight. Jessie has something planned that he said was a surprise, and I am literally bouncing on the ground in excitement to see what it is.

"Tell me, tell me, tell me!" I had pestered him last night and this morning. Following him around his apartment as he shook his head and laughed at me. I even waltzed around naked, refusing to let him touch me unless he told me his secret. The bastard was still too strong-willed and managed to get me to fold. Pulling out that magic dick, stroking himself while staring hungrily at my body. I relented, of course.

"Have you filled any of those trainer spots yet for the self-defense classes?" Elle asks as she follows me out of the studio.

"I have a friend who has volunteered to help, so I might be able to get classes up and running first thing in the new year." I fill her in on

Ethan's offer.

"Oh, that is so exciting!" She claps her hand, and when we round to reception, my heart does a little happy dance in my chest. Unable to stop any of my excitement, I skip through the waiting area and leap into Jessie's arms with a squeal, planting my lips on his.

His big lumberjack arms catching me with ease, and he laughs into our kiss.

"Happy to see you too, sunshine." I cover his face with kisses because it still shocks me that this guy is still around after the way I ragdolled the crap out of his trust, but he looks at me with those eyes, and says things with that delectable mouth, and then it no longer shocks me, because I feel the love Jessie has for me deep to my bones. The one thing I know I never have to be unsure of in my life is how much he wants me, how important I am to him. That I am a priority and always will be.

"How come you're here? I thought I was seeing you tonight?" He drops me back on my feet and gives me an incredulous look.

"You eat your lunch?"

"Yes," I lie.

"No, she didn't." Elle, that traitor. I hit her with a look over my shoulder and she winks at me, disappearing into the studio for her next class.

"Okay, in my defense, I assumed your plans tonight involved food. I didn't want to spoil it." And I bought a new set of incredible lingerie and I didn't want to be bloated, but I wasn't going to tell him *that*. He narrows his eyes at me and pulls a paper bag from his pocket, grabbing my wrist and forcing me to take it from him.

"Eat it." Shivers run down my spine, and I have to bite my lip. In an effort to distract him, I reach up and push his messy hair from his forehead.

"Mmm, I like it when you boss me around." He groans, his eyes rolling until they're closed, and then he grips the front of my sweater and pulls me against him, slamming his lips onto mine.

I relax against him, twirling my arms around his neck and melting into his delicious lips. Before I can get too lost in them, he pulls back slightly and says against my lips, "Eat. Your. Lunch."

"Or else what?" I challenge, and the stupid sexy man hits me with a grin that has desire ruining my panties.

"Or else I won't eat *you* later." He winks, and I almost combust from how hot he makes me.

"No fair." I smack his chest but turn and head for the staff room. I feel him hot on my heels, and when I spin to question him more about tonight, the studio entrance opens and the words die on my tongue.

"Grace?" Jessie spins, and I feel him go rigid next to me, bless his soul. He knows what had happened last time she was here, and he was ready to storm over to her place and set her straight. So that he doesn't do or say anything stupid, I walk ahead of him and stand in front of her. Ready for a fight, if that's what she came here for. Except the closer I get, the smaller she looks, sunken in on herself, dark circles under her eyes.

"Grace, what's wrong?"

"Can we talk?" she whispers, her eyes still avoiding mine. I turn to look at Jessie and his frown pulls deeper, but he nods. Taking a few steps up to me, kissing the top of my head with a cheeky slap to my ass, he takes the lunch bag. "I'll wait in there," he says and points to the staff room.

"What's up?" I ask, not moving from where we stand. I'm not overly interested in taking her into a private room to be scolded again, and she must sense this because she looks around the room nervously before she shifts on her feet, avoiding eye contact with me at every chance she gets.

"I'm sorry, Casey," she practically whispers.

"Sorry, what was that?" I heard her, but I'm going to need her to repeat herself so I know I'm not imagining things. She looks up at me incredulously before rolling her eyes and speaking louder.

"I said, 'I'm sorry.'"

"What's this apology for, then?"

"All of it." She sighs and runs a hand down her face. I stare at her for a moment, and this time, she holds my gaze. Lets me see it all, a window to her heart, and it has my shoulders slumping forward. I nod at her and tilt my head for her to follow, pulling her into an empty studio. I close the door and we sit on a mat each.

"I have been so rotten to you, Case."

"You have." She looks up at me and grunts before she fidgets in her lap.

"But you're also smothering. You always have been," she says, but there is no hatred in her words, just acquiescence. Like it's a fact.

"Sorry?" I ask with a scoff because, *excuse me?!*

"Don't give me that. You have forever been like this; it just really put me over the edge after everything I've been trying to handle, and I couldn't do it anymore."

"Okay, I don't need to hear any of this," I scold her and go to leave, but she raises a hand.

"Wait, just... I'm not saying any of this properly. Let me try, okay?" I analyze her for a beat and roll my eyes, plopping myself down on the mat again.

"Happy birthday, by the way," she says, pulling her lips into a smirk. I give her a tight smile but wave my hand for her to speed this along. She takes a deep breath and prepares.

"You're a super annoying people pleaser." I rear back at the slap.

"Okay, thanks for coming by to tell me that?" I go to leave again, and she stands, grabbing my wrist, and I pull it from her grip. "You came all this way to apologize and then slap me across the face? I am well fucking aware that I have an issue with helping people who don't deserve it. Sorry I cared about you, Grace. I'll remember not to moving forward."

"Casey, stop!" she shouts at me, and I know the whole fucking studio can hear us now. I'm surprised my broody caveman isn't storming in to save the day. "What I meant is, you're always trying so hard to pretend like things don't affect you. You smooth things over, let go of shit that pisses you off. You never make people feel bad for inconveniencing you or insulting you. You try to be there to fix shit you have no business fixing. You try to make everything perfect and try to *be* perfect for everyone, and growing up, that was so fucking exhausting," she says everything in one breath before she closes her eyes and breathes deeply. I recognize the familiar centering breath and graciously allow her the moment to get her bearings. Opening her eyes again, they seem a little sadder but a lot more sure as she continues. "Then you kept doing it as adults, and it just made me constantly feel like a failure. Mom and Dad were always comparing my shittiness to your perfectness, and I resented you for it." She breathes hard again, her cheeks pink with her frustration, and I have to take a deep breath myself, biting my tongue, giving her the room to continue.

"I just wanted you to be my sister. I wanted you to mess up and complain like I did. I wanted you to get annoyed and frustrated, to throw a tantrum and yell at our parents. To steal my shit and pretend like you didn't when I caught you. I wanted a sister, and instead it was like I just got another mom." She throws her hands in the air, all the calm breathing out the window as I watch her temper rise with her voice.

"Grace, you act like I had a choice. You were a mess as a teenager," I shout back.

"I was a normal teenager." She rolls her eyes.

"Okay, then. Normal, sure. But because our parents were so busy fighting with you and fighting each other *because* of you, they missed dance recitals. Mom forgot to pick me up from study group. One time they forgot to feed me dinner because you ran off and they spent the entire night worried about you. I barely existed to them anymore. Why the hell do you think I learned to cook so goddamn early?" My voice gets progressively louder and I see the way recognition hits her face, the way her mouth drops open and her eyes widen. She shakes her head and goes to speak, but I interrupt her.

"The only way I could help stop their arguments was to make sure there was nothing to fight about. So, I cleaned up your messes. I made sure I fed myself dinner, packed our lunches. I organized my own rides to dance and to the library. I kept track of your keys. I put away your laundry. When they weren't fighting each other over you or fighting you, I had my parents back." I take a few steps forward and jut a finger into her chest, noticing the tears pooling in her eyes, having thoroughly shut her up.

"I just wanted a sister, too, but you were too busy being a rotten teenager that you missed that memo as well. Sorry that I only managed to love you in return." My voice lowers and I go to storm out of the room, but she grips my arm and pulls me against her, throwing her arms around my torso and squeezing me in a hug.

Shock has my arms out by my sides, trying to understand what's happening. It isn't until I feel her body shudder against me and I hear her sob that I return the hug and wrap my arms around her tightly.

"Casey, I'm so sorry," she says between sobs and I just hold her as she cries. After a few moments, she pulls back and I wipe a few of her tears. She does the same to me, and I hadn't realized I was crying at all.

"For the record, I know I have a problem with giving more than I should. Jessie is actively trying to stop me from doing that." A little laugh leaves my lips, and I have to wipe my slobbery nose from my tears. Grace steps back and does the same, a little laugh leaving her, too.

"Jessie Jenkins, hey?" she says, a little smile hitting her lips, and she nudges my shoulder with her fist.

I nod and release a dreamy sigh, remembering that my big grump is out there waiting for me. "Yeah, he's great."

Grace laughs and nods. "I'll say. I had a huge crush on him back in the day." That has my eyes darting to her in a frown, and after a moment, she bursts out laughing and lands her hands on her knees. I laugh with her, but also, *umm...?* She must read the trepidation in my face because she rolls her eyes and waves a hand at me.

"He's stupid good looking. Any teenage girl was going to crush on him." Fair, also true. "I love Evan and I'm not about to cut your grass, Case. I was just poking fun. I'm happy for you." She squeezes my arm and I smile, nodding at her.

"I am sorry, Casey. I didn't mean to snap at you all those times. I do appreciate everything you've done for me. I had no idea all my drama caused so many problems for you. I... I miss you and I want to be sisters again, or like sisters for the first time. I feel like we have missed out on something by being who we were." Her face drops as she speaks, pain and sadness, and I hug my arms around my waist.

"I'm sorry, too. For smothering you, for pretending I was okay when I wasn't. I am trying to be better at that. I miss being your sister, too. I do really want to be able to hang out and just bitch and moan instead of walking on eggshells." She laughs lightly, nodding her head.

"Umm... also, about the studio—"

"Oh, I never saw that lawyer," I clear up.

"Oh, thank god." She laughs gently, and her eyes bulge with gratitude. "I do love working with you, Case. I love this job, and I love the studio. I really didn't want it to go." I nod, knowing. I was hoping she'd come around because I equally didn't want our partnership to end.

"Let's be better sisters?" she asks, and I pull her into another hug that she returns.

"We can certainly try. As long as you stop being a bitch." I joke and she hoots a laugh before withdrawing and rolling her eyes at me. We head for the door. "Ugh, you're already going to be insufferable. Maybe I should take it back." I laugh with her, and as we open the door to leave, I'm not in the slightest bit surprised to find Jessie leaning against the wall opposite the room. A deep frown on his face instantly assessing me before leveling Grace with a stern look, his arms across his chest, his body vibrates with a menacing energy and I have to smother a giggle.

"Geez, he never outgrew the predator vibe, did he?" Grace says under her breath, and I shake my head, no longer able to hide my smile. I wink at him and he nods slightly before disappearing back around the corner, and I walk Grace to the door.

"You coming back to class soon?" She nods enthusiastically.

"I am! I..." She clears her throat and looks around the room. "I started seeing a therapist. For the grief. Evan and I are seeing a fertility doctor, and we're going to wait but try again soon. But I want to get back to a normal life."

"I'm so proud of you, Grace. Your usual classes are ready for you when you are." She lets go of a big breath. We say our goodbyes and my heart is practically beating out of my chest with joy as I skip back into the staff room, finding Jessie scrolling on his phone. It's promptly discarded when I enter. I walk up to him and he pulls me to stand between his legs from where he sits on the dining chair, his hands tickling the backs of my thighs as his eyes scan my entire face.

"You playing guard dog?" I tease.

"I heard her shouting. I was getting ready to intervene," he says, a lethal air to his words.

"I can handle Grace," I assure him, brushing his hair off his forehead, the perpetual mess that it is. His grip tightens on my thighs and he pulls me closer.

"I know you can. You just don't have to handle it alone anymore," he says gently, and I bite my lip to hide my smile. His eyes catch there and I watch them darken with desire.

"I'm looking forward to tonight," I whisper, and he grunts in response.

"I'm thinking about skipping straight to dessert."

His voice oozes with a dirty promise and I lean down to whisper in his ear, "But then you'll miss the lacy gift I got you." When I pull back, I'm thoroughly satisfied with his pain as he bores those stunning eyes into me and something like a growl works its way up his throat.

"It is inappropriate for me to be hard as a rock at your workplace, Ace." I giggle and walk backward, pulling him up to stand. He wastes no time shoving the lunch back in my face. "And I'm not leaving until you finish this. You need to eat."

I roll my eyes at him. "You're no fun."

"I'll be plenty fun later, with you spread out below me when it's my turn to eat." I feel my cheeks blush, and I have to swallow the moan his dirty words elicit from me.

Jessie, motherfucking, Jenkins.

dessert is served

Casey

"Jessie?" I call for him as I enter his café. It's dark out, the snow was relentless today, and it's absolutely freezing. I shiver as I step into the shop, the fireplace to the left heating the space and setting a romantic, warm glow across the space. My chest warms, and I can't fight the smile that spreads across my face. I take a few more steps in and look around the shop. It's different at this time of night. None of the ceiling lights are on, only the fireplace and a corner lamp light up the room, the back of the shop disappearing in darkness. Only flickering light coming from the mezzanine above the counter.

"Jessie?" I call again, now slightly breathless. Either the desire to see him or the romantic setting stealing my breath. I have no idea at this point.

"Hey, sunshine." His deep voice from close behind startles me, and I turn quickly, almost tripping on my feet, but his strong hands dart out to catch me, pulling me against him. His smile is devastating, his eyes hooded as he looks me over. "You look delicious." He hums and leans down to steal my lips in a kiss. I sigh into it and let him kiss me for a few moments before he pulls away. "I have a surprise for you." He turns and drags me by the hand up the stairs to the floating second level. This is usually just a reading space; books line every wall and there are reading couches and silent areas gathered in the center. Except, when we crest the top level, most of the center furniture has been pushed aside and there is a simple table and two chairs lit up with candles everywhere, a stunning bunch of marigolds lay across the table and I have to smother the squeal from my throat. He walks us to the table, lifts my hand to kiss my knuckles, and hands me the bunch of flowers.

"They're beautiful," I breathe as I take them from him and hide my blush from his gentlemanly act.

"I have to admit something," he says with mischief.

"Oh?" I raise an eyebrow at him and lay the flowers back on the table as he pulls me into his arms.

"I watched *The Notebook* today." By the look on his face, he is mortified at the admission, and it has me giggling like a schoolgirl. Jessie starts to sway us in the open area of the top level, an arm wrapped around my lower back holding me to him, his left hand holding my right,

"Did you love it?" I ask, not able to hold back my smugness because I've been trying to get him to watch that for weeks. He just shakes his head and rolls his eyes.

"The book was better." He hums slightly and I tuck this piece of information away, as he continues to sway us in a waltz. I roll my eyes at his statement and he just smiles.

That's when I notice the background acoustic music.

"Are we dancing right now?"

"We are." He nods, his incredibly handsome smile beaming across his face.

"Happy birthday, *stella mea*," he whispers and steals my lips in a delicate kiss. Tentative and searching, a greeting and a declaration all in one. I let go of his hand and wind my arms around his neck to pull him closer, to deepen the kiss, and he holds me firmly around my lower back, groaning as I swipe my tongue against his. His grip tightens on my hips, and he withdraws on a chuckle.

"Not going to make it to the end of the night if you keep that up."

"Good, let's just skip to the end part," I pant and try to pull him against me again, except he stops me, chuckling. I roll my eyes at him, but settle into his embrace as we dance gently to the acoustic music.

"You didn't have to do all of this for me, Jess."

He just shrugs and I can hear the smile in his words, "You're Jessie's girl. You watch me with those blue eyes, love me with this incredible body, and holding you late at night, like this, is something I dream about." I blink as his words settle in, and when I pull back to assess his face, the cute blush across his cheeks, I almost burst with laughter.

"Did you just paraphrase Rick Springfield?" I accuse, not able to wipe the humor from my face, and he just smiles wider, chuckling with me as he points to his ear, gesturing for me to listen. That's when I hear it. The song we are dancing to is an acoustic instrumental of Rick Springfield's song, *Jessie's Girl*. The same song I played when I told him I loved him for the first time. A huge laugh howls from my throat, my head thrown back, and I feel Jessie's body shake with humor with me.

"Oh, Jessie, you're a massive cheeseball," I say between chuckles, and when I look back at him, only love and adoration hit me in those eyes.

"I know." He sighs, shaking his head gently at me. "I can't even help it. Loving you has ruined all my masculine street cred," he jokes, and I slap his chest.

"I'm the best thing that ever happened to you, *actually*," I joke back, raising my eyebrows at him and turning to walk toward the table he has set. He doesn't let me get far, coming up behind me, his hands firm on my hips, pulling my back to his front as he nuzzles my neck.

"The greatest, and there is no getting rid of me now," he whispers, his hot breath fanning against my neck, and I nearly melt into a puddle. I lean my head back on his shoulder, combing a hand through his messy hair as he kisses my neck.

"I wouldn't dream of it," I whisper back–or basically pant. It doesn't take much for Jessie to get me worked up. One kiss, even a little look with his stunning hooded eyes, the uptilt of his pretty smile, and I'm a goner.

Like he is also struggling to fight the rapidly growing desire between us, his grip tightens on my hips, gently thrusting into my ass, amplifying the need we have for each other.

"I think it's time for dessert," he grounds out, and I meet his thrust with my own, practically dry humping each other as I claw at his hair and struggle to control my breaths.

"We haven't even had dinner yet," I breathe.

"It's your birthday. Consider it a gift." And before I know what's happening, Jessie has me spun around and lifted onto the table, my legs spread. He stands between them and seals his lips on mine in a demanding kiss. His expert hands tour my whole body, unzipping my jacket and peeling it from my shoulders. He makes quick work of peeling my top from my body, which exposes the gift I have for him, that I was hoping would be revealed later.

"You're spoiling part of your gift," I say, and when he pulls back, his eyes bore into my chest, at the pale blue lace bra that cups my small breasts perfectly, barely covering anything, the material see-through and leaving my puckered nipples visible.

"This fucking blue." His attention is stuck in the middle, though, at what I knew he'd enjoy, the small silver star charm that hangs at the material between my breasts. I watch his eyes turn predatory and he drags a delicate finger between my tits, playing with the charm.

"Part of?" he chokes out, his eyes glued to the star charm.

"Well, if you keep removing my clothing, you'll see the rest." His eyes snap to mine and his lips pull into a devious half smile that has me almost whimpering. I swear, sometimes, the way he looks at me could make me come. No touching needed.

"You know, it's *your* birthday. You're not supposed to get me anything," he says, but his voice is a tease. His hands dig into the waistband of my jeans, the button and zip are flicked with his expert hands while his eyes remain on mine.

"Maybe it's an early Christmas present, then," I whisper. He slowly peels my jeans from my body, and when there is nothing but my thong and bra covering me, he takes a small step back and examines me. A groan leaves him as he drags a hand down his face and rests his hands on his hips. His eyes trailing me everywhere. The slow and deliberate perusal sends shivers across my body.

"Fucking masterpiece," he whispers, and then in another breath, he is on me. Capturing my lips in a demanding kiss, swallowing my moans as he gradually lays me down on the table, his lips eventually leaving mine to kiss down my neck and across my collarbone.

"*Stella mea*," he whispers. So much longing in his voice. *My Star.* I know this man has a love for nicknames, but every time he calls me his star, I feel my heart explode. It would be almost impossible to love him deeper than I already do, but somehow, every time he says it, I fall even more.

His lips find mine and kiss me back, desperately, his hands working frantically, dipping under the front of my panties and trailing a finger through my middle, so gently, teasingly that it has me pulling from the kiss in a gasp.

"I love how wet you get for me. How quickly I can have you dripping," he pants, his voice full of arrogance. "Who do you want tonight, sunshine?" he asks, his lips trailing a path back down my body, alternating between bites, licks and kisses.

"The animal or the gentleman?" His fingers curl around the edge of the G-string, pulling them slowly down my legs.

"I just want you," I whisper in response, and it is his undoing.

The underwear discarded, his knees hit the floor, and his mouth descends on me like a beast starved. His tongue expertly licking the length of me before drawing in my clit and sucking.

"Oh my god," I moan, my back arching off the table, gripping my fingers through his hair to hold him in place. *I guess it's the savage then.*

With no mercy, he devours me, thrusting three of his fingers into me. "So fucking tight," he grinds out, his hand picking up the pace while the other reaches up and tucks itself under my bra to flick and squeeze my nipples.

"Holy shit," I groan, because, animal he is, with his tongue teasing my peak and his fingers curling to thrust against that sensitive spot, the orgasm hits me in no time and I convulse around him as he continues to lick me and tease me.

"This blue is exquisite," he whispers, placing one more delicate kiss to my center before withdrawing himself, grabbing my hand and sitting me up so that our chests are together, bringing his lips to mine. "But the greatest gift of all was you letting me into your heart." He kisses me passionately, tasting myself on his tongue, and I moan into his embrace.

"You're not so bad at gift giving either," I pant and he chuckles, his warm hands searching my bare back as he unclasps my bra from behind.

"And we've only just begun, *stella mea*. When I'm done, you won't be able to walk out of here." He punctuates with a nip to my neck and I gasp.

"I can only hope."

Jessie and I broke the table. But he was adamant to continue our date, so we currently lay on a blanket from the back room by the fireplace, utterly naked and sated from an evening well spent. He wasn't joking about not being able to walk. After my first gift, Jessie bent me over the table–hence it now being broken–the savage that he is, followed by a passionate declaration of love from the gentleman. I was four orgasms in for the night when he heard my stomach grumble and was adamant we should eat before he gave me any more.

"I have something else for you," he says, dropping the plate of Scottish macaroons–yes, you heard correctly. For my birthday, Jessie got my family cookbook from my mom and spent the last twenty-four hours making some of my favorite recipes so he could feed them to me on my birthday.

"Jessie, if it's your penis, can I have a nap first?" I groan as I pull the blanket around me tighter from my spot on the floor and he chuckles, disappearing for a bit.

After a few moments, I feel a delicate finger brush my cheek and my eyes are peeled open. I hadn't realized I drifted off, but now, my head lays in Jessie's lap, his stunning mixed-colored eyes staring down at me as he caresses my cheek. "I didn't realize I had *actually* wrecked you." The bastard is smug, but God, he is delicious when he looks at me like that. I chuckle and sit up slightly.

"Here."

"What is this?" I say, but know exactly what I'm looking at. It's a manuscript. Except it's not the one I stole, it's a different one, with his name on it and a new title. "*Finding Home*?" I read it and look at him. He scratches the back of his neck.

"The first one was therapy. An outlet, a way to get all the pain out. This one…" He gestures to the manuscript in my hand. "This one is a healing. This one holds my heart. Like you do. Do you think…" His eyes scan the ceiling, and I don't miss the curse he mutters as I see the embarrassment and shyness over take him. Discarding the manuscript, I crawl toward him and climb onto his lap, straddling him as the blanket falls away, both of us still as naked as the day we were born, and feel him stand at attention immediately.

"I can give it to Rosie." His eyes connect with mine in gratitude, and a light blush hits his cheeks.

"Your writing is truly incredible, Jessie. I can't wait for people to read your words and know how amazing you are," I whisper, and his hands land on my hips, slowly but lovingly grinding me down further.

"You haven't even read this one." I shake my head.

"I don't need to." I kiss each of his cheeks and then climb out of his lap. His grunt in disappointment has me giggling. "Relax, caveman, I'm getting your present, too."

"That wasn't all I got you." He sounds chastised, and it makes me laugh more.

I quickly reach for my bag and grab the gift I got for him, and head back to the fireplace. I go to perch next to him, but Jessie isn't having that. He pulls me into his lap, forcing me to straddle him again. "It's your birthday, Ace. You shouldn't have got me anything at all."

"I couldn't wait until tomorrow to give you this one. It's your Christmas present. It's nothing, really."

He watches me for a beat, but then takes the gift from my hand and starts unwrapping it. He pulls out the book I had bound, the black and silver canvas with his favorite blue foiling that reads *the Odyssey*. "I know it's not much. But you were reading this when it all started. I wanted to make one for you. Plus, I also added this." I pull out the small leather journal with '*JJ*' engraved on the front. "I thought maybe you could use it as an idea's notebook. So, while you're working, you could write down anything you think of." I shrug self-consciously and his eyes watch me, heavy with love and gratefulness.

"Ace, baby, this is... amazing. It's too much, but I do love it. I love you," he says, a slight croak to his voice as he admires the gifts again, discarding them and firmly wrapping his arms around me to nuzzle my neck.

"Thank you," he whispers. We stay that way for a bit, something about the intensity of his emotions hitting me in the chest before he pulls back. "Last gift." He hands me a box and kisses the tip of my nose as his big, warm hands gently tickle my lower back.

When I open the box, I see a journal almost identical to the one I got him, except larger, with a pale blue leather cover, and *Stella Mea* engraved on the front. A white ribbon bookmark hangs out the bottom, with a diamond star charm hanging from it, and I have to blink back the tears that sting my eyes.

"*Jessie*. It's so beautiful." He doesn't say anything, but when I look up to his eyes, they shine with joy, and he juts his chin. "Open it." My brows furrow slightly and when I do, I realize it isn't a journal at all, it's a book.

Every page has a different quote. All the quotes he recited from his classic novels, all the lyrics I've repeated to him. All the words written or sung by famous people that we had used to communicate our love for each other when we couldn't find our own.

Tears drip down my cheeks and I can't fight the smile as I feel his heart beat faster.

"Oh my god," I breathe. "Jessie, it's... it's *everything*." I close the book and hold it to my heart as I sob.

"Oh, sunshine, I didn't want to make you cry." He chuckles gently and pulls me to his chest as his hands comb through my hair.

"I love you, Jessie. So damn much it hurts." I sob into his chest. He pulls back, his firm grip framing my face while his thumbs swipe away my tears.

"I love you, too, Casey." He kisses me gently, then whispers over my lips, "So damn much it gives me hope."

THE END

EPILOGUE

ten years later

Casey

"JJ!"

"Yeah, sunshine?" I roll my eyes.

"Not you." Sighing, I head to the open window over the sink that looks out at the yard and shout at our second eldest, "Jeremy! Get your butt in here and wash up for dinner!"

"We really didn't think about this naming situation." Jessie grumbles as he toes off his shoes at the back door and I chuckle at him.

"That's your fault. Where are the girls?" I continue with the prep for dinner. I'm making mom's casserole because the full force of winter is now upon us and we need something hearty to warm us up. It is also Christmas eve, which happens to be my birthday, so I got to pick the meal.

"Moira is helping Allie get dressed," he replies, joining me in the kitchen. His magnetism still sets me alight, even after all this time. Crowding me against the kitchen sink, his huge form enveloping me, and I let myself fall against him, resting my head on his chest as he wraps his arms around me and kisses my neck.

"What time is bedtime tonight," he whispers.

"Right on eight," I reply through a chuckle. He'd made some big promises for my '*birthday present*', but I think we are both dying for some alone time. Before I can say any more, crying interrupts our little moment of peace.

"I'll get her," Jessie assures me with one final kiss to my neck. He pretends like he is tired of it, but my big grumpy lumberjack is as soft as butter for his newest baby girl.

Jessie heads up stairs to the nursery and I take the time to admire the life we managed to build together. Feeling my heart inflate with so much joy and love. Jessie happened to knock me up only a year after we got together. Papa Baker was less than impressed, but after our first blessing, Moira, was born, any hostility quickly evaporated. That little bundle of joy was the light of both my parent's eyes.

Jessie and I stayed in New York for another couple of years, where the studio grew to being one of the top studios in the city. The New York Times article had me in tears for a week. '*A world of its own: The Baker sisters have given the residents of New York a place to be at peace, to grow and become stronger versions of themselves.*' My dream had come true just as Jessie's second manuscript was published. Andersen Schulz & Meyers, the publishing company where Rosie was an editor at the time, accepted that Jessie wasn't interested in following through with the first manuscript, but they loved the second even more.

It became clear that we were outgrowing the city when Jessie published his second book and started touring... and he knocked me up *again*. The arrival of Jeremy made us a family of four. So, I sold my share of the studio to Grace, and Jessie managed to contact that developer again and sold the bookshop café. Between that and the sales of his books, we had enough to build our family home. So, we left the city and headed back to Great Falls. We snagged just over an acre of land that already had a small little lake, and as he promised, Jessie built us a gorgeous country style home with a wrap-around porch. Of course, we made sure to hire professionals. Despite his big muscles and masculine need to '*build me a home*', he relented and understood this was better in the long run.

In the winter, Jessie takes Jer out to the frozen lake to skate. The kid was actually surprisingly talented for the age of five, so we recently got him into lessons at the local rink.

We opened a small bookshop café in town, where Jessie has an office and does most of his writing. I looked into another studio too, but not long after we built our forever home, Jessie's stupidly fertile sperm gave us Allie, baby number three. I thought that was it, that we were done, but life has a way of surprising you sometimes. When Allie turned two and started full time day-care, I thought I finally had the time to think about a studio... but Jessie and his magic penis had other ideas, and six months ago, the final piece to our family arrived in the form of our beautiful baby girl, Hope. As much as I love our big family, that was the perfect icing on the top.

Needless to say, I made sure Jessie booked that vasectomy ASAP.

"Why can't I skate for longer?" Jeremy storms in from the lake, of course trudging snow and mud all through the back door.

"Hey, wipe your feet, mister! And you need to hop in the bath. I don't want your mud all over those new dining chairs."

"Bullshit," he mutters as he wipes his feet.

"Jeremy Jenkins, you watch your tongue." And I make a note to reprimand the teacher of those words later, too. Rolling his eyes at me, he turns to head for the stairs, finding his grumpy father at the foot of them delivering a stern look at his mini-me.

Heaving a sigh, Jer turns back around and reluctantly walks over to me and wraps his arms around my legs.

"Sorry, momma. Love you." I can't help but chuckle a little, re-turning the hug and bending to kiss the top of his head–a mop of dirty blonde hair, just like his daddy. Who, by the way, looks freaking edible, nursing a bundled and babbling Hope in one arm, carrying Jer's skate bag in the other.

"Love you too, JJ," I whisper into the top of his head.

"What have we said about speaking to your momma that way, kid?"

"To not to." Jer sighs like he has the weight of the world on his shoulders and I have to bite my lips to hold my laugh in. I've learned laughing at Jessie scolding our kids for their potty mouth makes them think it is a joke. Though, he is never worried about their language, until it's directed at me.

"Take this to the laundry room and clean it out or you'll stink up the house," Jessie tells Jer, who reluctantly follows instructions.

"You know, he learned that from you." I point at his chest when he joins me in the kitchen, bouncing hope in his arms.

"I warned you that would happen." He winks and hits me with that devastatingly handsome smile. "You married me, anyway." He closes the distance and places a soft kiss on my lips. The only thing stopping me from mauling him right now is the attention seeking baby in his arms, who has now latched onto my hair. Taking her into my arms, Jessie kisses the top of her head and threads his fingers through mine to kiss my knuckles. "Fuck, I can't wait to have you to myself," he whispers, and despite the way his words still ruin my panties, I have to smack his chest.

"We literally just discussed your potty mouth around the kids." Identical to his son, Jessie rolls his eyes and chuckles.

"Hope doesn't know what words are yet. We still have at least another twelve months."

"You're incorrigible." Thumping footsteps from the stairs, sounding like a stampede, hit us and the terror twins come bounding into the kitchen.

Moira was stoked to have a sibling when Jeremy came along, but when Allie was born, the light in Moira's eyes shone so bright. "A real babydoll," she had whispered, and ever since, she has adored helping her dress up and teaching her how to brush her hair. She also loves to take on the role of Mom and pretends to feed her with pretend bottles, and when it's nap time, Moira comes and reads her a story.

"Momma, Allie won't wear the cardigan you put out for her," she tattles, and Jessie turns to pick up a nagging Allie from where she pulls at his jeans.

"No cargan," Allie whines.

"That's okay, no cardigan is fine, you're all staying inside, anyway." I brush a few strands of auburn hair off of Moira's face and she throws her head back in defiance.

"But she has to wear it! Aunty Rosie said it goes perfect with leggings!" Jessie snorts a laugh and bends to get eye-level with his first baby while Allie snuggles into his neck. "Sometimes Aunty Rosie doesn't know what she is talking about."

"Don't let her hear you say that," I mumble, and Jessie delivers me an incredulous look before he pulls Moira in for a hug.

"We don't always have to get our way, *Stellula*. If Allie doesn't want to, she doesn't have to. Just like yesterday when I asked if you wanted to try to skate with Jer. That would have made you pretty sad if I forced you out there, huh?" Moira nods slightly, not making eye contact with either of us, her bratty pout perfected.

Watching Jessie parent never fails to set my ovaries on fire.

I will never forget the moment in that hospital room, the day Moira made us a family, and the nurse handed her to Jessie, the tears flooding his cheeks. I had never seen him smile in the way he looked down at his baby girl. He stroked her cheek, kissed her forehead, and whispered, *"Stellula,"* his 'little star.'

Moira heaves a sigh, but before the lecture could continue the oven pings and we are saved by the bell.

"Food!" I turn and shout up the stairs for Jeremy, who wastes no time in running down the stairs.

Jessie gets the girls settled into their seats as I place Hope in her highchair. I serve up each of their plates with Jessie's help, and he places them on the table. We settle in, Jessie filling my glass of wine. "Happy birthday Momma." He smirks at me from across the table, raising his glass, and the kids join in.

"Happy Birthday, momma."

"And Merry Christmas Eve!" Moira shouts, and we all break out into a laugh.

"Alright, rascals, it's almost eight, it's bedtime." Jessie tickles Jer and Moira with them huddled under each of his arms in an effort to get them moving off the couch. Hope went down an hour ago and I had Allie completely out to it in my arms. We join them all upstairs, ensuring they brush their teeth, have their *one* story before lights out and after thirty minutes of nagging, complaining, *'I forgot my bottle of water,'* and, *'I need to pee again,'* all four were tucked away, and it was finally Jess and me.

"Finally," I breathe as I fall into Jessie's embrace. He places gentle kisses to the top of my head as he rubs a warm hand down my back. Pulling back, I look into his gorgeous eyes, "So, about those promises..." The heat and desire I never get tired of seeing is reflected back at me and a sly grin slowly forms on his face.

"Not just yet, *stella mea*. I have a birthday surprise for you." He kisses my lips quickly, only leaving me wanting more, before he pulls back to say something else, except he can't because we're interrupted by a knock at the door.

"That's weird. Who'd be here this late on Christmas Eve?"

Jessie just winks at me and heads down the stairs, letting in our guest.

"Mom?"

"Hi, baby!" she whisper-screeches. I make my way down the stairs and she pulls me into a hug, except I struggle to return it because I am still confused.

"I'm so happy to see you, but also still very confused."

Mom pulls on a knowing smirk, but looks over my shoulder to JJ. My gaze shoots to his and then back to Mom. "Okay, what is going on?"

Jessie

"C'mon, sunshine, we'll be late."

"Well, you didn't really give me much time to work with, did you?" Casey grumbles from the other side of the bathroom.

Bev is here to watch the kids while I take Case out for her birthday surprise. I am antsy for it; I had spent so long organizing this, I can't wait to show it to her. Of course, both her parents know about it. It's really hard to lie and sneak around a woman whose intuition is as spot on as Casey's, but with their help, I managed to work around it for the last eight or so months.

"I already told you; you don't need to dress up, we aren't doing anything crazy and we aren't seeing anyone." In fact, it would really be simpler for me if she wore *less* clothing. But I wasn't going to say that in front of my mother-in-law.

Casey, as expected, has made sacrifice after sacrifice for our family. From the moment Moira was born, to four years ago, when we had an intimate wedding ceremony in our yard with our closest friends and family, to postponing going back to work between each kid. I know her dream is to have another studio, but she also keeps burying it, and I know it is because she thinks it's selfish to want things for herself. Despite her always making sure my own dreams come true. So, I took it upon myself to make it happen for her. To give back in the way that I can.

"Okay, okay, I'm coming. Mom, are you good? Do you need anything?" Casey sounds breathless as she comes out of the bathroom. Dressed in her jeans and pale blue sweater. Her hair is half tied back with her signature ribbon, some light makeup on, and looks breathtaking, as always. Before I can appreciate her look, though, she is zooming past me and into another room and then she's gone again.

"Caseyyyyy."

"Alright, alright, settle caveman. I'm coming." Then she finally looks at me as she smiles brightly, her bright blue eyes sparkling with excitement, and I can't help myself.

"C'mere," I practically growl and wrap my arm around her waist the moment she is in reaching distance. I thread a hand through her hair and steal her lips in a kiss I've been waiting all damn day to give her.

Just as I run my tongue along the seam of her lips to deepen it, falling further into my desire for her. A cough comes from our right, making us realize our surroundings and pull back.

"Sorry, Bev," I mutter and give her a guilty look. Casey's flushed cheeks tell me she was just as lost in that as I was.

"Don't be sorry, just don't hang around here all night doing that. Get going. I have everything under control here." Bev gives us an honest smile before shooing us out the door.

"So, where are you taking me?" Casey leans on the center console between us in the car and I rest a hand on her thigh, completely unable to go a moment without touching her.

"Well, it wouldn't be a surprise if I told you, now, would it?" Her eyes narrow in suspicion, but there is a playful smile there, too.

The rest of the car ride is in a peaceful silence, one neither of us gets too often, the sound of the road and the low volume of the radio, the only sounds as we pull up to the destination.

The main strip in town is quiet. In the late hours of the night before Christmas, there are only a few couples walking to and from late night venues and restaurants. It's the perfect amount of peace I wanted for this moment. We pull out in front of a shop in a line of newly constructed commercial buildings, the building I have spent almost the last year getting ready for her.

"What is this?" Casey queries as we step out of the car, looking up at the building we pull up in front of. The signage still wasn't done yet, so it added an element of surprise, which I was suddenly grateful for. I send her a knowing look but remain silent as I gesture for her to head through the door first.

The moment she steps in, I see her spine snap straight, a hand flying to cover her mouth.

"*Jess.*" I'll never tire of hearing her whisper that name. "What am I looking at right now?"

I come up behind her and wrap my arms around her.

"Your new studio," I say gently, letting my lips linger on the shell of her ear, allowing her intoxicating scent to envelop me.

"I don't understand." She spins to look at me. "When, and how...why?"

"Because you were never going to take the time to do this yourself. I've spent the last eight or so months working on this. Grace agreed to a partnership deal again, if you wanted, so you can both still be in it together just in different locations, a third studio. Or you can make it completely your own. The signage isn't done, so it's your choice." She looks at me with a mix of appreciation and wonder before the dam breaks and tears spread down her cheeks.

"Hey, baby, I didn't mean to make you cry." She chuckles, wiping at her tears, and falls into my chest. I waste no time wrapping my arms around her and burying my nose in her intoxicating floral scent.

"They are happy tears. I have wanted to get back into a studio so badly. It just seemed like so much, having to organize it all." She pulls back, her arms still wrapped around my waist and her blue eyes shine behind her tears. "Thank you, Jessie. I honestly don't think thank you is enough; I love you so damn much." I have to blink back the sting in my own eyes as I lean down and give her another kiss. I try my best to not let it get away from me, wanting to show her around before we christen the place. But Casey stands on the tips of her toes, wrapping her arms around my neck, before her tongue sweeps into my mouth and steals the breath from my lungs.

"Easy, sunshine. Let me give you a tour. We can try out the yoga mats after," I say as I rest my forehead against hers. She chuckles and bites her bottom lip, giving me a gentle nod. I reach for her hand behind my neck and interlace our fingers and pull her further into the studio.

We walk around for a few minutes. I show her the different studios–there are three in total and one room that is slightly smaller but has a thicker padded flooring for the self-defense classes. They have become fan favorites in the original studios back in NYC. The added addition to this one, though, is the kids' corner. "I figured there may be days you either need the kids with you or want them here, and this is a safe and fun little space for them." I gesture to the small TV and kid-sized armchairs with the gaming console. A small bookshelf stocked with kids' books and a trunk full of toys that would suit a toddler and a five-year-old.

"Jessie, you thought of everything!" she boasts and bends down to check out the books. "Hey, this could work for the mom's and bub's classes, too." She beams, her gigantic smile setting me alight, and this time, I can't fight it anymore. I pull her against me.

"I'm glad you love it, sunshine." I kiss her forehead and she hums happily as she wraps her arms around my waist, settling into my chest where she fits perfectly. "I was nervous. I wanted it to be everything you had wanted it to be."

"It is, Jess. It's everything." Her grip around me tightens, and she breathes a heavy breath before looking up at me and I frame her face with my hands. Swiping at her soft skin with my thumbs as she continues, "This life, with you. I never could have imagined something so perfect, and yet it has been everything I've ever dreamed of. It's everything I hoped for, and so much more." Emotion clogs my throat. I can barely breathe, but I feel my chest constrict with all the love I feel for the woman I hold in my arms. The gratefulness that she has given me so much in this life. I could never imagine my world without her in it. I lean my forehead against hers, breathe her in and bask in this feeling with her.

"You're everything I ever hoped for. *You* are my everything. This," I wave a hand around the studio, "is the least I could do."

"It's our forever?" She smiles up at me, biting her bottom lip with her sparkling blue eyes.

"Yeah, sunshine. It's our forever."

thank you for reading!

If you enjoyed this book, I would be so grateful if you could please leave a review!

Goodreads and Amazon are both good platforms that other readers will visit to be able to see your review and decide if this book is the one for them! You can leave a review on either site, but I'd appreciate if it could be both!

Want to stay in the loop with upcoming releases, events and announcements, connect with me, or subscribe to the newsletter on my website!

@authorbrittanyrianne
www.brittanyrianne.com

acknowledgments

Another story done, and it feels surreal to be publishing my second book. This book came to me a lot smoother than Fury, but it holds a special place in my heart all the same.

Again, I have so many people to thank for helping me make this dream a reality and to bring this story to life.

My amazing readers of Fury who loved and hyped it up, I am so incredibly grateful for you, and I wouldn't be where I am on this journey if it weren't for you!

Again, to Nick for putting up with the many, many late nights of being stuck in the writing cave, for dealing with my grumpy moods from lack of sleep and the complete insanity of the dialogue I was constantly having in my head. You're the true MVP.

There are many people who have been my village through this whole experience, but Jeni, you have and always will be my biggest support, my number one fan and the first reader of every single chapter—before I even know where the story is going! I appreciate you endlessly, and I can't wait to have you by my side as this journey continues!

My amazing bookish friends! I don't really know what a street team is, but if I was going to have it, it would be you guys! Kim, Zoe, Erin, Aimee, and Elleni, you guys keep me motivated. The edits you send for these characters, the hype you build, and your ability to keep secrets are unmatched! I am so sorry for putting you through the lengthy waiting game, but let's be honest, you LOVE the teasers.

The book community as a whole, I would be nothing without you, the support is crazy and unmatched. I've never been a part of a community like this, and I am so glad to have found my people.

To all the readers that are now along for the Central Sparks ride, I hope you're buckled in because, boy do I have some stories to come that you don't want to miss!

Thank you all for putting up with me, and I can't wait to see where my insanity takes me next!

xx
BR